The CROSS FIRE

J.B. STEPHENS

Interior Formatting: J.B. Stephens

Cover Design: Silver at Ever After Cover Design

Paperback ISBN: 979-8-9893366-0-9

Ebook ISBN: 979-8-9893366-1-6

Disclaimer

The author does not condone some of the actions that occur in this book. It is strictly for fictional pleasure and contains content that some may find triggering. This includes: detailed sex (bondage, choking, dub-con), profanity, graphic violence, gore, alcohol/substance use, attempted sexual assault (on page), and mentions of domestic abuse (off page).

The book is narrated in English, Jamaican Creole, and Italian. There is a glossary at the back with (contextual) Italian translations.

For more information about the author and her books, visit:

FOR THE SIX-YEAR-OLD WHO DISCOVERED HER LOVE FOR WRITING AND
NEVER STOPPED CHASING HER DREAMS.

&

FOR MY WATT-FAMILY WHO STUCK WITH ME EVERY TIME I CHOSE PROBLEMS
INSTEAD OF PEACE.

Chapter One

Chayanne

The community I lived in was violent. It used to be a haven, but now it was like almost every other place in Jamaica. Whenever it got this bad, it seemed I lived in Spanish Town instead of Steer Town. Mama always said, 'Back in my day, people cuda sleep wid door open, and nun bad wuda happen a nighttime. Or daytime, fi that matter.'

Mi never have dat. Mi witness people rushing home as soon as streetlights come on and being wary fi sidung pon dem veranda pon a sunny afternoon. Every day mi go school, she seh, 'Grandbaby, nuh idle after school. Mi heart cya tek the loss of another daughter.'

A mi third week ina fifth form, and me carry Mama advice wid mi every day. We only have each other, so mi always try do sum nice fi her — like saving a portion a mi lunch money fi buy her KFC every Friday.

Mi glare pon everybody ahead of mi ina the line. Mi nuh know why dem hungry belly people ya cya cook a dem yard!

The girl in front of me laughed, turning around. "Wa do you?"

Mi pout. "Mi waa go home."

"Yu too miserable. Me will buy the food fi yu. Go sidung." Chezzy hold out her hand fi the money.

Mi smile as mi put it ina her hand, then walk weh. Is a miracle mi find a seat ina the sardine tin. Mi wipe it off wid mi kerchief before mi sit.

It tek twenty minutes fi she reach the cashier, and another thirty fi get the food. A after seven now. To how mi tired from thinking how long it a go tek fi get taxi, mi a try mi best nufi drop *bluff*, cause Mama will drop *pleng*.

While we walk to the taxi stand, Chezzy tek out her phone. Mi have a phone, but me cya bring it to school. Mi foreign Aunty cuda only afford fi send one phone fiwi gwan juggle. It more reliable than the banga, but Mama nuh fuss wid it. Still, mi granny-proof it fi her: police and Aunty Simone number deh pon speed dial, and sticky notes with emergency contacts paste all over the house. Mi pray Mama nuh eva afi call fi help. Mi rather sum do me than her.

"Mek wi tek one a your taxi dem." Mi walk weh before Chezzy could disagree. Steer Town taxi drivers sometimeish whenever the violence surge. Money nuh worth more than life, but two hours passed already. Mi cya wait anymore. Mi foot dem tired and mi hungry!

"Yu forget where yu live, Chichi?" She grab mi hand, pulling me to a stop.

"No, but yu need fi go home to Aunty." Ignoring her protests, mi tug her toward the Mamme Bay taxi stand. The mouthwatering KFC tease mi the entire journey while I worried. Me never walk from Chezzy house this late before. Then again, the violence had never been this bad...

"Chezandra, yu phone doh work?!" Aunty jump to her feet, running over fi hug we by the door.

"Mi battery dead, Mommy." Chezzy pull away from Aunty thick frame fi look pon the TV.

Aunty sighed at me. "Mi cya carry yu home, Chichi. The car deh a the mechanic, and Dale nuh deh here fi follow yu—"

"I will follow her. Come, Chichi." Chezzy follow me to the half-distance mark between her house and mine, then hug me. "Mago call Mama and tell her yu on the way. Nuh badda wid the slow walking." She break the hug after me nod, and we walk away in the opposite direction.

Most of the streetlight dem blow, a flicker, or stolen. The barely visible moon a guide me along the twenty-minute walk. Mi almost half—

Pow!

Eyes widening, mi heart skip a beat as mi dive off behind the nearby car. Mi live ya long enough fi know gunshot from clappaz.

Pow! Pow!

Mi blousecup! A up the road dat!

Mi crawl to the side of the car, weh face away from the road, and blend into the darkness. Bush brush mi skin, making it itch while ants bite me.

Pow! Pow! Pow!

Bullets soared past the other side of the car. Feet scattered stones.

Biting my cheeks, mi clutch the bag to mi chest. Grease soil mi uniform. Mi never deh pon the road before when gunman a gwan wid dem antics! I was *always* inside the house with Mama, who'd be praying to her gods while I worried a bullet would fly through our concrete walls.

I wasn't sure how long the commotion lasted. Mi nuh breathe until it stilled to an eerie silence.

Exhaling a quiet breath, mi brush off the ants and dry mi tears with mi sleeve. Footsteps strolling toward the car made me freeze as I tried standing. The person lean pon the car, weed filling the air. A mek dem a mek demself comfortable?! It nuh look like me a move from here so tonight!

Mi nerves go haywire when another set of footsteps jog toward the car.

"Dem get weh," panted the newcomer.

"Wa dat ina yu hand?" asked another. Dem voice familiar. Mi cya place a name to it; mi heart a pound too loud.

"A gun."

"Exactly. You have a fucking gun and never use it?!" He kicked the car's tire, making me scream so loud, my throat stung.

Feet shuffled about, stopping a short distance from me. The click of their guns made me tremble while forcing myself to look at them. Me wuda faint if adrenaline nehna keep me painfully aware of the situation: me, Chayanne Arya

3

Bailey? Dead. Dead like dog.

"Get the fuck up!" His grip tightened around the trigger while I glanced at the sky, begging God to spare me. "Nuh mek mi repeat miself!"

Frightened to the point mi cuda pee miself, I jumped to my feet. Their guns followed me as I took unsteady steps toward them, stopping beneath a flickering light and keeping my head low.

"Wait... Chichi?" Him eyes widen as mi raise mi head, nodding weakly. Him conceal the gun. "Yow, wa yado?! Mind yu shoot mi sister!" Trav hissed at the man, who lowered him gun while Trav step toward me. Trav pause when mi step back. "Yu good?"

"Yes, sir," I whispered.

"Nuh eva call mi 'sir', Chichi. Wa wrong with yu?" Kissing him teeth, him lean pon the car and put the spliff in him mouth. "Come here. Wa yu see?"

Shaking, mi stand before him. "Nothing."

"Streets nuh safe dem time a night ya. Nuh mek mi ketch yu out ya again."

As mi tek up mi foot dem ina mi hand, approaching footsteps startle mi. Trav lean off the car, stance rigid along with the other man. Thinking quickly, I ran behind Trav, wishing the cracked ground would swallow me.

"Who that?" the newcomer asked, his tone cold.

"Chichi, mi sister." Trav step aside.

I clutched the bag tight to my chest, focusing on the stones beneath my feet. Mi shoes waa polish—

"*Chichi?*"

"She neva see nun. She a go touch pon fi ar base now."

"She can speak fi herself."

Gulping hard, I lifted my head, and my lips parted.

The flickering light bulb did him no justice, but he was about six-foot-four. A dark-colored hoodie covered his head, hiding his face. Danger rolled off his looming figure in icy waves, sending ripples of fear through my trembling body despite the distance between us.

"I didn't see anything," I whispered.

"Carry her home," he said, and my grip on the bag slackened.

"Fawud, Chichi." Trav lead we away while mi glance over mi shoulder. The man was gone. "Why yu out late?" him ask, bringing my focus to him.

"I was getting food for Mama. Why are you in that gang?" I asked, but he didn't answer. "Asia know?"

"Leff that alone," him seh, and mi purse mi lips until wi reach my house. "Nuh mek night ketch yu pon the road again. If yu need food fi Mrs. Saanvi, shout me," Trav seh while me open the door.

Not answering, mi run inside, not bothering to walk backward so duppy nuh follow me. Mi slam the door shut, muttering a prayer while sighing.

Opening my eyes, mi run a hand along the wall. The switch flicked on, revealing Mama. She a sleep ina her favorite chair, her chin resting on her chest. She a loosely clutch waa empty mug ina her hand. Tears swelled in my eyes as mi drop mi things, rushing over to hug her.

Mama stirred awake. "Grandbaby, yu finally reach."

Mi blink away tears. "Yes, Mama."

"Mi can go to bed now."

"You eat dinner already?" mi ask, and she nod, making her Bindi glisten.

"Mi pinch off some of Simone mackerel rundown. Mi leff most of it fi yu," Mama seh, and mi glance pon the food mi bring.

"Come to bed, Mama." Mi tek the mug from her and rest it pon the table before mi lead her to her room. Mi help her into the bed, throwing waa crochet blanket over her.

She smile. "What would I do without you, grandbaby?"

"Goodnight, Mama." Mi kiss above her Bindi before mi leave the room. Mi march to the KFC, then throw it ina the trashcan. Mi soiled uniform taunt mi, so mi yank it off and bin it, too.

Disheartened, mi go mi room. Mi text Chezzy before hopping in the shower. I scrubbed my skin raw, but the fear wouldn't wash away.

Chapter Two

CHAYANNE

Supposedly, black nuh crack. Mi nuh sure if that true. Mama ano eighty, but she look half-dead to me.

Regardless, she hearty. She usually wake up before mi on weekends and start chores. Me need fi go tell her fi stop work herself, but mi nav the energy. Mi waa stay in bed, hiding from the world.

Tears pricked my eyes, and I shot up, gasping.

If mi allow the memory fi tek permanent residence in my mind, mi nago find the strength fi leave the bed. Wiping away the tears, I got up.

Our bungalow was split in two. One side was an open-concept living room and kitchen. The other had two bedrooms and a shared bathroom.

Mama's room was across from mine. She paused entering it when mi open my door. "Morning, grandbaby."

"Morning." Mi walk into the bathroom, closing the door fi do mi business.

"How yu come in so late yesterday?" she ask, and mi blood run cold.

"Never see the time. Yu worry too much," mi seh, and she chuckle.

"Mi cya wait till drum beat before mi grind mi axe."

"Mi hate when yu talk like that. Nuh you say *cock mouth kill cock*?"

"Yes, but mi nav goat mouth. Mago lay down," she said, and mi hum as she close her door.

Sighing, mi stare at mi reflection. I had full, plump lips, a straight nose, and dark eyes, weh usually shine bright pon mi heart-shaped face. Dark circles a mek seventeen-year-old me look like thirty with a trailer load of pickney.

Mi comb through the knots ina mi shoulder-length, jet-black bob until it pin-straight. Mi hair easy fi tame cause mi get it from Mommy, whose family was Indian. People seh mi a waa carbon copy of her, but mi nuh think so. Mi nuh look like the 'average' Desi girl. Mi nav Mommy light brown complexion, mi have mi wukliss Pupa smooth, dark skin.

After mi done ina the bathroom, mi eat, then mek the house spick and spang by the time Mama fi wake from her afternoon nap. Mi cya wait fi graduate so mi can get a nice paying job and spoil her—

Something knocked on the door, making my heart race. Sas Crise! The man dem come fi finish the job?!

Mi tiptoe to the window, peeking through the curtain. "Mi a mad?" Mi open the door, resting my hands on my hips as mi look around.

Nothing was out of the normal: two cars parked parallel on the street, heavy winds ruffled tree leaves, and mongrels barked in the distance.

"Mi must a mad—" A mouthwatering aroma hit my nose. Snapping my head in that direction, I spotted a stuffed KFC bag atop the down-turned plastic chair.

Fadda God, wa dis?! Dem waa fatten mi up fi slaughter mi?!

Mi naa mek mi belly lead mi astray, but mago tek it up cause mi nuh waa nuh mongrel tek residence pon mi veranda. Mi step toward it, and a gust of wind blew a small piece of paper outta the bag. Gasping, mi snatch it up. A could never waa food bill dem fling pon mi—

About yesterday, this is for your uniform.

Brows furrowing, mi unfold the rest of the note. Mi eyes widen at the ten crisp five thousand dollar bills.

Mi scan mi surroundings, searching fi who leff dem greasy chicken and dutty money so mi cuda fling it ina dem face, then run go call police. A parked car drove off, and my grip tightened around the money as mi read the license plate. "Watch me and him." Mi go back inside, placing the bucket of chicken pon the kitchen counter. "Later mi fling yu weh."

Grabbing the sticky notes, mi write a note seh mi deh Chezzy. Mi slip on a nicer dress and Crocs, then leave.

Trav lived in the worse part of Steer Town — Godsto. I usually avoided that area like the plague, but my anger wasn't allowing me to see reason. As mi reach the Square, Trav car trickle off the lane. Him betta smell the rat! Gripping the money tighter in my hand, I stepped before the slowly approaching vehicle.

It halted.

Trav hopped out from the passenger's side, walking over with his fists clenched. "Yaa idiot?!"

Gulping, mi look at my feet. "Sorry," I muttered to the rocky ground, and him huff. E too late fi mi put mi Crocs in sports mode and run weh?

"Wa yu want? Talk fast," him seh, and mi look up, offering him the money. Him eyes soften at the same time smaddy ina the car call him. Him jog ova, then return a minute later. "Gwan ina the car."

"W-wa?" Mi eyes widen while him drag him hand down him face.

"Mi nav time fi dis."

Against better judgment, mi obey. Mi eyes glue pon Trav as him sidung across from the driver, whofa face mi cya see. As the car drive off, the one beside me stop stare through the window fi look at me.

Mi nearly faint when mi look pon the man. He had a nice, golden-brown complexion, a square-shaped face, and light stubble on a jawline sharp as steel. His tapper fade had a few long strands of curly, black hair touching his forehead. Dark-brown eyes reeled me into a sea of oblivion, settling me on a seabed of naughty thoughts. God must have spent an extra day or two with the sole dedication of sculpting this strikingly handsome man.

"It's rude to stare," he said.

Pause! Weh mi hear dis voice before?

Diving into my memory, I froze. Then, mi yank at the locked door. "Let mi out, or mago scream!"

"Wa yado now?" the driver asked.

"Mind yu spoil the door," Trav said.

8

I yanked harder. "Help! Murder! Rape!"

"Relax," said the stranger. The finality in his tone made me quiet like he had control over my mouth.

"Stop gwan like me nuh got yu," Trav added.

Mi huff and stop fight the door. Plastering myself against it, mi scowl at the passing scenery. The space in the car got smaller with each distance between me and safety, all because of the man beside me.

He was still looking at me.

No, staring.

Blatantly staring like I'd done to him.

The driver took a turn off the main road, heading onto an abandoned rocky path. Tall, leafy trees deh pon either side of the path. Waa cluster of men and nondescript vehicles deh up ahead.

Afta me escape death last night, a today me a meet my untimely demise?

Deevn frog back salt like me.

Chapter Three

Chayanne

The car park a distance away from the others. Driver and Trav exit the car, and mi glare pon the unlocked door. Mi yard far from yaso, it nuh mek sense mi come out. Nuh think mi even have a choice. The man beside me have a dark aura, weh mek mi scared fi attempt an escape. The silence in the car deafening, adding to my anxiety-ridden state, but mi remain calm.

Crossing my arms beneath my breasts, mi glance pon him. His eyes snapped up to mine, and I scowled. Mi nago mek discomfort kill me! Mago outside until Trav come back.

"Why do they call you Chichi?" him ask, and mi pause reaching fi the door.

"Mi nuh know..." I murmured.

"What's your real name?"

"Chayanne."

"*Chayanne,*" he repeated. My name dripped off his tongue like honey, making me inhale a deep breath. A so mi name did nice all this time?!

I met his gaze, its beauty reeling me in. He had long eyelashes, and for a moment I envied him. Why was this man so good-looking? He was the most handsome man I'd ever seen.

He blinked, and I stopped fixating on him, looking away. His hand shot out, grasping my chin while I tensed. He turned my head, tilting it upward. I tried pulling away, but his grip tightened, captivating me with his icy stare. There was no escape except through him, and I knew better than to put up a challenge.

"You didn't strike me as shy," him seh after a while, loosening his grip.

Mi quickly pull away, opening mi fist toward him. "Mi think a yours this."

"Was."

"Me cya accept it. Mi nuh know yu like that, sir."

"Do you want to know me?"

"No."

"Sure?"

"Yes." I licked my lips, keeping my bottom lip trapped between my teeth.

He locked onto the action, then dragged his eyes to mine. He leaned in, and my breathing grew short. Stopping inches from my face, he pressed his thumb against my lip. Tingles ran through me as he pulled it free from my teeth, then trailed it with his thumb.

Maybe me a imagine it, but it look like him waa kiss me. If he did... I'd kiss him back. Just because mi nuh want him kill mi.

Seconds passed before he moved his hand.

I released an uneven breath.

"Are you uncomfortable?" he asked.

"Wa yu think?" I retorted, and his brow raised.

"Why?"

"Yaa gunman," I said, and his brows lowered.

"Something like that." The spark disappeared from his eyes.

"Mi nuh want nuh trouble with nobody, sir," I rushed out, frightened by how fast him mood switch.

"Favio. Not 'sir'."

A knock came on the window, and Favio bring down the window. Trav open him mouth, shutting it when him see me.

"You can say whatever in front of her. Right, Chayanne?" Favio look pon me, and mi nod quickly.

"Mamme Bay man dem a plan fi push," Trav seh, and Favio jaw tick.

"Carry her home." Favio pulled out a gun. Coldness wash over me as him check the clip, then look pon me. "See you around, Chayanne."

Nodding, mi watch as him exit. Him walk to the other vehicles while mi put a hand over mi chest. Mi heart a beat too fast. Mi lips still a tingle. When mi blink, mi see him face.

Trav enter the car, driving away. "Gov?" him ask, and mi nod.

Every inch between me and Favio mek mi breathe more freely. There was still one thing bothering me, though. "Weh him come from?"

"Kingston. Slitta a good youth."

My brows crinkled. Wa good bout a man weh nearly mek mi pee miself last night, and a mek mi feel ants under mi skin today? "Good fi him."

Approaching the Square, Trav bring down the window. "*Psst*, browning."

"Mi nuh ina nun wid yu," the girl replied.

Snickering, mi bring down mi window and push out mi head. "Me either," mi add, and Trav scowl.

"Mi nuh believe ina apology. Get that outta yu head," him seh to me. Him glance pon the thickaz as she sidung pon the front, then drive off.

"Weh unu a come from?" she asked.

"Ask your man," I said.

"Me nav nuh man," she said, and Trav kiss him teeth.

"Unu leff again?"

"She cya leff," Trav seh, and Asia scoff.

"Wish yu cuda say that bout everybody ina yu life, don't?" she ask, and Trav grip tighten round the wheel.

Tension fill the silence until Trav park before mi gate.

"Bye, Chichi," she said, and mi nod while exiting.

"Nuh know when Trav and Asia a go bill," I mumbled, walking to the veranda while the car drive off. Dem two years older than mi and deh from mi ina grade six, yet all now dem cya change.

Mi enter the house and freeze. Mi eyes widen at Mama, who sit round the table a box off the KFC. It took all the energy in my body not to run over and slap it outta her hand. "Mama!"

She paused taking another bite. "Grandbaby, why yaa frighten me like this?"

Nervously chuckling, mi walk toward her. Mi gulp as mi look pon the half-eaten food. "Wa yado?"

"Me think yu bring this for me..." Her shoulders slump while more crinkles appear pon her forehead.

When since me can afford chicken bucket, fries, biscuits, and corn?! Mama musi have dementia.

Mi glare pon the food. Suppose it poisoned?! Trav wouldn't allow that, but Favio? Mi nuh sure.

Would a man who gently caressed my lips, despite the coarseness of his fingertips, kill off waa helpless old woman? Mi nuh think so.

"Yes, Mama, eat," I urged.

She smiled before taking a big bite out of the chicken, washing it down with a sip of lime life tea.

Hoping for the best, mi go mi room. Mi change into my yard dress before laying in bed. Mi have nuff homework fi do, but my mind drifted to someone I shouldn't think about.

Chapter Four

FAVIO

C hayanne.

She sparked my interest.

It wasn't every day a person had a gun aimed at them and didn't shit themselves. I knew she was terrified — it was obvious by how she shook while clutching the KFC bag — but she held her composure.

Unlike dem crosses gyal ya, Chayanne wasn't weak.

I liked that.

Moments ago, her flowery perfume lulled me close like a sailor to a siren. Her beautiful face bewitched me.

Tightening my grip around the pistol, I forced her away. I wasn't here for leisure, and I wouldn't allow Chayanne to distract me.

My focus was a bigger picture than the petty crimes Blood Paw was involved in, but the company got me involved sometimes. Mamme Bay's gang, Shottaz, a push bay badness since the other day. If dem keep up dem fuckry, it would disrupt my meticulously calculated plan.

I couldn't have that.

I hated things being out of my control.

The vehicle I sat in took a sharp turn, parking at the side of the road. I exited, my eyes scouring the area covered by vegetation. The driver's door opened, and I narrowed my eyes at him. I always kept Blood Paw at an arm's distance, but now

I had to keep track of everyone. I didn't know this man, but his hesitance to take out his gun wasn't lost to me. "Yu eva fire a gun?" I asked coldly.

He held the gun tighter. "Yes."

I walked away, stopping by the furthest car while waiting for a call from Josiah, who was scouting the closest Shottaz hideout. He had yet to call, but that didn't come as a surprise to me. People were incompetent. I never expected much from them.

A ringing erupted from my pocket, making birds squawk as they flew from the trees high above me. I grabbed my phone and turned on the silencer while checking the ID. My jaw ticked as I answered, waiting for them to speak first.

"Waa gwan down there?" he asked, his accent thick.

"Thing gov." I gripped the pistol tighter, aggravated the longer the call lasted. I'd need to release some steam later.

Chapter Five

CHAYANNE

Despite my family being Hindu, I was Christian. Maybe they allowed me to pave this path because I was a first-generation Jamaican. Mi never very religious though, so me rarely go church.

Chezzy a the opposite. She cya miss church cause a Aunty. If mi waa visit, me afi wait until dem reach home.

Me reach minutes afta dem finish eat dinner. Now, me and Chezzy ina the backyard. She stand before the concrete sinks, weh attach to the wall like extra limbs. Me sidung pon a crate ina the shade beneath the guava tree, hoping pickle mickle nuh drop pon mi.

"Mommy seh mi need fi learn fi manage mi time more wisely, so she neva wash my clothes yesterday. Anyway, tell mi wa yu did waa tell mi," Chezzy seh.

My heart skipped a beat at the mention of the purpose of my visit. Then, mi tell her everything. Her expression changed from shock to disbelief, then excitement.

"Yaa mad?" Mi brows raise while she laugh.

"Why yu seh that?"

"Yaa grin off yu face like yu nuh hear mi seh mi fraid of who the man be."

"Girl, yu ex-man a scammer."

Shrugging, mi pick few grass strands and weave dem into a ring. "Him neva own a gun. This one's different—"

"A the big buddy energy! Fuck him!" Smiling while mi scoff, she grab a pin off her green blouse. She walk to the line with her big batty a wheel behind her.

"Yu nuh hear mi seh the man a gunman—"

"Yes. But yu have bad taste in men so mi naa medz dat. How it feel when him rub yu lip?" She walk over, kneeling in the grass and beaming at me.

"It was nice. But ano cause of how him touch mi, a how him look pon mi. Mi wish yu cuda see him, Chezzy. He has this coldness to his eyes, but when he was rubbing my lip, him did look... soft." Mi look away as him face pop in my memory. Not that it ever left.

"Fuck him!" Chezzy squealed, and mi cover mi ears.

"Fi a virgin, why yu stay so?"

Chuckling, she move mi hands. "How? Him sound nice!"

"And goodly have a gungyal fi shot mi."

"True. Nuh ready fi put yu to rest yet," Chezzy said, and we laughed as she moved to the sinks. "Seriously though, mi feel seh yu nufi judge a book by its cover. Maybe him nuh so bad. Give him a chance."

Was Chezzy right? Which side of him should I judge, anyway? The side I knew was dangerous? Or the side that showed me kindness since we met?

Coward man keep sound bone.

Mi know, but mi have bad taste in men.

The worst, actually. Red a mi favorite color.

"Mi nuh want nun happen to me." Mi stand, walking toward the rose trees, weh line the inside of the high concrete walls.

Aunty love gardening, so Uncle ensured she had a large garden. The Tomlinsons live pon the better part of a more expensive scheme than mine.

"Nun nago happen to yu," Chezzy assured.

"How you know that?"

"Badman always tek care of them woman," she seh, and mi almost give miself whiplash fi look pon her.

"Me ano him—" I paused. It nuh mek sense fi argue wid her.

Chezzy was a romantic. Though she wishy-washy with her feelings, she loved love. I couldn't blame her. She was like this because she grew up in a loving two-parent home. Being her best friend meant some of her

'I'll-meet-my-Prince-Charming' ways rubbed off on me.

My Prince Charmings a never people me cuda introduce to mi family, but that was beside the point! She planted these thoughts in my mind, and it festered with thoughts of Favio.

No, blossomed... From his handsomeness. How eloquently he spoke. Him being a skyscraper beside my five-foot-four frame. How good he smelled, especially with that drop of risky behavior I'd always been attracted to.

I was getting ahead of myself, but I never dated a person this dangerous before. Time too perilous fi mi go stick mi hand ina fire, but suppose mi nuh get burn?

My boring life could use a likkle razzle dazzle.

Minutes after I left Chezzy's house, the universe played a sick joke. Mi almost reach the Square when waa familiar car stop a mi foot. The back window went down, revealing the flame I was tempted to touch.

Favio.

Two emotions ran through me: excitement, then fear.

My grip tightened around the bundle of roses as mi stare into his eyes. The atmosphere sizzled around us. My lips parted slightly, wanting to say something, but unsure what would be best.

The front window went down. Trav push him mawga arm through the window, swaying it. "Weh yaa come from?"

"Mind yu business," mi seh, and him grin.

"Hop in. Mek mi drop yu home."

Mi glance pon Favio. Him a stare pon me, his expression not revealing much. Swallowing some of the fear, mi enter the car. Goosebumps rose on my skin. Waa invisible force dare me fi draw closer to him, but mi brush it off.

Clearing my throat, mi look pon Favio while Trav drive off. "We have to stop meeting like this."

"You need fi stop walk by yuself pon the street." Favio's eyes narrowed pon the bouquet. "Boyfriend?"

"My mother."

"Your mother?" Trav asked, and I nodded.

"It good. I'll walk," mi seh as Trav reroute.

"Nuh diss mi. Slitta, we a mek a stop." Trav shift him focus to the phone after Favio nod. "Asia, hang up the phone before mi come a yu yaad come fuck yu up." Kissing him teeth, him move the phone from him ear.

Favio eyes widen when the car park before the cemetery.

"I'm okay, Trav..." I mumbled as Trav reach for the door handle. Mi hurry outta the vehicle before them say nun.

Trav always ina mi corner, but now mi doubt the finality of death bother him as much as I used to think. Favio probably nuh phased by it either.

The door slam behind me, and mi shake mi head as mi continue through the rows of graves. If a person nuh know where dem a go, dem a go lost. But not me. Mi trod this dirt path many times before.

The cemetery was littered with enormous trees and overgrown shrubs. Graves weren't numbered, and strangers rested in reserved family plots. Squatters built dandy-shandy board houses at the back, always returning after police run dem. This was more of a patty shop than a cemetery.

A moment later, I arrived at my family's plot. My grandfather bought it when he settled down in Jamaica after moving from India. Mama always said, 'We came here for vacation, and Ishaan fell in love. We never went back to India because him seh a yaso him waa dead.'

I sighed at the two graves beside each other.

Ishaan Sharma... Him dead when me a baby. Mi nav no memories of him.

Mi throat tighten as mi stoop before the next grave, replacing the withered roses with fresh ones. Footsteps stopped behind me, and mi swallow a lump as mi look over mi shoulder. "Yu hard-of-hearing— Sorry. Thought you were Trav."

Favio place him hands ina him pockets. "Disappointed?"

"Surprised." Mi look at the black and white tiled grave.

Mikeila Sharma... Death was so unfair. She should've been here to watch me grow.

Mi lips tremble as mi reach out, tracing her name. A powerful gust of wind wafted by, whipping my hair in its direction, and carrying away a mix of my perfume and Favio's cologne. Goosebumps pricked my skin as the wind swirled around us, bringing tears to my eyes.

Maybe I was too superstitious, but I convinced myself this was Mommy, reminding me she watched me from heaven.

Blinking away tears, mi face Favio. Mi cya read him expression, but mi know wa deh pon him mind. "You want to know."

"Do you want me to know?" he asked, and I smiled. That was new. Different.

Mi stand beside him. "Cancer. She did alright. I mean, me did know seh sum do her, but she always stayed strong around me. So, mi did believe she alright, until she couldn't hide it anymore... All the medicine. Doctor visits. How fast she was losing hair.

"I was eight when Mama get the call that we should come to the hospital as soon as we can. The treatment wasn't working, and her health took a turn for the w-worse. We were in the taxi when... w-when we got the call. I still remember how Mama cry out, and how w-we were too l-late to s-say b-bye—" My throat tightened and my eyes stung. Too weak to stand, mi wrap mi arms round Favio's waist, burying my face in his chest and soaking his shirt.

Why did Mommy have to die?! Why did I have to lose her like that?!

"I-I miss her," I cried, my throat aching and raw.

Favio didn't reply.

He wrapped his arms around me and held me tight.

Chapter Six

CHAYANNE

Me late fi school!

Usually, me wuda catch a taxi and save a spot for Chezzy. Wid all waa gwan ina Steer Town lately, we have a backup plan: if me nuh come within twenty minutes, she fi go school and lie bout why mi late.

"Taxi must deh pon strike," Mark said from beside me. Putting one foot on the low wall behind us, him brush him Clarks. "Feel fi go home."

"Yu know yu madda will fist yu dung," I said, and him laugh.

"Tell him again," Asia added, brushing a speck off her sixth-form uniform.

"Pay diss Asia diss mi. She know how fi mek it up to mi, stills," Mark seh.

"Yaa gwan until mi man kill yu," Asia said, and I nodded. Trav nuh ramp bout him red woman all when dem deh pon the worse terms.

"Mi nuh fear no man weh cya treat dem woman good."

Asia quieted. Her mind probably flashed to the argument she and Trav have pon the phone a few minutes ago. She smiled at me, but it nuh reach her eyes. "Mi leff one of mi notebook dem. Mi soon come back."

Mark shake him head as Asia walk off. Him chat to me fi the next few minutes, telling me how him a go save him lunch money fi buy sex from Lyrica this evening. Him pause as waa strange car stop nearby.

The small group of skoolaz gawk pon the criss, yellow BMW. Mi nuh know the

21

model, cause mi nuh know nun bout car except that dem have four wheels and an engine. The window went down. Ignoring everybody, the driver focused on me. Mi heart pace as Favio motion him head ina the car.

Ano every roof a shelter.

Who mi be fi turn down free drive? If him kill me, people see him. Including Mark, who seh mi fi beg ride fi him. Mi open mi mouth fi ask Favio, but him bring up the heavily tinted window without hesitation. Mi give Mark an apologetic smile before mi sidung ina the front seat. Mi gawk at the custom full black interior while vanilla filled my nostrils. "Good morning. Thanks," I said, and he nodded, driving away.

Today, he traded his hoodie for a white tee that gripped his forearm muscles. A big face silver watch was around his wrist. Simple as he was, him look good to the point me cuda—

Clearing my throat, I widened my legs and dropped the schoolbag on the floor. Favio tek him eyes offa the road, glancing where mi dress ride up and expose my thighs. Fixing my dress, I smiled sheepishly at him.

"Think we did a go stop meet like this?" I asked.

"Where would you like to meet?" He curled a hand around the top of the wheel, resting the other elbow on the windowsill.

"Mi nuh know yu like that fi meet yu anywhere."

"You're in my car."

"Fair. Why yu stop fi me?"

"Because I saw you."

Mi roll mi eyes. "Yu girlfriend must sick a yu."

"I'm a free man."

With a face and body like that? Me born big?

Him glance pon mi when mi scoff. "You don't believe me?" he asked, and I shook my head. "Get to know me. I'll consider it a thank you."

Sitting more upright, I fired off the first question. "What's your name?"

"Favio Welsh."

"Are you from here?" Mi brows furrow when him nod. "How old are you?"

"Twenty-three," he said, and my interest peaked. "You?"

Six-year difference aside, mi soon legal. "Seventeen."

Favio's brows raised as him glance pon mi. "When were you born?"

Mi smile. "July twenty-seven."

"The year?" him ask, and mi tell him.

"Problem?"

"No."

Satisfied him nav a problem with my age, we fell into silence for a minute before mi talk again.

"Yu nuh talk much, don't?"

"I do to you," he said after a moment's pause. Him vaguely ansa mi other questions fi the rest of the journey to St. Mary. Parking before mi school, him pull out him phone and offer it to me. "Give me your number."

Kiss mi neckstring! Nuh the latest version of my phone dis?

Mi hurry and lock mi mouth before him think mi nuh used to things. "Say 'please'," I teased, my thumb hovering over the keypad as he glared. "Rude," I mumbled, tapping in the number before returning the phone. "Text, don't call. Thanks for the ride." Mi exit the car.

Him drive off in a cloud of dust, capturing the attention of my schoolmates, who were idling by the gate.

Chezzy ran toward me. "A him dat?! Tell me everything!" she demanded, and we walk through the gate side-by-side while mi tell her everything.

How sexy he looked, all cool and collected.

How inviting his lips were.

How good his cologne smelled on his skin.

Mi stop walk, shrugging my bag off my shoulder. Mi sigh after looking inside. "Cho, blousecup! Mi leff mi perfume."

"Yu soon leff yuself. Ano time fi perfume, tell me bout the man. Yu betta fuck him ino," she seh as we enter we first class.

"Me walk and fling mi crochiz pon everybody?"

"Mi want yu get some good sex so you nafi go back to dutty Dayshawn."

"Mi wudn deh back with him…"

"But yu mek him fuck yu so it bound fi happen—"

"Wow, Chezzy, that was *one* time!" I hissed, and she scoffed while we teacher enter the class.

"Time yu let the bwoy go. Yav a don ina yu life now."

Dayshawn ears must did a ring since me and Chezzy chat him this morning. Why as we reach Ochi bus park, him a the first smaddy we see?

"Hide me!" Mi duck behind Chezzy bag and her big batty.

She crossed her arms. "Him see yu already."

I sighed and straightened myself, watching Dayshawn approach us. Him turn twenty-one the other day and was a college dropout. Him easy pon the eyes, but such man look bet—

"Chezzy," Dayshawn greeted, and Chezzy kiss her teeth, grabbing my hand and trying to walk away.

Mi pull weh mi hand. "Me waa talk to him."

Chezzy glare. "Yu know mi tired fi talk to yu?"

"Gwan yu ways and stay outta husband and wife argument," Dayshawn hissed.

"Yu lucky than me, Chichi." Chezzy walk away, stopping a short distance away from us. She took out her phone.

Sighing, mi look pon the man. "Yes?"

Dayshawn flashed me that two dimpled smile. It used to make me weak, but all it do a sick mi stomach these days. "Yu naa hug yu man?"

"We nuh deh," mi seh, and him sigh.

"Babes, how much time yago mek mi apologize? Yu deevn a link mi again."

"Yu nuh realize school start back? Me tell yu fi use yu subjects do sum wid yu life except *that* alone, and yu always gwan like a foolishness mi a tell yu."

Him kiss him teeth. "Bill offa that nuh, babes. Mi miss yu..."

"Don't lie to me," I hissed.

He opened his mouth, closing it as him look behind me.

Following him gaze, mi jaw clench. Mi look at him, scowling at him fake innocence. "A she yu cheat with?"

He shook his head. "No. A different one."

Mi heart drop to mi batty. Mi talk to nuff man before, but none a dem neva have a buzz like Dayshawn. Giving him a chance a mi biggest regret cause him a nun but a crosses. Mi cya stand the lyad, busy buddy bwoy.

"Leff mi alone," I snarled. Mi walk away, and him deevn stop mi. Him nuh rate mi, yet mi a try convince miself him a go change.

Sometimes, I wished red flags were green.

Or, at the very least...

Yellow.

Chapter Seven

CHAYANNE

Mi fi stop mek everybody feel like hummingbird. Imagine, after me wait up all night fi such man text me, all now him deevn fawt pon mi.

"Me nuh know why mi care," mi complain, walking toward the school gate.

Chezzy shrug on her green jacket. "Cause yu like him."

"No. I'm intrigued. Mi start understand wa other girl mean when dem seh badman have a buzz."

Reaching the gate, we greet Sikki.

Sikki greet we before him walk to waa car, weh park close to the gate. Him return a moment later and seh to me, "A yu brother. Him come pick yu up."

Surprised, mi walk toward the car. "Wa yaa do here?"

Trav was about to answer when the back window went down. My heart paced when I met Favio's eyes. They always looked dark.

"Get in," Favio ordered, moving over.

Mi kiss mi teeth. "A so you do people?"

"How? We're dropping you home."

"Mi friend afi come, too." My bench nuh travel widout the batty.

"Friend?" Favio look at Chezzy, who a stare in our direction. Him look away momentarily when mi nod, then look back at me. "Get her."

"Thanks!" Smiling, mi run toward Chezzy. Mi grab her hand, tugging toward the car. "Favio a bring we home."

Chezzy froze. "Gunman Favio?"

"Yes. Why yaa worry? Mi bredda dih deh."

"Alright. Mi will come, but as yu bodyguard. If anything happen, mi know you alone cya go fight."

"Just collect the shot dem ina yu batty," mi joke, and she laugh as we approach the car. "Yago like him. Him nuh as bad as him seem."

Chezzy sidung a front. Me sit beside such man, my nerves jittery. Favio was wearing a different cologne today. I had a good nose for scents, but I couldn't place what it was. It was expensive, though.

Trav and Chezzy were my closest friends, but they never met, so I introduced them. "Trav, this is Chezandra. Call her Chezzy."

Trav lift him chin. "Pree?"

Chezzy smile. "Hey."

Favio pon the other hand? Antisocial and bad breed. Him nuh seh kem to her, and Chezzy nuh seh kam.

The ride was silent minus the music and cool swish of the AC. The silence was stifling, and me only like when one thing choke mi. I tried making conversation with Favio, but as I turned to face him, him phone ring.

Him ansa the call. Him grip tighten round the phone while listening, causing the color to drain from his knuckles. "I'm handling it. Nuh send him nuh weh," he hissed, hanging up.

He turned to look at me, and mi snap round quickly. Favio's fingertips brushed mine, taking my hand in his. Surprised by the gentle action, my lips parted as I looked at where our hands joined.

His large hand swallowed mine, but it was a nice fit. A smile tugged at my lips as I looked at him. Him a stare through the window.

A loud voice from the front tugged me into Chezzy's and Trav's conversation.

"Curry goat fi eat with rice and peas!" Chezzy declared.

Trav kiss him teeth. "White rice alone fi touch curry."

"Yu nuh used to good food."

"Chichi, talk sense ina yu idiot friend."

"Unu leave me outta this," mi seh, despite agreeing with Chezzy.

We arrived at Chezzy's house shortly after. The men were well relaxed despite being in Mamme Bay.

Standing outside the car, Chezzy wag a finger at Trav. "Drop her home safely."

"Nuh worry boh her, Cheesy." Trav reverse, taking the long way to Steer Town. Him turn onto the rocky road weh Favio caressed my lips and left me wanting more. Him park, exiting the vehicle.

"Oye, come carry mi home," I said.

"Easy nuh. This a tek a minute." Trav walk toward the small cluster of vehicles.

"You good?" Favio asked, and mi look pon him. Every time mi see him, is like him get more handsome.

"Yes. You?" mi ask, trying not to stare at his lips.

"Always good."

Ketch lie! Anybody who tense fi waa entire car ride cya 'always good'.

"Why yaa do this?" Mi release him hand, and him bring it to him side.

"Do what?"

"You could've killed me, but you didn't. Now yaa act... a way. A nice way. Yu nuh seem like the type fi care bout anybody, so this a confuse me."

Favio eyes widen before him recover quickly. Him expression harden, then him exit the car. Seconds later, him yank open my door. "Get out."

"Why?"

"Get. Out," him repeat through clenched teeth, and mi gulp while reluctantly complying. "On your knees."

"W-wa?" Mi eyes widen, my breathing quickening.

"Doh mek mi repeat miself." He pulled out his gun. Him flick off the safety, and mi blood run cold.

Tears roll down mi cheeks as mi lower miself to the ground. Sharp stones press into mi knees, and mi wince. Pairs of footsteps run up to we, but mi vision too blurry fi see who come witness mi execution.

A bewildered yell came from before me. "Slitta?!"

Waa flicker of hope come to life inside me, but Favio killed it.

"Shut up," Favio hissed, aiming at my forehead and making me tremble as mi eyes slam shut.

Mi cya feel mi heart a beat anymore.

All mi senses gone dormant, leaving me sure of one thing: mago dead today.

"Yu ungrateful nuh fuck. Man spare yu life, and yaa ask mi fuckry. A dis yu want?" Favio asked, his tone cold.

More tears spill from mi eyes as mi force miself fi look at the fuming figure above me. His handsome face was twisted into the meanest scowl, washing away my belief that he could be soft. Him a nothing but a stone-cold murderer, and me a him next victim.

"Kill who?!" Trav shrug off the hands holding him back. Him run over, standing in front of me. "Yafi kill mi first."

Mi struggle fi breathe as mi shut mi eyes again. Mi nuh waa witness we death, so mi force miself fi focus pon sum else.

The inaudible muttering of gang members.

Birds singing while ruffling tree leaves.

Vehicles blazing in the distance.

A phone's ringing.

Mi eyes open, locking on Favio. Him glare pon Trav while moving the phone to him ear.

"*Che cosa*? Maa fawud." Favio lower the gun, but mi couldn't relax. Him a stare pon me like a neva me hold him hand after him call upset him.

Yet, me ungrateful?

Wa sweet a mouth, hot a belly.

Mi bury the silly fantasies about this man as him walk weh. Everybody else leff while Trav pull mi to mi feet.

"Swear dem drop that youth pon him bloodcleet head when him a baby." Trav brush off my knees. Him use him shirt hem fi wipe weh mi tears. More replace them, and him sigh. "Yu good, Chichi?"

Me a cry, shake, and unsure if Favio pull the trigger and this a the afterlife.

No, mi neva good.

I'd never be good again.

Chapter Eight

CHAYANNE

I sighed while Chezzy eat a box lunch, waiting for me to tell her what I didn't get the chance to do last night. I cleared my throat. "Trav carry we waa place. Me and the man did leff ina the car, and mi ask him waa question—"

"What question?" Chezzy asked.

"Why him a be nice to me. I guess I struck a nerve... Him draw gun pon mi," mi seh, and her eyes widened.

"Wa?! Yu good?" she ask, and mi shake mi head.

"No, but... it's whatever. Mama seh *if mi get mi hand ina devil mouth, tek it out*. A dat mago do."

"Yu know damn well mi nuh understand all of Mama's sayings," she joked, and mi smile at her attempt fi lighten the mood.

"Certain things nuh shock me because of where me live, but it different when I'm the one in the situation. Yu get me?" mi ask, and she nod.

"Mi happy nun worse nuh do yu, Chichi. Yado the right thing by leaving him alone. What a good thing yu neva fuck him."

Nodding, mi tell her mi will see her after school before mi walk away.

My God... The man handle mi like mi come a him yaad come thief ripe mango. If mi see Favio Welsh again, mi a run like dog a chase mi. Mi cya afford fi bite off more than mi can chew.

A knock on the front door pull mi from my homework. Curious who a visit at eight p.m., mi hop outta bed and cautiously approach the door. "Who is it?"

"Trav," him ansa, and mi tense.

"Nobody nuh deh here."

"When since 'eedyat' write pon mi farid? Open dis." Trav knocked the door louder, and me glance toward Mama's room

"Mind yu wake Mama. Wa yu want?"

"Open the door. Ano so we grow."

Clenching my jaw, I slipped the safety chain intact. Mi open the door, peeking through the small space.

"Wa this fa? Mi can still come in." Trav slip him hand through the space. Him start undo the latch, and mi slap him. Grinning, him bring him hand to him side.

"Ano so we grow."

"Exactly. So come talk to me."

Mi open the door, stepping onto the veranda. Mi sit pon the railing while Trav lean pon a column.

"Yu good?" he asked, making memories push through my mental barrier.

"Me good..."

Him sigh. "Mi waa apologize pon Slitta behalf—"

"Yu can keep dat. No apology cya mek up fi—" I paused, unable to finish.

"Him sick ina him head sometimes."

"*Sometimes*?" I mocked.

"Ah, most times. But him a good youth—" Him laugh when mi glare. "Yu know yu eyes cya do mi nun."

Waa door slam, and mi look over mi shoulder. Mi smile at Asia, who walk ina the yaad wid waa KFC bag.

"You good, Chichi?" she asked, and I nodded. She smile, placing the bag ina mi hand. "This is for you. From Trav."

"Mi know how yu love yu belly, but mi did fraid fi carry it come when yu did still vex. Neva waa yu dash it weh," him seh, and Asia chuckle. Trav pull Asia to him side, grabbing a handful of her ass and making her redden.

"Unu good now?" mi ask.

Trav kiss Asia neck. "We always good."

Mi glance at dem complimenting outfit. "A weh unu a come from?"

"She nuh feel good, so mi carry her go hospital."

"Yu good?" mi ask, and she clear her throat, nodding.

Trav kiss him teeth, pulling away fi hug me. "Ago good?" him whisper, and mi nod. "Ah. Hail Mrs. Saanvi fi me." Him pinch mi before dem leave.

Mi go inside and tek out three piece of breast, some fries, and waa corn before returning to my room. Mi eat mi dinner two hours ago, but mi cya mek the food waste. As mi tek the first bite, mi phone ring. Why Dayshawn nuh leff mi alone?! Mi tired fi block number now! Mi kiss mi teeth and answer. "Wa yu want?"

"Who yaa chat to, Chichi?" him hiss.

"You! We leff from August, but yu won't lowe mi."

"We nuh leff. We cya leff," him seh, and mi kiss mi teeth. "Babes, yu did vex with me over fuckry. If yu pree it, a your fault mi cheat."

Mi laugh dryly. "Wow."

"Me change, babes. Come link me weekend, mek wi talk things out."

"Why you nuh link me?" Mi smirk when him nuh ansa.

"Joke thing yu deh pon... Please, Chayanne?"

Dayshawn always call mi by mi nickname, so this surprising. Mi nuh like how him seh mi name. It nuh sound like when F—

Mi fist tighten, my nails digging into my palm. "Okay."

Chezzy tell mi nufi visit Dayshawn, but mi stubborn, so mi nuh listen.

Dayshawn stop kiss mi neck, pulling away with a brow raised. "A wa?"

Mi glare. "You said you wanted to talk. This isn't talking."

"We can talk after. Let's try again—" Him pause when mi push him off mi, getting out of bed.

"Me tell yu mi hungry, and yu nuh offer me nun fi eat besides dick."

Him scratch him neck. "Yu know me cya cook. Mi will run go buy a box food."

Mi kiss mi teeth, searching fi mi Crocs. Him did yank dem off ina him haste fi get mi pon him air mattress. Mi nuh judge him cause everybody afi start somewhere, but him nuh interested fi elevate. Mi tek feel up pon hungry belly fi seven months, and mi tired now!

"Yaa leff mi wid this?" Him walk over, grab mi hand and press it pon him buddy. Him kiss him teeth as mi pull weh. "Then yu vex when mi fuck next gyal."

Mi glare. "Keep disrespect mi and see."

"See wa? Why mi naa stop tell yu yaa fuckry?"

Chuckling, mi grab mi handbag and leff him one-room house. Mi nuh know weh him a scam fa. A must man him a try impress with the bottle a liquors ina dance, plus name brand clothes and shoes.

Mi walk go KFC, weh ina the middle of St. Ann's Bay. After mi get mi food, mi go Western Union. Groceries a run low, so Aunty send money. Mi collect the money and a leave out when mi bump ina smaddy.

Dem wrap dem arm round mi waist and mi grab dem shirt, preventing my fall. Mi eyes widen when mi see Favio. Mi waa pull away, but mi cudn move.

People walked around us, oblivious to how this dangerous man held me captive in his gaze and powerful arms.

Swallowing to dampen my dry throat, mi tug free. Him hand shoot out, his fingers circling my wrist. Tingles shot up my arm.

From fear or excitement? I didn't know.

"Let me go or I'll scream," I warned.

"You won't," he dared, and mi chest heave faster.

"Me nuh waa talk to yu, sir." Mi gulp when him grip tighten.

"*Favio.* I want to talk to you." Him drag mi toward him car, weh park across the road. Ignoring the people gawking at the car, him open the door while giving me a pressing stare.

Mi tremble as mi sidung, wishing mi did have mi phone. Mi wuda tell Chezzy fi call police cause the man a kidnap mi.

Him enter the car, driving toward Priory. Him park pon the beach, facing me while me keep my gaze straight. "I want to apologize. I took things too far."

"You did," I said.

"I'm not the best at verbally expressing how I feel. I'm better at showing," him seh, and mi glare at him stupid, handsome face.

"Wa dat supposed to show mi? Seh yu waa kill mi?!" mi yell, and him eyes widen, but mi nuh care.

"It's fucked up, but I was trying to show you that even though I can, I wouldn't do you anything," him seh, but I was unmoved. "You wouldn't understand."

"Clearly. Can I go now?" Mi tripe a twist cause the Zinger scent a tease mi.

"It won't happen again."

"It won't happen again because mi nuh waa see yu again—" Mi belly grumble, and mi eyes widen. Mi glance at Favio as the corner of him mouth twitch upward. "Sorry!" mi rush out.

"Eat."

Mi nuh waa deh round him, but Steer Town deh far from yaso. Mi eat while him watch mi choke when the spice kick mi tastebuds. Favio release sum like a chuckle, and mi nearly bruk mi neck fi look at him. Him cough, and mi glare.

"It hot," mi seh, and him mouth twitch again.

"Yu cya manage hot things?"

"Taste it since yu better than mi." Taking large sips from the drink, mi use mi eyes fi tell him fi tek a bite.

Favio open him mouth, and mi eyes widen.

Gulping, mi rest the drink ina the cup holder. Mi flip the sandwich upside down, directing it to him mouth. Him eyes lock on mine as him take a bite, then pull away. Him swallow without a fuss.

Mi roll mi eyes. "Yaa talk nuff today doh."

"I'm not a mute," him seh, and mi scoff. Tha one deh funny star!

"Says the gang leader of Steer Town. Yaa must waa busy man, why yaa spend time with me?"

"You intrigue me, Chayanne."

Every time this man call mi name, mi heart somersault. Mi intrigue him? Ouu, mi cya wait fi tell Chezzy dis!

Blushing, mi look weh. Mi cuda feel him eyes pon mi — looking at every perfection and the smallest imperfections like I was a specimen under the microscope of a scientist. "How so?" mi ask, barely getting a hold of myself.

"You're still here after what I did. I intrigue you, too."

"Yu ego big doh."

"Ano dat alone." His eyes shone as mi choke. "Let's go for a walk," him seh after mi stop.

I should run, but what could I say? Yellow was becoming my favorite color.

"Mi vex yu nuh waa mi go in." Mi pout at the glistening water while mi swing mi Crocs ina mi hand. Mi cya swim, but mi love the beach.

Favio glance at me from head to toe. "I had my reasons."

We a walk toward the end of the beach, away from the crowd. It more peaceful out yaso. There was no noise except the waves crashing onto the beach, and the insects in the bushes.

"Unu liff up from yaso," Favio hissed.

A boy and girl around my age were in the bushes. She deh pon her knees. Him pants round him ankles.

Favio sidung pon a log, glaring as them struggle fi straighten themselves while running away. Favio look at me, patting the space beside him. "You know you're too trusting?" Him stretch a conch shell toward me.

Mi accept it, moving it to mi ear. Mi smile while the ocean fill mi ear. "How?"

"You trust people too easily. That's not a good trait."

"Not trusting is a bad trait." Mi rest the shell ina the sand, walking toward the water. A squeal escaped my mouth as Favio lift me from behind. Mi wrap mi arms round him neck, glaring while him walk into the water. "Put me down!"

"You sure?" he asked, and I nodded. Him mouth twitch upward before him drop mi ina the water.

Mi tightly shut mi eyes. Water fill mi ears and mouth before mi cuda push miself to the surface. Mi wipe weh the hair sticking to my face, seething at Favio, whose eyes a glisten. "Why yu do that?!"

"Nuh you seh put yu down?" Him stretch him hand toward me.

Mi lay mi hand in his, smirking before mi tug him into the water. Mi laugh till mi nearly dead when him head break the surface. "See seh it nuh funny?"

"I have spare clothes in my car. You don't," he said, and I shut up. "See seh it nuh funny?" he mocked, and I chuckled.

We walk out of the water together. We clothes drenched, but we naa complain.

"Wait," he said, and I paused. Him take bits of seaweed outta mi hair, then trail him finger down the side of my face. Him stop beneath my chin, lifting my head. "Do you know how beautiful you are?"

Blushing, mi look away.

Him grip mi chin tighter, forcing me to look at him. "Don't look away when I compliment you," he said, and I nodded. Humming, him brush him thumb across my bottom lip, reminding me of our moment in the car and how badly I wanted to kiss him.

His lips were more inviting now.

Meeting his eyes, I tipped. He was still too tall, so he leaned down. Favio's lips met mine, and my breath hitched. He slowly kissed me. His lips were softer than I imagined. Our kiss was salty, but I didn't care. I only cared about the sweetness of this moment. Bliss replaced the fading world while our lips moved in sync.

It was a sin to indulge in pleasure from a man like Favio Welsh, but I never claimed to be a saint.

He was an amazing kisser. I couldn't pull away even if I wanted to.

Chapter Nine

FAVIO

I dropped Chayanne home two hours ago, and she was still on my mind. Even as I smoked on my veranda.

The gate opened, and my head snapped up while my hand reached for my gun. Seeing who it was, I relaxed.

Travis walked toward the veranda, bumping his fist with mine before he sat. "A check yu pon a thing," he said, and I raised a brow. Cya tek the fuckry right now. "Mi likkle sista," he said, capturing my attention. "Waa yu intentions?"

"*Wa*?"

"Chichi," he stated, as if anyone else had such a stupid nickname. "She young, and mi naa try diss yu, but mi nago sidung and watch nuh man try use her—"

"Me a use her?" I wasn't aware.

Travis shrugged. "Nuh know waa gwan between unu. Mi hear a thing, so mi a seh a thing."

"Yaa seh too much." I took a long drag from my spliff. Weed always increased my tolerance for whatever bullshit people had to say. For example: Travis. The shit he spewed from his mouth was ridiculous, but I listened.

"Slitta, she a good girl. If yu nago serious boh her, lowe her. Memba a me one yu tell yu naa stay a Steer Town afta yu done business. Chichi need smaddy weh a go deh ya fi her. Get wa maa seh?"

Wa him a try seh? The man know the bagga gyal thing nuh interest me. One was time-consuming and annoying enough.

Fuck whatever Travis had to say. I always got what I wanted. I was me.

Chayanne didn't know it yet, but she was mine. Because of her bravery. Beauty. That snarky attitude and willingness to look past the shit I was involved in.

I didn't want to ruin her innocence, so I'd do my best to shield her from this life. Not that I'd have much of a choice if Antaro found out there was someone else who snagged my interest. And if he ever did, well...

"Get wa yaa seh," I said.

Travis nodded, taking out his phone from his pocket. He sighed at the screen before looking at me. "Need mi fi handle nun?"

"No."

"Ah. Ina e lates." He reached over to bump my fist. "Mago link mi woman, then check mi sister. Yu know mi nuh fraid a yu unlike dem other man ya, so blood afi run if yu fuck wid her again."

I smirked.

Chapter Ten

CHAYANNE

Mi push open the door, peeking inside the room. "Me a leave now."

"Be safe, grandbaby," Mama said, making me swallow guilt as me go outside to Favio's BMW.

Him lean off the car, blowing fumes into the air.

"Good morning. It too early fi dat." Mi fan away the smoke while him scoff.

"Get in." Him open the door, and mi enter. Seconds later, he entered the car. As him drive off, mi realize him dash the tail somewhere. "Is your friend coming?" he asked, and I nodded.

Chezzy ina her sometimeish phase right now. As the bad decision-making friend, she know she cya change mi mind about letting Favio drop me at school.

Mi take my travel-sized perfume outta mi bag, spraying like mi nav sense.

"*Fuck*, Chayanne." Favio coughed, bringing down the window.

Apologizing, mi stop spray miself, then direct him to a shortcut. Favio use one hand steer the vehicle, stretching the other toward the back seat.

Me turn round, looking at the black hoodie. "Yu waa mi get it?"

Favio shook his head, struggling to grab it while maneuvering around the potholes. Him look weh from the road, and the car swerve. Mi hand shoot out, pressing against the dashboard.

Him get the car under control quickly, glancing pon me. "You good?"

"Yes. Mek mi do it before yu kill wi off." Mi reach for the hoodie.

"No—"

Too late.

Coldness seeped into my palm.

"Yu nuh listen?" He glared while mi look from the pistol to him. "Put it in the glove compartment."

Anybody see mi dying trial?!

Mi about fi protest, when mi realize him need fi focus pon driving. Nodding, mi wipe off weh mi touch, then put it in the compartment. Mi slam it shut and rest the hoodie pon mi lap.

"It's registered," Favio said, amused.

"Better safe than sorry."

"Smart."

Chezzy friend tug her away as we step through the gate, so mi a walk to class alone.

A laugh came from behind me. "Which man yaa gimi bun wid?"

Mi gasp at the hoodie tossed over my arm. "Sorry."

"Me hate when yu flaunt man ina me face. Me waa yu flaunt me," she seh, and mi laugh as she link our arms.

"Fi yu deal wid mi like yu other gyal dem?"

"Never! You're my Number One."

"So yaa seh until dem try beat mi."

"Me we report dem cause dem fi know dem place," she said, and we laughed. Yolanda Montgomery was my second closest friend at school. She was of Hispanic descent, had blue braces, and was one of the prettiest girls in school.

"How me a yu Number One and mi hear seh yaa deal wid new woman?" mi ask, and she kiss her teeth as we enter waa empty classroom. Sitting, mi lay Favio's hoodie across my lap.

"A must Stosh Foot fly ar mouth. This a why me nuh deal wid lower form gyal. Dem nuh know fi shut up."

"Dem probably feel special seh yu want dem."

"Me tried fi tell dem fi stop want me, cause me nuh want a soul. Oh, before me forget, sign this fimi." She pulled out a permission form for a class trip.

"Why yu mother nuh sign it?" I searched my bag for my pencil case. Mi sigh, realizing mi leff it pon the kitchen table.

Yolo hand me a pen. "A so me wish me gyal dem dee forgetful when dem see me wid next woman. And me forget fi tell Mommy."

Humming, I forged the signature. I learned to forge at a young age cause mi nuh like bother Mama. I only did this for Chezzy and Yolo. Although Chezzy nuh approve, she use me to her advantage sometimes. The other times, she seh she nuh waa mi get ina trouble.

Finished, mi hand Yolo the form and pocket her pen.

"Whofa hoodie yu thief? Watch her a smile! You and Dayshawn good?" She wiggle her brows.

"A someone else own..." Mi smile widen while looking at it.

"Tell me bout the man weh a try tek weh me favorite woman."

"There's nothing to say." I didn't know what Favio and I were doing.

The car drop mi at the entrance of mi lane. Mi tek mi time walk home, then open the door quietly. It was nearing six p.m., so Mama should be praying. Entering the house, mi smile when mi see her on her knees with her hands clasped.

Leaving her to it, mi grab the phone and go mi room. Mi tek off mi clothes while checking the notifications. Waa strange number text mi. The person nav up a picture, so me nuh know a who. A must Dayshawn a come provoke mi peace afta mi block him!

Fuming, mi call the organized crime unit. "Hello, I'd like to make an anonymous report of suspected scamming."

Afta mi file the report, mi return to the chat. Mi bout fi block the dutty bwoy when a new text pop up.

UNKNOWN: Hey. It's Favio.

Mi baxide! Look how mi send such man gone a jail when a the other such man text mi!

Oh well! If Dayshawn get lock up and suspect seh a me, mago tell him *mi nuh know how wata walk go pumpkin belly.*

Smiling, I sat on the floor and replied to Favio's texts.

Think yu fling weh mi number...

FAVIO: No, I changed my number and thought I texted you.

Oh...

Neva mean fi yu touch nuh strap today.

It's okay.

No. Neva waa involve yuh ina certain things.

Too late for that Favi.

Favi?

Too soon for nicknames?

No.

I smiled.

Favi... Mi think mi like that more.

Mi bout fi reply when sum fall somewhere ina the house.

"Mama, yu alright?" I shouted, but she didn't answer. Me tell Favio mi soon come, then go to the living room. Mama a kneel before the altar Grandpa mek fi her, fixing a statue. This area was sacred. I always respected it by keeping my distance.

"Mama, yu alright?" I asked.

"Mi peepee miself," she whispered, her head hanging low.

Mi glance at the wet spot beneath her. "That's fine, Mama. Can I come closer?"

She nodded, and mi help her stand. Mi lead her to the bathroom while she look back pon the mess.

"Nuh worry about it, Mama. Accidents happen sometimes."

Mama sigh as mi help her outta the soiled clothes. "Me wish yu neva afi take care of mi, grandbaby."

"Mama, stop the foolishness. A me fi tek care of yu. Memba mi a yu one and only," I joked, and she chuckled.

"Always bragging."

"Yup, cause Aunty and Tate nuh look like dem waa give yu waa grandbaby."

"If me cya get turkey, mi afi satisfy with johncrow," she seh, and mi gasp. She laugh while mi help her into the shower.

Mi bathe and dress her, then hot up some of the Sunday-Monday pon the stove fi ar. We have a microwave, but Mama nuh like eat from it.

While she eat, mi clean the altar. After mi done, mi bathe, then join her at the table. Mi call Aunty Kenzie so Mama could talk to her. Mi deevn realize how much time passed until Mama eyes start droop. I helped her to bed, then kissed above her Bindi.

"Mi put the chimmy beside the bed if you cya mek it to the bathroom," I said, and Mama nodded. Yawning, mi return to mi room and lay in bed, checking the new notifications. Mi see Favi text and slap mi farid. "Forgot to reply."

Still here?

It's late. You should get some sleep.

Goodnight Favi.

Goodnight miserable.

A nickname!

Cheesing, mi rest the phone aside. Mi close mi eyes, falling asleep with him at the front of my mind.

Me a season turkey neck fi dinner tomorrow. Mi tired a soup, and a dat Mama wuda mek. She can help herself to an extent, but she nuh strong like one time.

It too late fi a cook, but me a occupy mi time while mi wait pon Chezzy call. We have a project together, but she nuh finish her part yet. Mi waa review it tonight cause mi nago have enough time fi dweet before class tomorrow.

My phone rang. I grabbed it, smiling while trying to make my voice sound sweeter. "Hello?"

"Chayanne, weh yu deh?" he asked urgently.

"Home. Why?"

"Make sure you stay inside tonight."

The dial tone fill mi ear, and mi furrow mi brows. Leaving the kitchen, mi resume the movie pon the TV. An hour later, mi phone ring.

"Mi done. Yu can come fi it," Chezzy seh, and mi look pon the clock.

"A afta nine. Yu need fi manage yu time wisely fi real," mi seh, and she sigh.

"Sorry. Mi did afi watch mi bredda dem earlier, so mi cudn focus. Hurry and come. Mommy a sleep, and mi nuh waa she see mi a leff the house this late," she seh, and mi hang up.

Mi step toward the door, freezing as Favi's words play ina mi head. I should listen, but this project worth a chunk of my exam grade. Mi naa fail school, ah sorry. Mi leave out, taking long strides in the darkness until mi reach HalfWay. Chezzy give me the project, then mi retrace mi steps.

The place eerily quiet. Deevn the peenie wallie dem mi naa hear, and mi hate it. Putting more pep in my step, me mek a turn when sum grab mi from behind one a the shop dem pon the side of the road.

Mi heart skip a beat, and mi open mi mouth fi scream.

Dem slap dem hand over mi mouth, muffling me.

Mi squirm and fight, and dem hold mi tighter.

"Relax," they whispered, and I stiffened.

Favi?

"Be quiet," came another hushed voice.

Mi look at the shop before we, seeing Trav and a man. Dem dress ina black while mi ina waa hot pink dress like Frighten Friday. Nodding against Favi, I watched as five masked men ran off the street mi did deh pon. Dem head further into Steer Town.

Favi stirred from behind me. Trav and the man sneak out behind dem.

Favi spin mi around, seething while looking at me. "Yu nuh know how fi fucking listen?!" he hissed lowly.

I opened my mouth to respond, screaming as rapid gunfire filled the air.

Favi slapped a hand over my mouth, muffling my scream. He pushed me against the wall, his body shielding mine as he peeked up the road.

The gunfire was rampant, deafening.

My heart was going to combust. Favi's heavy body made it harder to breathe.

He pressed my head further into his chest, wrapping an arm around my head. His palm flattened against my ear. The gunshots weren't as loud anymore, but I could hear the blood pumping through my veins.

Favi raised his gun, waiting a few seconds before firing up the road.

The project dropped from my hand. I gripped his shirt tightly, burying my face into his chest as I tried making my body smaller.

I tried thinking of my happy place for however long it would last, but my mind brought me to the beach with Favi.

I loved how he held me.

Kissed me.

Stared at me.

I got lost there until finally... silence.

I took my head off his shirt, looking at him. His jaw clenched as he looked at me, prying my hands off him gently. Favi moved the gun to my head, and I stiffened as the hot barrel brushed the hair from my face.

"You good?" he asked, and I nodded. He looked from me to Trav, who jogged toward us.

"Yu good, Chichi?" Trav pull me from Favi, inspecting me while mi nod.

"Clean her," Favi ordered, and Trav nodded.

"Come pon mi back." Trav turned around.

I jumped onto his back, bile rising in my throat as he jogged past the dead bodies splayed on the road.

"Don't look," he said, but I couldn't tear my eyes away.

I'd seen dead bodies before, but never up close.

There was so much blood. Brain matter. Everywhere. On everything.

I gagged. "Trav, me waa vomit."

"Swallow it. Yu cya leff nuh trace a you yaso," he said, and my stomach churned as I swallowed.

Trav maneuvered us through the darkness to his house. He took me to the bathroom, setting me to my feet and handing me a towel. "Wash everywhere properly. Use this toothbrush to scrub your fingernails. When yu done, put yu clothes in this bag, tie it, and put it in the corner. Mago put some clothes pon the bed fi yu."

I nodded, entering the shower after him leave. Mi scrub mi skin until the icy water sting mi. After mi done, mi exit the shower and go to the room. A sweatpants and shirt deh pon the bed. My hand a shake too much, mi cya put on either fabric, despite knowing dem too big fimi.

A knock came on the door, and I jerked.

"Mi can come in?" Trav asked.

"Yes," I croaked.

Trav peek inside, sighing before walking over. Him put the shirt over my head and direct my legs into the sweatpants before removing the towel from around me. "Yu good?"

"Is Favi okay?"

Him squeeze mi trembling arm. "Slitta can wul him own. Focus pon yuself."

"Yu think mi a mek a mistake?"

"Mi cya ansa dat fi yu."

"Asia know wa yu do?"

"She know seh mi scam—" He paused when my eyes widened. "Nuh badda wid the lecture. Time hard, mafi do wa mafi do. Whether or not yu waa deal wid the man, dat up to you. If him try diss yu certain way, a dirt."

"Yu cya put yuself ina trouble fi me. Him mad."

"Me mad, too."

The ajar door opened, and Favi entered. Mi release a breath as him walk over, holding my project.

"Thanks." I accepted it. It neva dirty up.

Favi didn't answer. Him too focused pon where Trav hand rest pon my arm.

His eyes darted to mine, narrowing. Mi step outta Trav's hold.

"Come mi carry yu home," Trav said.

"I'll bring her," Favi said.

Trav glance pon me, and I nodded. "Ah, lata." Trav hug me, making Favi's glare deepen before he left the room.

Favi turned around, and mi tek that as a sign fi follow him. We go ina waa ProBox, and mi stare through the window while him drive mi home. This a the car him did rub mi lips, then tell mi fi go pon mi knees.

Tonight was another preview of our future. Could I be with this man?

When plantain waa dead, it shoot.

Favi parked before my gate. "Get in the back," he said, and I raised a brow but complied. Now sitting beside me, he asked, "You good?"

Looking at his flawless brown skin and long eyelashes, weh frame the most captivating dark brown eyes, mi lick mi lips. "Yes."

Him narrow him eyes pon mi. Mi a get fi understand him do this when him a think. Wa him a think bout now? The same thing as me?

Kissing shouldn't be on my mind after wa mi witness, but his kisses were a welcomed distraction.

Fyah deh a mussmuss tail, him think a cool breeze.

I closed the space between us, kissing him hard. I took him by surprise, but he kissed me back.

My body steadied as I melted into a puddle of electricity. A dangerous combination, but a better death than what I witnessed.

Favi's fingers laced beneath my thighs, bringing me over to straddle him. He gripped my ass roughly while his tongue slipped inside my mouth. He tasted like weed, but I didn't care right now. I accepted everything this man gave me. It was too sweet to deny.

He pulled away, trailing kisses up and down my neck. He sucked on my sweet spot, making me moan while my pussy throbbed.

My breasts pressed against his chest while my fingers snuck under his shirt. I clawed at his back, and he pulled away with a hiss.

"*Fuck*," he cursed, and my eyes widened as I pulled away. He released my ass, pressing his hand against his shoulder and wincing.

"You okay?" I rushed out, crawling off him.

Him adjust the crotch of him pants. "Mi good."

"Wa do yu shoulder?"

"I said I'm good."

"And me ano idiot." Mi turn on the ceiling light. Ignoring his protests, mi liff his hoodie, and my mouth dropped.

Favio Welsh had the coolest tattoo I'd ever seen.

A realistic snake head was on the left half of his abs. Blood-red roses with thorny green leaves wrapped around the snake's body, which crawled around his side. The snake's mouth was open wide, showing two pointed fangs dripping venom. It hissed at the words on the right half of his abs: *SOLO DIO PUÒ GIUDICARMI.*

Mi nuh try decipher the language cause sum else catch mi attention.

A gory bullet hole.

Chapter Eleven

CHAYANNE

Tears swelled in my eyes. "Why yu neva get this checked?!"

"I'm go—"

"Yu nuh good, Favi! Come inside let me—"

His face blanked. "No. Mi good."

"And me seh yu doh good! Yu bring mi home instead of get it checked, it's the least I can do. Please, Favi." I wiped away tears to see him clearly.

Jaw clenching, he nodded.

Mi exit and lead him toward the house. "Tek time and walk. Mi granny sleep soft," I said, and he nodded. If my grandfather or mother could see wa kinda man me a bring ina dem house, dem wuda shame a mi. But the opinion of the dead nuh hold much weight right now. Favi was alive. Mi neva ready fi lose him. Opening the door, mi look over mi shoulder. "Walk backward."

"What?"

"Mi nuh waa duppy ina mi house," I said, and the corner of him mouth twitch before him follow mi order. I did the same, closing the door and turning to see him looking around while placing my project on the table. I wrapped my fingers around his arm. "Come." Mi lead him into mi room. The space was smaller with this enormous man in it. After him sidung pon mi bed, mi go to the bathroom fi the first-aid kit. When me return to the room, he had his shirt off. Mi eyes widen at his sculpted build. "Focus," I mumbled, kneeling before him. Doing my best fi ignore his gaze on me, mi rummage through the kit.

"Do you know what you're doing?" he asked, amused.

"Yu nuh ina pain?" mi ask, and him shrug.

"Been through worse. Stand. I'll show you how."

I stood and followed his instructions. The bullet went through, so it was easy to tend to. However, concentrating hard when him a watch mi every action.

"You're shaking," him seh.

"Because yaa watch me."

"I make you nervous?" he asked, and I bit my lip, looking away at the bloody gauzes on the floor. He wrapped his arm around my waist, tugging me down to straddle him.

I would've thrown my arms around him if mi never worried bout him shoulder.

Favi gripped my chin, making me look into his eyes. "I'm good. Stop worrying."

I nodded weakly, and him eyes flicker to my lips, then back to my eyes. Mi think him wuda kiss me, but he didn't. Instead, he lifted me and placed me on the bed.

"Get some rest. I'll close the door." After me nod, him walk toward the door, then pause. "Next time I tell you to do something, don't disobey me."

"Mama, me a leave now," Chezzy said to Mama, who was sitting on the sofa.

"Alright, Simone one gyal. Mek grandbaby give yu some tohtoh," Mama said.

"Yago mek mi fat, Mama." Chezzy rub her eyes. She come over earlier fi help wid the changes to wi project, and she start bawl fi eye pain a few minutes ago.

"Yafi maintain the weight so yu nuh sidung pon yu back like grandbaby," Mama said, and Chezzy laugh while mi gasp.

"Mi have batty. It just small compared to Chezzy trailer load." Mi go cut the tohtoh before we leave.

Approaching the ball ground beside the Square, we spot Asia and Trav pose up pon him car. Dem a nyam off each other face. Mi smile as mi walk toward dem wid Chezzy behind me.

"Unu gwan a unu yaad wid dat," mi seh, and them chuckle and pull away.

Asia lean pon Trav, and him wrap him arm round her shoulder. "Who nuh waa see wi fi lock dem eye."

Trav snicker. "Weh yago?"

"Me a follow her home." Me glance pon Chezzy, who a rub her eye. "Weh unu a do here so?"

"Did a come check yu," he said, and mi smile vanish.

"Mi good. Like how yu see me, yu can do sum fimi?"

"No," Trav seh, and mi roll mi eyes.

"Yu can carry home Chezzy, please?" Mi nuh waa walk past where mi witness five man get killed last night. The news deevn mention dem. Wa happen to the body dem?

Bucket wid hole a bottom nuh belong a riverside.

Trav glanced at Chezzy. "Sure. Come in, Cheesy," he said, and Chezzy gasped.

"Babe, she name Chezzy," Asia seh, and Trav scratch the back of him neck.

"It good…" Chezzy muttered, and I sighed as she enter the car. She hate when people mess up her name. Trav better get it together before she hate him.

"Lata." Mi close the door behind her while declining Trav's offer to drop mi home. A long-time mi nuh stretch mi foot dem, plus the Saturday cool and nice. When mi reach home, mi do some homework until a call distract mi. "Hello?"

"Yado?" Favi asked, his voice sounding deeper through the phone.

Glancing at the books on the bed, mi sigh. "Study."

"Come study at my house."

"Yu cya seh 'please'?" mi ask, and him nuh answer. "Where yu live?"

"Godsto."

I closed my eyes, wanting to block the flashbacks of last night. I shouldn't have. They were more vivid now.

"Mi nuh waa come deso…"

"Nun naa do yu. I'll come get you," he said.

"Okay." Mi smile. Why a the smaddy weh a cause turmoil ina the community, a the one weh mi find comfort ina?

Fyah deh a muss-muss tail, him think a cool breeze.

Mi hop outta bed and gather mi belongings. Mi write a note and post-it pon the fridge. Favi come fi mi minutes later.

"How's the shoulder?" I asked as he drove off.

"It good."

When we reach Godsto, people move outta the way like him a king. Mi nuh really come here, so mi tek in everything: grass growing in patches on the road; zinc houses and concrete houses, some having a gate and others without; barefoot likkle pickney playing pon the road.

We slowed before a blue and white painted two-storey that had a remote-controlled gate. A concrete path led to two steps that stopped at a veranda. Flower trees and a well-kept lawn were on both sides of the path.

He drove through the gate and parked. Mi fly out.

Him come stand beside me. "Next time, wait for me."

"Why?"

"To open the door," he said, and I smiled. Mi think dem sum deh only happen ina movie! Mi afi go tell Chezzy so she can like him again!

He led us into the house and paused in the living room to ask if I wanted a drink. I declined.

We went upstairs to a decent-sized bedroom. A king-sized bed was against one wall, and behind it, a wooden headboard and window. Through the somewhat translucent curtain, I saw a grill over the window. There was a desk and chair, two bedside tables, and a closet pressed against the adjacent wall of a table. Before the bed, a large TV hung on the wall above the dresser, which was beside the bathroom door.

My eyes dragged to Favio. He took off his shirt, leaving him in a shorts. The top of his boxers peeked above it. I didn't get to appreciate him enough last night, and my, my... Favio was ripped. His six-pack and defined pecs made me gawk.

"See something you like?" him tease, and mi blush, looking away.

"I-I'm not answering that." Mi drop miself on the bed, taking out my books.

"You could've used the desk."

"I prefer working on the bed," I said, and he nodded before sitting at the desk and powering on a laptop.

We fell into a comfortable silence for the next half an hour. I kept peeking at him because his back was turned to me. He was looking at a bunch of spreadsheets that were too complicated for me to understand.

My buzzing phone tore my attention away from him. Cho, blousecup! Weh Dayshawn a call mi fa?! Mi decline the call, and him call back.

Favi look over him shoulder. "You good?"

"Homework a frustrate me..." mi lie, and him walk toward the bed. Mi eye him V-Line as him lay beside me. Him cologne flood mi senses, but mi still couldn't figure out its name.

Favi poked my shoulder. "Chayanne."

My eyes snapped to his. Jesam. Him did a talk all this time? A fi him fault mi zone out! Him do sum to mi upstairs and downstairs all when him naa try.

"I said if you need help?" he repeated, and I nodded.

Trav usually help me with my homework cause mi head tuff sometimes. Right now, him busy a stress ova Asia, so mi nuh waa bother him.

"Do you understand?" Favi asked after him done, and I nodded before doing the equation. He hummed after I finished.

Mi surprise him have this much sense... Then again, my brother a Trav. Him a the smartest person mi know. Mi fi stop think seh everybody weh tek up badness a idiot. Based pon how Favi articulate him English words, him educated.

"Which school did you go to?" I asked, and him tell mi the name of waa all boys school ina Kingston.

"Who taught you to do it like that?" him ask as mi start the next equation.

"My brother."

"Travis?"

I furrowed my brows and looked at him. Him jealous or mi imagine it?

"Is he your biological brother?" he added quickly.

"No... It's a long story."

"We have all day."

"Ketch fass," mi joke, and him mouth twitch. Ugh! Wa mi wuda give fi see him smile! Propping mi elbow up, mi rest mi head ina mi hand and do mi favorite thing: talk. "We went to basic school together, but we never became friends until primary. Mi grow up know miself as Chichi, and some older boy used to tease mi. Yu know how Trav short-tempered?" I asked, and he nodded.

"One day, him see me a cry, and him go beat up the bwoy dem. Since then, dem nuh bother mi and Trav look out fimi," I said, wishing Trav would listen when mi seh fi go back to school. He had a promising future.

Favi nodded.

Mi realize him nuh talk much. Mi nuh know how him put up wid mi cause mi love chat once mi get comfortable wid smaddy. "Do you have any—" My phone vibrated. Knowing a Dayshawn, mi groan and drop mi head pon the bed.

Favi shuffled about. "Who name Dayshawn?"

Mi look pon him, seeing him wid mi phone. Mi nuh know how fi answer. Favio Welsh sick ina him head, but ano like we deh.

"My ex."

Favi glanced at me, eyes narrowing. "Him nuh know boh me?"

Aye, mi giddy-headed bad! Watch how mi sense dem a float weh while mi smile like chimp! Hiding my smile, I teased, "Mi single last time mi check."

Him turn the phone toward me. "Open this," he ordered, and I did. The more he scrolled, his anger intensified. Muttering sum ina dat language mi nuh understand, him look pon mi. "Yu waa mi kill him?"

My eyes widened. "Wa? No!"

"Block him."

Mi shake mi head. "Him a go text pon next number. Him soon stop."

"Why him a text yu so much?"

"I... called the organized crime unit because him upset mi."

"Nuh try dat fuck wid me," he said coldly, and mi nod.

My phone vibrated again. Favi reach fi it, but mi toss it outta him reach.

"Mi neva know yaa the jealous type."

"I don't share what's mine."

"I'm yours?" I asked, but he didn't answer cause him still angry. Swallowing mi hesitance, mi push him back and straddle him. My hands trailed over his defined abs, and I licked my lips.

His hands found my waist as I brought my face closer to his. "Mi nuh kissy-kissy, Chayanne."

I pulled back, my brows furrowing. "You kissed me before."

Him narrow him eyes.

"Alright." I trailed my mouth up his neck before licking his ear. I smirked as his dick twitched. "Think yu neva kissy-kissy?"

"Shut up." Favi flipped us over, pinning my hands above my head. He kissed me hard, forcing his tongue inside my mouth and making my eyes flutter closed. Moving a hand beneath my dress, he fondled my breasts. He was heavy atop me, but I locked my legs around him, pulling him closer.

We kissed until Favi pulled away, breathless. He tugged my dress over my head. He took a moment to trail his eyes down my body. The hair on my skin rose from his attention and made me shy, but I couldn't look away from him.

He looked at me like I was the prettiest thing he'd ever seen. I loved that because I felt the same about him.

Favi's body was perfect...

Licking his lips, he took my bra off. He tossed it in a corner of the room before taking a nipple into his mouth, licking and sucking.

"Mm," I moaned, feverish from Favi's talented mouth.

His hand trailed to my panties, running a finger along the waistline. He popped my breast out of his mouth as he looked into my eyes. "Can I?"

"Yes." I wasn't one to give it up easily, but this man had been on my mind since I saw him. I wanted him— no, needed. I needed him now and logical thinking wouldn't deter that.

Favi's finger latched onto the waistband, and he paused. "Are you a virgin?"

"Yes—" I paused as he tore himself away. I sat up, covering my chest while he gathered my clothes. "Wa happen?"

"Nothing," he answered, but his tone said the opposite. Refusing to look at me, he handed me the dress. "Get back to studying."

Confused, I nodded and redressed. He sat on the edge of the bed, facing away from me while tapping on his phone. I frowned at his back.

The snake's body crawled around here, maintaining the wrapped-in-roses aesthetic. With each twist and turn, the tail created square-shaped swirls that seemed to dance around the rose at the center.

"Yu tattoo really nice," I said in awe, breaking the tension.

"Thanks."

"Waa the purpose of the roses?"

"Rose that grew from concrete."

"And the snake?" I asked, and he tensed for a second.

"I'll tell you another time."

"Okay... Mi can touch it?"

"It doesn't bite."

Chuckling, mi crawl toward him. Hesitantly, mi place a finger against his skin. I trailed the tip of the tail, stopping at the rose when he shivered. "What do the words mean?"

Favi's pronunciation was excellent as he repeated the phrase. Mi nuh know why mi think him a one a dem fully dunce people deh weh tattoo next language pon dem body, and cya seh the first syllable widout bite dem tongue.

"Only God can judge me," Favio translated, and mi brows raise. Him believe ina God? Kiss mi neckstring!

"Having the tattoo is inviting people to judge you. Yu nuh think that ironic?"

"I don't care about the opinion of people."

"Do you care about mine?" I whispered.

He nodded slowly.

Chapter Twelve

FAVIO

Shottaz man dem a the biggest set a pussy mi eva encounter.

Over the years, the only times Blood Paw and Shottaz warred were because of petty fuckry.

Robbery.

Greed for more turf.

Lately, dem a tek Blood Paw lightly, trying to fuck with what we established.

Antaro didn't seem to understand that.

His sole concern was how soon I could tie up loose ends and return to Kingston to handle more pressing matters. Man neevn business seh mi cuda get mi three points tek.

Not that I needed the bastard's pity. I had my mother.

She was in Antaro's office with us, tending to my bullet wound. It looked worse than it felt, but *Mamma* and Chayanne refused to believe that.

The only pain I had was the ache in my eardrums. Antaro was a nuisance, yapping on and fucking on about what I already fucking knew.

He glared at me. "You need to be in Kingston. This Shottaz thing a tek too long. I don't care what you must do, do it. Dem need fi know wi nuh tek intimidation. If you need to kill their wives and children—"

Mamma glared at Antaro, silencing him and making me smirk.

In all my years, *Mamma* was the only person who challenged him and lived to tell the tale. Life being the gamble it was, there'd always be one thing, or person, that could cost someone everything.

Mamma was his.

Taking the glass of Hennessy off the office desk, I drained it, then slammed it down. I'd need two more glasses or something stronger to handle Antaro's nonsense for the rest of the night.

There was nothing I hated more than when he called me to Kingston for lectures. I was a grown fucking man. One day, he'd understand that. Hopefully, before I gouged his eyes out and fed them to him with a golden fucking spoon.

"I'm handling it," I said coolly.

Mamma tossed a bloody cotton ball into the bin. "You shouldn't have to deal with this. I told you not to get him involved with this!"

Antaro scoffed. "He should learn. Th—"

"No!" *Mamma* walked toward Antaro, stopping before him to glare. "Doh seh it! All of this is your fault because yu nuh listen to me!"

"I did what was best."

"For your flesh and blood or yourself?" she asked, and he clenched his jaw. "Exactly." *Mamma* scoffed, turning to walk away. The door slammed shut behind her, and Antaro sighed.

Shaking my head, I stood. Grabbing the Hennessy bottle, I headed to the backyard. *Mamma* hated smoking in her house. I sat on a chair by the pool, its water gleaming at me while I lit a pre-roll. I took a long drag, blowing the fumes toward the dark sky, which sparkled with hundreds of stars. Given my predicament, the cool night air paired with the drink and spliff made me as relaxed as possible.

I was trying to get in touch with the leader of Shottaz. Usually, Blood Paw had no problem turning a community into a bloodbath, but I was trying to leave Steer Town with minimal bloodshed.

Too much blood meant too much cleanup.

Too much cleanup left room for error.

I couldn't afford a minor slipup. It'd ruin my career.

Or lead back to her.

My phone rang, and I hissed my teeth. "Who the—" I sat more upright, accepting the call. "Chayanne?"

"Hey," she greeted, making the corner of my mouth tug upward. Her voice was sweet over the phone, a delightful addition to the peace I got beneath the sky. "When yaa come back?"

My jaw clenched. "Not sure. Why?"

"Mi miss yu..."

Choking on fumes, I yanked the spliff out of my mouth. "What did you say?"

She chuckled. "Yaa get deaf, Favi?"

She and that nickname.

"Hold on." I switched to a video call.

She turned on the light in her room. Her face filled the screen.

Fuck.

There she was.

She was easily the most beautiful girl I ever saw. Her eyes. Her smile. Her pouty lips with a hint of the tiniest smile. Chayanne was perfect.

"What did you say?" I asked, desperate for her to say it again.

She smiled, and I locked onto the action. There was that smile.

"I miss you," she said shyly, and I moved the Hennessy bottle to my lips, hiding my smirk.

After a quick sip, I moved the bottle away. "Surprising."

Her smile washed away, her brows knitting. "Why?"

"Thought I made you uncomfortable." Why did she have to be a fucking virgin? Most men would've salivated at being the first to get their dick wet by a virgin pussy, but not me.

"You didn't, Favi. Yu surprise me, though."

"How?"

"Because you didn't want to... Why?"

Neevn a go deso wid she. Neevn sure if mi waa lock her down anymore.

Chayanne was fucking stubborn, and I hated headaches.

I liked control.

Last night proved she'd be hard to control.

"Nuh worry yu head." I took a drag from my spliff while she sighed.

"Okay... I have to go. Goodnight."

"Goodnight," I said, and she hummed. "Wait."

She wasn't looking at me anymore. "Yes?"

"I miss you, too," I blurted.

The light returned to her eyes.

There wasn't any in mine, but if there was, I wasn't sure if it would've faded. That wasn't what I intended to say, but seeing her return to her chirpy self did something to me.

My focus wasn't on the alcohol, weed, or sky. The only power I had over myself was what she allowed me to have. This girl's smile and bright eyes captivated me; I couldn't look away.

Fuck. What was she doing to me?

And what was I going to do with her?

Chapter Thirteen

CHAYANNE

The evening, me and Chezzy a walk to my house from hers. Ina the Square, waa car pull up a wi foot.

"Pree, Chichi?" Trav look pon Chezzy. "A yu curry friend dis?"

"Behave. Carry mi home if yu waa sum fi do," mi seh.

"Me nago wid him." Chezzy cross her arms, looking toward the football field.

"Walk then." Shrugging, Trav open the back door. "Come, Chichi."

Mi grab Chezzy, dragging her ina the car.

Trav drive off. "Weh yu carry Sandra in ya fa?"

Chezzy scowled. "Mi name Chezandra."

"Nuh dat mi seh?"

"No. Mi deevn expect sense from smaddy weh eat curry goat with white rice."

"Jah knows. See why mi seh yu friend a idiot, Chichi?"

Mi roll mi eyes. "Unu behave unuself."

"He started it," Chezzy said.

Trav gasped. "Me?! Yu lie nuh—"

"Trav!" mi exclaim, and dem huff.

"Wul this." Trav stretch waa big chocolate bar over his seat toward me.

Mi smile, accepting it. "Thanks! A mi birthday?"

"Mi cya do sum nice fimi sister? Jah knows... A Asia mi buy it fa, but she seh she want the hazelnut one instead," him seh, and Chezzy look pon him, her eyes shining. "Nuh give Sandra none of it."

"Mi neva waa none." Chezzy kiss her teeth, looking through the window.

Trav park before mi house seconds later. "See unu ya," him seh, and mi thank him while exiting. "Yu nav no manners, Sandra?"

Chezzy kiss her teeth. She walk toward the veranda, waiting fimi open the door.

Trav push him head through the window. "Next time mi see yu a walk by yuself, mago run yu over!" Trav laugh as him settle ina the seat.

"A when you give Chezzy drive?" I asked.

"The other day, mi mek a spin through Mamme Bay and see ar a walk, so mi drop her home. Shuda mek shi pay fare cause all now she deevn tell mi thanks." Trav glared at Chezzy.

Humming, mi look pon him plaid shirt and jeans. "A weh yago?"

"A go check mi woman."

"Hail Asia—"

Trav kiss him teeth. "Me a breeze she. She a get pon mi nerves, Jah knows."

Mi brows raise. "Yu deh wid smaddy new?"

"Kinda question dat? A Asia alone have mi heart. A go link a one B."

"Yet yu beat up Dayshawn when yu find out him a gimi bun?"

Trav grin. "That different."

"E nuh different. Yu too miserable."

Trav sighed, looking at his lap. "Asia head too easy fi chip, and she supposed to be mi peace. Mi tired fi tell her fi bill cause every day coming like the same old shit ina different toilet, Jah knows. Sometimes, when mi want a break from the fuckry a mi yard, mi cya go to her. Mi afi hitch up a Slitta or Eltham yaad like mi love man."

"Yu mother start up the foolishness again?" Mi frown as him nod. "Mi door always open."

Smirking, Trav looked at me. "Yu nuh see how mi tall now? Mi cya sleep ina yu sofa again."

I chuckled, remembering when Aunty was in Jamaica a few years ago and mi ask if Trav could sleep over. Aunty did think a man mi waa tek, but mi neva interested ina dat yet.

"Joke maa run. Mi nuh believe ina bun. Ago buy the chocolate and watch a movie wid mi headache. Lata. Gwan go study." Trav blow the horn until Chezzy look ova pon we, kissing her teeth. Laughing, him drive off.

Me walk toward the veranda and open the door. We enter the house. Mama ina the kitchen a sweep.

"Mama, stop hackle up yuself." Chezzy walk toward Mama and try tek the broom.

Mama shrug her off. "Too much sidung bruk breeches," Mama seh, and Chezzy give me a pleading glance while mi shrug.

Chezzy sigh, following me into my room. "I don't like that boy."

Mi grab the phone, replying to Aunty's texts. "Yafi get use to him personality. Yu soon like him."

"Me good."

"So yaa seh, wid yu wishy-washy self," I said, and she laughed.

For the next few hours, we revised our project. Chezzy drop asleep before me, so mi go the kitchen fi nyam and talk to Yolo.

"This a why me cya stand dem gyal ya. Imagine, afta me tell Eva Bless nuh tek picture of me under style and post it nuh weh, me go home the night and see meself pon her status. Now Gold Mine vex wid me," Yolo complain.

"Which one a Gold Mine?" mi ask.

"The fourth former, who still wear bubbles," she said, and I laughed.

"Hush. Just memba yu motto."

"As one gone, a next one born! Mi young and too much gyal ina the midfield fi anybody wul me down."

I laughed, tears rushing to my eyes. "Yu finger dem a go rotten off."

"Me have eight more can use."

"Mama seh *cow nuh know the use of it tail till it cut*, so you stay there," I said, and she chuckled.

"Mago sleep now, Number One. Me deevn dee see the time."

Mi glance pon the clock pon the stove, jumping to my feet. "Kiss mi neckstring, a one o'clock! Lata."

"Bye, love of my life," she said, and I smiled.

Ending the call, mi go the bathroom fi brush mi teeth. A next call come in pon mi phone. My eyes brightened when I saw the caller ID. I cleared my throat before answering. "Hey, Favi."

"I just got back," Favi said, and I perked up.

"Think yu neva sure when yaa come back?"

"I wasn't, but you said you missed me—" He paused. "Come outside."

As much as mi miss him, mi nago outta door! Mama seh a dem hours ya rolling calf walk. "It's late... I'll see you tomorrow."

"Come outside or I'm coming inside to you." Footsteps drifted into the line.

"Alright! Give me a minute."

"Thirty seconds." Him hang up.

Mi naa tek him lightly, so mi hurry and done brush mi teeth. Cya go outta door wid mi breath a kick like actor ina karate show. Dem onion rings deh did deadly.

Mi go mi room and find a hoodie ina the darkness. Slipping it on over mi big T-shirt, mi sneak through the front door. Mi cross mi arms beneath my breasts and walk toward Favi, who lean pon a SUV. "Weh yu car?" mi ask.

"This is my car." Him open the door of a metallic black BMW.

Mi go ina the car and sit down, and him sit beside me.

One thing wid Favi car dem? It a go radiate wealth. This one had a fresh aroma like the crisp morning air pon a school trip. Its interior was blue.

Favi tell mi the name of the model, and mi stop look round wid mi nuh-used-to-things self. "Is that my hoodie?"

"It's mine now." It smell like him, so mi nuh wash it.

Humming, Favi easy back into the seat, parting him long leg dem. "Was supposed to be here earlier, but I had a meeting run late."

"Meeting?"

"You thought the name Welsh was for show?"

"Yu own Welsh's?!" Mi gasp when him nod. Kiss mi neckstring! Mi neva know him that rich!

Welsh's a waa fancy wine company. It nuh sell ina regular supermarket. People afi buy it from Welsh's high-end stores or selected alcohol retailers.

Favi's so young and him have an entire company under him name. Knowing him a do sum meaningful wid him life nuh only mek mi more curious why him involve ina wrongs, it make me very proud of him.

And more attracted...

"That's impressive for your age," I commended, and he shrugged, making me frown. "Wow. Nuh do that."

Him brows furrow. "Do what?"

"Act like yu accomplishment likkle! Yu nuh see how yu big like house? I'm so proud of you."

His eyes shone as he looked down. A shadow cast over his face, hiding his expression. "Thanks."

Mi smile. "Look at me teaching you manners."

Scoffing, he adjusted the seat before him and pushed it forward. He sat more upright, patting his thigh. "Come here."

"What?"

He patted his thigh again. "I want you closer to me."

My smile stretched as I straddled him. The soft material of his sweatpants brushed against my panties as he cupped my ass. Heat rushed to my skin as he stared into my eyes, trapping me in them. He wasn't touching me much, yet goosebumps rose all over my skin.

Favio Welsh was a work of art. From his chiseled jawline to those lips and body beneath the hoodie he wore. I wanted to rip it off and lick his skin, but I moved my hands before the urge overtook me.

Brushing back the strands of curly hair grazing the top of his brow, I smiled. He needed a haircut, but his long, messy hair was sexy. It should be a crime for one man to look this good.

He moved his hands to my thighs. "Why are you looking at me like that?"

"H-how?" I shivered as his fingers crawled up my thigh.

"Like you want me to fuck you when I'm trying not to."

"Stop trying." My breath hitched as his fingers paused close to my groin.

Favi smirked, wetting his lips as he glanced at my lips, then eyes. "Kiss me."

I leaned forward, pressing my lips on his. Favi's tongue slipped into my mouth, making my eyes flutter closed while the world faded. He squeezed my ass while my hands snuck under his hoodie, caressing his hard body. My pussy throbbed as our tongues tangled, making me pull away to breathe hard at the ceiling.

Favi kissed my neck while I laced my fingers in his hair. He hardened beneath me, poking against my panties, and heightening my hormones to carnal greed.

"Favi," I moaned, resting my hand and his chest and easing him away.

"Chayanne..."

Jesam, why him so sexy?! Mi cya do dis anymore. I needed him now. I never had sex in a car before, but I wanted Favi's big hood a slam ina mi. And to see his face. There was nothing sexier than a man's ecstasy when him a come.

"Do you have a condom?" I asked, and his arousal vanished as he looked away. "Favi?" I held his face, making him look at me. "You don't want to have sex with me?" I whispered, shame and bitterness filling my gut after seeing his far-off expression.

"I do, but..." He paused, and I came off him.

Look how me did a go skin out mi crochiz and the man nuh waa mi. Hair ina mi face? Deevn Chezzy mi cya tell dis to how mi shame.

"Yu vex ova dick?" he asked, amused.

Mi deevn a go ansa! Him nuh worth mi breath. Mi waa go in go rub mi clit.

"Nuh hear mi a talk to yu?" he asked coldly, and mi kiss mi teeth. Him grab mi chin, roughly turning me around to look into his eyes. As my phone vibrated and I tried pulling away, he held me tighter. "Cut that fuck. I have my reasons."

"Kinda reasons?"

"Me nago fuck yu ina car back like you're a whore, Chayanne. I respect you more than that."

My anger washed away, giddiness taking its place. Butterflies settled in my stomach. My heart ran a mile per second. Ouu, him like mi! But mi nuh like how mi can feel the wetness between my thighs, which him refuse fi tend to. Mi nuh want respect, mi want hood!

Mi naa go tell him dat, though. Mi a save what dignity mi have left.

"Okay..." I said, and he released me. Mi grab mi phone. The bright light from the screen nearly blind mi, despite not being bright like the caller ID.

"Wa mi tell yu boh tha bwoy deh?"

Mi block Dayshawn. "There's nothing there... Mago inside."

"Ah."

"*Ah*?" Mi glare while him look through the window. Maybe a cause horny a ride mi, but it irritate mi. "Cho, lata! Yaa upset mi."

"Who yaa talk to, Chayanne?"

"You!" Bolting outta him piece of car, mi slam the door shut. Mi walk to mi veranda, ignoring another slam. Mi a open the door when sum grab mi from behind. A shriek almost tear from my mouth as Favio press mi against the wall, his fingers curling around my neck while he glared at me. "Let me go or mi scream," I warned, hating how rage increased his sex appeal.

"I know you're not going to," him seh, and mi glare. "I need to do something about your attitude."

"What? Kill me?" I taunted, and his grip tightened.

"No. I'm going to fuck the attitude out of you."

I smiled. "Right now?"

Favi loosened his grip, stepping away.

Mi grab him wrist before him could turn away. Mi stand before him. "Can you talk to me, please? Mi know yu nuh talk much, but yu behavior hard fi read."

He sighed, prying my hand off him. He used the same hand to brush my hair out of my face before saying, "My first year of college, a girl said I raped her."

My eyes widened. "W-what?"

"I didn't do it."

"I believe you."

His eyes searched mine for a second before looking away, focusing on the strands of hair twirled around his index. "She was a virgin, and her father was religious. When he found out we were fucking, she lied about what happened."

Sneering, mi fist clench at mi side. A gyal like dat mek it hard fi actual victims!

Mi pry mi hair outta him hand, then hold him face. Tipping, mi give him a chups. Mi pull away, smiling while him eyes open. "This is why you should've made me finish speaking," I said, and his brows furrowed. "I'm not exactly a virgin. Well, mi nuh know. It complicated. With my ex, the head kinda go in, but it

67

hurt too much, so mi tell him fi stop. I'm not exactly a virgin if that makes you feel better. I'd never lie on you like that cause *quatti buy trouble, but hundred-pound cya pay for it.*"

Him brows knit. "What?"

"Nothing." Smiling, mi kiss him again.

He wrapped an arm around my waist, pulling me closer. I smiled into the kiss while his cologne wafted into my nose. Pulling away, him tug mi bottom lip between him teeth.

"Can we have sex now? And me nuh mean right now, mi mean whenever yu comfortable—" I paused as the corner of his mouth tugged upward. "You smiled."

"You talk too much," he said, and mi frown. "We can."

"How that sound so?" mi ask, and him smirk.

"We need to work on your attitude, don't we?"

Chapter Fourteen

CHAYANNE

Chezzy follow me go market so Mama nafi hackle up herself. Mama know she nuh strong like one time, yet she love chat wid everybody and feel up every pumpkin fi mek sure dem nuh overripe.

Mi thankful she nuh come today. A Favi money mi use buy healthier food cause it nuh mek sense fi buy new uniform. If Mama did deh ya, she wuda ask weh mi get so much money. Even doh Aunty always send as much as she can, we cya afford fi spend above wi means. It feel good buying nice things, even if a just food. Big up the big pocket brown man anyweh him deh!

"*Psst*, Coolie," seh waa man.

Cho, blousecup! Why mi a think bout the best man and a scabby a disrupt mi?

Chezzy glare pon him. "She have a man."

Watch mi friend, who nuh too ina Favi since him draw gun pon me! Mi wuda smile if the dutty foot man neva start walk wid we.

"Ano her man me a look," the dry head man seh.

"Mi nuh interested, sir," mi seh as nice as mi can.

"And her man a gunman," Chezzy add, and him eyes widen before him fall back. Chezzy laugh.

"Mi thankful fi yu, Chezzy." Mi smile, watching her carry few a the bags fimi.

"A Mama sake why mi follow yu." She stick out her tongue.

"Mind the stinking water scent stuck pon yu tongue."

"Pay things yu gwan wid." She laugh as we approach Trav car. "A first yaa see mi?" Chezzy glare at Trav, who a stare pon her.

"First me a hear smaddy laugh so brawlin. Yu nav no home training?" Trav ask, and she gasp, about to give a rude response.

"Give mi the bag dem," mi seh, and she hand them to me. Mi load dem ina the trunk. "Cho, mi soon come back. Mi forget fi buy the tomato dem."

Trav chuckle. "Yu soon leff yuself."

"Mi tell her every day." Chezzy join Trav's laughter. They stopped suddenly, sneering at each other. "Hurry and come back," Chezzy snapped.

"Nafi dog mi up so..." Mi go back up Market Street, buy waa bag of tomato, then retrace mi steps. Mi freeze a distance from the car, my eyes widening.

Trav lift him shirt, flashing a gun to a man, who scurry off. Chezzy nuh see the gun, but mi nuh want mi bredda put himself ina trouble. Mi hurry ova while Trav seh sum to Chezzy, and she nod. Him put him hand pon her lower back, leading her to the front seat. Mi reach as Trav close the door.

"Wa happen?" mi ask.

"Him did a look her and make her uncomfortable." Shrugging, him open the back door fimi.

Mi go in and touch Chezzy shoulder. "Yu good?"

"Yeah." She glance pon Trav as him come ina the car.

Speeding off, Trav blast the music while making a call. "Yu ready? Wa yu mean 'no'? A from morning yado hair and cya done? Mi a drop a yu foot ina twenty minutes. Tell the slow hairdresser fi hurry."

Roughly twenty minutes later, we enter waa scheme in Drax Hall. Trav slow before a house.

"Go the back, Sandra." Trav blow the horn, glaring at the house.

Chezzy sit up, her brows knitting. "What?"

"Yu ina mi woman seat."

"Sorry..." Shoulders slumping, she come ina the back.

Mi deevn medz her. Me busy a read Yolo messages.

YOLO: Me hate dem gyal ya isi! Long Back a move stingy with her pussy.

Mago through withdrawal Number One. Mi afi go ask Mommy fi check me ina Bellevue.

Yu cya check yuself ina madhouse.
We nuh buy the big house pon the hill fi wi people dem yet.

"Mi soon come." Trav glare through the rearview mirror.

Mi bruk mi neck fi see Asia a come outta waa taxi. Trav walk toward her, then dem start cuss. Shaking my head, mi turn round. "Yu good, Chezzy?" mi ask, hating how she quiet. Mi hope mawga Trav neva seh nun to her when mi leff dem!

"Yeah, of course," she seh as a ringing erupted in the vehicle.

Nodding, mi look weh fi answer mi phone.

"A so long yu tek fi answer?" a the first thing him seh.

Mi roll mi eyes. "Mi never take long."

"Are you back yet?"

"Soon."

"Let me know when you're back. I'll come get you," him seh, and mi blush.

"Put it pon speaker," Chezzy whisper, and I did.

"Me naa come nuh weh," I said, even though mi waa run go a him yard fast like horse a Caymanas Park. I'd never been this needy for a person before... especially one me nav no business a fool round wid. Forbidden things always had a fun, tantalizing thrill.

"Chayanne Arya Bailey..." Favi trailed off.

"Favio Matteo Welsh."

"A call out mi name so fa?"

"Nuh you dweet first? Miserable like." I smiled when he chuckled.

"Nuh know wa yaa do to me..." him seh, and Chezzy slap her hand over her mouth, muffling a squeal.

"Wa yu mean?" I fished for more compliments.

He mumbled inaudibly, then said, "Hurry and fawud."

"Okay." I hung up.

"Girl! Yafi tell mi everything afta him angle triangle yu!" Chezzy exclaimed.

"Me a come back wid story this time, mi promise. Mi naa run like wid

Dayshawn," I said, and she grinned. "Mi surprise yaa tell mi fi do this."

"Mi still nuh really like him, but me waa yu get a good fuck so yu can stop go back to Dayshawn."

Trav and Asia come into the car. The tension between them so thick, waa rusty cutlass cya cut it.

"Evening," Asia muttered as Trav drove off, his grip tight around the wheel.

"Yu hair look nice, Asia." Mi smile at her braids. Sometimes mi wish mi hair did kinky so mi cuda wear dem nice hairstyle ya.

"Yeah. It looks nice," Chezzy agreed.

"Thanks." Asia smile. It nuh reach her eyes cause she keep a glance pon Trav.

"A run go Ochi, cause mi cya touch the road later. Yu mind come wid wi, Sandra?" Trav asked.

"*Zandra*," Chezzy hissed.

"Just ansa the question."

"Yu nafi talk to her like that," Asia seh, and Trav kiss him teeth. "Know wa? Nevermind! Carry dem home. Mi will handle mi business pon mi own time—"

"Mi a carry yu go do the thing, b."

"Mi nuh bother waa yu carry mi," Asia snapped, and Chezzy shifted around while me purse my lips.

Sighing, Trav drive to Mamme Bay and drop off Chezzy. Her bredda dem a play ina the front yard.

"Later, Chichi and Asia." Chezzy glance at Trav. "Thanks, Trav."

Trav nuh ansa, and Chezzy look shame while she exit the car. Lata mi tell ar nufi tek it personally. A so Trav gwan whenever him and Asia ina hot water.

We drive ina silence to Steer Town. Trav get angrier when him see him mother a walk pon the road ina waa shorts and bra. Him park a the side of the road, patting him pocket before exiting the car.

"Wa unu a argue bout?" mi ask as Asia grab Trav phone outta the cup holder.

Scowling, Asia stop scroll. "Trav a gwan like him always afi know mi whereabouts. Mi lie seh mi still a do mi hair, cause me go somewhere and think mi wuda mek it back in time."

"Yu nuh think that look a way?"

"No. Cause me cya ask him bout certain things." She quieted when Trav reentered. She laid her hand on his thigh as he drove off. "She still loves you, babe."

"Nuh lie to me, b." Him bring her hand to his mouth, kissing it. As Asia move her hand to her lap, Trav raise a brow. "Mi nuh tell yu fi stop search mi phone, Asia?"

"Sorry..." She put down the phone. Fi the rest of the journey, she talk to him until him relax.

After Trav help mi unpack the bag dem, mi follow him to the gate. "Nuh badda wid the fast driving if unu start cuss again."

Him sigh. "Me naa medz ar."

"Unu too much alike," mi seh, and him chuckle.

"A mi baby. Shi just mek mi waa fuck her up sometime. Later." Him hug mi, and mi smile against him boney chest.

"Bye, Mawga Boy," I said, and him pinch mi before running toward the car.

Mi go inside, put away the groceries, then bathe. Mi pack a bag wid the necessities fi after Favi done beat mi likkle coochie up.

Ouu, mi excited! Hood deh pon mi mind since last night, is a miracle mi go to bed widout rubbing the sensitivity outta mi clit. Mi nuh sure about many things about this brown man, but him buddy? Mi surer than sure! Even if me cya tek it, mi a go mek miself tek it!

Mi put mi bag ova mi shoulder and exit mi room, about fi sneak out. Mama should be sleep—

"Where you going, grandbaby?" Mama's voice came from the kitchen. Cho, blousecup! A when she wake?

Mi go to her. "Mi a go Chezzy."

"Drink some of the tomato juice mi mek." Mama poured the thick, yucky liquid into a cup.

Mi hate when she mek mi drink this. Mi nuh want no cleanser when me a go tek buddy, next thing mi afi run go bathroom when the man a damage mi. "Lata mi drink—"

"Take a sip. Nuh medicine nuh taste good."

Sighing, me tek three sip so she can satisfy. Mi gag as it go down. She smile,

73

taking the cup from me before grabbing at my crochiz.

Mi jump backward. "Mama!"

"Go put on tights. Mi tell yu fi stop walk wid all your pokie outta door."

Grumbling, mi go put on tights, then go back to her.

She feel mi up, smiling. "Walk good. Donkey seh the world nuh level."

"If mi follow you, mi nuh go nuh weh."

"Earth a run red, mi cya lose mi one grandbaby."

"Yu naa lose me." Guilt grew inside me as my mind drifted to where me a go. *If yu lay dung wid dog, yu get up with fleas.*

Forcing down a sigh, mi go brush mi teeth. After me done, mi run outside to Favi's vehicle. Once seated, mi kiss him. "Back to my favorite car."

Him drive off. "You haven't seen all my cars. How do you have a favorite?"

"Mi just know," mi seh, and him chuckle.

"Nuh know wa mi a go do wid yu."

"That's what you're saying now." I bit my bottom lip as I watched the veins in his hand flex while he gripped the wheel tighter.

Did they look that nice around my neck last night?

Favi sat on the edge of his bed while I stood by the door. Nerves a nyam mi. How me fraid so?

"Why are you so far?" he asked.

"Suppose a yaso mi waa stay?" Mi heart race as him stand, walking toward me.

He stopped before me, looping a finger beneath my chin. His sexy smirk made my clit throb. "Shy now?"

"I-I-" I couldn't say anything else before his head swooped down, capturing my lips. I didn't have to think about kissing him back. It was as natural as breathing. My eyes fluttered closed as I surrendered to the feeling. My lips tingled sweetly.

Goosebumps peppered my skin as he lifted me into his arms. Mi neva heavy like calf, but mi surprised how effortlessly him liff mi without breaking the kiss. Wrapping my arms around his neck, I moaned as he led us to the bed and gently placed me down.

He broke away, his lips grazing mine as he whispered, "Sure about this?"

"I trust you, Favi."

He smiled against my lips, and it made my heart beat faster. Giving my lips a last kiss, he broke away to get rid of my dress. He freed my breasts from the bra, tossing it aside. I lay back, and his eyes raked down my body. In a smooth motion, his head swooped down, capturing one of my hardening nipples with his mouth.

"Oh," I moaned, loving the swirl of his tongue while his next hand massaged my other breast.

Favi's eyes met mine, and I broke the stare to look at the ceiling. Something about his stare always held me captive, and I was scared to look into his eyes at a time like this. His tongue circled my nipple. His brazen fingers trailed my abdomen, pausing at the waist of my tights. He stopped sucking and kissing to ask in a low, hushed tone, "Is this okay?"

"Yes," I said, missing his touch.

Accepting that I wouldn't run, Favi stood and pulled me to the edge of the bed by my ankles. He tugged the panties and tights off, tossing them aside. He spread my legs wide with his knee. Cold air grazed my throbbing clit as a wave of self-consciousness swept over me. I was tempted to close my eyes and hide my body, but one look from him made me rethink.

Slowly, my eyes made their way up — passing the tent in his gray shorts, tattooed abdomen, and clean-shaven chest — until they settled on his eyes. They burned with a sensual flame, making them appear a darker shade.

Favi hooked onto every feature, committing them to memory. He met my eyes, and my cheeks burned. "You're sexy as fuck, Chayanne."

I covered my face with my hands. "Thanks."

Chuckling, he moved my hands. "This shyness isn't going to work."

I kept quiet, and he smirked.

"I'm going to break it out of you." He leaned in, and a chill ran through me. He stopped an inch from my face, and my quick breaths brushed his face. "Little."

He kissed the valley between my breasts. "By little." He kissed above my navel.

Then he dropped to his knees.

My lips parted. My brows flew up. Wa him a go do? Mi find it hard fi believe seh a badman like Favi a go eat—

My thoughts got washed away by his fingers, sinking into my thighs, and spreading me wider. He circled my swollen clit with his thumb, and I bit into my lips to silence a breathy moan.

He stopped rubbing. "Stop that. Let me hear you."

"O-okay." My chest heaved as he slowly inserted a finger inside me. My walls stretched, clamping around a second finger.

"Open wider."

My legs parted, exposing the juices flowing from me. I was almost embarrassed by how this man made me drip, despite barely touching me.

Favi brought his face closer, licking up my juices. Stunned by the sensation, my back arched off the bed. He looked at me, his eyes shining.

Unable to look at him, I glanced at the ceiling as his tongue swirled around my clit while two fingers moved in and out, curling slightly.

"Oh, God!" I moaned, pulling his hair.

Favi picked up the pace, pleasing me like no one had ever done before.

He removed his fingers from inside me, replacing them with his tongue. His thumb pressed against my sensitive clit, sending me to another dimension while his tongue worked inside my pussy.

"Mm," I moaned. My voice didn't sound like my own.

Favi worked my body like magic. My entire being was aflame as a tightness built in my abdomen. My loud moans, paired with the wet sounds of his fingers going in and out of me, drove me insane.

"Favi!" I cried, tears rushing to my eyes as he sucked my clit. My eyes slammed shut, but I could feel him watching me. "I'm—" My words turned gibberish as my hips raised from the bed.

The tension snapped, and I painted his face with my release. Stars blinked behind my closed eyelids. My legs and entire body shook from this powerful orgasm, but Favi didn't stop his maddening pleasure until I rode out the high.

I dropped onto the bed with a huff, my eyes opening to see Favi focused on licking away all traces of the aftermath. Mi neva know head nice so!

Placing a kiss on my clit that made me shiver, Favi stood to his full height. Smirking, he wiped the back of his hand across his mouth. "When I said I wanted to hear you, I didn't mean deafen me."

"Stop!" I bit back a smile, wiping tears from my eyes while he grabbed a pillow.

"Up," he said, but I couldn't move. Snickering, he lifted me and tucked the pillow beneath my lower back. "You good?"

"Yes." I nodded weakly cause mi body still a shake. Wa him do to mi? I never had an orgasm like that before.

Favi chuckled, taking a condom out of his pocket. He tugged his pants and boxers down to his ankles. His big, veiny dick saluted me, and my mouth dropped while my eyes widened.

A who dat a go ina?!

Favi's eyes glistened. "Still sure?"

"Y-yes."

He ripped the condom open with his teeth. "Good."

Mi gulp and mentally prepare miself fi get stretched like I'd never been before. Oh, God... It too late fi get up and run?

Favi slipped on the condom, then gripped his dick in a hand. He rubbed it in my wetness before positioning it at my entrance, making me whimper. "I'm going to be gentle," he said.

"I know," I said, shocked by how much trust I put in him.

Looking between us, he slapped the head against my clit, making me shudder. He pressed against my opening, about to thrust inside, when his phone rang.

Mi nuh know if mi fi be thankful or bawl. Mi a expect him fi ignore it cause him have more pressing issues at hand, but him scowl and pull weh.

Him grab him phone from outta him shorts. "What?" he snapped. "Wa the fuck yu seh? No, stay. Me a fawud." Ending the call, Favi yanked up his boxers and shorts. Him grab mi clothes, handing dem to mi while mi sit up. "I—"

"It's okay. Mi understand." Mi crawl off the bed, putting on mi clothes. Deep down, mi disappointed and relieved. That deh cocky look like it will cripple me.

It neva feel so big last night.

Favi go the bathroom, closing the door, and turning on the pipe. When him come out, him ina waa change of outfit — full black, even the watch round him wrist. "Stay inside tonight," he said, checking the clip of the pistol in his hand.

Slipping on my Crocs, I nodded weakly. I didn't want to be in the middle of another shootout, and I hated not being able to stop him from being in another.

"Josiah a go drop yu home. And I mean it. Stay the fuck inside, Chayanne."

"I'll stay inside."

He walked toward me and held beneath my chin. Mi blink away tears as mi meet him eyes. They were swirling with many emotions mi cudn place. He didn't say anything, but mc know wa him waa say: 'I'm good.'

Chapter Fifteen

CHAYANNE

Gunfire rang loud and rampant since late Saturday evening into this morning. Blaring sirens were added to the mix by nightfall. Anytime police got involved, the wul Steer Town know a sum serious. During them time deh, the boldest of smaddy nuh dare set foot pon them veranda. Whoever had plans to pay bill or buy food, remain fixed ina dem house wid no light and a hungry belly.

Death from natural causes was better than a bullet ripping through the many layers of skin.

Mama beg mi nufi go outta road to Chezzy, but mi neva interested ina that. I could only think about Favi and Trav. Mi nuh hear from them since yesterday. They were probably doing bad things to people, but I didn't want anything to happen to them.

Finger never say 'look here', it say 'look yonder'.

The harrowing howl of a dog drifted from in the distance. A shiver ran down my spine. I glanced at my phone, then back to the news on the TV.

A female anchor was at the Drax Hall gas station, mic in hand, as the camera focused on the barricaded entrance to Steer Town. "Behind me is the abandoned road leading into the ZOSO communities Steer Town and Mamme Bay. Police and military personnel are on the scene, trying to de-escalate the rising tension between two rival factions. Residents are urged not to leave their homes until the all-day curfew lifts."

The news cut to waa annoying advertisement.

"Tek mi! Do a beg, tek mi!" Mama cried.

"Stop it, Mama," I said, and she ignored me. Sighing, mi reach fimi phone. Mi quickly scroll past Favi and Trav number, then call Aunty.

She answered on the first ring. Warmth bloomed inside me because of her familiar voice. "Chichi baby, unu good? Mi a watch the news."

"The gunman dem nuh near fi wi lane, but it sound like a ina the backyard dem deh." I sighed as Mama cried louder. "Aunty, talk to Mama—"

"I doh waa Kenzie talk to me. This gingeration lost its way, and the next one a go be the same cause wa the goat do, the kid follow," Mama seh, and Aunty sigh.

"Nuh pay Mommy nuh mind, Chichi baby. Yu contact school?" Aunty asked.

"Yes. Mi teachers a go give mi extensions," mi seh.

"Good... Tate is home. Mi will call yu later."

Ending the call, mi pull my knees up to my chest while watching Mama.

"I not leaving! This has been my home and a yaso me a go drop dung *ploof* and dead!" Mama declared.

The violence a waa never-ending cycle. Mi nuh waa become more used to it. Dealing with Favi meant no escaping.

The weight on my heart and mind grew heavier, and I sighed.

Nothing was more eerie than falling asleep to loud turmoil every night for an entire week, then waking up to a bone-chilling silence.

Did I get shot in my sleep, leaving behind everyone I loved? Or did they die, too?

"Ano everything weh soak up water a sponge," came a voice.

My head snapped in that direction, relief flooding me. "Wa yu seh, Mama?" I asked, braiding her hair.

She always kept it in one big braid over her left shoulder. It stopped at her waist.

My hair needed a cut. It was at my armpit.

"There must be a reason for the silence. Turn on the TV so we can see the afternoon news."

We didn't have cable, and the two channels pick and choose when fi show good. Mi nuh know if it safe fi go outside go turn the antenna. Flicking between the two channels, mi settle on the one with the best feed.

"We have apprehended a group of lawbreakers and they're now in a secure location undergoing questioning. There were many gang-member casualties—" said the Police Chief, and I leaned off Mama, sitting at the edge of the sofa and holding my breath. "—a few within the security forces, and injuries among civilians. I can confirm that the situation is under control, and the lockdown will lift at six p.m. If you have any information that may help with the ongoing investigation, contact the nearest police department. Thank you."

The camera switched to the anchor, and mi focus pon the background. The military presence was lighter!

Me run toward the front door, ignoring Mama's cry fi sit dung mi likkle baxide. Yanking it open, the song of crickets filled my ears while a dog's barking disrupted the melody. The cool wind caressed my skin, dousing it with the scent of my neighbor's pot of fried chicken. A mix of voices was in the distance, and I smiled. I would have people to talk to again!

Chapter Sixteen

Favio

*D*espite Antaro's beliefs, I was a business executive.

I hated being linked to fuckry.

Glaring at two boats sailing toward the sun, I relaxed my jaw and turned away from the crimson sand.

Buonanima.

Stopping by the car, I shoved the bloody hacksaw into an acid-doused trash bag. The suffocating fume stung my nose as I secured it with a zip tie before handing it to the man standing beside the car. "Mek dis nuh exist," I said, and Lizard nodded. "Teeth?" I asked the other. While the mocking crash of waves cleansed one of my many sins, I vividly heard my next burdens. They clicked against each other within a small plastic container he held. I took it from him, handing it to Lizard. "Yu know wa fi do."

Nodding, Lizard walked away. The other man attempted to follow him.

"You," I said, and he froze. "Stay."

He turned, gulping. "Yes, Slitta?"

"A you kill the Shottaz man dem and mek dem run dung pon we the other night?" I asked, despite knowing the answer. He opened his mouth, but I continued speaking. "Suppose mi neva get intel, how dat wuda go?"

"Slitta, hear mi nuh—"

"Hear?" Chuckling, I took my knife out of my pocket, opening it. "How yu expect

mi fi listen when you can't?" I taunted, and he staggered backward.

Travis pushed him forward. "Listen to the man."

"Tell me what I said," I demanded.

"Nuh step to nuh Shottaz man unless dem push badness first. But mi did out fi mi old man funeral, and a youth tell mi yu seh anything we see, we fi dirt."

"Who?" I asked, and he told me. "Order came from a higher-up?" I clarified, and he nodded, making me exhale a sharp breath. "Travis, hold him."

"Slitta, please! Please!" he begged as Travis grabbed him, forcing him to kneel.

Knife clenched in my hand, I approached him. "A yu first mistake dis. Mi nago kill yu," I promised, and he nodded. The color drained from his face as I added, "But I don't like people who don't listen. You don't listen, and mi cya allow yu fi act stubborn twice pon my watch. Mek dis be a lesson."

I grabbed his ear. He struggled to get free as Travis held him steady. Pressing the knife against the tip of his ear, I made a clean cut with the sharp blade. Blood gushed from the slant cut, and I scowled while pulling back.

Travis released him, and his hand shot to his ear, red painting his fingers. His screams intensified when I dropped the flimsy flesh onto the sand. Stepping on it, I walked away with Travis by my side. We stopped by the van he drove here, and he grabbed a bottle of water and poured it into my hands. I furiously scrubbed my hands. My skin crawled as the water turned from light pink to a clear hue.

"A go good yaso?" Travis moved the bottle, and I nodded. He bumped my fist, then hopped in the van and drove off.

I walked toward my car, taking my place behind the wheel. My phone rang, and I grabbed it. It was the old man; he was good at getting information. "Update?" My grip tightened as I listened. Releasing a huff, I hung up, driving toward the safe house to clean up.

Minutes later as I slipped on my watch, a text came in. Who the fuck was texting this early? Texts came with redundant greetings instead of getting to the point. I hated being bothered.

CHAYANNE: Good morning!

The corner of my mouth ticked upward as I read the message once.

Twice.

Then called her. "Chayanne."

"Why yu always afi greet me like that?" she asked, and I imagined her doing her cute little pout. The one that made me want to kiss those soft lips. "Favi?"

I cleared my throat. "Chayanne?"

"Yago busy today?" she asked, and I hummed. "So, me naa see yu tonight?"

"Not sure." If she didn't have school, I'd see her all day.

"Okay," she replied, and I forced down a sigh.

She had explained her phone situation to me, and I needed to buy her a better one. Whenever I wanted to talk to her or see her, I needed to do so.

Instantly.

Spontaneously.

Whenever I fucking wanted.

Her being young and having all these other responsibilities would hinder my access to her...

Fuck. What was I doing with her?

"Favi?" she said.

I rolled my shoulders before glancing at my watch. It was almost seven a.m. I needed to leave soon. "I'll talk to you later," I said, about to hang up.

"Wait," she rushed out. "Remember fi put yu right foot first when yu reach wherever you a go deh today."

My mouth did that uncontrollable tick. "My right foot?"

"For good luck."

"Mi nuh entertain fuckry, Chayanne."

"Ano sheggry. Do it, it works."

I didn't believe in luck. If a person wanted something, they had to get it themself. Luck was not real. Only initiative, hard work, and making a way where there wasn't one.

"Have a good day at school, Chayanne." I hung up, leaving the room and passing by Josiah, who gave me a nod of respect. Ignoring him, I hopped into my BMW, taking the highway toward Kingston.

I had an important business meeting, then I needed to return to St. Ann. I fucking hated everything related to Steer Town, but lately, I wanted to be in that hellhole every second of each day.

"*Mamma, is it necessary for you to do this?*" *I asked.*

Mamma glared at me, then glanced at the boy standing beside her. "*Cover yu ears.*" *After he complied, she scowled at me.* "*Go suck yu madda, Favio. He says he wants to see his nonno, so I'm bringing him. He is your family. The sooner you stop disowning him, the easier your life will be.*"

My jaw ticked, and I turned away to open the door.

"*Let's go see your grandfather before his meeting.*" *Mamma led the boy through the doors while he glanced at me.*

I entered the office, left foot first, and Chayanne's words replayed in my head.

Fuck that right-foot bullshit. Since his mother called and told me to get him, I was reminded there was no such thing as luck. Even if there was, mine ran out many years ago.

The door closed behind the last board member, and my focus shifted to the man sitting at the other end of the table. The fucker grinned at me.

"*Well done, figlio. The board knows the right choice is you,*" *he commended.*

Ignoring him, I stared at the wrist of my white shirt. It was clean, exactly how I liked it.

There was nothing I hated more than messes, and what Antaro did was the epitome of messy.

My head snapped up, my eyes narrowing at him. "*Wa the fuck dat yu do?*"

His grin washed away, his lips curling into a devious sneer. "You were taking long."

"I had a plan."

"It was a stupid plan. We're dealing with lowlife criminals. Most of them do not have an education. Why do you think a sit-down with Truko would work?"

"Not everyone craves chaos."

"Then you're not a criminal mastermind."

"I'm not a criminal," I muttered, and he cackled. "Yu feel seh telling Rush fi drop a message ina my name was a 'criminal mastermind' thing fi do?"

"Don't take that tone with me, figlio." Antaro straightened his tailored suit before approaching the screen. "Numbers went up."

"I don't want to talk fucking numbers."

"No?" He glanced over his shoulder. "You said you're not a criminal. Why wouldn't you want to talk numbers?"

"You did it out of spite."

Turning to face me, Antaro smirked. "I don't do anything out of spite."

"Bugiardo! If ya go fuck up the operation, keep me out of it. We have a deal."

"I'm sticking by it," he said, and I scoffed. Him tek mi fi a big, fucking claffy.

Unclenching my fist, I stood and walked toward the door. It was six p.m., and I didn't want to be in his presence longer than necessary.

"Figlio," he said, and I paused, turning my head slightly. "Is it done?"

What kind of stupid fucking question was that? For a person with hardly any interest in this, Antaro knew I was thorough. I never left room for error, and I didn't plan on starting now.

Chapter Seventeen

CHAYANNE

Lingering tension blanketed the community, adding to the morbid feeling tight in my gut. The sky was stone blue, and no birds flocked toward it. Minus my feet hitting the paved road, the rattle of chains around the necks of busy-bodied dogs pierced the eerie silence. Maybe I should've heeded Mama's warning and not go to school.

Gulping as I reached the Square, mi approach the small bunch of skoolaz and working adults. Usually, the Square would be more crowded than this. Mi deevn see Asia or Mark.

Stopping by the wall, mi gulp down more of my budding fear.

Something terrible happened, and I was scared to know what it was.

Yolo tugged me into a hug as soon as I stepped through the school gates. "My Number One! Oh gosh, me dee miss yu!" She kissed both my cheeks, then hugged Chezzy. "Me big batty friend! Me miss yu, too."

"Mi cya badda wid yu, Yolanda." Chezzy chuckled while returning the hug.

Yolo break the hug. "Unu better badda wid me. Cause unu mek me watch news like old woman."

"A old people watch news?" mi ask, and she nod. "Me watch news every night, even before this."

"You a waa special case, Chichi," Chezzy seh.

Yolo link her fingers with mine as we walk off. "So much happen when unu gone. Wa unu waa hear first? How two a me gyal dem bruk big fight ova me, and me cut dem off cause me nuh play dem game deh? Or unu waa hear how Mr. Black get waa drop, weh yu cuda stay from anywhere and hear?"

Mi eyes widen. "Him alright?"

"Yes, love of my life. Yu favorite teacher alright," she seh, and mi kiss mi teeth.

Chezzy chuckle while putting on her green sweater. "Ano her favorite teacher."

"Exactly. Him grade mi harder than anybody else, but mi glad seh nun worse nuh dweem," mi seh.

"Me nuh know how fi feel. One less man ina the world a good sum," Yolo said.

"Why?" Chezzy asked.

"Because me can have more gyal." Yolo winked at a third former who a past by, and the girl blush. Poor thing. Once she out of earshot, Yolo grin. "Afi get ar."

Mi feign anger. "Watch ar a flirt wid next gyal round mi."

"Sorry." She kiss me cheek, and me smile, thankful to be around her. She was always amusing, and I needed laughter now.

I was yet to hear from Favi and Trav, and I couldn't express my worries to Chezzy. When mi did bawl to her during the lockdown, she ask wa mi expect fi happen to gangsters. She tell mi fi stop deal with Favi, and mi hang up cause mi nuh waa hear dat.

For the entire day, worry plagued my mind and heart.

Especially when the taxi drop mi ina the Square the evening, and the first thing mi notice a waa news crew. The community was awake now. People were gathered by the wall, and mi walk toward dem fi fass.

"A week ago, a violent turmoil shook the communities of Steer Town and Mamme Bay, leaving behind a civilian casualty," said the anchor.

A chill ran down my spine. The people round mi start whisper among themselves, but mi block dem out fi focus pon the anchor.

"Behind me is where they met their untimely end." The cameraman turned the camera at Godsto, and my blood ran cold. "Wait. It appears the mother of the deceased is making an appearance." Rebecca covered the mic and lowered her voice. "Zoom in!"

My eyes widened and mi heart drop to mi batty as a short, black lady made her way off Godsto.

No.

Nuh you.

God, *please.*

Tears rushed to my eyes when she took the mic from Rebecca, tightly clutching it between her chubby fingers. Her face was tear-stained, her eyes red and puffy. She was a mess in her ripped skirt and mucus-stained blouse.

"Asia a did mi one pickini," Miss Olive forced out. "Yu know when yu roast breadfruit, most a dem bun up, but one come out perfect? A before mi husband pass, mi finally get pregnant with my one roast breadfruit. We neva get the chance fi go market before the lockdown, so mi tek wa likkle mi have gi to her—" Miss Olive choked on a sob, and Rebecca squeezed her shoulder.

"Asia neva like seh mi hungry while her belly full. Mi beg ar fi stay ina the house cause me wuda be alright. But she neva listen... She neva listen." Miss Olive hung her head low, shaking it. "Sh-she did a try see if nuh shop open w-weh she cuda buy sum fi mi get f-fi eat. She neva come back at all. She fight ar hardest dung a hos-hospital fi outlive the bullet, but she neva mek it. Mi one lik-likkle roast breadfruit." Miss Olive drop pon Rebecca, wailing.

Rebecca held her close, rubbing her back in small circles. She signal fi the cameraman cut the feed.

I stepped backward, bumping into someone.

"We need justice!" the person cried.

My heart was heavy. My throat dried. Words couldn't explain what I felt.

Asia... Asia died?

I ached for Miss Olive. Trav. My shaken community, who walked over to console Miss Olive.

The community hosted a candle lighting for Asia that night, at the shop it appear she did a head to. Pon the concrete step leading into the shop, candles of all shapes and sizes burned bright flames. A blown-up of Asia's prettiest picture was posted on the shop door. Her smile was stunning; Trav had told me it was one of the first things he loved about her.

And now she was gone.

Miss Olive stared at her one roast breadfruit picture through soulless eyes.

Where was Trav? He should be here.

Searching the crowd, mi spot Favi. Him lean pon a wall — not too close to the candlelight, but not too far, either. Him a smoke, his eyes focusing on me. I gulped, looking away from him. I was relieved to see him alive and well, but I was wary of him.

Was Favi involved?

The question plagued me until the candlelight ended. The crowd dispersed, and I found Miss Olive before she cuda disappear into the shell of her home.

"Miss Olive," I called out, and she cudn force a smile as she look pon mi. Mi walk toward her, giving her chubby form the biggest hug I could muster. "My condolences, Miss Olive. Smaddy afi pay fi dis."

Miss Olive pulled away. She focused on the ground. "Police nago do nun, mi dear. Asia is nun but another statistic to them."

My heart plummeted. Mi wish mi cuda do sum fi help her. Mi wish wa she seh bout the police a neva true, but deep down, mi know a the truth. I'd seen this happen too many times before to expect any difference.

I sighed, discreetly sliding five grand into her hand. It wasn't much, but it could help with the funeral.

Miss Olive squeezed my hand. "Thanks, Chichi. Tek care."

"Alright, Miss Olive," I said, and she nodded before walking away.

Someone else pulled her into a conversation.

When Mommy died, I remembered not wanting anyone to talk to me. Other times, people were all I wanted around me.

Wiping away the tears brimming my eyelids, I walked away. When I was a few steps away from Favi, him lean off the wall and walk toward me.

"Chayanne," him seh, and mi walk faster. "*Chayanne.*" Him grab mi hand, pulling me to a stop. Him mek mi face him, using him finger fi liff mi chin. The concern shining in his eyes made tears rush forward again.

Favi toss the tail a him spliff into the nearby bush, tugging me into a hug. I froze for a second before relaxing, wrapping my arms around him. Him liff mi bridal style, and I curled into a ball in his arms as he walked toward his house, weh further down the street. Him bring me ina the house and lay me pon the bed. Him step backward, and I clutched his shirt.

"Stay..." I croaked.

He hesitated before lying beside me. Holding me close, him kiss my forehead. This was the first time me neva giddy cause Favio Welsh was showing me the part of him no one else saw.

I was too confused. Angry. Sad.

Why death always afi rip people from mi life?

A strained noise ripped from my throat, and I buried my face in his chest. My tears soaked his shirt, sobs rocking my body.

I held Favi tighter. I didn't want to lose him. Ever.

I'd hate for him to go out like Asia, but I didn't know what I could say to make him leave this life of violence behind. After all — live by the gun, die by the gun.

I waited for Mama's voice to remind me that *if yu born fi hang, yu cya drown,* but her voice never came.

My eyes fluttered open. When did I fall asleep?

Favi gently squeezed my shoulder. "You good?"

I forced a smile, surprised he stayed. "Not really…" I confessed, my voice hoarse.

He sighed. "Sorry. Stupid question "

I snuggled closer to him, throwing a leg over his body as he continued to trail a finger up and down my arm. "You apologized."

"Don't start."

"Where's Trav?"

"Nuh know."

If there was one thing me know bout my brother, him like disappear when things bother him. I'd give him his space, but as soon as mi reach home, mi a go text him fi mek sure him nuh do nun too crazy.

"You knew her?" Favi asked, and I nodded. "I'm sorry…"

My heart skipped a beat, and mi lean offa him. "For?" I asked, and his expression blanked. "Did you…"

He glared. "Did I *what*, Chayanne?"

"Kill—" Mi pause when him kiss him teeth before moving to sit at the side of the bed. Tears swelled in my eyes and my heart raced. "Answer me, Favio."

"I didn't kill her, Chayanne. The police did," him seh, and mi gasp.

"W-wa?"

Sighing, him take him phone outta him pocket. Afta a few swipes, him put the phone before mi face. A material stained in red flashed before my eyes. I tore my gaze away, bile rising up my throat.

"Look at it, Chayanne," Favio demanded, and mi snap mi eyes shut, pushing the phone away. "Look pon the fucking picture."

"Mi nuh waa see that, Favio," I cried.

"How else yu a go believe seh ano me nor the gang kill her? It's a picture of the bullet hole. The size of the puncture doesn't match the guns Blood Paw uses."

I peeked open an eye. Him phone move, so mi give him mi undivided attention. "How yu so sure?"

"They used semis during the shootout. I think a bullet ricocheted and hit her."

"How yu get the picture?"

"I have people."

"Sorry for accusing you..." I mumbled, my heart rate decreasing while him nuh ansa. "Yu sure yu nuh know weh Trav deh?" mi ask, and him look away. "Favi, please tell mi if yu know," mi beg, and him sigh.

"I don't want to lie to you, but I don't know if you can handle the truth," him seh, and mi sit more upright, swallowing a lump.

"Is he... Is he d—" I inhaled a sharp breath.

"No," Favi said quickly, and I released my breath. "What the Chief said isn't the whole truth. They made some arrests, and Travis is with them."

"He's in jail?" I asked, relieved and worried as Favi shake him head.

"No. I don't know where they're holding him, but I'm working on it. Yu brother a go good."

I nodded, trusting him with my whole bleeding heart.

Mama always told me education was the one thing no one could take from me. They could rob me of my money, my clothes, and my life, but never my education. It was embedded in me like DNA, the one thing that could get me out of the ghetto.

Mi approach Mr. Black desk. "Morning, sir."

"Morning. You have until the end of class." Mr. Black hand me a test paper.

I thanked him and took up a desk and chair, bringing dem outta door. Mi place dem before the entrance so Mr. Black cuda watch me while him teach. The first question mek mi brain blank like dunce pickney book. When sir teach we dis?

Mi skim through the questions, groaning when mi realize the first few questions a from last month. Mi nuh study none a dat, but mi know all wa him teach this month like the back of mi hand cause of the lockdown.

"*Rain never fall a one man door,*" mi remind miself before getting to work. An hour later, I finished and entered the class while mi classmate dem leff.

Mr. Black take the test. "I am expecting you to ace this test, Miss Bailey."

"Sir, me never hear yaa tell the other girl dem seh yu only want an A," mi seh while him scan the test.

"I encourage all my students, but I give extra pushes where I see fit. See you tomorrow," him seh, and mi nod and leff.

Cho, blousecup! Mi nuh know wa do dat mawga man. A must Trav 2.0—

I stopped walking.

Trav.

Mi really hope him okay...

Saddened, mi go find mi friends. We walk to the gate together.

"A the man dat yu tell mi bout?" Yolo whispered, and mi look in that direction.

"Yeah." Mi smile at the yellow BMW while mi heart race.

"Watch her a blush! Yu neva tell me a rich man! Him have a sister or aunty? Me neva fuck a big woman before."

"Ano waa man dat weh yu waa con," Chezandra seh, and mi glare pon her while Yolo scoff.

"Man wicked, but me wickeder than dem." Yolo hug me, squeezing mi batty.

"Bye, fish." Mi pull away so she can hug Chezandra.

"Your *favorite* fish, doh forget the title. Unu lata. Me have court," Yolo seh.

"All the best." Mi give her a thumbs-up before she walk off. "Yu really a do this?" mi ask Chezandra, and she roll her eyes.

"Wa mi do, Chichi?" she ask, and mi glare.

"Yu know wa, so nuh act smart wid mi."

"Yu expect mi fi go ina the man car when last time him put—" She lowered her voice. "—a fucking gun to yu head?! A time yu stop deal wid him, Chichi—" She pause when mi kiss mi teeth, crossing my arms.

"Yu cya tell mi who fi deal with."

"I will when yaa act fool. This ano waa joke anymore—"

"A did joke when yu tell mi fi sex him even doh dat neva deh pon mi mind?"

"Ano dat mi a talk boh. Mi nuh like how yu act fool once yu ketch feelings."

Gasping, mi jaw clench as mi shut mi mouth. "Mi really nuh bout fi argue wid yu, Chezandra."

"Yu think mi waa argue wid you?" She roll her eyes, looking away while crossing her arms. "Go see wa him want. Hurry back so we can go home."

Mi deevn grace her wid a response before mi walk toward the vehicle.

The front window went down. Favi's brow raised. "You good?"

"Good evening. Yeah, mi good..." I said.

Him glare pon Chezzy. Him hand move to the pistol pon him lap.

Mi step closer to the vehicle. "Wa yaa do?! Put up dat before smaddy see you."

"I don't give a fuck about any of these people. Get in the car." Him release the gun, and mi sigh.

"Me cya come... Chezandra nuh waa come."

"Taxi stop run?"

"No, but we always go home together. Plus, mi afi stop at mi Aunty," mi explain, and him stare pon mi before him bring up the window, revving as him drive off. Mi sigh as the car speed down the road. Mi walk toward Chezandra, kissing mi teeth as mi step pass. "Come mek wi go get a taxi."

She nuh ansa, and mi thankful fi dat cause mi nuh like when mi tongue get loose. Chezandra a test mi. We nuh talk until we reach her house. Aunty pick up pon the tension.

"Wa unu a quarrel ova?" Aunty asked, and we didn't answer. She chuckled. "Yu know seh me and Mikeila give birth to wiself? Unu soon kiss and mek up, so mi deevn a fawt pon unu. Chichi, the rundown deh pon the kitchen counter."

I nodded and went to the kitchen. The twin dem trail behind me. Chezandra come ina the kitchen seconds later, grumbling while she share dem dinner. Mi go talk to Aunty until she enter moments later.

"Bye, Aunty," I said, and Aunty smiled.

Chezandra slip on her green yard slippers and follow me to HalfWay. "Mek mi know when yu reach home."

"Like yu care?" mi ask, and she glare.

"Yu think a foolishness me a tell yu?"

"Me never seh a foolishness, but—"

"But what?" She grab mi arm, pulling me outta waa car way.

"But—" I paused, realizing she wudn understand how Favi mek mi feel.

Comfort. Appreciated. Pretty. No one understood us but ourselves.

"Mi nafi explain miself to yu." Mi kiss mi teeth, walking away. Instead of going home, mi go Godsto. Approaching Favi's gate, mi gulp when mi see two man pose up wid guns tuck ina dem waist. Keeping my head low, mi try step past them.

"Oye. Weh yago?" One of them grab mi arm, making me stiffen.

"Bredda, wa yaa do?!" The other pried the hand off me. "A Slitta own dis."

I looked at him. Piece of him ear gone, but him look familiar. Wait deh, nuh Driver dis? Sas Crise! Mi shuda tek Chezandra foolish advice!

"Fuck! Sorry. Nuh tell Slitta mi put mi hand pon yu," seh the one weh did hold mi. Him sound genuinely scared, and I hated to admit it, but I liked the power his fear gave me.

I smirked. "Me will think about it," I said, and him eyes widen.

"Slitta nuh deh ya," Earzas seh.

"Weh him deh?" I asked, but him nuh ansa. Sighing, mi walk off, freezing when mi spot where Asia died. This shrine had more flowers than the shop.

It was my first time being here, and this hurt a lot. My throat tightened. It was so difficult to breathe. I wanted to find Favi and run into his arms, but my feet brought me to the shrine.

Mi wish mi did pick some of Aunty roses. Maybe Asia would've liked them.

Sighing, mi about fi leave when the phone ring. Mi leff the banger pon the charger for Mama, so she cuda get mi whenever she worry boh mi today.

"Yes, Aunty?" mi answer while staring at Asia's shrine.

"Chichi baby, yu reach home yet?" Aunty asked.

"No, Aunty. Mi did stop a Aunty Simone. Mi on mi way home now."

"Hurry and come offa the road. Anyway, mi call cause Tate Mommy sick, so me afi tek money outta yu exam fees," Aunty said, and my eyes widened. Fees needed to be paid by the end of this month, and I had one subject left to pay for. "Mi a go try replace it ina four weeks. If not, the late fees can go up to January, right?"

"Yes. Mi understand why yu do it. Yago send it ina four weeks, so no rush," mi seh, and she sigh.

"Alright, Chichi baby. Me did just waa notify yu. Later." Aunty hung up, and I put the phone into my pocket.

Someone approached from behind, stopping beside me. I glanced at them. It was a man in his late forties to early fifties. His graying hair was dyed black. His most prominent feature was his fat nose.

Him focus pon the shrine. "Sad, isn't it? Wa yu think happen?"

"One a the gangs, right?" mi ask, despite not intending to lie. Mi gulp when him glance pon mi before looking at the shrine.

"I guess so."

Sum boh tha man ya nuh sit right wid me.

I needed to leave.

Now.

"Well..." Mi step backward. "Have a good rest of your evening, sir."

"You, too." Him nuh look pon mi.

I was thankful. Him wudn afi see me do the fastest walk-away in history. And I would've done it if him neva talk again.

"Reconsider who yu choose fi lay dung with, Chayanne."

Chapter Eighteen

CHAYANNE

M i skin up mi face. "What?"

"Who the fuck yaa ansa so? Fix up dat."

Between my thighs throbbed, and mi put a hand between it. Wa wrong wid Fat Ma mek she a gwan so? I cleared my throat. "Yes, Favi?"

"That's better," he said, and I imagined him smirking. "Come outside."

"A almost twelve. Weh yu did deh wul day?"

"Nuh ask mi fuckry. Mi link yu and yu nuh fawud," him seh coldly, and mi swallow mi guilt.

"Sorry..."

"Outside in five minutes." He hung up. Cho, blousecup! Why this man so controlling?

Mi push mi books aside and put on him hoodie over mi shirt. Mi brush mi teeth, then go outside. Him lean on the car a smoke. Him dash weh the tail fi open the door fimi. Mi go inside and fold my arms, waiting fi him sidung.

Adjusting the seat for more leg room, him raise a brow. "You good?"

"No," mi ansa, and him move closer.

"What's wrong?"

"Mi come a yu yaad and neva see yu. Weh yu did deh?"

"Nuh ask mi fuckry," he said, and mi kiss mi teeth, making him glare. "Come here," he said, patting his lap. Him rest him hands pon mi waist after mi straddle him. "You know you wouldn't have to ask if you came, right?"

"Where yu go?"

"The beach."

"Why?" I asked, but him nuh ansa. Mi sigh, changing the topic.

While we talk fi the next few minutes, me smile like an idiot while him smirk.

"Yu nuh waa fawud?" him ask as mi lay pon him chest. Him caress my ass, making me smile.

"I can't. Mi afi stay wid Mama, and mi never stay away from her so long before."

"I'll have you back by Saturday." Him pause. "Please?"

Mi jolt up, my eyes widening, "Yu just seh please?" mi ask, and him glare.

"You're provoking. Don't make me repeat it. Yes, or no?"

"Yes, only because you said please." Smiling, I leaned forward and kissed him.

He kissed me harder, tightening his grip on my ass as his tongue swiped across my bottom lip. I opened my mouth, and his tongue slipped inside. Favi tasted of weed. I didn't like it, but I didn't shy away because his kisses made me insatiable.

I craved the way my eyes fluttered closed.

How my lips tingled.

And how my entire body was aflame.

When Favi kissed me, I never, ever wanted it to end.

Even as we pulled away for air.

My breathing was heavy as I kissed along his neck. I licked his ear, tugging it between my teeth.

"*Fuck*, don't do that." He groaned, and I smirked while releasing his ear.

"Why?"

"You're making me horny," he said, and I chuckled, grinding myself against his hardening length.

"I know." I continued teasing his ear while trailing my hand to his waistband.

He raised his body, allowing me to pull his sweatpants down. I caressed the bulge in the darkness. My clit throbbed, aching for the release he wouldn't give.

But I wanted to please him. His dick was hard, pressing against the fabric. I knew it must hurt.

I broke the kiss and slipped my hand inside his boxers. Favi leaned his head back, and I chuckled. "You good?"

"Always," he replied, his voice gruff. He was holding back, and I wanted to tell him that mi nuh care if wi first time a ina waa car, but mi appreciate his respect for me. And himself.

Mi definitely a back mi clit when mi go inside.

"Okay..." I looked from his face to his length. Mi like seh him circumcise, so mi nafi peel hood like banana. Mi spit ina mi hand, stroking him to his full length, then gasping.

His eyes snapped open. "What?"

"Why it so big now?" I asked, and he chuckled. Mi hear bout growers, but wow! A really alladis mi waa go ina mi? Nuh stitches mi a go need afta dis?

"Scared?" Him smirk when mi shake mi head.

"No..." Mi kiss his ear, licking and nibbling on his lobe.

His moans were low, yet him still so sexy. "Faster."

I picked up the pace, my grip tight around his dick as I pumped it and rubbed the tip with my thumb. It leaked pre-cum, and I wanted to lick it away or stick my finger in my mouth, but I controlled myself.

I peppered kisses along his cologne-doused skin. My tongue circled the base of his neck, and I smiled as an uneven breath passed his lips. I retraced kisses to his jawline, then his mouth. He kissed me back, biting my lip when his body stiffened. Lines of cum shot onto my hoodie.

He kissed me through his orgasm. My clit throbbed at how sexy he sounded. He didn't allow me to break the kiss until he came down from his high. I smiled at him as I pulled back.

"What?" he asked, his eyes hooded.

"Nothing. You owe me a hoodie." Mi release him dick while him smirk at the white lines on the hoodie.

"I'll get you a new one."

"Mi want one weh yu wear..."

"Okay," he said, and mi smile. "Get off so I can get something to clean you."

I sat beside him, watching him stretch him long self fi sum ina the glove compartment. Hope ano the gun... "It's fine," I rushed out. "Mi will go inside—"

He looked over his shoulder. "Fuck yu tek mi fa?" He grabbed a pack of wipes. He pulled one out, wiping the white streaks off the hoodie. Him did completely concentrated.

It deevn cross mi mind fi talk. Mi did only waa watch him. Favi was so handsome.

Finished, his eyes drifted to mine, and I looked away, blushing. Him wipe off himself before gripping my chin between his fingers. "Tomorrow, I'll fuck you how I want to. For now, go inside and get some rest. And don't touch yourself. I can see how bad you want to."

"Yav yu phone and get vex money?"

"Yes, Mommy," mi seh, and she laugh.

"Stop call mi dat. Being the firstborn and oldest daughter is a lot of work."

"We good now?"

"Yeah... Mi just scared boh yu safety, Chichi. Please mek sure yu keep yu phone pon yu. Mi have yu location if—" Her words come out muffled as mi slap mi hand over her mouth.

"Yu worry too much. Wa happen deh behind we. Favi wudn hurt me," mi assure, and she sigh, moving mi hand.

"For your sake, mi hope so. Me a go give this to Mama fi yu, and me will check pon her bright and early tomorrow morning." She tek the KFC from me.

"Thanks, Chezzy. You're the best." Mi smile, and she return it.

"See him a come outta the car deh like him more impatient than anybody else."

Mi look behind me fi see Favi a lean pon him car. Him cross him arms over him chest, resting a foot on the wheel. What a fine piece of brown man!

"Mi know wa unu a go do, so nuh leff out none a the details," Chezzy seh, and mi laugh and hug her before mi walk toward the man.

"Evening," mi seh, and him nod, opening the door.

"Get in," Favi seh, and mi comply. Him enter the car seconds later, driving off while mi throw mi overnight bag pon the backseat.

"Oh, mi need fi change. Mi cya check in ina mi uniform," I said, and him park at the side of the road. Mi go rounda back. "Don't peek," mi warn, but him still glance pon mi ina the rearview mirror. If mi neva fraid smaddy ketch we, mi wuda tease him. After mi redress, mi return to the front and spray on mi perfume.

Favi coughed, bringing down the window. "Swear, yaa try kill me."

"Naa try kill yu yet," I said, and he chuckled, causing a big smile to stretch across my entire face. Mi chat off him ears to the hotel ina Ochi, shutting up when we reach ina the room. Mi nuh frighten fi things, but a so hotel room always nice?!

The whitest sheets deh pon a king-sized bed, contrasting with the light-brown furniture. The glass doors were opened. Ocean breeze drifted inside, beckoning me to go to the balcony and gawk at the glistening sea below.

"You good?" Favi asked, and mi shut mi mouth.

Why mi so big and embarrassing?! Man must a wonder wa kinda country-come-to-town gyal him tek up.

"I'm going to shower." Mi grab some clothes and head toward the bathroom.

"I've seen you naked. You can change in here."

"No." Being naked for sex and stripping to shower were different levels of intimacy. Mi run go lock up ina the bathroom.

All ina the bathroom nice and fresh. No sah, look pon dem complimentary soap ya! Dem smell nice, eeh? Me a thief dem when Favi naa look.

Ratid, watch hot water! This nicer than when mi afi heat water wid the kettle fi bathe a morning time.

Mi tek a nice, long shower. Mi redress ina the bathroom and spray perfume everywhere, including mi ankles, before mi exit. The room darker cause the balcony door shut, and the curtains drawn. Favi lay shirtless on the bed, tapping on his phone.

"Weh mi a sleep?" mi ask, and him brows furrow as him look pon me.

"On the bed with me, Chayanne." Him hold out him hand toward me, and me lay beside him.

Mi trail him abdomen tattoo with mi finger. "What language is this?"

"Italian."

Mi brows crinkle. "Yu can speak it?"

"*Sì*."

"When yu learn it?"

"Spoke it all my life."

"Yu nuh sound Italian."

"I was raised here. *Mamma* is Jamaican. Her husband is Italian."

How me never know all these things? Mi need fi question him more. Mi lean off him, and him stop type fi mek four wid my eyes. "Do you have siblings?" mi ask, and him look back pon him phone, resuming typing. Mi will dash weh the phone ino! A cause mi cya afford fi buy it back.

"No."

"Tell me more about your family."

"There's nothing to know."

"You know all about mine. It only fair if yu tell me about yours."

"Do you always ask this many questions?" he asked, and I grinned. Him sigh, putting the phone aside before making me lay on him. "Antaro came to Jamaica years ago on vacation. He met *Mamma* at the hotel where she worked. They fell in love and had me."

"You've been to Italy?"

"I was born there. It's beautiful. I'll bring you one day," him seh, and mi smile.

We talked more about Italy, his company, and some aspects of our childhoods. Him nuh fond of talking about it, but mi nuh mek dat bother me cause him nuh love chat.

"It's nice that you're in touch with both of your cultures. My family nuh teach me much about India... I can't even speak Hindi."

"They should've taught you. Italian was my first language, then I started speaking English, Patois, Sicilian, and a bit of Spanish."

"Watch educated badman," I joked, but he didn't laugh. I frowned. "Why yu involved ina wrongs? You have a company, I don't understand—"

"You don't need to know about that part of my life."

"But—"

"Drop it."

The iciness startle mi. Mi pull miself outta him hold, grabbing my phone. Mi text Yolo, rolling my eyes when Favio change the TV from cable to local TV. Mi chuckle at sum Yolo seh boh her father, and Favio glare pon me.

"Who yaa text?" him ask coldly, and attitude pitch pon the tip of mi tongue.

Nuh everything good fi eat, good fi talk.

Afta him cya do mi nun!

"My man," I stated firmly, and him grab the phone.

"Nuh mek mi mash up this fuck—" Him pause when him see seh a waa girl. Him toss the phone toward me. "Yu so-called boy ina prison."

"Dayshawn?" I asked, and him glare. "Mi mean, who?"

"Nuh you report the boy? Mi ensure dem follow up pon yu tip."

"Maybe me shudn call. At least him did honest wid me," mi grumble, and Favio glare deepen. Gulping, mi move outta him reach, and him sigh.

"Come here," he said, and me shake mi head. "I won't hurt you, Chayanne. I promised you."

Oily tongue nuh must tell truth.

Him never lie to me before.

Mi go to him. Him motion fi mi lay down, then hover above me.

"What I do is complicated, I'd rather you not know about it," him explain, and mi search him eyes before mi gi him a chups. Favi mek up him face. "Wa kinda kiss dat?"

Giggling, mi give him a proper kiss this time — parting my lips so he could slip his tongue into my mouth and control me however he desired. He kissed me long and hard before breaking away. He left feather-light kisses down my neck, a trail of heat remaining in its wake.

My back arched off the bed as his tongue teased the sweet spot of my neck. I released a breathy moan as he sucked the skin, not moving until he left a mark there. He kissed up to my mouth, sucking my lower lip into his mouth and making it tingle.

"Sure yu want this?" he asked, and I nodded. "Words."

"Yes, Favi. I want you. Now. Please."

"Yu cya fuck nobody after me. Got it?"

"Yeah." Nobody deevn deh pon mi mind except him.

Smirking, his hand crept down my abdomen, slipping into my dampening panties. He trailed a finger around my clit, making me tremble.

"Favi," I moaned, parting my legs wider as he slipped his index inside me.

"Patience."

I whined, and he smirked before taking his finger out. He quickly removed our clothes. A chill ran down my body, and I covered my breasts.

"Stop hiding from me," he warned. His eyes were dark, but his voice was soft.

"O-okay." Shyly, I moved my hands away to reveal my hardened nipples.

He did a take of appreciation of my body, then kissed down my abdomen to my pussy, spreading my legs wider. My breath hitched as he kissed my clit, making a shiver run through me.

I gasped as he moved away suddenly. "Favio!" I exclaimed, and he chuckled, tugging me to the edge by my ankles.

"Yu love too much tongue. Come tek fuck." He leaned down, his lips brushing mine while he rubbed the tip against my clit. "I'm going to fuck you raw. I want to feel you for the first time. Is that okay?"

I nodded eagerly. "Yes, Favi... Just go slow, please."

He smirked against my lips, leaning up to press his erection against my opening. A hiss escaped me as my walls stretched to accommodate him.

"Relax around me," he coached. "And breathe in and out... Good girl."

"It hurts." Tears pricked my eyes. Now mi memba why mi run from Dayshawn. As Favi stopped and pulled away, I grabbed his forearm. "I want you."

"You have to try relaxing. I don't want to hurt you," he said, and I nodded.

He pressed against my opening again. I bit into my cheeks, snapping my eyes shut as the tip settled inside me. An uneven breath passed our lips.

"Open them. Look at me," Favi said, and my eyes did at will. Leaning in, he whispered against my lips. "You feel so fucking good around me, Chayanne."

I moaned, and he smirked against my lips while thrusting.

In and out.

So slowly, yet it felt so good.

Great.

"Feels good?" he asked, still working the head inside me, and I nodded. He leaned up, lips parted slightly as he looked between us, watching his dick go in and out of my pussy.

"Oh, God," I moaned as he gave me another inch. My walls tightened, welcoming him inside as I locked my legs around his waist.

"Want me to go faster?" he asked, his eyes mirroring mine as I nodded.

"Yes," I begged, and Favi delivered.

He picked up his pace. My moans were loud and unfiltered in his ear.

He felt great. I felt great. *This* felt great.

Sex fi so nice?

His breathing was heavy in my ear.

On my face.

I was hyperaware of everything between us.

How tight his grip was around my neck.

How he fondled my breasts.

How he pulled out and slammed inside, giving me most, but not all of him.

"Faster," I begged.

He slowed to throw my legs over his shoulder. He rested his hands on either side of me, driving more of his dick inside my pussy.

"Favi!" Tightness grew in my abdomen as I grabbed at the sheets, nearing a high I'd never been on before. I didn't know if I wanted to stay here or go higher.

Favi chose for me.

"Come for me, Chayanne," he urged, and my walls clenched as I came.

"God!" I screamed.

He glared at me and slapped my ass. "Favio."

The wetness paired with the slapping of skin filled my ears, driving me senseless. Dots winked behind my closed eyelids, still blinding my vision as I dropped flat with a huff and opened them.

"A go deaf mi one day," he teased, and I laughed. Gently, he moved my legs off him and pulled out. He turned me around.

I arched my back, putting my ass as far as possible into the air. I was drained, but excited. A regular mi practice arching mi back. I could hold it as him slip inside.

And sent me on another high.

Then another.

While him slap up mi batty and haul me back on him in the nicest way. I was stuffed and tired, but his stamina was incredible.

"Whose pussy is this?"

"Yours!" I screamed. "I'm yours."

"Mm, *fuck*." His grip on my waist tightened. His strokes turned into sloppy, long, hard pounds that made me bite into the sheets.

I lost my arch, and he descended with me, settling his hands on either side of my body. His thighs slapped against the back of mine as his orgasm drew closer and closer. His dick sent ripples of pleasure throughout my entire body, and I gripped the sheets, trying and failing to not fall into insanity.

"You can take it," Favi said from above me, his voice husky.

I mumbled an answer, my words muffled by a mouthful of sheets. I was only aware of Favi's hands moving from my sides, gliding up my arms and settling atop my hands. His fingers laced with mine, tightening into fists as he continued his hard pounds.

Groaning, he stilled as warmth flooded my insides. Favi didn't pull out until he finished emptying inside me.

"Wow," I said breathlessly, rolling onto my back as cum leaked out of my pussy. My chest heaved, between my thighs stung, and I felt so... empty. Mi cya move again even if mi want to.

Favi chuckled. "You good?"

I smiled. "I'm great."

Chapter Nineteen

FAVIO

The table was a three-seater. To my right, Antaro. To my left, Hudson Graham, a pot-bellied old white man whom Antaro and I agreed to do a sit-down with.

Unless he was visiting Italy, Antaro never left Kingston.

Ever.

For anything.

But occasionally, if it was something to create havoc, he'd be there sooner than I could make my decisions.

I didn't want to be here either. I'd rather be upstairs with Chayanne, fucking her or listening to her talk off that pretty little mouth.

Yet here we were.

"I can come to a settlement. A sum of forty-five million could make me reconsider my decision to buy YaleD," Graham said.

As much as mi waa look pon him like him tell mi bout *Mamma*, I kept calm. I took intimidation from no one. But forty-five million? That was audacious, even for me.

I reached for my drink on the table, taking a swig.

YaleD was the company that supplied workers to Welsh's vineyards. They were excellent at what they did. They were worth forty-five million, plus more.

Two of the first things Antaro taught me about business were:

One. Acquire as many links as possible.

Two. Never pay the competition to back off. Hit them back, harder.

I could easily get another company to supply workers, but YaleD was the best. Despite our longtime business relationship with YaleD, they were considering Graham's proposition. His new wife was the cousin of their CEO.

I would teach Graham why Welsh's was such a successful business for many years now.

I placed the glass on the table. "Are you sure this is the route you want to take?"

"Unless you have a higher offer, I don't see why not." Graham grinned at Antaro, who observed silently.

"You're prioritizing the wrong thing for a man whose stepson is missing," I said, and Graham's smile vanished.

"H-how do you know that?" His eyes widened as I relaxed into the chair, tapping a finger against the tabletop. "Mi seh, how yu know that?" Graham hissed as the tips of his ears turned red.

I glanced at Antaro. We smirked before looking at Graham.

"*There's* the person I heard so much about. I wondered when you'd show me the real you. The one who has an admirable, and I use that term loosely, brandy company," I taunted, and Graham opened his mouth. I cut him off by holding up a finger, wagging it slowly. "I'm not done speaking. Tell me, Graham, how would your wife feel when she finds out her son is missing because, allegedly, you owe the wrong people?"

"I don't owe anyone money—"

I paused bringing my drink to my lips. "You owe me forty-five million." I placed the glass atop the table. "Plus, twenty for my troubles. I should be elsewhere right now, but I'm wasting my time on you."

Graham glared at me before sending an equally fierce one at Antaro. "Tell yu boy doh fuck with me, Antaro."

"Yow." I knocked on the table with my knuckles twice, dragging his attention to me. "A me run dis now. Mi need mi money by next Saturday. No later than twelve p.m."

"B-but—"

"B-but I need my money by twelve p.m.," I said while Antaro smirked. "You should've thought this through before you came here. What? You thought I'd be fazed by forty-five million? A chump change that and nuh links nuh frighten mi. Come on, Graham. You know there are two things I don't play about. Help me, will you?" I held up the finger I wagged.

He skin reddened as he gulped. "Your money," he said, and I raised another finger. "And your—"

"Enough." Antaro glanced at the exit of the hotel's dining hall.

Smirking, I looked at the face of my watch. It was one p.m. What was she doing now?

"Get out of here, Graham, and bring your bruised pride with you," Antaro said.

I swallowed the last of my drink as Graham scurried away from the table. I stood, about to take my leave. I hated many things, and at the top of the list, was being around Antaro longer than I needed to.

"*Figlio*," Antaro said, and I paused shrugging on my jacket. He smirked, his eyes shining... from pride? No. It couldn't be. "You'll do well as Welsh's CEO."

And I was about to do better.

I hated people who tried to one-up me.

I didn't answer before I left the dining hall, calling Chayanne. She said she was by the pool, so I headed there.

Antaro should've left already, so I wasn't worried about him finding out about her. I couldn't handle what'd happen to me or her if he did.

I ignored everyone around me as I arrived at the pool area. I didn't have to search to find her. She stuck out like a white stain on the blackest of souls.

My soul.

Chayanne was consuming me whole.

Chapter Twenty

CHAYANNE

Mi roll over with a big stretch. The wul a mi joints crack up like old iron, and mi drop pon the bed with a smile. I snuggled into the comfortable bed, then sat up ina flash. A weh mi deh?!

The room was silent minus the swish of the AC, and the drawn curtains mek in here darker. The big TV at the front of the room made everything come back to me... Last night, Favi big hood cripple me and put me to bed. Is a miracle the wul a mi crochiz nuh tear out to how him handle me.

Speaking of, a weh him deh?

I reached for my phone on the bedside table and gasped. A rose bouquet was on the table. They were arranged nicely in a shiny, white ceramic vase. A napkin was beside it. I moved the napkin, revealing a pack of emergency contraceptives.

"Ketch romance!" Smiling, mi lean forward fi smell the roses. I tore my head away when the door opened, and in came Favi with food. Mi squeal, throwing the blanket over mi head.

"Fuck do yu?" him ask from above me. When him come so close?

Mi hold the sheet tighter so him cya tek it off. "Mi nuh wash mi face yet, and mi hair look like a bird's nest."

"Can't be worse than how I made it last night."

"Favi!" I exclaimed, and he laughed, making me smile. Did he actually laugh? Or me a imagine things cause him sex mi senses outta mi?

"I bought the two breakfast combos you wanted. Nuh know wa kinda fuckry this yaa eat ina the morning."

"Neva afi add the last part," I muttered before flying outta the bed and into the bathroom. Mi blush at my reflection. Watch hickey pon mi breasts and neck! Him a must vampire. After mi do mi business, mi return to the room and sit pon the bed. "Thanks for the roses."

He sat beside me. "You're welcome."

"Why though?"

"You always smell like them. I thought you'd like it."

Mi waa scream and cry! Why mi heart a beat so fast? This cya healthy! "Thank you," I said, my eyes shining as I looked at him.

"Yu scamma boy never buy yu things?"

Mi bubble burst, and mi roll mi eyes. "Gwan go bathe. Yav a meeting in two hours," I hissed, and he snickered.

The truth was mi never waa him see how mi shame. Mi used to bring mi own food whenever mi visit Dayshawn. The most the man eva give me a taxi fare and drinks when we go party. There was also that time him give me money fi buy lingerie, but mi buy a pack of composition book instead. Nuh know why mi stay wid him so long, but mi glad mi wise up and get the crosses outta mi life.

I was with a real man now.

I smiled, turning on the TV while mi eat. Favi settled himself between my legs, swiping on his phone while I ran my fingers over his low-cut hair. I preferred it when it was long, but him cut it fi the meeting.

His phone rang. Mi strain mi ears, but mi cudn hear wa the next person a seh.

"Sì, Mamma?" him answer. "Why mi wuda do dat?" he hissed, then laughed. "Stop provoke mi. Lata." He hung up.

"A so yu talk to your mother?"

"A mi g dat," he said, and I smiled sadly. His smile washed away, then him pat him lap. After me straddle him and lay pon him chest, him kiss atop mi head. "I didn't mean to—"

"It's fine. Nuh start pity me now."

Him sigh, kissing me again. Him use one hand stroke mi back while the other scroll pon him phone. Mi stop eat fi pay him mind, why him naa do the same?

"Pay mi attention," mi seh.

"I am, *fiore*."

Mi lean off him, my brows furrowing. "Wa dat mean?"

"Flower," he said with the hint of a smile.

Me? Cya hide this smile even if mi try! Him a try turn mi ina ground provision, but mi nuh mind at all! Call mi Farmer Chichi.

I couldn't help but leaning in and kissing him. Him kiss me back without hesitation, and I broke away to tease his ear and neck.

"Oye, nuh badda hickey me up," Favi said, and mi pull away fi glare pon him. "It's not because I don't want you to, so nuh start. I can't show up to a business meeting with hickeys all over me."

"Sometimes I forget how much older you are than me." I loved how responsible he was, cause my head come and go more while.

Him stare pon mi with an unreadable expression, then tap mi ass. "Up. I need to get ready."

Mi come offa him, and him go the bathroom. Mi eat while watching the TV.

The anchor said, "A body and head were found at sea. The eyes were gouged from the head, and the teeth were removed. It might take a while to identify the man because of the decomposition."

Favi walked into the room, buttoning around his wrists while looking at the TV. Favi was sexy with or without clothes, but him in a suit was in a category by itself. The black material perfectly hugged his tall frame; it looked tailored. A dis name look good enough to eat!

Favi disrupted my thoughts. "This doesn't bother you while you eat?" Favi ask, and mi shake mi head while gesturing him over. Mi kneel pon the bed fi fix him tie. "You're not normal."

Mi chuckle. "How?"

"Most people would be disgusted by the details."

"Mama always mek mi watch news, and a Steer Town mi come from."

Muttering a thanks after mi finished, him return to the bathroom. Him shut the door this time. Low talking drift through the door until him come out. Him grab a briefcase off the chair, stooping fi kiss mi forehead. "I'll see you later."

"Bye." Mi turn off the TV as the door close behind him. I called Chezzy, and she tek one look pon mi, then squeal. "Deaf mi, Chezzy."

She smiled. "Yu fuck him?!"

"Yes," I answered, and she squealed again. Mi did waa tell her mi get suck too, but as much as me love chat, me know mi limited. "A weh Aunty deh fi tell yu fi stop mek noise ina the place?"

"She leff mi wid her pickney dem and gone fi Daddy a the airport—"

"Yu never tell mi Uncle come back."

"Daddy is the top marine biologist in the Caribbean. Deevn him nuh know him schedule. Mi nuh waa talk bout my Daddy. Tell me about *your* Daddy."

"Fi a virgin, yu love sex too much," I said, and she grinned. "Girl, it was something else. We do two round last night — ina the bed, then shower."

"Watch rabbit! A true seh sex feel weird with condom?" she ask, and mi look weh. "*Chichi.* Nuh tell mi seh—"

"Him buy pill gimi," mi seh, and she purse her lips. "Anyway, mi nuh see the hype wid shower sex. Wul time him brace mi pon the wall, me fret seh wi wuda slide, drop and dead. Imagine Mama a hear seh mi did a tek hood before mi wash mi likkle pokie and gaa mi bed," mi seh, and Chezzy laugh.

"Mi happy fi yu— Jordan and Jordane, stop the ramping! Cho, lata we talk. Mi a go check pon mi bredda dem. Dem a play and sum bruk."

Mi eyes widen. "Pray seh ano figurine or fine China."

"Mi hope not cause a me a go get blame." Chezzy kiss her teeth, ending the call.

Mi go throw weh mi garbage and change mi clothes. While mi stand up a rub mi belly and think boh the next meal, the door knock.

It was room service. Mi go explore the hotel so dem can do dem job. Mi a walk bout the place when Yolo call.

"Yu wudn believe wa happen last night!" she seh, and mi chuckle.

"Wa dat?" mi ask.

"Remember when Gold Mine dee vex wid me? She unvex and invite me to her house, but me nuh go cause me naa mek nuh gyal set me up. Me go so boom and sweet talk one of the man dem in my inbox. After him send the money, me block him. Me carry Gold Mine go movies and we end up get the wul theater to weself. Me seh the b suck the life outta me pumpum, it deh ya shrivel up and need likkle CPR," she seh, and mi laugh.

"Wait deh! Mi think yu neva like dem things deh?"

"Me nuh like it, but the way Gold Mine handle me, me realize the other girl dem neva know fi use dem tongue. I need to stop being a giver and start receiving, cause a ten outta ten Gold Mine get fi dat."

"Mi happy fi yu," mi seh, and she smile.

"Anyway, me cya talk long. Me soon afi get ready fi court."

"You good?" mi ask, and her eyes droop before she smile.

"Of course! But let's not talk about that."

"Yol—" Mi pause when mi see Favi. Mi know tha head back deh anywhere!

He sat at a table with two men — waa fat, white one in a gray suit, and the other white man ina waa navy blue suit. Mi cya see Blue Suit face good cause him back turned to me.

"Number One?" Yolo seh.

"Sorry. Continue." Mi walk away because mi nuh waa Favi ketch mi a fass.

"A some a tha head deh me waa give yu. I provide my closest friends with moral support whenever dem dutty man ya naa treat dem right!"

"You mean oral?"

"Same difference." She laughed, then we said goodbyes cause her Mommy seh shi fi get ready.

I found the pool. People of all age, size, and race a chill out here, sipping on tropical cocktails and engaging in conversation. Is a pity me cya swim, or me wuda tek off tha dress ya and go splash round.

Mi sit pon one of the lounge chairs, basking in the blistering sun and cool breeze. Mi ask smaddy fi tek pictures of me, then thank dem wid a smile.

Minutes afta dem leff, smaddy step before me, blocking the sun. Putting a hand above my brows, mi squint at them.

"Yu lost?" mi ask. Me nuh know this short, black bwoy from nowhere.

He flashed a lopsided smile. "No. GPS lead me to you."

Cringing, mi continue scrolling through the pictures. "Not interested."

"Yu deevn get fi know me. How yu nuh interested?"

Yu shake man hand, but yu nuh shake him heart.

"I just know." First off, him a my age. Plus, mi have a man-weh-ano-mi-man-but-a-mi-man, who have a gun.

"I have money," he added, and mi liff mi head fi tell him which part fi put him money, but the words died off when me sense Favi.

Mi snap mi head in that direction. Wow, there he was! Him have one hand tucked in his pocket, and the other held his briefcase. The sun hit his skin at the right angles, making his sunkissed skin glow.

His eyes brightened as he strolled over. No one else was in his path except me, and I loved it. He stopped beside me. His mouth pulled into a straight line after seeing the bwoy. "Fuck yu still a do yaso? Move before mi kill yu."

My eyes gleamed as the boy hurry away. Maybe me get drop pon my head when mi younger, too.

Favi held out a hand toward me, and mi lay mine in his. Mi wrap mi hand around his arm until we reach the room. Mi sidung pon the edge of the bed, watching him undress. Him rest a pistol atop the dresser, then step toward the bathroom.

"Can I touch it?" I blurted, and him pause, glancing at me.

"Sure." He walked over with the gun. Him take out the clip and check the chamber before placing it beside me. Him go lock himself ina the bathroom with him phone and the clip.

My fingers wrapped around the cold metal, lifting it. It wasn't as heavy as the first time. Mi walk round the room and point at everything, pressing the trigger over and over. "*Pew! Pew! Pew!*" I whispered, thrill rushing through my veins.

Shuffling come from the bathroom. Mi run go put the gun pon the dresser, then sit on the chair.

Favi peeked his head out. "Come shower with me."

I nodded, and he disappeared into the bathroom. Sas Crise! Suppose him waa sex mi again? Mek mi seh waa quick prayer before mi go in deh.

I whispered the prayer, then stripped and joined him in the shower. The overhead stream poured down on us. The droplets bouncing off his dick were hard to look away from, so I slowly dragged my eyes to his.

He smirked.

"You have a big ego, you know that?" Mi grab the rag and soap it up.

While we showered, mi ask about him meeting. Him give one-word answers.

Jesam! It hard fi seductively wash mi front compared to how mi wuda skin out without a care ina the world.

"Do you usually shower like that?" he asked.

"How?" mi ask as embarrassment box mi up. Mi know mi shudn come in ya! Last night, we neva bathe together after the shower sex cause him did afi tek an important call.

"Stosh."

"Mi nuh bathe stosh!" mi exclaim, and Favi buss out the loudest, most ghetto laugh mi eva hear ina mi life!

Him eyes crinkle at the sides. Him mouth widen as him throw him head back. Despite how him a laugh mi to shame, I smiled, then laughed. We laugh like idiots fi minutes. Whenever we glance pon each other, we start laugh all over again.

"You do. Probably can do it better than you," him seh, laughter still in his tone.

"Yu deevn have a vagina."

"I know everything about pussy. Let me shower you." He took the rag from me, kneeling. He threw one of my legs over his shoulder, handling me with utmost care while washing my most private area.

I couldn't take my eyes off him. Even as he stood, lathed the rest of my body, then himself, and turned on the overhead shower to wash us clean.

He helped me out of the shower, wrapping me in the towel. "Go into the room. I need to make a call."

Cho, blousecup! A call center him a run? Annoyed, mi nod and go ina the room. Mi put on clothes, then lay pon the bed. My feet pressed against the headboard while me snap selfie pon mi phone.

Mi nuh ready fi return to Steer Town. Mi waa stay here forever with Favi. I had no nagging granny. No stress from school. No community violence.

Only me, these four walls, and the sexy man in the next room, who knew my body like we'd known each other all our lives.

Mi cudn ask fi a better weekend. Fat Ma nuh stop jump since last night. All the teasing build mi up to the nicest sex a mi life!

I wanted him again... Mi nuh know when we a go get a next chance fi do it. Soon as we leff yaso, a back to *the same old doodoo in a different toilet,* as Trav would say.

Favi enter a the room minutes later. A towel wrapped round him waist, water trailing down his defined, tatted abdomen. Him use another towel fi dry him hair. "Lock yu mouth before mi put sum in deh."

"I want you to put sum in deh," I said, serious as a judge.

Him freeze. "It's soft."

Smiling at how shyly him seh it, mi roll over onto my stomach. "I don't care. Let me suck it."

He stared at me for a moment. "Ah. Give me a second." Him enter the bathroom, returning a minute later with a small tent under the towel.

Wow. Him nuh waa feel it a grow ina mi mouth?

"Turn upside down," him seh.

Wetting my lips, I scooted to the edge of the bed. My head hung off the side, and he came closer. He dropped the towel, and his semi bounce before mi face.

"Open," Favi said, and I kissed his tip before parting my lips. He inched inside my mouth, leaning over to fit more of it into my mouth.

He stilled, and I swallowed, urging him to continue. My gag reflex was nonexistent. I could swallow his entire body if he wanted me to.

Favi slowly rocked back and forth. His dick grew to its full length as he drove it further down my throat each time. His moans were low while loud noises escaped my mouth. My mouth stretched wide to the point it stung, but I bore it because I wanted to make him feel good.

He slammed into my mouth like it was my pussy. The rough pounds made it hard to breathe. I moaned around his dick, loving the way he used my little mouth and squeezed my throat with the right amount of pressure.

Spit dribbled down the sides of my mouth and tears poured from my eyes as his balls smacked against my face. My pussy was dripping wet, and I rubbed myself through the panties.

"Fuck," he hissed lowly, his thrusts animalistic. His body jerked before he came with a long groan.

The large load rushed down my throat in one instant, almost making me choke. I swallowed as much as I could until he pulled out. Sitting up, I coughed.

"You good?" he asked, and mi nod while rubbing my neck.

"Yes. Yu just get too rough before yu come."

"Sorry. That's how I like head." Him wrap the towel around his waist.

"It's fine." Mi neva hear him complain when mi a try drown him.

"You have something right here." Favi point at the corner of his mouth, smirking as mi lick away the tasteless drop of cum. Him step closer to the bed, hooking a finger beneath my chin, and making me look at him. He leaned in, giving me a kiss that made me smile uncontrollably.

One hand resting on the wheel and the other swiping on his phone, Favi asked, "Yu need anything in the town?"

"Yes. Mi hairdresser must miss mi. Mi hair overdue fi a trim." Mi stare at my reflection in the visor's mirror.

"Why?" Him stop type fi look pon me.

"I prefer it here." Mi point at mi shoulder.

He placed his phone on his thigh, reaching over fi release mi hair from the grab clip. It cascade down to mi bra strap, and the corner of his mouth quirked upward. "You look prettier with it like this. Grow it out."

"I would, but when it's long, it's expensive—"

"Let me know when you need it trimmed, and I got you. For anything. Got it?" Him drive off after mi nod while smiling.

Mi reach ina mi bag fi mi phone so mi can snap few picture, and mi groan. "Favi, we can turn back? Mi leff mi phone."

"Too fucking careless." Him grip tighten around the wheel while my shoulders slumped.

"Sorry..." Mi play with my fingers atop my lap while him do waa illegal U-turn, speeding toward the hotel. Mi go speak to smaddy, then return to the car. "Mi get it back," I said, but him deevn fawt pon me. Frowning, mi turn weh from him for the rest of the journey.

Wi nuh talk to each other, but silence neva nyam mi cause music a blast. Why him this angry? Afta ano fi him phone.

We past Trav mother pon the road side. She dressed ina waa bra and shorts while she look sale fi her front. She even realize him missing?

Mi sigh as him park before mi house. "Thanks. Be safe..."

"Nobody cya run up pon me. Gwan in go rest yu throat," him seh, and gasp while him smirk.

"Wow. A your fault mi voice hoarse!" mi hiss, sounding like mi smoke nine pack of cigarette every day fi the past seventeen years.

Smirking, him tap him lips. Mi lean over fi kiss him.

"Bye, Favi," mi seh while pulling back.

"Bye, *fiore*."

I loved hearing him call me by my government, but this nickname did something to me. Blushing, mi exit the car and walk to mi gate.

Mi neighbor ina him yard, watering him plants while watching me. Mi tell him evening, but him nuh ansa. Shaking my head, mi enter the house. Favi car speed off while mi smile at Mama, who deh by the altar. Entering mi room, waa stack of books greet me, and mi sigh.

The fairytale was over.

Back to reality — exams. Passing with flying colors a mi only goal. I needed to make Mommy, Mama, Aunty Kenzie, and myself proud.

Chapter Twenty-One

CHAYANNE

Rubbing the sleep outta mi eyes, mi get up from round the desk. Mi wait until all the other girls leave the classroom before me enter and place mi test pon Mr. Black desk.

"I hope you did better than last time," Mr. Black said sternly as him tek the paper from me and hand me the test mi do last time.

Mi heart stop beat when me see the score. "Mi nuh do bad, sir!"

"An eighty-nine percent is good enough? One extra percent would've given you an A. You need to stop being okay with good enough and aim for the best."

Mi sigh, looking away. Why him a gwan like a Cash Pot number mi get?

"Are you okay, Miss Bailey?" him ask.

No way me a go tell mi teacher seh since mi come home from hotel days ago, mi cya sleep a nighttime. Mi miss the man arms a pull mi closer to him during the night. Mi body a gwan like me nuh sleep by miself fi years without so much as a goodnight kiss.

"Yes, sir." Mi force a smile before me leave. Mi go find Yolo cock up ina waa classroom a finger waa girl under the table. Shaking mi head, mi exit the classroom, waiting fi dem come out.

When they did, the girl go in the opposite direction, while me and Yolo go the bathroom.

"Yu finger dem soon drop off," mi seh while she wash her hands, and she scowl.

"A must ina Big Lip it a go drop off ina. Nuh know how fi her pussy so deep. Must gold me dee a dig fa."

"Wa happen to Gold Mine?" mi ask as we walk toward the gate, and she smile.

"Added to my list of favorite eaters. Anyway, yu still miss the man?" she ask, and mi sigh.

"Yes."

"Me dee a expect yu fi lie fi spare me feelings cause a long-time me waa yu. Me need fi up me game?" She wiggled her brows, and I laughed. "On a real though, sure yu good? Yu look like yaa mad out. Deevn when Dayshawn dee a treat unu relationship like Easter holiday, yu neva look so."

"Neva afi seh it so... Mi good," I lied, and she sighed.

We reach the gate. Chezzy deh nearby with her friend, chatting and laughing. A small group of girls deh next to them, waiting for taxis.

"Later, Number One. Memba fi send me the Maths homework," Yolo seh, and mi nod. Favi's method been real helpful fi me and mi friend dem.

I missed him... Him supposed to come from Kingston this evening or tonight. Me mek sure pluck the bird cause one way or the other, me a fling it up!

Mi walk toward Chezzy, and we look a taxi, then go her house. Mi smile when me see Uncle, Aunty, and the twins in the living room watching TV. "Evening," I greeted everyone.

"Evening, Chichi," Uncle replied.

"Evening. Chezandra, go fi waa bottle of water fimi, please," Aunty seh.

"Mi deevn reach in good," Chezzy grumble.

"Stop back talking to your mother," Uncle scolded.

"Mi tell yu she a get rude, Dale. She gwan like a the world me ask fa anytime mi tell her fi do sum," Aunty said, and mi purse me lips as mi follow Chezzy into the kitchen.

I held her arm before she could leave with the water. "Nuh pay them nuh mind. A so some parents stay."

Chezzy dragged her eyes from the floor, settling on mine while her brows pulled together. She stare at me for a moment, then forced a smile. "Share the rundown fi Mama, and mek we leave."

I nodded and found the tupperware that was exclusively Mama's. Mi share the food before returning to the living room. "Uncle, when yaa leave?"

"I'm going to Grenada tomorrow. Not sure when I'll be back, but— Oh, I forgot to give you the keyring I brought back this time." Uncle started getting up, but Aunty placed a hand on his arm.

"Rest yuself. Yu have a long day tomorrow. Mek Chezandra go for it. It's the red one on the dresser. It's beside your green one," Aunty said, and Chezzy's jaw ticked before she went upstairs, returning quickly.

"Thanks, Uncle!" I smiled at the keychain from Saint Kitts and Nevis. It was shaped like the largest island, and had the flag printed on it.

Uncle nodded. "You can knit it like you did with the others."

"She nuh knit anymore, Daddy," Chezzy said, and I nodded.

"Alright. Hurry and gwan off the road," Aunty said, and Chezzy and I left.

Chezzy held my arm when we were at HalfWay. "H-how's your brother?"

"Favi find him and a work pon getting him free. I miss him," mi confess, and Chezzy hug me.

"Me, too," she said, and my brows pulled together. "I-I mean, I understand. Him a go good, Chichi."

I relaxed into her hug. "I hope so. Later." Mi break the hug, walking away. When me reach the Square, mi see Mark and Miss Olive. This a the first me see her since Asia candlelight, and she lose nuff weight. Mi walk toward them. "Evening. How are you, Miss Olive?"

Smiling weakly, her puffy eyes crinkle at the sides. "A tek it day by day."

"Dat is it, Miss Olive. Life sheg up, but we move," Mark seh, and mi glare. Him nuh see cause him a brush him Clarks.

"That's insensitive," mi hiss.

"It's fine, Chichi. The coroner dem a release mi pickini body. Me start the planning already cause me waa put her to rest. The nine-night a tomorrow and the funeral a next Saturday," she seh.

"Yu need help with the funeral planning?" Mi nuh mind skipping a night of studying to help with Asia homecoming. Trav would've wanted this.

"No, dear. We family from Hanover a come help mi."

"Alright. Take care, Miss Olive." Mi slap Mark, running away before him slap mi wid the brush. Mi tek mi time walk home, then go bathe. After mi done, mi sidung pon the veranda wid Mama, eating rundown.

Mama skin up her face as Paul step past we house. "Cya expect nun from a pig but a grunt."

"Stop it," I said, despite chuckling. Me and Mama talk until nightfall. Mi lay in bed fi hours, but sleep wudn come. So, me do sum stupid... I told Favi to come over.

I knew it was selfish to call him after his long week of dealing with business legalities, but I couldn't sleep without him. Mi hope Mama still a sleep. When him text seh him reach, mi go pon the veranda.

Favi looked like a thief in the night in his full black outfit. Him cologne fill my senses as him hug me, kissing atop my head. "You good?" him ask, and mi shake mi head while pulling away.

"I can't sleep," mi seh, and him step toward the door. Mi grab him. "Yafi go through mi window," mi seh, and him nearly bruk him neck fi look pon mi.

"Mi ano thief, Chayanne," him seh coldly, and mi put a finger to mi mouth, shushing him.

"Keep down your voice." Mi sigh as him jaw clench. "Fine... But tek time and walk. Foot dem big like."

He glared when I pushed him out the house cause him nuh walk inside backward. Him enter the correct way the second time. When we reach my room, him shut the door behind him. Him tek off him hoodie, resting it pon the back of my chair. Mi already have three a him hoodie dem, but mi a go tek dat.

"Do you want me to spend the night?" He placed his pistol on my dresser.

"Can you?" Mi smile as him nod while stripping down to his boxers and socks. After him join me in bed, mi smile widen.

Craven choke puppy.

Favi throw waa arm over my waist. "Why can't you sleep?"

"Wul heap on my mind."

"Like?" him ask, and mi face him.

"Asia— Oh, yu buy the red brief fi Trav?" mi ask, and him glare.

"No. Why the fuck would—"

"So Asia duppy nuh badda him. Cho, never mind. Mi will see if mi can buy some round a market back tomorrow, then mi will give it to you," mi seh, and him sigh heavily. "Anyway, the next things on my mind are exams and you…"

The moonlight streaming through the window highlighted his brows as they creased. "Me?"

"Yes. Yu secretive bad. Me worry about you a lot, and mi scared fi miself. Mi nuh waa nun happen to me cause a wa yu involved ina."

"Nothing will happen to you," he stated firmly.

"Yu cya promise that," mi seh, and him turn mi round.

"I can. Sleep."

"It's not that easy."

"Just close your eyes."

"Tek time talk."

"You always have man over here?" him ask, a trace of anger in his tone.

Mi roll mi eyes before closing them. "No. Only you."

"Good." Him hold me tighter.

A moment later, mi eyes open. "Really, Favi?" I hissed while him hood press against my ass.

"Stop wiggling your ass."

"Yu always horny, so nuh blame it pon me."

"I'm not—" He paused when I scoffed. "*Fiore?*"

I smiled. "Mm?"

"My dick hurts."

"Not under my granny roof," I said, and he sighed. Seet clear him waa send me to the deepest pits a hell. "Back yu fist."

"Mi nuh back fist."

"Sucks to be you," I teased, and him sigh, moving him arm from round me. Mi face him. "Yu fi help mi sleep."

"Cya help yu sleep wid dis." He motioned to the tent in his boxers.

How him get hard this quick? Him lucky mi waa him help mi sleep.

"Nuh you seh we naa fuck?" Him brow raise as mi sit up, sticking my hands inside his boxers.

"Changed my mind." Adjusting my body, I spat on my hand and on his dick. I sucked the tip and stroked him to his full length, then I straddled him. My pussy was ready for him because sucking dick made me wet.

"Wait." Him halt mi hand as mi slip mi panties aside. "You're really loud."

"So?"

"Yu waa wake yu granny? Because I like hearing you scream my name. I don't care who hears." He smirked.

Reality crashed into me, and mi crawl offa him.

Him chuckle. "Feelings?"

"No," I lied.

Humming, he scanned my room, then got out of the bed. He returned with my school tie and a belt.

"Wa yado?" Mi eyes widen. Me look like goat?!

"Rather wake your granny?" he asked, and I shook my head. He smirked, stripped, then straddled me. He gagged me with my tie, then strapped my wrists to the headboard with the belt. "Tight?"

Testing the restraints, I shook my head while my heart raced. This had never happened to me before. Scary as it was, it excited me more than words could explain. The only proof was the wetness between my thighs.

Favi kissed my forehead before giving all his attention to my breasts. His tongue swirled around my nipple, pulling it with his teeth while his other hand kneaded my left breast. My muffled moans poured into the gag as I leaned into his touch. He trailed kisses to my left nipple, then down my stomach.

His breath fanned my clit, and I tensed. His head snapped up, his brows pulling together. "You good?" he asked, removing the gag.

"I... I don't want you to do that." I looked away.

He gripped my chin, making me look at him. "The shyness," he scolded, and I gulped. "Why?"

"I don't like it..." I said, and his brows raised, making me backtrack. "Not like that. I-I mean I like it. You're great, but..."

His brows knitted more. "But?"

"I always cry and shake every time you do it, and mi feel weak after." I realized at the hotel.

"You're afraid of how good I make you feel?" he asked, and I nodded. He leaned in to kiss me, long and hard, before pulling away. "You don't have to be scared, *fiore*. Sex is supposed to feel good. I'm supposed to make you feel good."

"Okay." I smiled while my worries slipped away.

"Do you want it?" he asked, and I nodded.

He stuffed the gag into my mouth before moving between my thighs and parting my folds. He ran a finger through the wetness, inching two fingers inside. "Me can barely see yu clit. It likkle like—" He smirked when I glared. He chuckled, his breath fanning my slit. "Nuh drown mi dung ya."

My laughter became a moan as his tongue circled my hardened clit, making my back arch off the bed. Two fingers thrust inside my pussy while his other hand caressed my breast. His tongue worked wonders while my thighs tightened around his head.

I was feverish and being sent into another dimension as a fire grew inside me, but I couldn't tear my gaze away from him. He watched my every reaction while I did the same to him.

"Mm," I moaned into the gag, writhing as his tongue replaced his fingers.

He rubbed my clit hard with his thumb while licking up my insides. My hands curled into a fist, my nails stinging my palm as Favi kissed and nipped my inner thighs.

"Gah!" I screamed, my voice muffled as my orgasm took me by surprise.

He latched onto my clit, sucking it into his mouth and sending me over the edge. My hips bucked as I tugged at the restraints, riding out my orgasm on his face. Tears poured from my eyes and rolled down the sides of my face, but I couldn't look away from Favi.

He held me captive.

By these restraints.

His fingers.

Tongue.

Eyes.

Everything that made him.

He smirked against my clit as I dropped flat on the bed, panting. He stopped fondling my breasts and lapped up the aftermath, placing a kiss against my quivering clit before pulling away. Kneeling, he removed the gag from my mouth. "Did that feel good?"

Inhaling a big breath, I nodded. It was better than good. That was intense.

Favi smirked as he untied my wrists. He leaned in, kissing my lips. Our spit mixed, and I tasted myself on his tongue. He broke the kiss, climbing off the bed to slip on his boxers.

My brows furrowed. "Aren't you going to—"

"No. Mi good," him seh, and mi glance at the tent in his boxers.

"Favi—"

"It good. Tonight's your night."

Ugh, this man! Him a go mek mi yam out ina mi young age!

He threw my shirt over my head before he took me up bridal style, heading toward the door.

"Wait. Suppose Mama see yu?"

"Me will tell her me a duppy." Him approach the bathroom while mi lay mi head pon him chest, listening to his heart and trying fi breathe like him. Chuckling, him set me to my feet. "Mind yu kill yuself."

"With what?" mi ask innocently, and him smirk before him clean me up, then wash him face. After him done, mi step toward the door. Mi freeze when mi hear peeing. Despite facing away from him, mi cover mi eyes. "Neva afi do that while me in here."

"Nothing you haven't seen before." He flushed the toilet, and mi open mi eyes. Him try touch mi, and mi jump back.

"Gweh wid yu nasty self!"

"Why do you scorn me?" Him pout while washing him dutty hand dem.

"Why yu waa touch me wid yu pissy hand?"

"You swallow my cum, but you're afraid of my piss?"

My mouth dropped. What a bright bwoy!

"Grandbaby!" came a disembodied yell, and mi heart nearly collapse.

"Stay here so," I hissed at Favi, and him kiss him teeth as me go Mama room. "Yu alright?"

"Yes, grandbaby. Mi did a hear waa noise and think a Paul cat reach ina the house," Mama said, and mi gulp.

"No, Mama. A probably the wind. Gwan back go sleep." Mi turn off her light and close the door. Mi return to the bathroom.

Favi raised his brow while throwing and catching a tampon. "Yu bad pon the lying, though."

"Shut up." Mi snatch the tampon from him, putting it on the shelf.

Him throw mi over him shoulder before leaving the bathroom.

Him ass firm, eeh? Mi slap it, and him jump.

"Fuck yu just do? Me a go scream and wake yu granny."

"Sorry." Giggling, I rubbed where me slap.

Favi grumbled in Italian before him fling mi pon the bed like cement bag. Him lay beside me. Mi grab mi phone and scroll through social media.

"Aww," I cooed, showing Favi a video of a poodle jumping through hoops at a dog show. "It cute, eeh?"

"Hardly," he muttered, and mi roll mi eyes.

"Yu too bad breed."

"I'm not. Do you want one?"

"One of what?"

"A poodle," Favi seh, and mi squeal, making him glare.

"Yes!" mi whisper as loud as mi can, and him nod.

Taking the phone from mi, him rest it beside the gun. Him pull me into a tight hug. "Go to sleep, *fiore*."

Chapter Twenty-Two

CHAYANNE

"Mi promise me a go alright, Chezzy," I said for the umpteenth time. Mi nuh know why she so eager fi come Steer Town.

"Alright, but nuh fraid fi call me if you need extra support. Lata, mi a go study." She hung up.

Mi toss the phone pon the bed, then slip on the pretty dress mi get ina barrel earlier this year. Staring at my reflection, a high ponytail and saddened eyes looked at me. It mek mi miss Trav more.

He should be here.

We deh at each other side through everything. Mi wuda trade the world fi deh wid him right now.

Sighing, mi look round mi room fi ensure me naa leff nun. Mi spot the bedsheet, weh mi ball up and fling ina the corner this morning. Favi woke me early, sex me, then leff cause him have an early online meeting. Mi dodge Chezzy as much as possible today cause me nuh know how me wuda explain me limp.

Mi enter the living room. "Me a leave now, Mama."

Mama paused dipping waa crackaz into the cup of lime leaf tea. "Send mi best wishes to Olive. Wish mi cuda mek it, but mi cya manage."

Nodding, mi walk toward the door, then mek a U-Turn. Almost leff mi key! After mi find it, mi leff out.

Minutes later, mi reach Miss Olive. The dead yard lively bad. Bands music a fill the air. People a mingle with either a beer or soup cup ina dem hand. Some bad breed pickney a run up and down like dem nuh see weh dem deh.

Me push through the crowd of people until mi find Miss Olive. "Night. Yu need help with anything?"

She took a big bag of ice out of the deep freeze, dropping it by my feet. "Night, Chichi. Can put this in the igloo by the step?"

Mi nod, doing as she seh. Mi use mi hand fi even out the ice pon the cold drinks dem, looking up when mi hear mi name.

"Chichi!" dem yell again, and mi spot Mark. Him smile and wave mi over, and mi hold up a finger.

Mi finish wa mado, then go lean pon the wall beside him. "Hey, Mark."

"Thing good?" him ask, and mi shrug.

"Naa brush yu shoes today?" I joked, trying to lighten the solemn mood.

"Time and place." Him glare pon the mingling crowd. "Doubt Asia know half a dem people ya."

"She didn't." Mi pour some of my juice pon the ground before taking a sip.

Mark did the same with his beer. "Surprised Trav deevn show him face. Did always know him nuh rate her, but it too late fimi show her any different."

I pursed my lips. Nobody could ever pay me enough fi bad mouth Trav. Leaning off the wall, mi hug Mark. Him sigh as him hug mi back.

"Mi nuh waa lie seh it gets easier. Me nuh over Mommy death, but mi live every day to the fullest for her. Sometimes, it mek mi feel better."

"Me a go tek yu word fi it, Chichi," him seh, and mi smile. Him smile back, but it fade as the crunch of gravel capture him attention.

Mi look over mi shoulder, my eyes widening at Favi. Mi tear weh from Mark like his skin burned, and him raise a brow.

"Who you?" Mark asked, shielding me with him body. Favi was a mountain before Mark, but Mark neva care. Him glare pon Favi, whose fist tightened.

"Mi know him, Mark." Mi side-step him and stand beside Favi. Hoping him nuh misinterpret anything between me and Mark, mi grab Favi arm and pull him toward a less populated area. "I wasn't expecting you—" I paused as his menacing glare settled on me. "A wa?"

131

"Who the fuck dat?" he asked, venom lacing every syllable.

"My friend," I answered.

"Yu hug alla yu friend dem like that?"

"Wait... Yu jealous?" I asked, and his jaw ticked. Mi nibble mi lower lip so mi nuh laugh afta him.

His jealousy was cute! Hot, even.

"Yu a go find it funny when mi kill him?" he asked coolly, and my smile vanished. "Don't fuck with me, Chayanne."

"Yu nuh own me," I hissed, ready to walk away.

Favi grab mi arm, and mi meet him ferocious glare. Mi try pull free, but him bring me to the back a the house. Our bodies blended into the darkness.

Him push me against the wall, hand snaking around my neck. "I don't what?"

"Mi seh yu nuh own me! And leggo offa mi!" I hissed, trying my best to ignore his cologne and hand around my neck. They were a dangerous combo.

Favi chuckled. In a swift action, he threw one of my legs over the crease of his elbow, bracing me pon the wall. A gasp ripped from my throat as him move him hand from around my neck and cupped my pussy.

Betrayed.

My pussy soaked the seat of my panties, making me snap my eyes shut tightly. My breathing was heavy as he rubbed me through the material.

"I don't own you?" he mocked, slipping the panties aside and thrusting a finger into my pussy. "Then why are you so wet?"

My lips parted, but no words escaped.

Only a moan.

He pressed his mouth against mine, silencing my moans and leaving the distant sounds of people to fill the void between us. Somewhere in the mess of him roughly kissing me to the point I couldn't breathe, he freed his dick and thrust into me without warning.

I gasped into the kiss, my walls stinging as he bit my lip before sliding his tongue inside my mouth. Our tongues tangled in fervor as he hooked my other leg over his elbow, slamming me down on his dick.

I broke the kiss, burying my face in the crease of his neck as he took me.

Hard.

Faster than he'd ever done before.

My pussy creamed on his dick. His rough breathing in my ears drew my orgasm closer by the second.

"Can he fuck you like this?" Favi asked, and my walls tightened.

His dick touched me at a spot it'd never been before. It burned, but the pleasure was so good. I was soaking wet, biting hard into his neck to stifle my screams. It was the only thing holding me to my sanity. Barely.

"Yu fucking belong to me, Chayanne. Which other man can fuck yu like this? Which other man can mek yu feel like this?" he asked, taunting me.

I freed his neck from my mouth, sure to leave a spot. I threw my head back against the wall, my back rubbing against it as he thrust into me while pulling me down. He wasn't giving me all his dick, but it felt like it.

I muttered gibberish to the air, watching his eyes shine with a devious glint as he lost more control. He released one of my legs, and I had to stand on my toes as he continued his relentless assault on my pussy.

"Who owns you?" Favi asked.

"You," I panted, and his head dipped down, his lips capturing mine in a fervent kiss.

His hand snaked around my neck. His thumb restricted my breathing, amplifying everything I was feeling.

My walls tightened, and I exploded as my screams died off in his mouth. His thrusts slowed, becoming sloppy as he neared his orgasm. He broke the kiss, and my nails sank into his arm as I looked at him and clenched my walls at will.

This pussy was his.

No one else's.

"Fuck." Favi groaned, slightly tossing his head back and closing his eyes while emptying inside me.

Neither of us moved nor spoke for the next minute. Only our heavy breathing penetrated the air.

Finally, Favi slowly pulled out of me, and I winced. My legs shook and mi grab the wall, glaring at him. Him put away him hood, smugness in his eyes.

He leaned down to my height, bringing his face close to mine. His low voice sent a chill down my spine when he spoke. "Run back to yu youth. Tell him who yu think bout when him bring chat to yu."

"It's nothing like that, Favi," mi seh lowly, and him scoff, walking away. I gasped. Favi a go leff mi wid cum a trail dung mi leg like snail? "Favio!" I yelled, and him stop walk, turning to face me with his hands in his pockets. "Come carry mi home."

"Mek him drop yu home."

Pity him nuh know Mark a bustekker like me.

"Favio, stop this." My legs wobbled, and I pressed both hands against the wall. "Please. I can't—" My legs gave out, and Favio rush toward me, catching me before I fell.

He pulled his brows together as I dragged my gaze to meet his. Jaw clenching, he swooped me into his arms and carried me bridal style through the dead yard. Mi never know if anybody a look pon we. All my focus was on him.

This deranged man whom I couldn't help but fall for more each day.

He placed me in the front seat of his car and secured my seat belt. After he entered, we drove away in silence.

I glared at the window. "Why yu come ina mi, Favio? Suppose yu breed mi?"

"I'll get you a pill tomorrow."

"If yu feed mi pon pill, it a go lose its effect," mi seh matter-of-factly. Chezzy drill that ina mi head after mi come from the hotel.

"I have money." Shrugging, him park before mi house.

Mi exit before him cuda open the door fimi. Limping toward the house, mi roll mi eyes when the car door slam behind me. Him enter the house after me, and mi thank God seh Mama a sleep. Favio sidung pon the edge of my bed, fuming while watching me undress. Mi vex, too! Look how the man nearly mash up mi crochiz! Mi nuh know why him ina Mama house. Mi hope Mommy box him ina him face!

"Yu nago bathe?" him ask as mi lay pon the bed.

"No." Mi look away as him strip down to him boxers.

"Nasty. Come mi bathe yu." Him reach fimi, and mi scoot away.

"*No*. Suppose Mama wake or yu try mash me up again?" Between my thighs hurt more than the first time. Mi nav the energy fi stand up fi bathe.

"Sorry..."

"Yu nuh sorry!" I hissed through clenched teeth.

Him nuh ansa as him lift me, carrying me to the bathroom. Him tek off mi clothes, then join me ina the shower. "Nuh piss pon mi hand."

"I should," mi seh, and Favio scoff.

"Give me yu foot."

"Naa tell mi nufi kick yu ina yu face?"

"Try it," he dared, and mi purse mi lips before resting my hand on the wall and giving him my foot. Him finish bathe me, then himself.

We exit the shower, and him swaddle me ina the towel like likkle baby. Mi grudgingly hand him a new towel, then we go mi room. Favio lotion me before putting me in a shirt. We lay in bed, and him wrap an arm around me.

Mi mek miself smaller in his hold, my anger dissipating. Me, Chayanne Arya Bailey? Naa run the man weh help mi sleep a nighttime. Mi doze off until him hand creep between my thighs. My eyes snapped open. "Favi, no."

"I'm not going to fuck you. I want to touch you."

"Okay," I said, and him start touch me everywhere — my breasts, stomach, pussy, and thighs. Him never do this before, so mi confused. "Are you okay?"

"*Sì.* Sleep."

Mi turn around, throwing a leg and an arm ova him. "Goodnight."

Favi kissed my forehead. "*Buonanotte.*"

Chapter Twenty-Three

FAVIO

She laughed — the one where she threw her head back while tears gathered in her eyes. I couldn't see her, but I imagined how gorgeous she looked with her face bright and her eyes gleaming like a shiny fucking star. Chayanne had a pretty face and a stubborn mouth that only a dick could silence.

I shouldn't have gotten upset over a wasteman a hands her up. I knew she only laughed like this for me. I knew that pretty pussy only got wet for me.

But I couldn't help it.

The thought of another man in her life made me see green.

Red.

Black.

I thought I'd grown past that.

I cleared my throat. It wasn't time to think about Chayanne like this when she was parishes away. Ano time fi think boh tha crosses woman deh, either. "It's not funny," I stated.

Chayanne laughed. "Stop lie, it funny! Wa happen afta yu mother come a the party fi yu ina her nightie and settaz?"

"She dragged me out by my ear," I said, omitting that I had puke on my shirt. It was an embarrassing first-year incident in high school.

"Murda!" Chayanne's loud laugh morphed into a yawn. This girl was something else.

"Tired?" I asked as she stifled another yawn.

"Yeah. Goodnight, Favi," she said, and I smiled.

I wasn't fond of people giving me endearing nicknames, but I grinned like a lunatic whenever she called me 'Favi'. Maybe it was because of how sweet her voice was, or because my heart raced whenever she said it. It was hard to tell because they were one and the same.

"Goodnight, *fiore*." I smirked because I knew she was blushing.

She'd grown to love that name. It suited her face and personality — pretty to look at, dangerous if mishandled.

I hung up and stood from the patio chair, walking toward the door while my phone vibrated. I contemplated disregarding it, then decided against that.

It might be Chayanne. She nuh wrong fi cuss whenever I took too long to answer. I chuckled upon realizing it was her.

CHAYANNE: Why yu hang up before mi ask mi question?

What did you want to ask?

Yu nuh waa talk to mi?

My jaw ticked, and I called her. "Nuh start wid yu fuckry."

"I was going to ask when yaa come back..." she whispered.

Fuck! I hated when she did that thing. It made my gut twist out of fear of hurting her. She was trying her best, but she couldn't handle all of me.

Not yet.

"Tomorrow." I loathed the thought of going to the funeral of a person I didn't care about, but I needed to support her. She was lonely without Travis.

"Why yu ansa mi so? Yu tired of me?" she asked, and my grip tightened around the phone.

"Chayanne, go to sleep. Stop provoke me."

"Night," she grumbled, hanging up.

I put my phone away and entered the house. I raised a brow at *Mamma*, who was fanning her cat with the dust brush. A small smile tugged on my lips. "You can do better than that."

"I wasn't eavesdropping," *Mamma* lied, and I chuckled as I headed to the kitchen to fix a drink. She followed me. "Who yu did a talk to?"

"Nobody."

"I'm your mother. Yu cya lie to me, Favio."

Between Chayanne and *Mamma*, I wasn't sure who was more persistent with nagging questions. They were too much alike. They'd be a fucking headache if they got close.

"A girl." I moved the glass of Hennessy to my lips while *Mamma*'s eyes shone.

"I knew it! Yu fi mek mi meet her. You never bring anyone around here."

"No." No way in hell would I allow Chayanne to cross paths with Antaro.

"Fabiano brought girls around."

"Fabiano is a *puttano*—" I ducked, barely missing the dust brush *Mamma* sailed at my head. It hit the refrigerator, clattering to the ground as I straightened myself. Must grieve her she cya beat me anymore.

"Watch yu language ina mi house, bwoy! Nuh cause yu big now yago tear dung mi house!" *Mamma* hissed.

"*Mi dispiace*," I said.

"I want to meet her."

"Fine," I agreed grudgingly, and she cheered.

The doorbell rang, and *Mamma* grabbed the dust brush as she left the kitchen.

A moment later, I stood more upright as voices approached. They entered the kitchen, stopping on the other side of the island. Taking a seat, one of them placed a badge and a gun on the counter before me. Was he trying to intimidate me? Amusing.

I moved my drink to my lips, taking a big chug.

Mamma glanced between the newcomers. "Would you like anything to drink?" she asked, and they declined. Nodding, she exited.

"Slitta," said the one seated.

I refilled the glass. "Only time mi fi see yu a pon TV."

"Favio, *zitto*," Antaro warned.

"Say that again," I hissed in Italian.

He pulled his pistol at the same time I did mine. We aimed at each other's heads, and he clicked off the safety.

"Not because you're my son means I'm scared to use it," he threatened in

Italian, and I smirked.

Of course, I expected him to shoot me. The first thing he taught me was to never pull my gun unless I planned on using it. I always kept the safety off when I was at this house. The opportunity to use it could arrive at any second.

"Who said I'm scared?" I asked in English, my smirk stretching. I needed him to tighten his finger around the trigger a bit more so I could end his pitiful life. I'd been dreaming of this day since I was thirteen, but I couldn't kill him unwarranted. It'd place a rift between *Mamma* and me.

Rush jumped to his feet. "Diana, they're at it again!"

Mamma ran into the kitchen, yanking the guns from us. She glared at us, and we gulped. "Yu cannot kill yu son, *amore mio*. Favio, please behave. Mi tired fi talk to unu bout unu behavior," *Mamma* chastised, fatigue lacing her voice.

"He has no respect for me," Antaro complained, and I hissed my teeth while grabbing the Hennessy bottle. Antaro glared. "I should send you back to N—"

"*Amore mio*, stop it!" *Mamma* hissed. She walked toward me, causing me to place the bottle on the counter. She laid a hand on my cheek, her eyes softening. "No one is sending you anywhere, Favio."

I didn't give her a reaction as she left the kitchen, taking the set of knives with her. Antaro straightened his jacket, taking a seat along with Rush.

"Speak," I said coolly.

"The beach incident. Gon need a likkle sum fi identify the body. Things nuh look good over yaso," Rush said.

"Lizard plant the teeth a Graham house."

"*Figlio*," Antaro said, and I looked at him. "You didn't have to take out the man's tongue or scrape off his finger and toe prints. It's making things harder for Rush. Sometimes, you go overboard."

"I'm a Welsh." I could've done worse.

"True," he said, his anger becoming pride. "Rush will get everything sorted, and the competition will be out."

Nodding, I left the kitchen. I found *Mamma* in the living room, watching reruns of her favorite sitcom. I grabbed my pistol off the table. The metal was like a second limb in my hold. "I'm leaving."

"So yu too big fi hug me?" *Mamma* lifted her cat off her lap, resting it on the sofa. She stood and walked toward me. "Memba mi soon dead gone."

"Soon can't come soon enough."

She gasped, and I laughed, throwing an arm over her shoulder while she wrapped her arms around my waist. Pulling away, *Mamma* grinned. "Favio, come outta mi house before mi tell yu bout yu mother."

Hours later, I was in a club's private section. I was drinking with the idiot who had the misfortune of me calling him a lifelong friend.

"Dawg find woman and dash mi weh," Jelani slurred, and I ignored him as our server walked over.

Her breasts spilled out of the too-small top as she bent over before me, winking seductively. Gyal ya need fi hurry and get the fuck out of my face. She disregarded my glare as she nibbled on her bottom lip, placing the shot glasses on the table before leaving.

I drank a shot. The alcohol burned in my throat as it went down.

"Welsh, yu soon start link mi again. All yu do a fuck and duck," he added.

What the fuck was this idiot saying? I hated too many people having access to me. Whenever I dealt with a woman, I never stuck my dick in anyone else. She knew she was obligated to open her legs only for me.

Unless she saw a casket she liked.

If that were the case, I had no problem laying her there — dead or alive — the instant I learned she allowed another man to touch her.

Scoffing at Jelani's comment, I swallowed the next shot. Fuck, I needed more. I could still see Antaro's annoying fucking face at the front of my mind. I wanted to slowly peel his skin, then dump him in a pool of acid while watching him dissolve into the load of shit he was.

Jelani laughed. "Watch the man! Memba when we deh college and a same so yu gwan over Amber and weh the next one name... Catty!" he said, and I stiffened.

"You talk too much when you're drunk," I said, forcing myself to relax.

He chuckled. "Been like this since college, dawg. Mi afi vibe fi the two a wi."

Deciding against drinking the last shot, I gave it to Jelani. I didn't want to get tipsy or drunk; I had to drive him home.

"Yu soon find a woman weh change yu," I said, thinking of the old saying that went *que sera, sera*.

Me neva know me cuda find a next girl mi rate enough that would make me consider settling down... after she graduated, of course. Chayanne was too ambitious to do it any other way.

I was good with that.

I was good with her.

Chapter Twenty-Four

CHAYANNE

G od had a sense of humor.

The bright sky and cheerful birds were a mockery to everyone gathered at the burial site. We were dressed in white, minus Asia's family, who were in lilac. We clutched dampened napkins in tight fists, hiding teary eyes behind shades.

This somber day couldn't end soon enough.

In the church, I wasn't brave enough to look at her lifeless body.

At the burial site, I didn't have a choice.

Asia's casket was open. Her eyes were closed, her mouth in a resting smile upon her powdered face. She looked asleep. My foolish hope was her waking up to ask where Trav was. They'd argue, then make up seconds later. His birthday was in a few days, and she loved making his day special.

"From dirt, we rose. To dirt, we shall return." The pastor stooped, grabbing a handful of dirt.

A pallbearer — her uncle from Cascade, Hanover — closed the lilac-colored casket. The pastor threw dirt atop it, and Miss Olive cried out.

As the church choir began singing, Asia's casket began its slow descent.

"Waii! No, mi baby!" Miss Olive wailed, thrashing in the arms of the men holding her back. "Bury mi wid ar! Bury me—" Her words died off into incoherent pleas, and I looked away.

Miss Olive reminded me of when Mommy died. Mama had almost jumped into the grave, too.

Miss Olive's cries were louder than the crowd's mix of singing and wails. It pulled at my aching heart. I couldn't stop my tears as they flowed.

An arm tossed over my shoulder, pulling me closer. I buried my face in Chezzy's chest, violent sobs rocking my body as I lost control.

"God, why?! *Why*?!" Miss Olive screamed. She was angry at the world. Herself. The police force, who were yet to admit their mishap. And at her daughter's boyfriend, who was yet to condole her.

Miss Olive, I couldn't answer your question. I'd been trying to figure it out for nine years, too.

After the funeral finish, me and Chezzy leave immediately. Mi heart cudn manage being ina the cemetery any longer. We stopped at the Square.

"Yu sure yu nuh waa come over fi get sum fi eat?" mi ask Chezzy, and she nod.

"Yu bredda still ina jail?" she ask, and mi nod. "Mi hope him come out soon."

"Me, too. Mi miss a cuss him every time him call yu Sandra," mi joke, and Chezzy's gaze flickered to the ground before settling on me.

"Me a leave now. Tell Mama evening." She hugged me, then left.

I walked home. Much to my surprise, Favi park a mi gate. He was smoking. Shaking mi head, mi walk toward him. "Yu smoke too much, Favi."

"I don't smoke enough," he said.

"Yu good now?" mi ask. Before me leave this morning, him pull up a mi gate, fuming. Him gimi some ruthless sex ina the backyard. Mi did think him come from Town still vex wid mi, but a him side lose dem match.

Favi nuh ansa. Instead, him lean off the car, opening the front door. He took out a vase of roses, and my face brightened as he handed it to me, along with a small gift bag. "Condolences, *fiore.*"

143

Smiling, mi hug him. "Thanks, Favi. You never come the graveside?" mi ask, and him shake him head. Him did sidung beside me during the service, but him disappear as the ceremony over.

"*Mamma* wants to meet you," him whisper, and mi draw back mi head.

"*Me?*" mi ask, and a small smile come pon him face.

"*Sì.*"

My heart raced as mi pull away, beaming at him. Mi never meet a man mother before! "Sure. When?"

"Next Saturday," him seh, and mi shoulders slump.

"Can't. Mago collect money weh Aunty a go send."

"We can go whenever works for you," him seh, and mi nod. Maybe if Aunty send the money early enough, mi will have enough time fi go during the day.

"What's her name, by the way? You never told me."

"Ask her when you see her."

"Why yu stay so?" Mi roll mi eyes while him grin. "Suppose she nuh like me..."

"She's going to love you."

"You sure?" I asked, and he nodded.

"*Sì.* Unu annoying alike."

I gasped, and he burst out laughing, making me feign anger. It hard fi be mad at him when him this relaxed.

"I have a surprise for you," him seh after him get a hold of himself.

Mi smile. "Really?"

"*Sì.*" He opened the back door, revealing a white toy poodle curled into a ball on the seat.

I squealed, almost dropping the vase and gift bag. It bolted up, ran in a circle, then wagged its tail.

"Him so cute!" Mi put the vase ina Favi's hands and take up the puppy. It licked my face, and I giggled.

"She," Favi said.

"Does she have a name?"

"I called it—" Him curse waa Italian bad word. "—when it did a shit up mi house before it got trained, but you can call it whatever you want."

Mi nuh waa bite mi tongue, so mi nuh try repeat wa him seh. Petting the energetic bundle in my arms, I said, "Marshmallow."

"Yu love yu belly too much, Chayanne," Favi said, and I grinned. Him shake him head before walking away to open the trunk. It was full of dog supplies.

Me almost melt. Why him so sweet?!

I tipped, kissing his lips. Mi neva care seh fass Paul outta door. "Thanks, Favi," I said while pulling away.

His eyes shone when he nodded, and my heart beat faster.

Faster than it ever did before.

I didn't know what this feeling was, but I loved it.

Favi blew the horn from outside.

Inhaling a big breath, I double-checked my outfit in the mirror. Mi ina waa simple, flowy red dress that stopped mid-thigh, brown slippers with gold accents, and a crossbody bag. Chezzy picked my outfit yesterday afta shi cuss seh mi fi stay home in case Trav come home.

Exhaling the breath, mi tell Mama seh me a go Ochi wid Chezzy, then go outside.

Favi lean pon the yellow BMW. Fi the first, him naa smoke. "Look how long mi a try tell yu mi reach."

I looked at the phone, chuckling nervously when mi see the missed call. "Sorry. I forgot I have a new phone. Me did a use the old one all day."

"How yu forget, Chayanne? Mi give yu that so when mi call yu, mi can get yu. Yu nafi worry boh sharing the old phone with yu granny," him seh, irritation and anger lacing his tone.

"Yu nafi call it waa old phone..." Aunty work very hard fi buy it. It neva fancy like the one him gift me last week, but it got the job done.

"Me never mean it like that," he said, and me nod. Cya hold it over him head when him used to getting the newest and best everything, while I wasn't used to that luxury. He took my hand in his, running his thumb over my knuckles. "You look pretty."

"Thanks." Mi smile.

Him look pon mi lips before releasing mi hand. "Where's your bag?"

Him blind? Mi pat the bag swaying by my side.

"I meant to spend the night," him seh.

"Yu neva tell mi dat, Favio!" I exclaimed.

"Watch how yu talk to me," him seh coldly. "And it slipped my mind. I have a business meeting tomorrow morning, and knowing you and *Mamma*, unu a go chat wul day. It's best we come down tomorrow."

"Mi naa go nowhere," I stated firmly. Mi hate how him can gwan like mi nav a life! Mi need fi study and eat off the curry chicken mi cook last night.

"Chayanne. You agreed to meet her."

"That's before me know we a spend the night. Mi cya deh a Town so long."

"Why?"

I looked at my white-painted toenails. "Mi nuh know Town," I whispered. Mi only go with Aunty Simone when a new school term so mi can buy school supply.

He lifted my chin. "I do, and nun nago happen to yu. We're going to Cherry Gardens."

Mi eyes widen. "How rich are you?"

"Very. Go pack. I'll suck your pussy when we get there."

Favi shook me awake when we arrived. I paused mid-stretch to gawk at the enormous house.

It was a modern three storey. White walls appeared freshly painted, and the sunlight reflected off glass windows. There was plenty of yard space; the grass green like primary school boy arm while the garden colorful like basic school pickney drawing. An angel-shaped water fountain in the center of the circular driveway.

Me nearly pinch miself, but mi never waa Favi think mi nuh used to things. "*Wow*. Yu mother live ina alladis?"

"No. Her husband lives here, too."

I nodded, hoping me get fi meet Favi father. Him nuh really talk bout him father, and mi waa know why.

"This is my family home. My house is close by," he said.

"Mi can see it?" I asked, excited to be in his world and far away from the antics him keep up in mine.

"When it done build." He exited the car. Him open the door fimi, holding my travel bag while leading us toward the door. Favi pressed the buzzer, speaking Italian in the intercom.

"Why yu nuh stop run up mi pressure? How mi supposed to know who 'it's me' be?" replied a woman's cheery voice, and mi giggle while Favi glare.

"*Mamma*, I'm here with Chayanne," Favi seh.

She chuckled nervously. "Oh! I'll be right down."

A moment later, the door open, revealing a round lady, who was a bit shorter than me. Her complexion was dark like mine, but me could see the resemblance between her and Favi. She had a warm, motherly smile, and it made me relax.

"It's nice to meet you!" She pulled me into a tight hug.

"You, too." Smiling, mi hug her back. She smell nice.

"*Mamma*," Favi hissed, tugging me outta her hold.

"*Dispiace*," she apologized, clasping her hands before her. Her Italian nuh fluent like Favi's.

"She doesn't understand Italian," Favi seh, and mi almost scoff at the hypocrisy.

"Oh..." She offer me a hand fi shake. "I'm Diana. Nice to meet you."

"Chayanne, but you can call me Chichi," mi seh.

"Please don't," Favi seh before asking her sum ina Italian. to which she replied in Italian.

A must chat dem a chat mi... Sighing, mi look pon mi feet.

Favi held beneath my chin, making me look at him. "You good?"

I nodded. How could I tell him I felt out-of-place? They were rich and spoke a unique language while me deh ya plain like white bread. Mrs. Diana was probably expecting someone different, but did she know what kind of person her son was outside of this gated community?

Favi didn't believe me. He was about to say something, but his mother interrupted.

"Please come in, Chayanne," she said sweetly, stepping aside.

I complied, gawking at the chandelier in the foyer while Mrs. Diana stepped away from the door. The door swung shut, almost hitting Favi. He hissed a sharp curse as he stopped it with his hand, and his mother smiled. I bit my cheeks cause mi nuh waa carry mi backa-bush laugh ina the people dem uptown house. Matter a fact, mek mi talk Standard English around her so she doh think mi a waa ghetto fowl.

Smirking, Mrs. Diana stepped toward me. "Come, Chayanne. Let me get you something to drink, then show you around."

I glanced over my shoulder at Favi. He stood by the door, glaring.

He was right. His mom and I were going to get along fine.

Favi disappeared all evening, and I got to know Diana (what she preferred me calling her) better. She was a housewife, whose only job was spending her husband's money. I didn't meet Antaro because he was away on a business trip.

We were in the kitchen, and I was watching her take a bite out of the chilled potato salad I made.

"Mm. This tastes amazing," she praised, and I exhaled a quiet breath. She knew I was a good girlfriend because pussy wasn't the only thing I had to feed her son.

"Thanks! It's my grandmother's recipe," I bragged. "I'm going to get Favi," I said, and she nodded.

Their house was a maze, but I found Favi's room after getting lost two times, despite Diana's tour. I entered Favi's room, pausing at the door. I skimmed past the fancy watch display cabinet and focused on him. He was shirtless on the bed with an arm thrown over his forehead. His sculpted abs beckoned me over to trail my fingertips or tongue across them. I would've if I wasn't on my best behavior.

"Favi?" mi whisper, and him move his arm, raising a brow. "You okay?"

"*Sì*, but I'm tired." Sitting up, him pat him lap.

Mi nuh hesitate fi go straddle him. My favorite place to be was in his skin. "You should sleep."

"I don't sleep during the day."

"Alright, superhero," I joked, and he chuckled, making me smile. "Come eat." Mi eager fi him try the potato salad. Diana did a go cook stew beef fi him, but mi tell her mi cya eat nor cook beef, so she change the menu.

"You?" he teased, and my clit throbbed.

"Yu cya behave?" I asked, and him chuckle.

"Did *Mamma* drive you crazy?"

"No. She's nice. Mi nuh know why you so bad breed," mi seh, and him scoff, flipping me over fi suck mi neck. "Your mother…"

He broke the kiss. "Maa big man, Chayanne. She nuh care bout hickey."

"But—"

"Shh, *fiore*." He kissed my lips before moving to my neck. He licked, sucked, and kissed my skin until he left a hickey. Pulling away, him sit up and mek mi straddle him. Staring pon the mark, him rest him hands pon mi waist.

Mi throw my arms round him neck. "You never told me what the snake means."

Him look from the hickey fi glare pon mi. "Everything you waa know."

Shuda box mi ina mi face!

"Nevermind, Favio…" Mi try get up, but him tighten him grip.

"Why yu so easy fi vex?"

"Mi nuh easy fi vex! Mi ask yu a simple question, and hear how yu ansa mi!" Mi yank miself outta him hold, marching toward the door. Mi day did alright until this big foot bwoy bruk mi vibes!

Favio slapped a hand against the door when I opened it, slamming it shut. He grabbed my wrist, spinning me around and caging me with both his hands on either side of my head.

"Move, Favio." My chest heaved while I stared into his angry eyes.

"Sometimes, mi cya badda wid yu," he said coldly.

"Me worse! Move, cause mi naa ramp wid yu!" Mi have a good mind knee him ina him balls! A cause me cya afford hospital bill mek mi nuh dweet.

"Look like maa play?" Favio asked, his low tone scaring me. "Wa the fuck this fi vex ova? Yu swear yu fucking mature, but half the time yu act like yaa eleven."

"Since me a eleven, yaa waa rapist."

His eyes widened. His hands dropped from the door as he stepped backward, and I immediately regretted my words.

"Favi—" I stepped toward him, and he put more space between us. "I didn't mean—"

He opened the door and walked out of the room. I wanted to chase him, but regret and anger rooted me in place. What did I do?!

Don't count ten toe in front a man wid nine toe.

Chapter Twenty-Five

CHAYANNE

For the rest of the day, I locked myself in the room. I was too ashamed to go out and face Diana after what me seh to her son. I was so angry at myself. How could I allow myself to say that?!

It was around nine when someone knocked on the door. Me sit up fast, hoping it was Favi.

"Chichi?" came Diana's voice, and I gulped, wiping away tears.

"Yes? You can come in," I said.

She entered the room with a tray, smiling gently while sitting on the bed. "Favio told me to bring you some food because you haven't eaten."

"Favi?" My heart skipped a beat as she nodded.

"Yes. Him seh yu love nyam, so..." She grinned while I chuckled sadly.

"Thanks." I accepted the tray, placing it aside. My stomach ached and my hands shook, but I was unable to eat. "Where's... Favi?"

"Upstairs."

On the third floor... Diana didn't show me up there. She said it was a mess because she was redecorating.

"Here's a little advice for being with my son." Diana laid a hand on my arm, and worry settled inside me. "Favio had a rough childhood, and it made him like having things in his control the older he got. When things don't go his way, he might take things to an extreme to ensure they work how he wants them to. My son means well. He just takes a while to give up some control."

It didn't sound like Favi told her about our argument, but she didn't know how much her words hurt.

Favi gave me control.

He told me a secret that still bothered him.

He made me see him at his weakest.

And I hurt him.

"Where exactly is he?" I asked.

"Upstairs is funny. Ignore all the side doors and head straight for the one on the back wall."

"Okay... Thank you," I said, and she smiled, then left. My belly grumbled, and mi grab mi shirt. The asparagus a mek mi mouth water, and the chicken so—

I jumped out of the bed. I needed to find my man and beg for his forgiveness.

Making a beeline upstairs, mi ignore the large photographs lined on the floor of either wall. Mi find the door and knock, waiting for an answer.

None came.

"Favi?" I pressed my ear against the door. Light footsteps padded across the floor, and me sigh. Swallowing my pride, I placed a hand on the knob, turning it. Pushing the door open, my eyes widened.

The room was full of snakes!

An entire wall was blocked off by large terrariums stacked atop each other. A thermostat was on the wall beside each one. A special light was in each enclosure, along with real plants, thick branches, stones, and hides. The adjacent wall was entirely glass. Lines of moonlight streamed through and stretched across the floor. My eyes widened at a green snake curling around a branch in its enclosure, peering at me through frightening black slits.

I gulped, shifting my focus to Favi, who was walking around while looking at the floor. "Fav—"

"Shut up."

Mi swallow mi shame. "I'm—"

"Shut up, Chayanne, and don't move." He took long strides toward me.

I looked at my feet, screaming as a snake slithered toward me. Its entire body was black, minus the white peel clinging to its body.

Favi sighed heavily. He lifted the snake with gloved hands before it reached me. My scream died off, but my heart continued racing as the snake curled around Favi's hand as if it was reuniting with a lifelong friend. He handled it with utmost care, placing it in a cage I didn't realize was open. The snake glided through the mix of red and brown substrates at the bottom of the terrarium, disappearing into the mix of vegetation at the back.

Favi closed it, then took the glove off, resting it atop a cabinet. He moved to sit on the sofa against the opposite wall. He grabbed the glass next to a bottle of Henny, taking a sip.

My brows knitted as he swallowed without a grimace. "Yu nuh chase Henny?"

"Why yu waa know? Waa throw it back ina mi face?"

Sighing, I closed the door. Mi stay close to the wall while walking toward him. "Neva know yu have snakes."

"Good. One less thing fi yu know bout mi."

I sighed, kneeling before him. "Favi, I'm sorry. Mi never mean it like that. It come out wrong." Tears pricked my eyes as him continue ignore me and sip him drink. Mi cya stand this tension! Mi grab the glass, resting it pon the table.

Him doh fawt pon mi. Instead, him get up and go stand before the glass wall. Him glare through it.

"I'm sorry, Favi..." Mi wish mi cuda tek out mi tongue and step pon it. Until now, mi neva understand when Mama seh mi fi *kibba mi mouth.*

The tension in the room was stifling. Mi couldn't breathe, not with the budding urge to cry tightening my throat. Maybe I should give him space...

Wiping below mi eyes, I glanced at him and his snakes before standing and walking toward the door. I placed a hand on the knob before he finally said something.

"Come here, Chayanne."

Mi go ova there ina blink, craning mi neck fi look pon him. "Yes?"

His jaw clenched as his brows pulled together. Even in his aggravated state, he was still the most handsome man I'd ever seen. His head tilted downward to look at me. A shadow fell over his face, making his eyes appear darker. "I want head."

Mi gasp, my anger surging. "Yu nuh talk to mi wul evening. Me try apologize, and a this yaa ask fa?"

"Yado it or not?"

I didn't want to when he was mad at me. But maybe this was what he needed to feel better. I kneeled, tilting my head upward and opening my mouth.

Favi avoided my gaze as he freed his semi-erection. Holding my head, he moved his hips to direct it to my mouth. "Wider," he ordered, and I did until my jaws stung. Favi forced himself inside with one powerful thrust, hitting the back of my throat and making me choke. His grip around my face tightened as he tilted my head more upward, slamming inside me with an unrelenting frenzy.

I choked and sputtered around his dick. Spit ran from my mouth, gathering below my chin. Tears streamed down my cheeks. My nose was runny. I couldn't breathe. He used it as an invitation to thrust into my mouth harder.

Faster.

Over and over as I swallowed his entire length.

"Mm—" Groaning, I squeezed his thighs, and he slowed before pulling out. "It hurts," I said, my throat aching as I wiped away the excess spit. Mi know him prefer rough head, but that a neva head! It was attempted murder.

"Okay. Take off your dress and arch."

Mi eyes widen. "In here?"

"*Sì.*" He kneeled behind me.

I did as he said, arching as best as I could. He came closer, pushing my back down further. My face pressed against the floor as he grabbed my wrists, restricting them behind me. My pussy was exposed to him, and I closed my eyes, ashamed that his manhandling made me this wet.

He ran his dick through me, slapping it on my clit and making me shiver. He thrust into me, burying himself balls deep.

"Ah!" I screamed. Pain became pleasure as he slammed into me repeatedly.

Slapping skin filled my ear.

The musk of our hot sex drowned out the air freshener plugged into the wall.

My entire body was in heat while Favi used me like a rag doll.

His grip around my wrists loosened as he yanked me up, lacing his arm through the crook of my elbows and pressing my back against his chest. The back of my thighs rested on the front of his as he slammed me down on his dick, punishing me with pleasure in a way he'd never done before.

"Favi!" My nails bit into my palms as his rough thrusts hit my cervix.

His harsh breathing fanned my ear as he picked up his pace. "Don't speak."

I didn't listen.

I screamed. Moaned. Cried.

For him to go harder.

For him to stop.

Continue.

Break me in the most beautiful way because I deserved it.

"I'm gonna—" I moaned, my orgasm drawing so close I could taste it. Goosebumps pricked my skin as my abdomen tightened.

Favi coaxed my orgasm closer... and closer... until he stopped, pulling out of me completely. He flipped me onto my back, throwing my legs over his shoulders before working his dick deep inside my aching pussy. His chain hung low in my face as he hastened his animalistic pace, focusing on my lips as I moaned at him.

I grabbed his arm, my nails sinking into his skin. "Favi, I can't..."

His eyes dragged to mine. "Can't what?"

"Take—" I moved a hand between us. My fingers pressed against the taut skin of his V-Line. "Favi, yu ina mi belly."

"Move your fucking hand." The curse rolled off his tongue so sexy yet intimidating.

I didn't have a choice but to obey him.

My back arched off the ground. My eyes rolled to the back of my head. Before my eyes shut, I glimpsed the snakes watching us.

I was getting used on the ground like a whore.

Favi's whore.

My pussy clamped around his dick tighter, my nails dragging across the floor as I screamed my release. Pleasure shot through my veins, rendering me senseless in that nerve-splintering moment.

After the wave passed, I dropped flat with a tired breath.

"Chayanne?" he said in that same gruff voice.

"Y-yes, Favi?" My eyes fluttered open. My vision was hazy.

"Don't fucking play with me again."

"I won't," I promised without missing a beat.

A glint ran through his eyes, and he smirked before leaning in. I puckered my lips, eager to kiss him.

Favi didn't kiss me.

He latched onto the unmarked side of my neck, sucking it roughly. His thrusts became sloppy, long, and hard as he neared his orgasm. His body weight pressed against me, stimulating my sensitive nipples as I clenched at will around him.

He stiffened, biting into my neck as his orgasm took control. Thick lines of warm cum shot deep inside me. Spent, he released my bruised skin.

We stayed there for a while, catching our breaths in silence.

A moment later, Favi pulled out of me. Cum leaked out of my pussy, running through my ass and gathering on the floor.

I sat up with a wince, placing my legs on either side of his body as I brought myself closer. "I'm sorry, Favi..." I murmured, but he didn't answer. Licking my lips, I went closer, hesitant as my lips brushed his. He didn't pull away, so I took that as a sign to continue. Placing my lips against his, I kissed him softly.

He took a few seconds to kiss me back.

There were no sparks. It was a plain, brief kiss that was better than nothing.

I broke the kiss, leaning back on my hands. "Mi never mean fi imply seh yaa waa rapist. You're not, and me really sorry fi tek it tell yu. If yu nuh waa share the meaning of yu tattoo or anything else until yu feel yu can trust me again, me understand."

"Yu good, Chayanne. Stop worry yuself. Yu too pretty fi a mek up yu face so." Him lean forward, kissing my forehead before pulling back. "I don't always say the right thing—"

"Yet yu always find it easy fi class me?"

"Sorry. Next time, I'll write you a letter," he joked, and I chuckled. He stood and dragged on his shorts. Him help mi stand, then redress mi. Him scoop me into him hold, and mi look pon the cum pon the floor. "I'll clean it later," he said before bringing me to his room.

We showered and played around before returning to the room. We sat on the bed. Him a watch me eat another plate of food after me box off the one Diana did carry.

"I made this for you." I offered him some potato salad, watching as his lips curled around the fork.

Pulling away, he chewed and swallowed. "It's *buono*."

"*Buono*... Good?" mi ask, and him nod.

"You're learning."

"I have to... Mi feel out of place when you and yu mother did a—" Mi shut up.

"Sorry about that. I was asking her if Antaro was back," he said, and I nodded.

"You should teach me Italian. Mi waa options fi when maa cuss yu."

"Hear mi second Diana," he said, and I chuckled.

We chatted and laughed for the next few minutes. He told me all about his watch collection and three different species of pythons. He had twelve snakes, and his favorite was his six-year-old ball python, Night — the one that scared me. His mom took care of them whenever he was in St. Ann.

"That's why them call yu Slitta? Because of your snakes?" I asked.

"No. I cut the throat of the second person I killed," he said casually, and my eyes widened. He shrugged. "Nuh like when nuh man deal wid mi certain way."

"How old were you when..."

"Sixteen. He was one of my teachers."

My blood ran cold. If mi neva know before, mi know now: Favio Welsh had several screws loose. I knew who he was, but he never seemed comfortable talking about that part of his life with me, and me never waa hear bout it, either. I liked being delusional that he was a good, upstanding business owner.

I cleared my throat. "Why snakes?"

"They're fascinating."

"How?"

He looked at his abdomen. "Snakes are perceived as bad, but they aren't. I like their nature to shed and start over."

157

Favi went to his meeting, so I spent most of my day with Diana. I watched as she tended to Favi's snakes, and I learned more about them because I wanted to be a better fit in his world.

Hours later, we were in the dining hall. She was putting batteries in her new clock while I sat at the table. Favi returned from his friend's house a few minutes ago. I didn't know he had friends.

"Antaro call yu?" Diana asked Favi, who released my hair from the grab clip and ran his fingers through it.

He started speaking in Italian, then glanced at me. "No," he said in English, and Diana sighed.

"Alright. Come put up the clock for me," she said, and Favi complied. After he finished, she told us she had to run errands.

After she leff, Chezzy call. She ina waa hoodie, wrapped under the green blanket mi knit fi her years ago. "Yu soon come down?" she ask, and before mi can reply, Favi tek the phone.

"Bye, Chezandra. We a go fuck." Him end the call while mi eyes widen. Him pocket the phone, then liff mi, laying mi pon the table.

Gasping, mi eyes dart round while him tug mi panties off. "Favi, not here!"

"Shut up and mek mi suck yu pussy. I'll buy them a new table," he said before his head disappeared under my dress.

Diana hugged me, pulling away to slap Favi. "Mek sure yu drive like yav sense.

Nuh go kill her off."

Favi scoffed. "Bay tuff chat with nun fi back it."

"A me bring yu deh here. Mi nuh fraid fi tek yu out." She tipped and ruffled his hair.

"*Mamma*. Lata mi call yu if mi feel like." Favi shrugged her off, brushing down his hair with his hand while we walked toward the car. "Trying to walk normally is making it more obvious."

"I wonder whose fault that is," I muttered while slowly sitting inside the car, and he flashed me that perfect white teeth smile.

He slammed the door shut as a black Land Rover pulled up in the driveway. A tall, formally clad white man exited the vehicle. He walked toward Favi, whose stance was rigid.

"Favio," the man said as Diana ran to his side. He bent to kiss her, and Favi scowled.

Diana looked like a midget standing between the men, who were about the same height. "Where's Chichi? Let her meet him," she said to Favi.

"*Chichi*?" Antaro said my name exactly how Favi did the night we met — surprise mixed with mockery.

"She's Favio's girlfriend," Diana said while me wonder if Favi a go keep mi locked ina the car. As a country gyal, him must shame a mi.

"Girlfriend?" A small smirk stretched across Antaro's face before he spoke to Favi in Italian.

Favi didn't answer. Diana sighed and said something to him in Italian.

"Fine," Favi hissed, opening the door. His eyes burned as he stretched his hand toward me and helped me out of the car.

"Good afternoon." I smiled, despite suffocating in the tension.

"Good afternoon." Antaro shook my hand. His hand was rough and calloused.

Favi yanked my hand out of Antaro's within two seconds. He wrapped his arm around my waist, pulling me to his side. Him better tek time wid mi! Every movement hurt up mi likkle vagina.

"*Bella*," Antaro said to Favi while staring at me. His accent was thicker than

Favi's.

"*Zitto.*" Favi opened the door. "*Entrare.*"

I smiled at his parents before complying. Mi bruk mi ears fi listen dem conversation, but them a chat Italian.

"Favio, ignore him. Mek mi know when unu reach. Love you," Diana seh.

Favi nod before him enter the car. Fuming, him tap him index finger against the wheel while waiting fi the gate open.

We drive off. Fi once, mi quiet.

Favi needed silence.

An hour later, mi a watch the scenes *whoosh* pass. Mi cudn live a Town. The place too congested, and country nuh so busy. Plus, the air nuh fresh like country breeze.

With all the comparisons in mind, mi doze off despite the loud bass of Favi's speakers. Mi phone wake me up a while later. "Hello?" mi answer groggily.

"Hello? 119?" the person seh.

"You have the wrong number." Mi rub the sleep outta mi eyes while glancing pon Favi.

Him a drive well-relaxed wid one hand. Him so sexy!

"119, help!" the person cried hysterically, and mi shot up, ignoring Favi's glance.

"Mama?!"

Chapter Twenty-Six

CHAYANNE

"Grandbaby, dem bruk ina the house!"

"Mama, calm down. Wa happen?" I asked calmly, despite my hands sweating.

"Mi deh pon the veranda when waa man push past me and go ina the house. Him rummage bout the place and gone wid the money Kenzie send. Mi bawl fi help, but it nuh look like Paul deh bout."

I stopped breathing.

"*Fiore?*" came Favi's voice, laced with concern, but I ignored him.

"Yu alright, Mama?" mi ask.

"Mi think so," she said, and I exhaled a breath.

"Mama, hang up the phone and call—" Me glance pon Favi. Him unpredictable, mi nuh need that right now. "Call the second number weh deh pon the sticky note on the fridge."

"119?"

"Yes, Mama." Mi hang up fi call Aunty Simone. While the phone ring, mi nibble mi bottom lip.

"Everything good?" Favi rest him hand pon mi thigh, squeezing gently when mi nuh ansa.

"Yeah." Sas Crise! Mi shudn go Town!

"Who's this?" Aunty ask, and mi tell her a me wid a new number.

"Yu can go check pon Mama, please? She nuh sound so hundred, but mi deh pon mi way right now."

"Lawd Jesus!" A rush of movement drifted from her end, followed by the jingle of keys. "Me a gwope deh right now! Chezandra, turn off the stove! Boys, unu go put on unu shoes and come!"

My hand shook as I moved the phone from my ear.

"Chayanne, you good?" Favi ask again, and mi fake a smile.

"Yes, Favi. We soon reach?" Mi look through the window. Wi deh pon the highway, approaching Ochi.

"Bout thirty minutes."

Despite feeling numb, mi nod. Mi stare through the window fi the rest of the journey. When Favi drop me at the street entrance cause mi tell him to, mi fly outta the car. Mi unsure if mi tell him thanks or drive safe back to Kingston. Mi run dung the lane with the bag swinging over mi shoulder.

Waa police car park before mi gate, and Aunty car deh behind it. Mr. Paul nuh deh home fi true cause him wuda outta door a fass.

Entering the house, mi ignore everyone and rush toward Mama. Mi kneel before her, pulling her into a tight hug. Tears prick mi eyes as her body tremble against mine. "Me deh here now, Mama. You alright?"

"Weh yaa come from, Chichi?" Aunty ask before Mama cuda ansa, and mi glance pon Chezzy, who gulp. "A me a talk to yu, Chichi. Mama seh yu did deh a mi yaad, and yu neva dung deh."

I pulled away, hating how everyone's attention was on me — especially the officer. "Mi did deh wid Yolanda."

"What's in the bag?" Officer asked, and mi grip tighten round the bag strap.

"Yu nuh have nuh grounds fi search mi bag. Why unu a question me? You should be searching for whoever robbed an old woman."

The police sighed, looking at the notepad in her hand. She scanned the paper, jotting down sum before saying to no one in particular, "Mrs. Saanvi didn't see the masked intruder, but she gave me a partial description. I doubt it can be of much help."

"So, we naa get back the money?" mi ask, and Officer pull her lips into a straight line, killing all hope. My shoulders slumped, my grip loosening around the bag.

"Sum a go work out, Chichi," Chezzy seh, and Mama nodded while taking a sip of her lime leaf tea.

"Yu need fi tell wi weh yu did deh. If yu find it so easy fi lie to me and Mama, who know wa else yaa lie bout?" Aunty seh, and mi force down the urge fi cry. Aunty rarely scolded me, and it hurt a little more this time.

"Mommy, Chichi wudn mek nobody tek the money. Dat nuh mek nuh sense," Chezzy seh, and Aunty scoff.

"Like unu lying to me for how long now? Yu call Kenzie yet?" Aunty ask, and mi shake mi head.

Officer grab her pen. "Who's Kenzie?"

Aunty glare while mi wipe weh tears. "Mama daughter, weh tek care of them from foreign."

"Me a go call her now." Mi stand, grimacing.

"Well, there's nothing much I can do right now. Please contact the station if you have any new information." Officer shake Aunty hand before she leave.

Mi go lock up ina mi room with the old phone, lowering myself to the ground with a wince. Mi call Aunty Kenzie and tell her everything. She tek Jesus offa the cross, pleading fi him strike who rob we.

Aunty Simone come ina the room moments after, taking the phone from mi. She leave the room while telling Aunty Kenzie bout wa me and Chezzy up to.

Chezzy come ina the room wid Marshy ina her hands. She sit pon the floor beside me. "You think Fav—"

"No," I said without missing a beat.

Favi family swim ina riches. He'd never.

If sum nuh go so, it near so.

Sighing, Chezzy lay her head on my shoulder while stroking Marshy's fur.

"Sorry seh Aunty a go beat yu when unu go home," mi seh, and she shrug.

"That a the least. Mi hope sum can work out fi you."

I didn't answer. Mi fixate pon the wall before we, detaching from the world. Mi spend mi whole life working toward an education fi tek mi outta Steer Town, and someone robbed me of it all.

Cya ketch Quako, ketch him shut.

Since the robbery, things get crazy. Aunty Kenzie a stress bout if she can get the money before the deadline. She and Aunty Simone vex wid mi cause mi still nuh tell dem where mi did deh. Aunty a come from foreign soon, and mi scared. How me a go tell her mi have man a sleep over most night?

My legs tightened around Favi as his tongue swirled around my right nipple before releasing it. He kissed along my jawline, finding my mouth while he used a hand to grab his dick, seeking my entrance. I winced as my walls stretched around it.

He broke away. "*Fiore*, you good?" he asked, and me shake mi head. Him pull out, lying beside me. "What's wrong?"

"I've been having really bad cramps."

"Your period came early?" Him reach fi him phone. Favi downloaded a period app; it was in sync with mine. Yolo think it weird, but Chezzy think it cute.

"No, it's not that."

"Yu waa go doctor?"

Shaking mi head, mi face away from him. "Aunty cya afford fi send mi go doctor right now."

"I can." Him pull mi fi lay pon him chest, and mi flick him nipple wid mi finger. Favi slap weh mi hand. "Cut that fuck. How long yu ina pain?"

"Since mi come from Town..." Missionary hotter than backaz, but dem backaz deh nearly cripple me. A did the first time mi tek alla him buddy, and wheelchair nearly pick me up. "Me cya go doctor, Favi. Mi Aunty will kill mi if it's because of sex."

"Your health should be her primary concern. Fuck the money. Tomorrow, I'll bring you to my godmother's private practice. Yago good, alright?"

I nodded, smiling while mi snuggle closer to him.

Suppose me a dead or worse... Suppose me a breed? Mi afi go kill miself before Aunty get the chance to. Mi need fi be more careful, but sex too sweet and Favi nuh like wear condoms or pull out.

"Chayanne, mi nuh waa yu feel obligated fi give mi pussy. If something's wrong, you need to tell me," Favi said after a moment's silence, and mi gulp.

"I will."

"Is this why yu nehna show mi nuh vibes since mi come back yesterday?" him ask, and mi tense.

Mi waa tell him cause me love how him tek care of me, but him busy wid him company. Plus, him head nuh screw on properly. There was no telling what he'd do, and mi nuh want him behind bars.

Learn how fi suck salt outta wooden spoon.

I forced myself to relax. "Yes."

Sitting in Dr. Merlgrove's office, my hands sweated a river. Mi wish Favi could stay ina the room with me, but Dr. Merlgrove tell him fi leave after she check me.

"Chayanne, whatever you say to me is usually kept in confidence. Do you understand?" she asked, and I nodded. She smiled warmly, holding my hand. "I understand this might be hard to talk about, but were you raped?"

"What? *No!*" Mi yank mi hand free.

"You've been having consensual intercourse?" she asked, and I nodded firmly. Her eyes searched mine before she smiled. "Your cervix's bruised." She tell mi boh deep penetration, rough intercourse, and that mi fi rest mi front.

Mi blousecup, this big buddy brown boy almost mash up mi good hole! Mi process the information, then inquire about birth control pills. Me cya afford it, so Favi a pay fi it. Him against me being on birth control, but me naa give weh mi future fi please him.

165

After mi get done, me meet Favi in the waiting area. We go outside to the car, and mi tell him everything. Him grip tighten round the wheel before him apologize profusely.

Mi cut him off wid a kiss. "It's okay. Mi deh pon bedrest, so no front for you."

"Your mouth still works," he said, and I gasped. "I'm joking." Chuckling, he took my hand and kissed my knuckles. "*Mi dispiace.*"

Mi yam field water as him release mi hand. It flourish when him drive go ina Ochi town, buying me food and a bouquet of red roses. "Thank you, Favi," I said, and he nodded as he drove off. "Why?"

"Every time mi do sum nice fi yu, yago ask why?"

"Me hate when yu talk to mi like that." Mi glare while him grip tighten round the wheel.

"I grew up watching Antaro showering *Mamma* with gifts."

"Aww! Ketch gun—" I paused as his jaw clenched. "*Businessman* with likkle romance."

"Nuff romance."

I snickered, diverting my focus to my phone. Chezzy texted. She nuh sure if she waa do nun fi her birthday next month, so mi give her ideas until we reach home.

Favi open the car door fimi, and mi tip fi kiss him. "Thanks, Favi. Later."

Favi nod, watching as mi tek quick steps toward the gate with a cheesy grin on my face.

Chapter Twenty-Seven

FAVIO

I leaned off the car, bumping my fist with his. "Welcome back."

"Respect. Nuh know how me can eva thank unu." He beamed at me and the lawyer.

"I'll be in touch, Mr. Bartley." Mr. Barnett nodded at us before walking away.

"Waa gwan upa yaad?" Travis entered the car while I did the same.

"Fuckry. Pig a roam the place," I said, and his brows raised.

"Wahm?"

Driving off, I shrugged. It didn't involve me or Blood Paw, so I didn't care. Regardless, I was on high alert. Antaro taught me never to be too careful.

"Me wi see wa mi can do," Travis stated, and I almost burst with pride. This was how a member of Blood Paw should operate — the opposite of that old man. He was lower ranked and good at finding information, but he wasn't very reliable. "Chichi good?"

Sometimes, I wanted to kill Travis for always asking about Chayanne. She was mine now. Mi nuh need nuh man a worry boh her. She good, always.

Reminding myself their relationship was platonic, I forced away the anger. "She's good. She's going to be happy to see you."

"With her miserable self." He chuckled, and I did, too. "Yu love her?"

I froze.

Amore?

Sure — I loved seeing her do her happy dance whenever I gave her food. Her dedication to getting a good education. Her curiosity, despite how nagging her questions could be. I loved her face and voice. I loved that she wasn't interested in my pockets, but in me as a person.

But... love? The thing where two people grew old together and lived happily ever after, like in those sappy sitcoms *Mamma* watched? That kind of love?

"It good if yu nuh have an answer right now. Long as unu happy," Travis said when I didn't answer.

Happy.

Chayanne made me happy. Happier than any woman ever did. Happier than I'd been since moving to Italy.

I hummed, and he chuckled.

"Mi did worried bout you wid her, but me know yu watch out fi her when mi did inside, so mi a put tha thing deh behind we."

That incident wasn't my proudest moment.

Chayanne did things to me. Strange things. I'd been with others, but no one like her.

Love. What else did I love about her?

I loved that *Mamma* took an instant liking to her.

I loved that I could show my worst sides to her, and she still accepted me.

I loved holding her for a few seconds longer than needed, savoring every moment we spent together.

I loved fucking her raw. She loved backshots, but I preferred missionary. Her back dimples were nice to look at, but it wasn't better than watching her gorgeous face contort from pain to pleasure. Mago breed her.

Cazzo. Cya fuck her right now cause of wa mi do.

I never meant to hurt her, but I took my anger out in her pussy instead of killing someone. I didn't know if choosing not to do the latter was commendable. If it was, I would admit that this girl kept me grounded.

If that was love, then maybe I loved Chayanne Arya Bailey.

But it wasn't time to love anybody. Not when fucking Antaro could use her to keep me trapped in Blood Paw. Not before that bastard Fabiano came out of prison and took his spot as the key player in Antaro's games.

"Can check if she home? Waa shout her," Travis said, pulling me from my thoughts before the rage could grow.

"Sure." I grabbed my phone. The corner of my mouth tugged upward when I saw her contact name. The other day, she complained she didn't like that her name was saved 'dry and soso', so she changed the ID.

She should've felt special. Everyone's caller ID, except for *Mamma*, was saved with their first and last name. If I knew their middle name, I included it, too.

Brushing away the memory, I texted her while glancing at the road. I would've called, but her voice made me horny. I didn't want my dick hard while I was stuck in the car with a man.

Weh yu deh?

FIORE: Home. Why?

I have a surprise for you.

ANOTHER DOG?!

Close enough.

I put the phone away. Travis and I listened to music until I drove onto Chayanne's street, passing by a pig's car. I glanced in the rearview mirror, memorizing the license plate. Wa the fuck a gwan?

My mind flashed to Chayanne. She'd been shying away from me for days now. Sinister thoughts swirled inside me, feeding the darkness I always tried to keep at bay.

Chayanne was smart. I hoped she knew better than to fuck me over.

Going against me was never something that ended well for anyone.

Chapter Twenty-Eight

CHAYANNE

Squealing, me run offa the veranda. Mi mek a U-Turn as mi foot hit the grass. Mi slip on mi Crocs, running outta mi yard fi jump into Trav's arms. Him wrap him arms around me, chuckling as him liff mi offa the grung.

"When yu come back?" mi ask, beaming as him set mi to mi feet.

Trav grin. "Today."

"Favi deevn cuda tell mi!" Mi glare pon Favi, who a build a spliff.

"Did fi come out last week, but fuckry happen."

Cya believe a already one week since the robbery. Police still nav no leads.

"Chichi, mi deh ya now. Yu can stop worry boh me."

"Mi so happy yu alright, Trav. Mi did miss yu." Mi hug him, smiling even though him ribs a juk mi. Mi never get fi hug him pon him birthday last week, so mi a cherish this hug.

"Gweh, a cause yu nav nobody fi put up wid yu chatting."

"I had Favi." I glanced at Favi, who glare pon Trav arms round mi. Mi glare back, holding Trav tighter.

Chuckling, Trav release mi. Him lean pon the car beside Favi. Favi light him spliff, and mi roll mi eyes.

"How've you been, Trav?" I asked, unsure how to bring up Asia.

"Gov. Mek me worry bout you." Him reach forward fi pinch me, and mi slap weh him hand.

"Yu cudn wait fi start pinch me, don't?" Mi laugh while brushing hair outta mi face. Mi hair deh mid-back now.

Trav groan as Favi smirk at me. "A me sista ino, bro. Yu nafi look pon ar like that round mi."

"Worry boh wa mi do when yu nuh round we," Favi seh, and Trav gag. "Come here," him seh, and mi gova.

Mi wrap my arms around Favi waist, craning my neck to meet his eyes. Him move the spliff from him mouth and place him lips pon mine. I hated the scent and taste of weed, so I quickly broke the kiss. A cloud of smoke disappeared between our lips.

Trav clear him throat, glancing at Marshy, who run outta the house toward him. Him chuckle as him pick her up. "A weh yu get tha likkle rat ya, Chichi?"

"Favi. She name Marshmallow, but call her Marshy," I said.

"I'll call you later." Favi kiss atop my head, then dap up Trav. "Let me know what you decide on."

"Ah, Slitta." Trav step weh so Favi could drive off. "A ina the house yu keep the likkle rat?"

"Ano waa rat! And yes," I said.

"Mi nuh believe ina house dog," him seh, and mi scoff. "Fawud a we spot."

Mi smile. "Neva know seh yu memba deso."

"Never forgot it."

"Alright, but come eat sum first." Mi tek Marshy, leading Trav inside.

"Evening, Mrs. Saanvi," Trav seh to Mama, who a watch the TV while eating crackaz and drinking lime leaf tea.

"Yu dash mi weh?" Mama ask while mi go share the food.

"Never. Mi did outta town." Trav smile while accepting the food from mi. Him talk to Mama while him eat. "A you cook this, Chichi?"

"Yes." Mi nod as him swallow the last rice grain. Only thing leff fi him eat a the plate and fork.

"Nuh wonder the food taste so bad," him seh, and mi gasp while Mama laugh.

"Nuh sit down pon cow back and cuss cow skin," Mama seh, and mi hum.

"Give me a next plate mek mi see if that one will taste better," Trav seh, and mi roll mi eyes and comply. Him shine the plate again. "It can gwan." Shrugging, him go the kitchen fi wash the plate.

"Mama, wi fi stop feed him," mi seh, and Mama chuckle before swallowing the last of her tea.

Trav return to the living room. "Later, Mrs. Saanvi and Starchy. We a go walk likkle," him seh, then we leave.

Our spot was the abandoned post office on the football field. It used to be well kept, but now the paint a strip and it mark up wid graffiti. The air always renk wid goat peepee. The last time we come here was the week before him beat Dayshawn and tell him nuh come back a Steer Town.

"How's school?" Trav ask as we sit on the concrete stairs, and mi sigh.

"Stressing... Yes, Trav, I'm studying hard, so nuh look pon mi like that," I said, and he chuckled. Silence fell over us for a few seconds, and I placed a hand on his knee. "How are you? Don't lie."

Him head hang low, sighing at the ground. "Mi cya believe she g-gone, Chichi."

Mi shoulders slump and mi draw nearer to him. Mi rub him back.

"Only Jah knows how me love Asia. When Slitta tell mi she... dead, mi bawl like a bitch ina mi cell, true yu deevn know. Day and day mi think boh all the fuckry we argue over, and mi just..."

"I know where her grave is if—"

"Yes." Trav jumped to his feet, wiping the back of his hand across his eyes. "Show me."

We walked side-by-side toward the cemetery. We passed by my family's plot, which had fresh flowers. Favi arranged weekly floral deliveries for me.

A moment later, we reach Asia grave. A weight lay pon mi soul when mi see seh her headstone put up. Trav was rigid and silent as him look pon the lilac-colored tiles. I slipped my hand in his. Him squeeze it to the point me think him wuda crush it, but I didn't grimace or move.

"I killed her," Trav seh, and mi eyes widen.

"Wa? *No.* Doh blame yuself."

"But I did. She did waa mi carry her go buy groceries, but we cuss and she change her mind. Mi still go buy it, but mi nehna go gi her it until she tell me weh she did a come from. A me cause this, Chichi, Jah knows."

"You didn't, Trav..." mi seh, and him sigh heavily.

"Remember when yu ask if Asia know mi ina the gang?" he asked, and I nodded. "She knew, but she didn't approve even doh mi only in it cause me nav a choice."

"No choice?" mi ask, and him inhale a deep breath, his grip tightening before it slackened.

"When mi did ina grade eight, mi... father... file fi me and mi likkle brother. Wi find out mi a jacket, so him tek him youth and cut. Mommy start do her thing fi provide fi wi, and ano seh mi ungrateful, but it tek a toll pon mi. Either way, the money weh shi did a mek neva enough. Mi lose mi scholarship and cudn afford fi send miself go school. Mi join the gang fi try stack food fast, but mi get stuck."

Mi brows furrow. "Stuck?"

"A one way outta the game, but mi neva waa this forever." Trav gulped as him continue look pon Asia grave. "When mi did ina the pen, the only thing keep mi peace a thinking bout Asia, you, and the likkle music from the guard radio. Me waa try do music, but dat hard, too."

"Why?"

"One way outta the game, Chichi," he repeated coldly. "And the Boss nago let mi go—"

"Wa yu mean? Me will talk to Favi," mi seh, and Trav chuckle sadly.

"Ano Favian me a talk boh, Chichi."

"Then—"

"Yu too fass." Him release mi hand and pinch mi. While mi rub the spot, him stoop beside the grave. Him kiss two of him fingers, pressing dem against Asia's name. "Blood afi run fi yu, baby."

"Trav, please don't put yuself ina trouble again," mi beg, and him snap round, glaring.

"Mi nuh believe ina letting things slide, Chichi. Think nobody can fuck round mi woman and it go so? She deevn experience life yet," Trav seh, his focus shifting to something behind me.

Mi glance over my shoulder at Miss Olive. Sas Crise! She was so thin, almost unrecognizable.

Miss Olive smiled weakly as she stopped beside me. Her smile washed away as Trav stood. "Mi nuh know wa she did eva see ina yu."

Trav sigh, unable to meet Miss Olive's eyes. "Condolences, Miss Olive."

"Wa mi fi say to that?" She walked toward him when him nuh ansa. She grab him arms, staring at him through frantic eyes while shaking his body. "Wa mi supposed to say to that, Trav?"

Trav pried her hands off him, then hugged her. He held her close as she broke down. Miss Olive's wails were as loud as they were at the funeral, and it brought tears to my eyes.

"E-everybody a seh dem sorry and a wish dem condolences, but nun a dat cya bring back mi one likkle roast breadfruit. Wa me supposed to seh, Trav?" she cried.

"I-I don't know, Miss Olive. Mi wudn wish this pain on anybody, Jah knows," Trav seh, his voice low. He held her until she calmed down, pulling away and leaving a wet spot on his shirt.

"Me a move go Hanover. Mi shuda leff long time, maybe Asia wuda alive now. As much as a that same house mi husband tek him last breath ina, it did hard fi leff Steer Town cause it remind me of him. Now all this place bring me a pain. Mi cya tek it anymore."

"Mek mi know if yu need anything at all, Miss Olive," Trav said, and I hummed even doh mi nav dry doodoo ina mi ass.

"It's fine, dears. Mi brother a come up here next week fi help mi move, but mi want the two a unu listen to mi carefully. If unu eva get the chance fi leave Steer Town, do so and don't look back. Unu young and have unu wul life a head of unu. Doh fall in with the wrong crowd." Miss Olive stayed with us for a moment longer before she left.

Me and Trav start head back to my yaad. Waa police car passed we ina the Square, heading toward another community.

"As mi see tha babylon boy deh, weh police did a do pon yu lane?" Trav asked.

Nuh mek yu left hand know wa yu right hand do.

"Smaddy bruk ina the house last week," I said before I could bite my tongue. Cho, blousecup! Mi neva waa tell him! Him already stressed, now this!

"The fuck?! Smaddy afi dead!"

"No. Yu forget where yaa come from?" Mi grab him arm, pulling him to a stop.

"Mi know Slitta naa mek nun do yu. And the other smaddy mi care fa, dead, so mi nuh fear death. Whoever rob yu get fuck."

"Doh tell Favi, please," I said as we resumed walking.

"Fi wa? We a go find whichever pussy do this. How much dem tek? Mi waa know how much shot fi geem."

"Trav, mek it stay," mi plead.

"Me might nuh mek it outta Steer Town, but yu nuh come so far fi smaddy tek that from yu. Mi naa drop it. Yu sick ina yu head?" Him kiss him teeth. "Walk up so mi can liff from yaso."

I sighed, worry embedding itself deep inside me. Why mi chat so much?

Our thoughts filled the silence between us until we reach mi yaad.

Mi smile when mi see Chezzy pon the veranda. She smiled and stood from the plastic chair. She run off the veranda and jump ina Trav arms, almost knocking him off his feet. My brows raised as Trav wrap him arms around her lower back while Chezzy hold him tighter around the neck.

Trav chuckle. "A really you dis, Sandra?"

"Exactly. A you dis, Chezzy?" mi ask while she pull away fi stare at Trav.

"I heard what happened. I'm so sorry," Chezzy seh, and Trav went grim.

"Just life. Yu good?" Trav ask, and Chezzy nodded, making my brows raise.

"Yes, I'm good. You?"

"Yah. Yu did miss mi, Sandra?" Trav smirk.

"I-I-" Chezzy stutter, and mi laugh.

"Of course, she did miss yu," mi seh, and she glare.

"Mi neva miss him," Chezzy seh angrily. She cross her arms, stomping toward the veranda.

"Later, Trav," I said, but him nuh answer. Mi look from Chezzy to Trav, who have him attention hooked pon her. Mi snap mi fingers in front of him face, and him shake him head, then look pon mi.

"Y-yah..." Trav pinch me, running away as mi grab a stone fi throw at him.

Chapter Twenty-Nine

CHAYANNE

"Why you deh so far from home?" me ask Yolo. She live a Highgate, St. Mary. She nav no reason fi deh a Ochi after school.

"Me go buy sum fi a project, check one a mi gyal, and now mi a wait pon Mommy." Yolo grinned, hugging me. She frown when mi quickly pull weh. "A wa? Mi mouth smell a pussy?"

"No. Mi just nuh waa none a yu gyal dem see me and try beat me," mi joke, and she pause cupping a hand before her mouth fi roll her eyes.

"Mi tired fi tell yu fi stop mek jokes bout abuse. A only me can do it cause mi traumatize," she seh jokingly, but hurt underlay her tone.

"Sorry."

"Yu good, Number One! Mi neva start run joke until mi quinceañera." She smirk, throwing an arm over Chezzy shoulder. "How yu naa pay mi nuh mind? Yu look happier than usual these days. Yu start plan we wedding?"

"Yes. Chichi a wi flower girl. When yaa plan fi breed mi?" Chezzy ask, and Yolo kiss her teeth.

"Mi hate roleplay wid straight gyal— Ratid! Nuh Mommy dat? Unu later. Mek mi run go over deh, cause she look tired." Yolo run toward waa high color woman, who ina long sleeves.

Mi go find taxi wid Chezzy. To how it pack, we afi text each other so dem people ya cya fass ina wi business.

SISTUR: Still cya believe him mash yu up.
Me fraid a sex now.

Until yu buss it open wid wa mi tell yu!

Chezzy sighed, and me glance pon her. One time, she did a talk to one a Dayshawn friend, but Aunty Simone mek a big fuss, so Chezzy stay to herself now.

Me? No sah. Gwan fuck fi wi.

Couple minutes later, the taxi drop mi ina the Square. Mi a go visit my man. Mi nuh see him since Sunday, and mi miss him. Mi step toward Godsto, pausing fi release mi hair from the grab clip. Continuing the journey, mi seh evening to everybody mi pass, including Trav Mommy. She too drugs out fi recognize mi.

Trav and Earzas deh by Favi gate a listen music and smoke. Trav spot mi first, raising a brow. "Weh yago?"

"Mi come read meter," mi seh, and Earzas chuckle while Trav lips pull into a line.

"Yu feel yu funny?"

"Hilarious," I corrected. "Obviously, a Favi mi come look fa."

"Mi nuh think dat a waa good idea right now, Chichi."

"Why not?"

"Ano waa good time. Yu nuh need no more explanation," Earzas seh.

"Mi got this, Eltham," Trav seh, and mi realize mi nehna call the man the right name all this time.

"Come outta the way or me a tell Favi unu nuh allow me inside," mi warn, and Eltham sigh while Travis and me have a stare down.

"Yu stubbornness a go fuck yu over one day, and mi nago dih deh fi save yu," Travis said sternly.

"Mi nuh waa yu save mi. Afta yano hero." Mi kiss mi teeth, stepping past dem into my man yard. The grill open, so mi walk inside.

Movement come from the kitchen. Mi drop mi bag ina the sofa before walking into the kitchen. Favi was shirtless with his back turned toward me. His muscles flexed as he reached for something in the fridge, creating an illusion of the snake moving.

"Hey." I smiled at his back, but he didn't answer. My brows knitted. "Fav—"

He spun around, his eyes storming. Fear gripped my spine, and I swallowed. Favi wouldn't hurt me, but I hated being in his presence when he was mad.

"Are you okay?" I asked gently.

Him close the fridge, walking outta the kitchen. Mi bout fi follow when the wine bottle on the counter catch me attention. This was the newest bottle in the line of fruity spirits. I wasn't much of a wine drinker, but when I was in Kingston, he made me try a bottle.

Smiling at the memory, mi return to the living room. Favi was on the sofa. A pistol deh pon the table before him, and a cleaning brush ina him hand.

I sat beside my bag that was on the opposite sofa. "Favi..."

Favi tek up the gun, disassembling it.

"My period's late," mi blurt, and him freeze, his eyes dragging to mine.

"You're pregnant?" Him nuh sound surprised or angry. Him tone and expression unreadable.

"I'm joking. It's the birth control. Dr. Merlgrove say it's normal until mi body get use to it," mi seh, and him stare pon mi for a few seconds.

"Chayanne, I'm only asking this once, so listen carefully. Why have you been lying to me?" Favi placed the gun on the table. The barrel was turned toward me.

I balled a fistful of my dress into my hands, forcing down a large lump as I looked at him.

"It's not loaded." His emotionless tone did nothing to help my unease.

"When me lie to yu, Favi?" I asked.

"I hate when people lie to me, Chayanne."

"I'm not lying."

"You have a tell," he said, and my brows furrowed.

"A tell?"

"You tense when you're lying," he said, and I gulped, surprised him pay that much attention to me.

"Believe wa yu waa believe..."

"You got robbed and nuh think yu shuda tell me?" He chuckled as I froze.

"H-how yu know that?"

"Doesn't matter."

Travis! Watch me and tha mawga bwoy deh! Next time him come a mi yaad, mi naa feed him!

"I was going to tell you, but mi nuh badda cause me nuh waa you do anything to anybody. Leave it alone, Favi. A the same thing me tell Travis. The police a handle it—"

Favi snatched the gun off the table, assembling it.

"F-Favi..." I whispered, scooting further into the sofa. It too late fi Travis come rescue me?!

Him put the clip ina the gun. "Yu know yu father, Chayanne?"

"No," I answered, and he flicked off the safety. The chilling *click* dropped my temperature by a few degrees.

"I don't like it when people lie to me, Chayanne," he repeated slowly.

"Me nav no reason fi lie to yu." I dragged my eyes from the pistol to him, my brows knitting.

Him lean back ina the sofa, resting the gun pon the armrest. Curling his finger around the trigger, him tap the muzzle against the armrest. "You've been lying to me for weeks."

I licked my dry lips. "W-wa yado?"

"What does it look like?"

My heart slammed against my chest. It was a miracle mi cardiac nuh arrest mi yet. My petrified eyes darted to his hardened ones, and my chest heaved. I'd only seen him look at his father like this. Tears filled my eyes. "Favi, p-please move the gun. I didn't mean to lie to you."

He stared at me for what felt like the longest moment, but was only a few seconds. Then, him look at the gun. Him flick on the safety, and I released a jagged breath. Him stand, walking away. "Lock the door when yaa leave."

Gasping, mi jump to mi feet. Mi wipe weh mi tears as anger replaced fear. "Yu nuh care?! Yu nav nun fi seh?!"

He continued walking. "I have nothing to say to you."

"Doh walk weh, Favio. Yu been a ask mi wa wrong, and see mi come clean deh. Yaa gwan like me keep more secret than you!"

Favio spun around, glaring menacingly. Him take long, powerful strides toward me, and me step backward until mi hit the wall. His nostrils flared as he narrowed his eyes at me. I balled my fists at my sides, glaring while breathing as hard as him. Anger blurred my vision, I wasn't seeing him clearly.

"Watch yu fucking mouth when yaa address mi. Nuh feel yaa mi woman fi size up wid mi certain way, zeen? Yaa just smaddy mi fuck, Chichi, know yu place."

My fists slackened and my shoulders sagged.

My lips parted, but no words came out.

Tears filled my eyes as he turned and walked away, leaving me weak while his words beat me down.

A tear fell from my eye, splattering onto the tile and joining my broken heart. One by one, more tears fell while I stared aghast at his back.

He disappeared, and a door slammed from upstairs.

His words weighed down my body, forcing me to my knees. Coldness seeped into me, but my brain could only process one thing.

I was nothing but Favio's whore.

Chapter Thirty

CHAYANNE

Chezzy slap mi pon mi batty wid a pillow. "Yu cya lay dung ina the bed forever. Get up."

"Leave me alone," mi groan, covering mi head wid the pillow mi did a lay dung pon. The movie Chezzy put on fi distract me a annoy mi. If mi did have the energy, mi kick her laptop off the bed.

Mi chest plate a bun mi. How could something so beautiful become this ugly?

I'd been wallowing in self-pity since yesterday. Mi cudn show mi face to Trav when mi walk past him a cry.

Despite how Favio diss me... I missed him.

I missed his voice. His rare yet beautiful smile. Him calling me *'fiore'* like I was the most beautiful girl he ever saw. His gentle kisses, and the rough ones, too.

I missed seeing him working hard for his company. How his eyes brightened when speaking about his snakes. Raging when a football match wasn't playing how he wanted it to.

I missed *him*.

Mi heart feel like it a get rip out and step pon with studded boots every time mi think bout how we nuh deh anymore... If we ever were.

"Yago alright, Chichi. Stop waste yu tears pon a man weh diss yu. Afta ano one man ina the world. You will get over him," Chezzy seh, and mi sniffle.

"I don't want to get over him. I love him."

Chezzy froze, but I was too drained to care. Mi nuh know when mi fall in love with Favio Welsh. Maybe it was the first time I saw him. Maybe it was when he broke my heart. All I knew was mi cudn imagine love if it wasn't with him.

Marshy scrape the door, and mi sigh while getting up. Mi open mi room door, staring at her through swollen eyes. She bark toward the front door.

"Come, Marshy," I said, and she barked while me dry mi tears, then grab her leash. Mi bring her outta door, and she walk up and down until she find a spot. Me look weh so she can have privacy.

A minute later, waa car drive pass, stopping at mi gate. The person weh exit nearly mek mi drop the leash.

"Aunty Kenzie!" mi exclaim, grabbing Marshy and running over.

"Chichi baby!" Aunty pulled me into a big hug, being mindful of Marshy. She put on likkle weight and look nice.

Mi smile against her skin, cocoa butter filling my nostrils. Mi nuh smile since Favio leff mi; neva know mi still capable of it.

Chezzy run offa the veranda, joining the hug. "Aunty!"

"Look how unu get big!" Aunty held us tighter.

"Aunty a gwan like she nuh see we last year." Chuckling, Chezzy pull away.

"Long time dat." Aunty turn away from Chezzy to pat Marshy's head. "When yu get puppy?" Aunty ask, and Chezzy open her mouth fi lie.

"A friend gave me. She name Marshmallow," I said while Aunty glance pon the taximan, who a exit the car.

"Unu help mi tek out the suitcase dem so mi can pay tha miserable man ya."

We help Aunty bring the bag dem ina the house. After Mama create excitement over her eldest daughter, Aunty Simone and the twins visit. For hours, we chat and laugh. We Aunty dem scold we bout the lying and disappearing, and me and Chezzy promise nufi dweet again. Ano like mi have nuh weh fi sneak weh to.

"Yu father hear seh yu deh ya?" mi ask Aunty Kenzie, and she raise a brow at me. Mi point pon the bat weh deh pon the ceiling.

"Mek mi father rest in peace nuh," Aunty seh, and Mama chuckle as she glance pon the bat.

Laughing, mi stand. Mi walk into mi room, closing the door behind me.

"Mi can get this?" Chezzy ask, smiling at a green hoodie in my closet.

"A Favio own..." mi seh, and her smile drop.

"Let's burn it," she seh, and mi grab it, holding it against my chest.

"Aunty ready fi leave," mi seh, and she sigh before exiting the room.

After our guests leff, me and Aunty Kenzie go visit Mommy.

"You alright, Chichi baby?" Aunty stroke a withering rose petal while mi nod.

"We can leave now? Mi afi study," mi seh, and she smile while we leave.

"Mi so proud of how hardworking yu be, Chichi baby. From yu likkle bit, we neva afi force yu fi do anything relating to school. Tate a send down the money sometime ina this month, so nuh worry bout the subjects."

"Mi happy fi hear dat. How him Mommy?"

"Better. She come out of the hospital last night," she said, and I smiled.

It faded as we approached the Square. A group of people lingered before the popular wall. Me cudn see one of them good, but I could sense Favio anywhere.

Him pause bringing a spliff to him mouth, eyes darting around before settling on me. Shadows fell over his face. I couldn't see if he was hurting like me.

The only thing me could tell was that him have two longtime big woman stand beside him. Dem a community mattress. Dem stiff wig fava the coconut brush Mama used to shine the floor wid before it get tiled. Yes, other woman cling to other man, but why dem afi hook up pon him?

"Nuh Trav dat? Mek wi call to him." Aunty cross the road.

Gulping, mi trail behind her. Mi eyes focus pon mi Crocs.

"As mi seh, any man weh fuck batty or suck pussy fi dead," one of them declared, and hums traveled through the group. "Get wa maa seh, Slitta?"

Mi snap mi head up. His focus was on me as he exhaled a cloud of smoke. Wa dis Favio deh yaso a chat bout wid dem man ya? Afta him nuh fraid fi nyam mi like Sunday dinner and lick mi like dessert.

"A battyman watch next man," Favio said coolly, and some men chuckled.

Aunty stop a short distance from the group. "Trav, come here."

Trav eyes widen. Him tek quick strides toward us. Him give Aunty a big hug before dem start talk. Mi nuh know wa dem a talk bout cause my focus deh elsewhere.

Favio's unreadable expression and the red mark on his neck.

Someone was speaking to him, but he didn't look away from me.

I couldn't look away, either.

The surrounding space closed in. The wind blew away everyone and left us by ourselves.

Until waa broad face gyal step before him, breaking our trance.

Mi tear mi gaze offa him, glaring at the woman. She seh sum to him, and him look at her, nodding. His eyes drifted to mine, a glint crossing them before him walk away with the two tuff turbit.

My jaw clenched, my hands balling into fists as I stepped forward.

"Chichi baby?" Aunty furrow her brows as mi retract mi step. "You nuh hear Trav a talk to yu?"

Brow raised, mi look pon Trav. Why him eye swollen?

"You good?" him ask.

"Mi good," I said tightly.

Him jaw tick as him look at the group a man, then at Aunty. "Me will see unu tonight. Lata."

Aunty smile as Trav walk weh. "You neva tell mi him a stay at the house again."

"Him cya bring himself fi go home cause him afi past Asia yaad," mi seh.

"Sad what happened," Aunty seh, and mi nod.

With each step away from the Square, Favio's face plagued my mind.

Just like the first night I met him.

Aunty ina the dining hall a talk to Mama. Chezzy and Trav ina mi room, keeping my company while mi push round the peas pon mi dinner plate.

"Yu nafi bark afta dem like that," Trav seh as Chezzy hang up her phone.

"Doh talk boh wa yu nuh know boh," Chezzy hiss. Her brother dem ask fi help wid homework, and she deny them. Dem neva ask fi help when she come from school earlier, so shi nuh waa dem ask when she come a mi yaad fi spend a relaxing weekend.

"Unu cya put the laptop pon sum better?" Trav ask a moment later, and Chezzy kiss her teeth.

"Nobody neva invite yu over here."

"Nobody nuh invite you either."

"Me a tek care of her."

"Me, too."

Mi groan loudly, tearing my gaze from the text thread with Yolo fi glare pon mi bredda and sista. "Unu can stop, please?" mi ask, and dem stop bickering.

"Ah, but mi a change dis." Trav get up outta the chair, approaching the bed.

"No!" Chezzy grab her laptop, scooting further away pon the bed.

Trav drop him long self pon mi bed, and the two a dem fight fi the laptop. Mi kiss mi teeth and come outta the room. If the laptop bruk, Chezzy better prepare fi get lick from Aunty. Mi go ina the bathroom, sitting pon the side of the bath while calling Yolo.

"Yu still a bawl ova man?" Yolo ask, and mi sigh.

"Yu nafi be so insensitive right now," mi mutter. A already one week since Favio leff mi. Mi wish mi cuda seh mi a do better, but that would be a lie.

"Sorry, Number One. This a why mi always tell yu fi give bun just in case. Mi nuh like when yu cry. Dry your face, please?" She smiled after I did. "Ketch pretty face! If him nuh love yu, me love yu, alright?"

"Mi love you, too. How the court case?" mi ask, and her smile disappear.

"Today dem bring up how him tek her from Portland and isolate her—"

"Yolanda," came a female's voice in her background while sum drop ina mine.

"Me nuh tell yu fi lack chat when yu see mi pon the phone?" Yolo kiss her teeth. "I'm starting to hate women as much as I do men. Lata, Number One." She blew me a kiss before hanging up.

Walking to the sink, mi wash mi face. Mi sigh at mi reflection, hating my puffy eyes. Mi wish mi cuda lie seh a period a mek mi this emotional, but it still late.

Mi about fi exit when the scissors ketch mi attention, and mi grab it. Turning away from the mirror, mi cut mi hair until mi mind tell mi fi stop.

Satisfied, mi put down the scissors. Mi return to mi room, pausing at the doorway with knitted brows. Chezzy lay dung pon her belly while Trav a massage her lower back. Dem look pon mi, and dem eyes widen.

Chezzy push Trav off, rushing toward me. Frowning, she grab some of the blunt strands between her fingers. "Wa happen to yu hair, Chichi?"

"Nothing." Mi side-step her and lay pon the bed. Mi resume the movie while forcing miself fi finish eat.

"Come back yaso, Cheesy. And tek up mi earring, weh yu mek drop out. It deh a the dresser foot." Trav pour alcohol ina him hand while Chezzy kiss her teeth, taking up the earring. When she offer it to him, him look pon ar like she fool. "Mi hand full of alcohol. Put it in."

She skin up her face. "No."

"But yu waa mi rub the pain outta yu big back?"

Sneering, Chezzy grab him ears and roughly put in the earring. Smirking as Trav wince, she lay down. "Tek time, and watch weh yu hand dem go."

"Nuh feel mi waa touch yu," Trav hiss, despite gently massaging her.

"Wa do yu?" I asked, my voice hoarse.

"This idiot mek mi drop offa the bed," Chezzy hiss, before dem start cuss again.

Sighing, mi look away from them. The food hard fi eat, so mi rest the plate aside. Bringing my knees toward mi chest, mi lay mi forehead pon mi knees and close my eyes. Trav and Chezzy too busy fi hear mi sniffling. I was thankful they cared about me, but I didn't want them here.

I wanted Favio.

And he wanted other women.

Every time mi awake, mi heart break off piece by piece, crumbling into nothingness. A waa painful reminder seh mi fi keep mi legs closed and mi heart pon a leash when it come to man. Mi hate fi compare the two, but as much as

Dayshawn a crosses, him never disrespect me like this before.

Sighing, mi get outta the bed and immediately regret it. Lately, all mi waa do a lay dung and think about Favio.

Chezzy gasped, and me turn round fi eye her. "Go bathroom," she said.

Mi sigh and go the bathroom. Mi pull dung mi panties and sidung pon the toilet. A red spot was on my panties.

God, yu neva mek no mistake! It a go be a long three days, but imagine the shame me wuda feel fi go to the man and tell him mi a carry belly fi him? Me rather go drink hot beer mix wid black pepper.

Smiling, mi grab a tampon. Mi fix up miself.

"Yu good, girl? We nafi bother go nuh weh," Chezzy seh from the other side of the door.

"Mi good." Mi wash mi hand before exiting. "No baby to the doll."

"Mi surprise yu period come. Way how you did have dat man a leff him pickney dem ina yu like yaa nursery," Chezzy seh, and mi chuckle dryly.

Truth be told, me did like it. When dat man a sink him big hood ina Fat Ma, mi senses float weh.

After Chezzy grab her jacket, we walk to the Square so she can buy sum from waa shop. While waiting, me stand at the door a tek cool breeze.

"December eighteen! That a next week Saturday at six p.m., is a big birthday bash pon Steer Town top football field! Ladies, bring a friend and unu wire waistline! Man dem, if unu doh know how fi dagga, rifle walk unu wukliss self back a unu yaad!" announced the promoter from a car exiting Godsto.

Chezzy chuckle as she stand beside me. "Since exam season start, we stop go out. If yu up fi it, we can go like how a the week before mi birthday."

"N—" My eyes widened as a BMW drove off Godsto, slowing a few feet away. It wasn't any of the three cars he frequented, but I knew this was Favio. My heart raced, and I stood more upright. Maybe I should—

The car sped off.

My shoulders slumped.

"Let's go." Chezzy held my hand, leading us away.

When we reach my house and lay on my bed, she hug mi. Trav did leave a few hours ago, so we could watch the vampire movie widout complaints.

Minutes later, mi phone ring. Mi sigh before blindly answering. "Hello?"

"Chichi?" came the voice, and mi sit upright.

"A who?" Chezzy whisper, and mi hold up a finger.

"Yes?" mi answer.

"Been a while. A car's coming to get you in an hour," they said.

"But me nuh—"

"Dat good. One hour." They hung up.

Cho, blousecup! Mi nuh waa go nuh weh, but mi know better than fi decline. Him will find mi yard, and mi nuh waa get ina trouble wid Aunty. She already realize sum do me, and mi did lie seh exam a stress mi.

Mi explain the call to Chezzy. Wi mek up a lie seh we a go study wid Yolo, and Aunty allow we fi leave. An hour later, we enter the house.

Mi fume the entire time mi sidung ina the chair, glaring at my hairdresser, who a grumble while she trim mi ends. She cya believe we spend years a work pon mi hair, fi mi chop it so nastily.

Ignoring her, mi seh to Chezzy, "Yes, let's go to the party."

"Yes!" Chezzy cheered, and I chuckled deviously.

Favio feel him still have waa claim to mi? Ah. Watch this.

Chapter Thirty-One

CHAYANNE

"Mek sure yu reach back by ten."

Gasping, mi turn round fi face Aunty, who ignore me as she continue play wid Marshy. "A eight o'clock!"

"Mi seh ten, Chayanne Arya," she stated firmly, and mi fight the urge fi kiss mi teeth as mi go mi room.

Mi cya stand Aunty sometime! Mi nuh know who shi feel a come back ten. Pon a Saturday? Must be joking! Me will come back eleven.

Smirking, mi spray on some perfume, then grab mi phone. Aunty did ask weh mi get it from, and mi tell ar Trav gimi. The only reason mi still a use it a cause it tek picture pretty, so mi hope the crosses nuh feel mi waa use the piece of phone. Hissing my teeth, mi return to the living room.

"Check if she have on tights, Kenzie," Mama seh, and Aunty give me a look.

Sighing, mi liff mi dress. "Happy?" mi ask, and Mama smile while nodding.

"Later." Mi walk outta the house and head down the lane. When me reach waa dark spot, mi tek off the tights and stuff it ina mi bag. Satisfied, mi continue the journey to the ball ground.

Mi find Chezzy, and we wul a vibes until the party stop go as planned. For starters, too many people deh ya. The music deh waa deafening volume, and every turn mi turn, smaddy sweaty or gyrating body bounce fimi. Me so annoyed. If mi neva have Chezzy, mi leff long time!

She a whine up her body ina the small circle a few feet away from me. She ina waa combat boots, black fishnet stockings, waa likkle bit a shorts, and waa green crop top. Me ina sneakers and a nice dress Aunty carry fimi.

The selector change the song, and everybody do waa routine dance while me stand up like statue. Poor me cya dirt bounce. Every time mi try, it look like gravel.

Chezzy realize mi naa dance. She tear weh from the crowd fi come yell ina mi ears. "Mek we get some drinks!"

We push we way through the crowd toward the makeshift bar. Chezzy order three white rum shots — one fi she and two fimi. After wi swallow the shots, we dance toward the raunchy crowd, stopping in the middle.

As a Coolie, mi a probably the biggest lightweight. The effects of the alcohol kick in fast. Mi neva push weh the man weh grab mi by the waist. Placing my hands on my knees, mi bend ova and gi him the whine a him life! Him buddy a poke mi ass, but mi deevn care to how mi nice! Eltham come try pull the man offa mi, and mi tell him fi stay outta mi water waistline business!

No sah, look how life nice! Me did really a mek one man stress me out? Lady Saw wuda shame a mi!

As a bad dancer, mi enjoy mi time wid the man while people cheer we on. Chezzy was the loudest. When him start gwan like him waa pick mi up and fling me a grung like sketel, Chezzy pull mi weh. All smiles, she carry we to waa less populated area.

"Watch big—" Her smile fell as she look behind mi. "Dayshawn deh here."

Eyes bulging, mi spin round. Mi nearly tip ova, but Chezzy hold mi steady. Mi eyes widen at Dayshawn. Sas Crise! Nuh kill the man come fi kill me?!

Wait, no. Him a dry hump waa girl. Ano me him come fa.

Him musi feel the look of disgust cause him look toward me. Mi yelp and spin round, forcing down the vomit weh nearly come up.

Chezzy sigh. "Him a come over here."

Mi inhale a big breath, prepping myself for the encounter. A weh Trav deh when mi need him?!

"Chichi." Dayshawn rest him hand pon mi shoulder.

Mi slowly turn around, gasping. "*Dayshawn*, mi neva see yu! Wa yaa do here?"

"Come check yu." Him scowl at Chezzy. "Pree?"

"Deh ya," she seh curtly, and him scoff.

Him eyes soften as him look pon me. "Been a while."

Mi chuckle nervously. "Weh yu did deh?"

"Bagga things gwan, b. Fawud ova deso—"

"She nuh waa talk to yu," Chezzy seh.

"Me waa talk to him!" I declared, and their eyes widened.

"See why yu fi mind yu business when it come to me and mi woman?" Dayshawn smirk while Chezzy glare.

"Nuh talk to her like that, Dayshawn. Chezzy, mi soon come. Go get me a water, please?" mi ask, and she shake her head before walking away. Mi look pon Dayshawn, urging him to speak. The world swayed before me, but mi notice how him much shorter than—

"Did afi go mi granny funeral overseas. Sorry mi neh tell yu," him seh, and mi release a quiet breath.

"Yu tell mi yu granny dem dead," mi seh, and him gasp, covering it wid a chuckle.

Nuh hide yu stick and lick man.

"One a dem did bat fi the same team... Weh yaa look pon mi so fa? Mi nav no reason fi lie to yu, b. Come here."

I didn't move.

Him step forward, pulling me into a hug. Him chest nuh hard and nice like—

Mi force miself fi relax, willing my skin to stop crawling.

"Nuh throw weh wi relationship, b. A modern times, everybody a get fuck pon. When yu do the Maths, yu nago find nobody loyal like me," him seh.

Mi close mi eyes as the image of Favi walking away wid two woman filled my mind. "When it did matter most, yu neva show me dat."

"Huh? Yu know me love you. And me change," him seh, and mi tear miself away, tears pricking my eyes.

"Yu nuh love me!" I yelled at his stupid face. Mi eight, nine, and ten man!

"Calm down, b..." Him pull me into him hold. Before my head could meet his bird chest, him arms get roughly pried off me. Him body fly back, landing with a *thud* in the dirt.

Mi blink rapidly. White rum can mek people hallucinate?

Dayshawn propped himself up on his palms, his eyes widening. Mi look side a mi, gasping at bad breed Favio. He had a gun in his hand.

"Why the fuck are you touching her?" Favio hissed through clenched teeth.

"A mi g-girl, g," Dayshawn rushed out. His voice didn't sound like his own.

"*Your* girl?"

"Stop..." Holding my pounding head, I groaned.

Favio turn him head to me, but keep him glare pon Dayshawn, who a shake like leaf. "Stay the fuck outta dis," he hissed, and mi shut up like obedient pickney, surprised mi head stop pound.

"Yu can have her if yu want her, m-mi g. Mi nuh waa trouble ova no bitch," Dayshawn seh, and mi gasp.

"*Bitch*?" Favio tightened his grip around the trigger.

"Favio!" Mi tremble when him look pon me, his eyes raging. "Stop! Please."

Favio's jaw ticked, and he looked at Dayshawn while lowering his gun. "Nuh mek mi see yu face again."

Nodding, Dayshawn scramble to him feet. Him run weh leff him ego.

Favio scowled until Dayshawn disappeared, then tuck him gun ina him waist. Him hold mi face ina him hand, and I leaned into his touch as him wipe beneath mi eyes. "You good?" Him eyes narrow after mi nod. "Are you fucking stupid?! Why the fuck would you go this far from the party with a youth?! A him yu did a whine pon?"

Tears rushed to my eyes. "N-no..."

Him release waa jagged breath, pulling me into a tight hug. The coldness of his watch seeped into my skin. His signature cologne wafted into my nostrils, clouding all rational thoughts.

"What am I going to do with you?" he asked, and mi mumble against him chest. "What?" Him pull me away, and my insides churned.

Before I could move away, everything rushed up my throat and spewed on his shirt and face.

Chapter Thirty-Two

FAVIO

Chayanne made me crazy.

Without her. And with her.

When I wasn't around her. And when I was.

It made me do obsessive things like watching her sleep.

She was beautiful. Even now, with her forehead sprinkled with drops of sweat, and her hair splayed above her shoulder. I hated the length, but she was still perfect. A wasteman saw that and thought it permitted him to touch my girl.

I gritted my teeth, my anger rushing through my veins. That night she tightly clutched my shirt, I made a vow to better distance her from this lifestyle, yet I almost killed someone in front of her. Sometimes, I acted senselessly when my judgment got clouded. I wasn't always like this. It was injected into me like poison, then it corrupted me whole...

"Favio!"

My name was called from somewhere.

"Amore mio, control them—"

Hands pulled at my body.

"Me?! A you mek dem like dis! You control dem!"

Bruised and raw, my knuckles stung as they pounded against skin.

"Cazzo—"

Gravel crunched from behind me. Strong arms wrapped around me, peeling me off the groaning thing.

My breathing was ragged as a haze lifted from my eyes, revealing the results of my destruction. A man was lying on the ground. His nose was crooked. His lips were busted. Blood smeared his face.

Panting, I turned to glare at the person who dared to restrain me. It was Papà.

"Fabiano!" A woman rushed toward the body. She dropped to her knees, clutching his sputtering frame. She barked orders for Papà's soldati to grab a first aid kit.

"Mamma—" I stepped forward, but Papà held me back.

Papà tugged me into the nearby shed where Mamma stored garden tools. "Figlio, what happened?" he asked in Italian, what we always spoke whenever Mamma wasn't around.

It took me a minute to gather my thoughts before I remembered all that made me see red. My fists clenched as my eyes darted to the door. I needed to be out there. I needed to kill Fabiano. Slowly. Painfully.

"He put his hands on Catty," I gritted out in Italian.

"A girl shouldn't come between you and your blood, regardless of what he did."

"That doesn't make sense."

"It does."

"How?"

Papà sighed, sitting atop the table beside the door. "I would've knocked sense into Ambi. You shouldn't have gotten involved in whatever they have going on."

"She's my girlfriend."

"You don't know why he hurt her?" His brows raised as I shook my head.

"It doesn't matter why. He put his hands on her, and I'm going to kill him."

"Figlio, your problem is you don't care about many things. When you do, you care too much. It makes you take things to an extreme—"

"Then you should understand," I said, and he scoffed. My nails sank into my

palms as my fists tightened.

"Figlio, you're not a kid anymore. You're eighteen. You can't resort to violence when you're pushed to your limit. Suppose you killed Fabiano? He's one less problem for me to deal with, but how would that make your mother feel?"

I didn't reply. Not because I didn't want to answer, but because I didn't know what to say.

"I'm sending you to Italy," he said, and my gaze snapped to his.

"I'm in second year—"

"You can do online classes or transfer to an Italian college. I hate to admit it, but you and Fabiano are fucked in the head—"

"Because of you," I muttered, and he pretended not to hear.

"You more than him because all your rationale disappears once something manages to make you lose your composure— Stai zitto e ascolta. Someone's always cleaning up after you and Fabiano, and Diana has had enough. Neither you nor Fabiano will ruin my marriage. Figlio, I said to shut up and listen.

"You will go to Italy and stay with my older brother for a few months. Years. However fucking long it takes to get you under control. You were raised how all men in la famiglia were, and we turned out fine. You should be no different, so I will try to fix this mistake." Papà stood, brushing off his suit. "Scusati con tuo fratello."

"No. He's no brother of mine," I spat in English, and Papà shrugged.

"Fine by me. I wouldn't either." He laughed. As the door opened and Mamma entered, he sobered up.

She didn't look at me as she crossed her arms, raising her chin as she met Papà's eyes. He nodded, and Mamma hummed before leaving.

Her rejection rooted itself deep within me. She never ignored me before, and now she seemed done.

I hated the look on her face. I never wanted to experience it again.

I willingly went to Italy. I spent time underground with the Italian mafia a Welsh built from the ground generations ago. I did things I could never admit to. I learned things I had to take to the grave. In those two years, I understood the conduct of made men.

Antaro was right. I wasn't provoked easily, but when I was, I released all my pent-up rage on whosoever was in my path. I was lesser than a sociopath; Nikola's psychologists and rounds of shock therapy proved I was born this way.

Antaro had fed into it when he first placed a gun in my hand, forcing me to kill a man who owed him money. I was thirteen, and that was my initiation. My fate was sealed when Mamma washed my hands clean.

Thankfully, at age twenty, I returned to Jamaica as a different man. I was made. I had better control of my impulses and violent urges.

When I stepped out of the airport, Antaro smirked. I didn't grace him with a response, but the need for vengeance boiled in me. He was the one who'd cheer on Fabiano and me when we fought. He was the one who taught us how to shoot. He taught us the right-of-passage of la famiglia, then turned us away when he could no longer control us.

Fucking Antaro. I loathed him.

I had space in my heart only for Mamma, who looked me in the eye for the first time in years. She knew I was doing better, and I wanted to continue being better for her.

I was displaying those unhinged traits again. I thought I was doing better.

No. I was doing better. Circumstances made me snap at Chayanne — the girl who'd grown to become the last person I wanted to cause pain.

No woman ever made me feel half of the emotions Chayanne did. No one else knew how to piss me off and make me happy within the next minute. No one else pushed my buttons and mek mi afi wul dat.

But like I always did, I reached my limit with her, too.

I was overcome by anger at the thought she was a pig's daughter, and by blood, a snitch. All I could think was: 'What a small fucking world. I could kill two birds with one stone.'

How could she not know the man when Josiah saw them speaking months ago? How could she not know him when him start act fucking funny since mi station him and Josiah outside her house during the lockdown? How could she not know him when he robbed her house and tried pinning it on Blood Paw?

These assumptions made me backtrack to the day I held her at her mother's grave. Unless she was the best liar the world had ever seen, Chayanne told the truth about her father. In the heat of the moment, it didn't seem like it.

I understood why a father wouldn't approve of his daughter dating someone like me, but that fucking man didn't know me. No one knew me. Only she did.

With her, I was cool and collected. I wasn't fucking Slitta or acting boss of another man's gang. I was simply Favio Welsh — CEO and a man deserving of a beautiful soul like hers.

Fucking Fabiano need fi come out of prison and free me from these shackles.

I hated being wrapped up in his shit. Whenever I was, the part of me that craved violence yearned to be released.

I must kill the elder for putting us here. I must teach Rush a lesson for not alerting me of the undercover officers in Blood Paw and Shottaz. I must decide how I would kill Antaro on the day Mamma died, because I couldn't do it while she breathed.

Looking at Chayanne, I sighed. Her brows knitted while she sweated profusely. I stood and found a clean shirt. I changed her clothes, wiping the sweat and makeup off her face. Why was she wearing this shit? She was already beautiful; she had nothing to make up for.

"Stubborn," I muttered, tucking the short, neatly trimmed strands of hair behind her ear before I adjusted the AC.

Chapter Thirty-Three

CHAYANNE

Being in Favio's bed was *not* something mi imagine cuda happen again. Slowly, me sit up and look round his room. Trying to remember all wa happen last night a mek mi head pound. But me remember bits and pieces: I was drunk; Dayshawn was there; I threw up on Favio.

Cringing, mi look pon mi clothes, surprised me ina Favio's shirt and boxers. It smell like him, and fit like me shop ina the Big and Tall section. Groaning, mi get outta him piece of bed and go his bathroom. Mi use the toilet and the toothbrush him give mi, back when mi used to show him how deep mi throat be. After mi done, mi return to his room. Mi nuh see mi dress, so mi keep on the shirt and drag on mi shoes. While searching fimi phone, the door open.

Favio paused at the door, his lips parting slightly. Recovering, him walk toward me and offer me a glass of water and a pill. "It's for your hangover."

Mi nuh waa nun from him, but mi need it fi real. Mi swallow the pill and water, then give the glass to him. Him place it pon the bedside table, his brows crinkling as him stare pon me.

Unable to bare his gaze, mi look at the TV, cringing at mi matted hair. I cleared my throat. "Did we...?"

"No. Do you remember anything?" he asked, and I shook my head. His shoulders slackened.

"What happened?"

Him look weh. "Nothing."

"Why yaa lie to me?" mi ask, and him look pon me, his expression blank.

"Who said I'm lying?"

"You have a tell."

The corner of his mouth twitched. "What's that?"

"Yu cya meet me eyes when yaa lie," I said, and his jaw ticked.

"I guess I shouldn't lie to you anymore."

"Yu shudn lie to me ina the first place!" I yelled, then ketch mi tongue. "Sorry. Shudn seh that cause we nuh deh."

"Chayanne, we a fuck raw fi months and mi spend mi money pon yu. Yu know we thing different."

I scowled. "*Different*?"

He nodded. "You're my girl."

Maybe a week ago that wuda mek mi head swell like the Number Thirty-One balloon, but I felt nothing. "When you ask mi fi be your girlfriend?"

"Are you being serious?" he asked, and I nodded. He sighed. "Will you be my girlfriend?"

"No," I said, and his jaw ticked. Smirking, mi walk toward the door. Mi deevn find the phone, but him can keep dat!

Him grab mi wrist and press mi against the wall, caging me in with his powerful arms. "Yu really waa do this right now?"

"Yes! How me a yu girl, but yaa smile ina gyal face?!"

Favio scoffed. "Smile?"

"Yu know wa mi mean! Did you have sex with them?"

"No."

"Mi deevn believe yu." Mi kiss mi teeth and try move, but him step closer.

His body pressed against mine, and hair rose on my skin. Holding beneath my chin, he lifted my head. Our eyes met — my angry ones clashing with his softened gaze.

"Chayanne, I..."

"You?"

His Adam's Apple bobbed. "I didn't know you were a lightweight. You blacked out after you threw up on me."

"Sorry," I murmured, embarrassed him see me like dat. A usually Yolo or Chezzy— Blousecup! Chezzy!

Mi slip outta him hold, searching fimi phone. Mi find it, and mi eyes widen at the wul heap a call and text from Aunty.

Alarmed, Favio asked, "What's wrong?"

"Mi afi go home—"

"I'll bring you home. Wait—" Him walk toward the dresser, returning with a small piece a paper ina him hand. Him give it to me, and mi eyes widen at the zero dem.

"Wa dis fa?"

Nuh look a gift horse ina the mouth.

"For your subjects. Is it not enough?"

"It's more than enough, but—"

"*Fiore.*"

My eyes watered as I looked at him. I couldn't resist tipping and throwing my arms around his neck, tugging him down a little so I could hug him. His arms wrapped around my waist, and I molded against him.

"Thank you." I smiled into his neck. Me always fraid fi ask him fi money, so I never did. But whenever him give mi things, who me be fi deny it?

"Does this mean you're no longer mad at me?" he asked softly.

Mi pull away. "No, mi still vex."

A voice came from downstairs, and Favio sighed. "Slitta?" came the voice again, and I ran out of the room.

"Morning, Trav!" I smiled at Trav, who was at the bottom of the staircase.

"Nuh mek mi diss yu, Chichi. Come me carry yu home cause Mrs. Kenzie a ring off mi phone wul morning." Trav glare at Favio while walking up the stairs. Before Favio could tell me 'bye', Trav grab mi hand, hauling mi outta the house.

Mi yank mi hand free when wi reach the Square. "Yu nafi handle me so."

"Mi think the man carry yu home. Mi neva know a him yard him carry yu."

"So nuh him yu fi vex wid?"

Him kiss him teeth. "If mi did know, me wuda come fi yu afta mi carry home yu friend."

Mi pipe up. "Chezzy? She's good?"

"She's great." Trav cleared his throat. "Yah. She good."

"She must a go kill me."

"If Mrs. Kenzie nuh kill yu first. Me neva sleep there last night. That's why mi neva know yu nuh reach home."

"Weh yu sleep?"

"Mi house. When mi did a talk to yu friend on the way to her house, she seh a thing weh mek mi waa face wa mi cause."

"It's not—" I paused as he glared. "Wa she seh?"

"Slitta nuh good fi yu. Anyway, mi did waa remember seh despite wa happen, mi always do mi best fi tek care of mine."

I laughed. "Chezzy waa hear seh shi a influence yu."

"She's not..." Him seh as we stop before mi gate. "Naa come in. Lata."

I nodded, running inside before him cuda pinch me.

Aunty was on the sofa. She jumped to her feet when she see mi. "Wa time mi seh yu fi reach here by?!"

"Ten..." I answered.

"Yu see the time, Chayanne Arya?!"

"I'm sor—"

"Weh yu sleep last night?" She glare while mi fumble fi waa ansa. "A man yaad yaa come from?!"

"No," mi seh quickly, and her glare deepen.

"Mi born big, Chayanne Arya? Nuh waa man shirt yu ina?!" She point pon the shirt, and mi gulp. "Heheya, nosah! A cya Mikeila one gyal pickney dis!"

"Aunty, me ano baby anymore—"

"Chayanne Arya, you are seventeen! Whichever man a mek yu smell yu arm, tell him it done today! You have exams soon, and yu outta road a idle wid man?! Yu think mi deh foreign a work two job fi yu form fool?!"

I clutched Favio's shirt as mi throat tighten. "The projects are on the timeline I'm working on, and I got a grant that can pay for the subjects," I mumbled.

Her wild eyes lost some of the heat. "You did?"

Nodding, mi hand the cheque to her. "Welsh's has scholarships."

Aunty's eyes widened. She hold her head as she sidung and stare pon the cheque. "Only God!"

"Me a go mi room, Aunty..."

She look at me. "Nuh mek dis happen again, Chichi baby. Ano so yu raise."

No one raised me... Mommy and Aunty been outta mi life from younger days. Mama too old fi run backa me. I didn't know my sperm donor.

Frowning, me go mi room and close the door. Mi sidung pon the floor before mi bed, calling Favio.

"Chayanne?" he answered, and I smiled sadly. His voice always did something to me, especially now when me feel so alone...

Mi wipe weh the tears, trying mi best nufi sniffle. "Yu mek mi Aunty a cuss me." My voice sounded stronger than I felt.

"*Dispiace*," he said, and I smiled. He was so sexy when he spoke Italian.

"Yu nafi apologize. Mi just call fi say 'thanks'... So, thanks."

"You don't have to thank me. Why didn't you come to me about it? That shouldn't have been something you kept as a secret," he hissed the last part.

I glared at the door. "Me know you naa talk boh secret, Mr. Yu-Always-Ask-This-Much-Question."

"Answer me."

"I didn't tell you about the robbery because me neva waa yu do anybody anything."

"Dat nago stop me."

"I don't think you should go through all that trouble for a girl you just sex."

He sighed. "That wasn't my proudest moment... I'm sorry, *fiore*."

My teeth clenched, hating how soft him sound. "*Sorry is a sorry word.*"

Him sigh again. "Me only seh it cause mi think yu did a try set me up."

"Who me know fi set yu up?" I asked, and him tek a second too long fi answer, so mi kiss mi teeth. "Lata, g."

"Mi rass! Who yaa talk to?"

"You! Mi tell yu mi hate how yu handle me when yu vex, and yu dweet again!"

"I'm sorry, *fiore*. Me rate yu more than life itself. Trust me pon dat."

"Whatever yu seh." Mi shrug, imagining him clenching his jaw.

"I want to make it up to you. Let me bring you out, then suck your pussy."

My clit throbbed, and mi slap a hand over it. "Behave," I whispered.

"Behave?"

"Not you," I rushed out, moving my hand to my side. "Me still a go vex wid yu."

"Declining head?" he teased, and I crossed my legs.

"Never. Come over when Aunty gone."

Aunty carry Mama gone visit some of her friends. Mi tell Favio fi come mad mi wid him tongue, then gwan him ways! Right now, him sidung pon mi bed. Me stand between his thighs while him hold mi hand.

"Yu neevn a go talk to me?" he asked, and mi look weh. "*Fiore.*" He held beneath my chin, making me look at him. Him bring my head close, placing his lips on mine for a slow kiss. Him pull weh cause mi nuh kiss him back. Sighing, Favi release mi hands and lay back. "Sit on my face."

My eyes widened. "Wa? No! Suppose mi stifle you?"

"Yu nuh see how yu likkle? Come."

"Favi—"

"The shyness, Chayanne. I'll be able to breathe, but if a yu pussy fi kill me, I'll die happily."

My clit jumped, and I stripped, crawling atop him. Him watch shake around him wrist as him fix mi pon him face. Him light breathing fan my clit.

"Yu can breathe?" My brows furrowed as me look pon him.

"Mm," came his muffled response as he brought his face closer, making me senseless for minutes.

"Oh my G-God!" I screamed, lacing my fingers in Favi's hair while his tongue flicked against my clit.

The doorknob rattled, and I gasped as I glanced at it. Blousecup! Mi never hear when Aunty come back. I tried getting off Favi's face, but him tighten him grip around my thighs, locking me in place.

Aunty knocked the door. "Chichi baby?"

I looked at the ceiling, panting. "Y-yes?"

"Why the door lock?"

"M-me did a bathe," I stuttered, moving against Favi's face faster while my legs tightened around his head. His tongue swirling around my clit was something dangerous. I never wanted him to stop.

"Alright. Mi carry back two patty fi yu. Mek sure yu eat dem before dem cold—"

"Ah!" I screamed as my orgasm took me by surprise. Shivers ran throughout my body, blinding me for seconds.

"Yu alright?!" Aunty yelled, and I slapped a hand over my mouth while Favi smirked against my pussy.

I moved my hand from my mouth. "Yes... Was a lizard," I lied, and Favi stopped licking away the aftermath to snicker.

"Okay." Aunty's footsteps departed.

My body sagged, and Favi loosened his grip so I could climb off him. I dropped flat on the bed while he sat up, looking at me. His light stubble glistened with my juices. Look how mi water park nearly drown the people dem one son!

He smirked at my weakened state. "You good?"

Blushing, I got off of the bed and tugged on my clothes. Him wipe off him face.

"Come here." Him nuh wait for an answer before him mek me straddle him. Him kiss the top of my head, then my lips. I licked his lips when he was pulling away, loving the taste of my pussy on his mouth. A now him fi go talk to him gyal dem! "Me a leave now."

Mi eyes widen. "Huh? No! Wait or go through the window."

He glared. "I told you I'm not a thief."

"Then wait. Yu have anything fi do?"

"Was going to check some records for the company, but it can wait."

Nodding, I walked toward my desk, which was stacked with school supplies.

"Come help mi wid mi project." Mi mek puppy eyes when him raise a brow. "Please? Yu seh yu waa mek it up to me."

"Fine," he said after brief consideration, and I grinned.

Marshy scratch the door, and mi let her in before closing the door. Favi scowled as she jump into the box of thread beside my closet.

"Nuh badda class mi dog," I warned, and Favi rolled his eyes, his gaze softening as he looked at me.

He patted the space beside him. "Come mi help yu, mi baby."

His baby.

He never called me that before.

Chapter Thirty-Four

CHAYANNE

The new year a move like it have sum weh fi go, cause a already the first weekend ina February. Mi nago seh nun big and exciting happen, but life a do better than it was during the time me and mi man leff.

Favi's an amazing boyfriend. Since we mek things more official, him always a spoil me — not only with gifts, but him a try be less controlling.

Him leff go Italy at the end of last year, and him come back earlier today. Him a carry me out to dinner. Mi a get ready, mi happy fi see him again!

Aunty Kenzie gone someweh and naa come home till late tonight, so mi a go enjoy mi early dinner as much as possible. Mama ina her room a tek a nap, so it a go easy fimi sneak out.

Mi spray on more perfume before mi go outside to him. Him look ravishing ina him suit. His tie and square matched the royal blue dress him buy fimi. Mi jump ina him arms, and him wrap an arm around mi waist. Him do a big waft of mi before him choke.

"You're going to make me lose my sense of smell." Pulling away, him continue cough. Him sound congested.

My heart race, my eyes widening at his red nose and drooping eyes. "Are you sick?"

He nodded. "*Sì*, but mi good."

Mi shake mi head, tears rushing to mi eyes. "Yu nuh good, Favi. Yu sick and—"

His brows knitted, and him take mi shaking hand in his. "*Fiore*, I'm good. I'm usually stuffy for a few days after I come from—" Him sneeze into him elbow.

"We're not going anywhere. Come inside. Mi will mek some of Mama special tea fi yu." Mi grab him arm, leading him inside despite his protests.

Favi groan as mi mek him sidung pon a chair ina the kitchen. Him look out of place ina the small area. Mi grab some of Mama different bush dem and prepare the tea. While it boil pon the stove, mi grab waa crochet blanket.

Favi sigh as mi wrap it round him. "Stop worrying. I'll feel better soon."

Mi pause walking toward the stove. Those words were so familiar. Look how that work out last time. Mi wipe a hand beneath mi eyes, then pour the tea into a cup. Mi walk toward him. "Open," I said, and him sigh before taking a sip.

Favi scowled, pulling away. "What the fuck is this? Poison?"

"Leaf of Life, Spanish Needle, and Jack in a Bush." Mi move the cup of unsweetened tea toward him mouth, and him glare. "No medicine nuh taste good. Drink it, Favio."

He stared at me long and hard. He coughed, and I returned the hard stare until he gave in. Gagging, him force down each sip until the cup empty. Him scowl. "Can we go now?"

"We're canceling. Mek mi get some Vicks—"

Favi grab mi hand before mi cuda walk weh. "I'm fine, *fiore*, I promise. We can order food if that makes you feel better?" he asked, and I nodded. Him smile, resting the blanket aside before leading us toward the car. Him grab a bouquet off the backseat, transferring it into my hands. "Flowers for my *fiore*."

"That did sound good ina your head, don't?" I teased.

"*Sì*..." he muttered, and mi chuckle.

"It was cute, though."

"You're cute," he said less awkwardly, and I beamed. He smiled, awakening the butterflies in my stomach as he opened the door for me. After he settled in the car, he drove us toward his house.

While we waited for the food to arrive, him tek waa call. Minutes later, him return, sighing as him sit across from me at the table.

"You good?" I asked.

"This—" He cursed in Italian. "—won't sign some papers. It's impeding the growth of my company."

"I know how to forge..."

Book learning ano intelligence.

"No. I don't want you doing anything illegal."

"You wouldn't make me go to prison," I said, and he stared at me for seconds.

Then, him get up and grab piece of paper and scribble pon it. "Forge this."

Mi scan the curves and lines ina him neat handwriting, then mi press the pen to the paper.

There. Done. Easy.

Favi look between the two, then write a full sentence. I mimicked it, and him glare pon me. "I'm not letting you do this again," he said, and I smiled as him walk weh. Him return with a document, and we scoured the internet fi the signature of the stubborn person. Favi found it, and I forged it without a struggle.

Ano same day leaf drop it rotten.

Favi smirk at the actual signature and the fake, his eyes gleaming as he looked at me. Him open him mouth fi seh sum, shutting it when a knock came on the door. He stood, kissing my forehead before leaving. A short while later, him return with the food.

Watching him plate my food, I said, "Remember me cya stay here long."

"Why?"

"Aunty will bruk my neck."

Favi kiss him teeth while sitting. "Me too fucking grown fi sneak round, Chayanne."

"Well, I'm not," I countered, and him shoot me a glance. "Sorry..."

"Stop that." He reached over, taking my hand in his. "It good. She soon leff so it neevn matter."

"About that... She waa meet you," I said, and his brow raised. "Yu been a send roses, gifts, and KFC come a the house. Aunty nuh born big."

"When does she want to meet me?"

"She a leave the end of this month, so Saturday?" I asked, and he nodded.

We ate over jovial conversation. After we done, we went to the living room.

Him a analyze a replay of last week's football match, complaining that the referee bias. Me a sneak videos of him while eating my dessert and his. Him neva want it ina the first place, but him order it cause him know one small slice of cake cya satisfy my long gut.

Finished with dessert, mi put the empty plate aside while the match go pon halftime. "Come here. I want to take pictures," I said, and him obey. Mi snap several pictures of us. Mi favorite a the one with me holding his chin while him kiss my cheek.

Favi scowled. "Mi look too white. Delete dat."

Mi roll mi eyes. "No. It looks nice."

"I look like Antaro. I don't like it."

"I think you look like your mother. Yu too miserable. Yu soon ketch back yu color." Mi smile at him while him scoff. Mi nuh know why him so bad breed, ano like him white like Antaro. Him just nav that sun-kissed skin right now, but him a still the sexiest man ever! "I'm ready to go. Mama seh when mi done eat, mi nufi sidung ina the same place and get hungry again."

"Do you have worms?"

"Wa dat yaa ask mi?" mi ask while we walk toward the door, and him shrug.

"I'm just asking. Nuh want me a e—"

Mi kiss mi teeth and him chuckle, making me roll my eyes. We reach outside, and mi gasp. The sky dark and the nighttime insect dem a mek pay noise. Mi walk faster toward the car. "Mi neva see the time! Aunty a go kill mi."

"If she tries to, I'll kill her."

Mi deevn ansa as mi stand beside the car door, glaring while him tek him sweet time. "Walk faster wid yu big foot dem!"

Favi walked slower.

Seconds later, him reach the car. Mi worry the entire time until we park before mi house.

Favi kiss him teeth. "Made me drive fast for no reason."

"Why yu so lie? Yu always drive fast," mi seh, and him snicker. "Sorry. Mi think shi did home."

"It good. Yago in now or...?"

I shook my head. He drove toward the end of the lane, parking in the darkness. Him exit fi go ina the back, while me slip between the two seats. Mi mek myself comfortable on his lap. Him rest him hands pon mi waist, and I ran mine through his hair. It nuh deh the usual length, but a enough fi pull.

"Why are you looking at me like that?" him ask.

Looking away from his hair, I met his eyes and smiled. "How?"

"Like there's a lot on your mind," him seh. Him sound less stuffy.

"There is."

"Such as?"

How me scared and excited fi see where life lead we. How much mi long fi feel the big buddy ina mi. Mostly the latter, though. We nuh have sex since the breakup. Mi hormones a ride me, and the oil ina him back must enough fi service a double shift at a fast food restaurant.

"You and yu cocky." My brows furrowed when he burst out laughing. "What?"

He grinned as his laughter died down. "I'm not used to you cursing."

"Whatever, *stronzo*."

Favi gasped. "Who taught you that?"

Despite how mi butcher the word, I smiled. "I've been practicing!"

He smirked. "What else have you been practicing?"

Mi roll mi eyes. "Nuh know why mi tell you that."

"What? How you used to hump your pillows as practice for riding dick?"

"A me and mi granny live. Mi have nuff time pon mi hands," I said, grinding pon him. "I want you so bad, but yu sick."

Him squeeze mi waist. "My dick is never sick, and stop doing that. I'm not fucking you in a car."

I frowned and leaned in, trailing kisses up his neck, then nipping his ear. Mi smirk as him inhale a sharp breath. "Yago mek mi beg?"

"*Sì*. Say please, Favio."

I released his ear, bringing my lips close to his and drawling seductively, "Please, Favi."

"Fuck," he cursed, slamming his lips on mine.

I returned his kiss with fervor, feeling victorious as one of his hands moved from my hip and crawled between my thighs. He slipped my panties to the side, pressing his thumb against my clit. He rubbed and fingered me until I was a leaking mess atop him.

Panting, he broke the kiss. "Up."

I rose off his lap, watching him shrug his jacket off, roll his sleeves up, then pull his pants to his ankles. "Might as well yu strip."

Favi scoffed. "Your pussy is too creamy. I can't soil this suit. *Mamma* bought it for me."

Mi chuckle. "Mi nuh waa think bout yu mother right now."

"Me neither." He gripped his dick at the base. "Sit. Let me make you a mother."

Mi pause sinking on him. "Favio..."

"I'm joking." He laughed, but his tone said the opposite.

A sigh passed our lips at the same time our bodies became one. Favi didn't give me time to adjust before he gripped my hips, thrusting his entire length into me while pulling me down.

My eyes snapped shut. My hand shot out, gripping the back of the seat. "Ah!" I moaned, my nails sinking into the material. I was barely holding onto my last shreds of sanity while this man ravished me. "Faster," I begged, moaning as he picked up his pace.

His dick fitted in my pussy like I was made only for him, and he was made only for me. Favi was hitting me at all the right angles, making me see colors behind closed eyelids.

"Keep squeezing me like that, baby," Favi coached, latching onto my neck, then sucking and kissing along my skin. His fingers sank into my ass, directing me up and down his length.

My entire body was sensitive to his touch as my orgasm came closer by the second.

With each thrust.

And every moan, sputter, and groan expelled from our mouths.

"Fuck," Favi said, his voice huskier. "I missed... this." He punctuated his sentence with a hard thrust that brushed my cervix.

"Oh, God, Favi!" I screamed, and he silenced me with a kiss.

His tongue slipped inside my mouth as I returned the kiss. My lips tingled and my abdomen tightened as I bounced up and down on him, meeting his thrusts and amplifying our pleasure tenfold.

Favi struggled to maintain his rhythm as his orgasm neared, and I coaxed it closer by fluttering my walls around him. He broke away from my lips and ordered against my mouth, "Come now, Chayanne. Me cya hold it."

God, his voice.

Him.

I trembled as my resistance snapped, sending me over the edge. Whimpers escaped my mouth as waves of pleasure rolled over me, leaving me boneless after the sweet sensation released its control.

Favi's grip on my waist tightened, and his thrusts became brutal.

I was still on the high from my orgasm, but I was breathtakingly aware of him.

The way his eyes closed, and how he threw his head back.

The way his lips parted, and how hushed whimpers escaped his mouth, along with strings of Italian.

Favio Welsh was everything.

And he was about to come.

"Wait," I rushed out.

He stopped thrusting. His hazy eyes snapped open. "Did I hurt you?"

I shook my head, climbing off him. My pussy ached as I settled onto the seat, glancing at his confused expression. "Yu naa come. That a yu punishment fi wa yu did seh."

Groaning, him toss him head back. "Bredda, yago leave me with this?"

Despite the car being dark, I saw the swollen head and veined length glistening with my juices. My tongue jutted out, wetting my lips. Mi waa suck him dick so bad! Or go sidung pon it again. But, mi neva tell nobody me a jockey, so mi a sekkle mi kekkle.

Smirking, mi stretch toward the glove compartment, grabbing the pack of wipes him always keep in there. Returning to my seat, mi wipe between my legs. "Hush, friend."

"Friend? Nuh fuck with mi right now, bro."

"Me ano yu 'bro'," I said, and him kiss him teeth while him put weh him hood widout accepting the wipes.

If Yolo fi see dis, she wuda proud. Mi cuda imagine her voice ina mi head: 'Yes, Number One! A so man fi get ride off, then after yu come, yu dismount the stallion!'

Mi go fi tease him when waa light shine from behind we. "Sas Crise!" mi curse, ducking.

Favi grab the pistol from him lock spot. "What?"

"Aunty..." Mi bring my hand to my mouth, chewing my nails. Mi a go dead tonight, and mi deevn put Mama ina waa mansion yet!

Favi kiss him teeth. "She can't see in here."

"Aunty ano idiot. She a go put two and two together because of this criss SUV pon the lane." I sighed. "Mago dead tonight— No, Favi. Mi know that look, and mi nuh waa yu kill Aunty. Wa wrong wid yu?!"

Him shrug, putting away the gun.

"Yu have gun ina alla yu car dem?"

"Not in my Ferrari."

"You have a Ferrari?!" mi exclaim, and him nod. Kill mi dead, a pay Bimmer this man drive! "How yu never drive me ina it yet?"

"I sent it to Italy before I met you."

"Why?" I released a quiet breath as the headlights turn off behind we. Mi a go sneak in likkle bit from now.

"Naa mash up mi car pon dem bad road ya," him seh, and mi chuckle.

"Goodnight." Mi kiss him, but him nuh kiss mi back. Mi chuckle as mi pull weh. "Yu vex?"

"No."

"Sure," I teased, and he glared.

"*Buonanotte*, Chayanne."

"*Fiore*." Mi wink as mi exit the car with my bag in hand. Mi tek uneven steps toward the house. When mi reach the gate, mi tek off mi heels.

Favi mek a U-Turn, stopping by Mr. Paul gate. Mi wave, and him blink the lights. Smiling, mi tiptoe toward the veranda. As mi reach fimi key, the door open.

Aunty crossed her arms, glaring while me smile nervously. "Yu start do this again, Chayanne Arya?"

"Sorry..." I mumbled as she look toward Favi car.

"I told you to introduce me to the young man so you can stop sneaking around, but me a draw the line tonight." She push past me, walking off the veranda.

"Aunty—" Mi grab her hand, and she shrug mi off. Mi drop mi belongings, running after her while stones pierced the soles of my feet.

Favi exit the car, slipping a hand ina him pocket. Sas Crise! Mi cya tek the foolishness!

Aunty give Favi a head-to-toe. "Goodnight."

His eyes drifted to my bare feet, then dart at Aunty. Him trigger fingers twitch, and mi loudly clear mi throat. Him jaw tick before him relax him hand. "Goodnight."

"You're the young man that has been dating my niece? Fayvio?" Aunty asked.

"Fav-io," mi correct, and she send mi a look weh shut mi up. Jesam peace! Wonder if she a smell the sex?

"*Sì*," he stated proudly. "You have a lovely niece."

"I know. *Grazie*," Aunty seh, and mafi go so boom and tek off mi glasses! Aunty deevn speak Hindi, yet she turn Miss Italy?

Favi's brow raised. "*Parli l'italiano?*"

She shook her head. "No. She told me you're of Italian descent, so I researched a few phrases for easier conversation."

"I see..." Favi eyes trail from Aunty to a white bundle weh fly past we.

"Marshy!" Mi run off. Cho, blousecup! Why mi neva lock the door?!

Aunty and Favi deevn help mi chase the dog up and down the street. Mi nuh know how she so fast! By the time mi catch her, her fur dirty, mi foot bottom cut up, and mi have stitches.

"Why yaa gwan like yu nuh have home training? Ano so mi raise yu. Yu naa get no treats fi waa week," I scolded, and she whined. Mi cut mi eyes. Mi nuh waa she sweet mi up!

Aunty and Favi laugh as mi approach the car. The way how mi shock, smaddy cuda stay from the Square and see mi wide eyes.

214

Favi noticed me first. "Chayanne, how yu neva tell mi a so yu stay?"

Mi stand beside Aunty. "How?"

"I was telling him how yu did likkle and nasty cause yu neva like bathe," Aunty said, and mi gasp.

Favi roared a laugh, and mi glare. Ano my fault mi did love ramp, and always too tired fi bathe after.

"Unu done talk now?" I asked, cutting their laughter short.

Aunty wiped tears out of her eyes, giving Favi a stern glare. "Remember what I said."

"I won't forget," Favi seh, and Aunty hummed before walking away.

"Wa she ask yu?" I pried.

"Chayanne Arya!" Aunty yelled over her shoulder.

"Me a come!" I shouted, waving Marshy's paw at Favi. "Bye, Daddy." I sighed as Favi sneered at Marshy. "Why yu hate Marshy?"

"I hate that she takes up so much of your time."

Mi roll mi eyes. "Bye, Favi."

"Goodnight, *fiore*." He kissed atop my head, and my eyes fluttered close while Marshy writhed between us.

I pulled away, wincing as I stepped toward the house. Favi lifted me from the back, and I yelped. Him carry me inside, resting me pon the bed. Marshy run outta mi hold while Favi tended to my feet. Aunty lock Marshy in the cage so she nuh nasty up the house. After Favi done, him kiss mi lips, then leave.

Aunty walk ina the room, crossing her arms as she lean pon the threshold. "Yu stay like Mikeila."

I furrowed my brows. "Wa yu mean?"

"Your father was way older than your mother."

"Really?" Afta me neva know dat! No one ever spoke about my sperm donor. Not Mommy before she died. Not Aunty before her husband filed for her. And not Mama after a we alone leff ina the picture. Ano like mi did eva care enough fi ask boh smaddy mi never meet, especially since mi get ina this relationship. Favi made me understand that if a man wanted to, he would.

Aunty nodded. "He really loved her, and she really loved him, but..."

"But?"

"Not everything lasts." She shrugged, her eyes narrowing at me. "Me can only wish yu the best. When I leave, please do better, Chayanne Arya. Yu cya leff Mommy by herself whenever yu feel like it, and outta road doing God knows what. You see wa the world a come to."

Mi shoulders slump. "Mi waa live while mi still young, Aunty..."

"Remember if yu scratch old woman back, she will let you taste her pepper pot."

"I know. That's why mi naa complain."

"Good. Now gwan go bathe. And mek sure yaa be careful." Aunty gave me a pressing stare before she leave.

Swallowing my embarrassment, mi grab mi vibrating phone. Looking at the notification, I gasped. It was a picture of my panties, paired with a text.

FAVI: Forgot something?

Chapter Thirty-Five

CHAYANNE

Leaving class, mi wipe tears outta mi eyes. Mi bump ina Yolo, and her smile disappear.

She lay her hand pon mi shoulder. "Number One, yu good?"

Wiping away more tears, I nodded.

Yolo sigh, pulling me ina waa empty classroom. She mek mi sidung pon a chair, then sit beside me. She rub mi back. "Mr. Black handle yu rough again?"

"M-mi n-uh understand why him a-afi grade mi so hard. M-mi have waa A ina alla mi class dem except fi him own, cause him nuh waa round up mi grade."

"Him tell yu fi work fi it cause things nago just hand to yu?" she asked, and I nodded. "Hush, Number One. A so him dee handle me when me dee have him class ina grade ten. We soon graduate."

The thought of graduation liff mi spirit likkle. Mi nod, wiping away the tears fi smile at her. "Thanks."

She grinned. "Me tell yu fi stop bawl ova man. If yu waa bawl, bawl tears of joy afta yu give dem bun."

Mi chuckle. "Yu love too much foolishness. Speaking of, how's court?"

Yolo sigh, her shoulders slumping as she start play wid mi fingers. "Any judge wid a drop of sense naa give him custody of me afta how him always mek Mommy admit ina hospital. Me a almost eighteen, plus me nuh see him ina waa year. Why him a do this?"

"Maybe—"

"Maybe because him a man?"

"Yu hate man too much."

"Wa me fi do, love them? Nuh mek me vomit," she seh, and mi chuckle.

"When yu realize yu gay?" Mi always curious, but mi never ask before.

"When me used to always rub me dolly dem crochiz together." She stop play wid mi fingers as the bell ring. She jump to her feet, grabbing her bag. "Mago find the girl weh have me textbook."

"Sure yu naa ditch mi fi go nyam crochiz?"

"Would never ditch yu fi dat cause me rather eat yours. But a me book mago fa, fi real. Me get me braces tighten so me deh pon diet. Later, Number One."

Mi wave at her as she left, then me leave, too. Mi find Chezzy at the school gate, and wi go her house. "Evening, Aunty," mi seh to Aunty, who a sweep the living room.

"Evening, Chichi. Mi nuh share the rundown fi Mama yet, so help yuself," Aunty said.

Mi nod, walking toward the kitchen with Chezzy. The urge fi pee tek mi, so Chezzy go share the food while mi relieve miself. Returning to the kitchen, mi pause when mi hear Aunty a cuss Chezzy.

"You are too selfish, Chezandra. Jordan simply ask if him can play game pon yu phone, and hear how yu bark afta him," Aunty scolded.

"Mommy, mi battery a dead, and Chichi leff her phone this morning. A far we a walk go, and anything can happen to wi pon the road. That's why mi nuh give him," Chezzy seh.

"Nuh that yu fi seh?"

"Yu give me a chance to?"

"Yaa backchat mi now?"

"No, Mommy," Chezzy muttered.

"Yu thief mi shape and face, now yu feel yu can size up wid mi." Aunty chuckled, and Chezzy laughed.

"Mi naa pay yu nuh mind, Mommy. A weh Chichi deh? Mi cold and wago bathe before night come," Chezzy said, and mi enter the kitchen. Chezzy smiled at me, then pinch her brothers' cheeks before we leave the house.

We neva go directly home. We detoured to Trav. Me knock pon the door, glancing pon Chezzy. She a tremble while brushing her hair back.

"Wa do you?" mi ask.

"Mi fraid a Godsto." She slip off her jacket, fanning her face. Cold bump deh pon her hand, but her farid lined with sweat. Chezzy bodily functions neva mek good to blousecup.

"Relax. Yu deh wid mi."

"Hear don wife."

"Stop that," I laughed, sobering up as the door opened, revealing Trav's mom; she was smoking, but she looked sober today. Mi look from her blouse to her face. "Evening, Miss Lyrica. Is Trav here?"

Miss Lyrica removed the cigarette from her mouth, blowing the fumes beside me. "Who yu be?"

"C-Chezzy," my best friend stuttered.

"A who deh the door?" Trav approached from the back.

Huffing, Lyrica walked past us and sat on the stairs. She put the cancer stick ina her mouth, taking a long drag.

"Sorry about her," Trav said to Chezzy, stepping aside so we could enter. Trav look pon me as Chezzy enter first, smiling at the sketches on the wall. "Mi text seh mi a come a your house instead, Chichi."

"She leff her phone," Chezzy seh, and Trav shake him head.

"Unu leff mi alone," I hissed, and they chuckled.

"Yu waa nun fi drink, Sandra?" he asked, and Chezzy glared. "Feel how the place hot? When yu start dead fi thirst, swallow yu spit cause mi naa offer yu nun."

Chezzy rolled her eyes, skimming the room and lingering on a picture of Trav and him bredda. Her eyes widened, then she cleared her throat and look at him. "The place nuh hot, it cold. Why yu have every window open?" she complained, shrugging the jacket on.

Clenching his jaw, Trav glanced at the veranda. "Mi nuh believe ina keeping window lock." Him nod toward his room. "Fawud."

"Unu gwan. A Chezzy need help wid studying, not me," I said.

219

Dem nod before dem enter the room, leaving the door ajar. Mi mek miself comfortable ina the sofa. Mi doze off until Chezzy wake me moments later.

"Mi ready," she hissed.

"A wa happen?" Mi sit up, rubbing my eyes as mi glance pon Trav. Him a stand by the veranda door, impatiently tapping his foot.

"All him do a upset mi. Mi nuh badda want him help."

"Tuff yu head tuff," Trav hissed.

Mi sigh. "Chezandra, put down the stubbornness and listen to Trav. Him know wa him a talk bout—"

"Mi nuh want him help!" Chezzy exclaimed, stomping out of the house.

Sighing, mi grab mi bag and walk toward Trav. "Mi a go talk sense ina her tough head, cause Aunty a go cuss boh why she wait so late fi seh shi need extra lessons."

"Mi nuh care if she fail or not, Jah knows. I only did this for you. You good with your classes?" He smiled as I nodded. "Good. Me wuda drop yu home, but mi nuh want yu friend ina mi car."

"Mi nuh mind walking. Maybe we can lose some weight."

"You nav no weight fi lose..." Trav glance pon Chezzy, who a fume by the gate. "Never mind. Mek mi carry unu home."

Confused by the change in his attitude, mi trail behind him toward the car. It tek five minutes fi convince Chezzy fi come ina the vehicle. Mi wish mi did deaf so mi neva afi listen to dem bickering during the journey to mi yaad. Mi fly outta the car as soon as it park, exhaling a breath when mi enter mi quiet room.

Dat silence last a few seconds.

"Why people nuh stop provoke me?!" Mi grab the phone off the bedside table. Mi heart skip a beat when mi see who it be, and mi answer quickly. "Hey, Diana!" A my girl dis! When Favi did deh Italy, me and her talk almost every day!

"Hi, Chichi! What's up?" she asked. Her voice was full of glee.

"Mi just come from school and a go study." Mi glance pon Chezzy, who grumble as she enter the room.

"Okay, mi nago hold yu long. You know Favio's birthday is coming up, right?"

I smiled. "Yes." February fifteen! Mi more excited fi him birthday than him! I'd been working on his gift, and mi waa bring him to the beach so him can look pon the sky. Mi also beg Chezzy fi cook beef fi him, and she agree. Mi wuda try dweet miself, but mi nuh waa give Mama a heart attack.

"I'm hoping to host a small get-together for him. It's going to be a special day,"she seh, and mi brows furrow. Get-together? That nuh sound like Favi, but a she a him mother. She know him better than me.

"That sounds nice…"

"It is! Will you help me with the planning?"

"*Me?*" I choked, and Chezzy stopped searching the drawer with her clothes, raising a brow at me. I waved her off, and she nodded before resuming.

"Please? I have a surprise for him, but I can't tell you because I don't want you to accidentally tell him."

"Oh "

"I just think he wouldn't be so against the idea if he knew you helped with planning," Diana said, and I nibbled on my bottom lip while thinking.

"I'd love to come, but I can't leave St. Ann. Can I help over the phone?"

"Of course!" She share her ideas fi the party, weh a go be the weekend after him birthday so I could come. "I'll call you when I'm at the store." Diana hung up.

"Watch daughter-in-law," Chezzy teased.

I chuckled and lay on the bed, scrolling through my messages. Mi sigh when mi nuh see none from Favi. Him have a whole day meeting wid him father and business associates, so mi naa hear from him till tonight. Sometimes, mi cya badda wid big man.

Tossing the phone aside, mi stand up fi strip from my uniform. "Trav gone?" She nodded. "Him talk to Mama likkle, then leff. Mi neva know dem close."

"My family loves Trav," I bragged.

"Mi realize. Mi never know him that nice…"

"Unu eva a cuss, how yu fi see? Yu just afi get use to him personality."

"Mi nuh waa get used to it."

"Yu better get used to it if yu waa ace exams," I said, and she sighed.

"Mi nuh waa talk bout that. How yago reach Town? Yu forget bout Mama?" she ask, and mi bubble burst. "Oh! Mi know! Me will sleep up here, just like old times. Mommy and Mama won't pick up pon it."

"That's why mi love yu," I said, and she chuckled. Leaving the room, mi go start cook dinner.

Minutes later, we round the table a revise when Diana call back. Walking through a supermarket, she tell mi she ordered Favi's favorite cake. She past by the alcohol section, she smiling at the variety of Welsh's wines. "It's almost unbelievable how successful Antaro and Favio are."

I nodded with a smile, proud of the brown, big foot man. "How old was he when he became involved in business?" I asked, nodding at Chezzy, who motion seh shi ago ina the room go study.

"For as long as I can remember. Sometimes, Antaro would take them to Italy to get them accustomed to some of the world's best wines, even when I told him they were too young to drink."

My brows pulled together. "*They*?"

She adjusted the phone in her hand while she tek up soda bottles off a shelf. "Huh?"

"Yu seh 'they'. We a talk bout Favi — one person."

Diana chuckled. "Silly grammar mistake. You know, even though I spoke English all my life, I mess up sometimes because of my husband."

"Why?" I asked. Favi limit mi interactions with Antaro. All mi know bout him a through Diana.

"He wasn't a good English speaker when we met, and he taught himself English to communicate better with me. I did the same with Italian." Her eyes glazed over before she looked at me. "Anyway, I see you're still studying, so I'll let you be now. Thank you so much for all the help, Chichi. I'll see you soon!"

I nodded, hanging up. Mi cya wait either! Favi won't be excited fi him birthday, so me will be excited fi him!

Diana and I made a ploy that she waa see me, so Favi bring me to Kingston. Me a go home bright and early tomorrow. As much as Chezzy deh there, mi still hate leaving Mama by herself. Thankfully, Favi have someone watching the house, and mi tell Trav fi drop by if him can.

Slowing before the gate, Favi scowled. "What the fuck is this?"

I smiled at him. "It's a party for you!"

"You knew about this?" he asked, and I nodded. Favi stared at me long and hard, making me gulp. He looked away, driving past the other vehicles. Him park ina the garage beside one of him many cars. Every day him complain seh him cya wait till him house done build so him can tek dem outta him parents' house.

"Diana wanted the day to be special for you. You only turn twenty-four once, you know..."

Favi turned the car off, looking at me. "When July twenty-seven come, you a go want waa party?"

"Then nuh must!" I said, and he sighed before exiting the car.

Him open the door fi me, and we enter the house. Everybody we past wish him a happy belated birthday, but Favi ignore dem. Cause mi nuh waa nobody feel shame, mi answer fi him.

"Thank you!" I said, beaming at everyone. Mi cling to him arm while him mek a beeline to the kitchen.

Diana was by the counter, swaying her body to the music with a glass of red in her hand. She was speaking to Dr. Merlgrove, but it didn't take long for her to notice us. "My baby!" Diana slurred, rushing over to hug Favi.

Favi gently pried her hands away. "Are you drunk?"

She giggled. "A little."

Favi clenched his jaw. "Put down the glass, Diana."

"Diana?!" She reached for her slippers. She nearly topple ova, and Favi catch her, swiping the glass away and placing it on the counter.

Chuckling, Dr. Merlgrove walk toward them. "I'll go let her walk it off. Happy birthday, Favio."

Favi nuh ansa, so I did!

"Thank you!" I said with a bright smile while she whisked Diana away.

Favi jaw clench as him grab waa Henny bottle and open it. Sighing, mi stand beside him. Mi wrap mi arms round him waist. Him lay a hand on mi lower back, moving the bottle to him head with the next.

"You don't like it?" I asked.

"I love it," he said dryly.

"I just wanted you to enjoy your birth week..."

"I know, *fiore*." Him look at me with an unreadable expression.

Mi neva did get fi carry him go the beach pon him birthday. Him did extra moody all day, so mi just tell him fi come fi the food. Who tell mi fi do that? Him cuss seh mi know mi nufi eat beef and cause mi love thief out him food, mi shudn give him it. Him throw it away, and shame did kill mi when mi lie to Chezzy seh him enjoy the beef.

I sighed, pulling away. Mi tek the bottle from him, resting it on the counter. "What's wrong?"

"*Mamma* knows I don't celebrate my birthday. I don't know why she's doing this." Favi reach for the bottle, and mi push it outta him reach. Him so uncomfortable ina him own house.

Wanting to fix this, mi tip, and him lean down so I had access to his ear. I whispered something naughty, licking his lobe before settling to my feet. The corner of his mouth twitched as he grabbed my hand, leading me upstairs...

I brought my head down, taking his balls into my mouth along with his entire dick. My hands were covered with spit. Some of it dribbled down my chin and fell on my breasts, but I didn't stop pleasing him.

I sucked him faster.

Harder.

Trailed my tongue over his tip in that slow, teasing motion he liked.

I was a girl starved, and Favi's dick was my last meal.

I couldn't breathe as tears stung my eyes and my nose ran, but it made my pussy soaking wet all because of him.

Favi laid a hand on the back of my head, pulling me closer as he thrust into my mouth. His hips jerked as he tossed his head back, inhaling a sharp breath through his teeth as he surrendered to the throes of ecstasy.

Lines of cum escaped his tip, and I hollowed my cheeks, allowing the cum to flow into my mouth. He looked so sexy locked in the dimension I sent him.

He stayed there for a moment, then his eyes fluttered open. He pulled out of my bruised throat. "Chayanne, weh yu learn fi suck dick like that?" Favi asked breathlessly.

Mi grab the towel mi did rest aside. Mi clean miself, pretending mi nuh hear him. Him think me a tell him a such man teach mi?

Hating my silence, Favi grab mi by the neck and pulled me to my feet. "You cya give weh this." He tightened his grip around my neck, and my pussy quivered. His free hand trailed between my thighs, roughly cupping my pussy. "Or this." He moved his hand from between my thighs and to my waist, pressing my body against his. His dick throbbed against me, and I leaned into his touch. "This belongs to you, and I'm never letting you go."

"I'm not going anywhere, Favi," I promised. Fi have a next gyal a mad over the tongue, buddy, and princess treatment? Must be joking! Him must nuh see seh me a proud yamduate with honors.

Favi smirked, his head swooping downward. He kissed me hard, placing a claim on the mouth that was wrapped around his dick.

God, this man.

He pulled away, lips brushing mine while he whispered somewhat inaudibly. "*Ti amo.*"

"What?" I asked against his mouth.

He answered in Italian, and mi roll mi eyes. Mi need fi hurry and get fluent ina Italian. Mi nuh know who tell this man me a translator.

Pulling away, him put away the big hood. "I'm going to make sure none of these idiots haven't fucked with my snakes. Soon fawud," Favi said, and I nodded as he left the room.

Mi go brush mi teeth, then lay pon him bed. Mi mek miself comfortable while

225

watching the news pon him TV.

"Renowned CEO, Hudson Graham, has been slapped with additional charges," said the anchor. "As reported last week, the mauled body found at sea was his stepson. This sparked an investigation into Graham, and officials found compromising evidence at his residence. Allegedly, Graham had been doing a lot of backroom deals to build his business empire, and his stepson got the short end of the stick. If proven guilty, Graham is facing twenty-five to life."

Favi entered the room, pausing at the door to stare at the TV.

The anchor continued, "The board had been urging Graham to resign as CEO to prevent the company from facing further backlash, but he refused. We received exclusive documents that Graham resigned and approved a new CEO, who will remain anonymous until the acquisition is complete."

Favi looked at me, his eyes gleaming as he extended a hand toward me. Something blossomed in me as I linked my hand with his, following him wherever he'd go.

He led us downstairs to the party. Who nuh drunk, ina deep conversation with the person closest to them. Favi bring mi to the kitchen fi feed me.

While him share the rice, him seh, "I figured out why they call you Chichi."

"W-why?" I asked, chuckling nervously.

"Yu know termite?" him ask, and my eyes widened as I sucked in a breath. Him burst out laughing.

"Leave me alone, Favi," I grumbled, and he grinned.

"Why? It explains why yu nyam hood like that."

"Sas Crise! Why yu stay so?" mi ask, and him chuckle. As much as mi love him smile, mi nuh like when him tek mi fi laughingstock.

Him done share the food, then give it to me. Grabbing his bottle of Henny, he stared at me while I ate.

"Stop," I mumbled.

He smirked. "Stop what?"

"Looking at me like that..."

"I can't look at my girl?" His smirk widened as I blushed. "*Sei bellissima—*"

"Guess who's home?!" a voice cut him off.

Favi froze, staring at something behind me as if it was a ghost. Swallowing the rice, mi turn round.

A stoic Antaro and a beaming Diana stood beside a man. He had Diana's complexion and was almost a spitting image of Antaro.

The newcomer spread his arms wide. "Baby brother!"

Brother?

Favio did a lie to mi all this time? Wow!

Mi turn round, glaring at him. His stance was rigid. His grip around the Henny bottle was so tight, me surprise it nuh break and cut him hand. Burning from anger, I hopped off the stool. Mi storm out of the kitchen.

"Fuck," Favio cursed before a heated Italian argument ensued.

Chapter Thirty-Six

CHAYANNE

Tears stung my eyes as I blazed upstairs. I was halfway there when the man call mi.

"Chayanne!" he exclaimed. His feet were heavy against the stairs as him tek long strides toward me.

Mi ignore him and hasten mi pace to him room. Why this man always find it easy fi lie to mi, but when me dweet, a problem?

Sadly shaking my head, mi grab mi travel bag outta him closet and gather mi things. Mi a leave *tonight*! Mi naa spend a night ina dis house wid lyad Favio!

"Who was that?" a voice drifted through the door.

"No one."

I froze. Wow! Mi a no one?! Alright, Favio Big-Foot Welsh!

"If I were you, I would've been happy to see my brother after almost six years."

"I don't have time for this."

His *brother* cackled. "*Papà* got me out early on good behavior. I've changed, I promise. Bygones?"

"Fuck off," Favio snarled before he entered the room, slamming the door shut. Him brows furrow when him face me. "What are you doing?" him ask, and mi ignore him. Favio released a heavy breath. Him walk toward me, grabbing mi arm. His grip was tight as him force me fi face him. "I asked you a question."

"Leave me the f— Leave me alone!" I yanked myself out of his hold. Spotting my Crocs under him dresser, mi stomp toward it.

"I can explain." Favio waited for a response I didn't give. Sighing, he walked toward me. "*Fiore*."

"My name is Chayanne," I spat, finding pleasure in the flash of emotion he couldn't conceal quickly enough.

"Okay, *Chayanne*," he mocked. "I can explain... Fabiano is their oldest son. I said I don't have siblings because I don't consider him my brother."

"Normal people would say dem ano the closest wid dem brother."

"I'm not normal people."

A must alien him be to blousecup.

"Honestly, Favio, mi nuh care. Yu can lie as much as yu want, just not to me anymore. I'm done, and me waa go home." Mi throw mi bag over my shoulder.

"Stop kill up yourself. Me and you nuh done."

"We are," I insisted, not backing down from his scorching gaze.

"Chayanne, you're not thinking rationally. Have a seat, please."

Rolling mi eyes, mi sidung pon him piece of bed wid a huff. Mi cross my arms.

"I never intended for you to find out about certain things this way," him seh, and mi tap mi foot, losing patience.

"Hurry seh wa yav fi seh. Mi nav time fi dis."

Him glare pon mi, then walk weh fi lean pon him piece of dresser. "After Antaro moved to Jamaica, he got involved with gangsters and corrupt politicians. He could've gone another route, but mafia ties and greed are in his blood. He made Blood Paw—"

"Yu already a lie to me! Yu seh a yours!"

"Chayanne, I never said that," he said calmly, and I shrank onto the bed. That a true, but everybody call him 'boss'. Everybody do wa him seh.

Oily tongue nuh must tell truth.

Exactly! Mi kiss mi teeth, looking away from him.

Favio continued, "Before the move, he was in the middle of creating Welsh's. It was easier to do it in Jamaica than in Italy, so he recruited ex-cons to help with his dirty work. They helped to make Welsh's into a tycoon by getting rid of competitors. In exchange, Antaro gave them whatever they wanted — guns, money, drugs, land. He allows the gang to do as they please so the police can't connect it to Welsh's, and only a select few know of its link to the company.

"Antaro raised us to follow in his footsteps. I'm fond of the business aspect of things, and Fabiano's interested in the illegalities. Fabiano's kind of... *come posso dire*... mentally unstable. When he took over Blood Paw, he did something that made Antaro put him inside..." He trailed off, focusing on the headboard.

I glared. "None a that nuh explain why yu lie to mi."

He didn't look at me as he continued speaking. "I like keeping my hands clean. I didn't want to be the CEO of a corrupt company. We've grown past that, so I've been tying up loose ends. That's why I came to Steer Town. I cut a deal with Truko and separated the company from Blood Paw, but I stayed back for you." Him look pon me, and my heart somersaulted as my arms fell from my chest.

"I'm not fond of violence because I tend to get too caught up in it," Favio confessed, his tone tugging at my heart. "But I've been working on that, and you're making me try harder. I know it wasn't fair to you, but I kept you in the dark because you looked past me being in a gang. I thought if you knew why I appeared in Steer Town, you'd start seeing me as a thug—"

"Fa—"

"Let me finish," he said, and I nodded. "I also didn't tell you everything because I've been lying to Antaro that you mean nothing to me. Oye, sidung back wid yu mad self. Yu know mi rate yu. Mhm, like mi a seh... Antaro likes having me in his control, and now he knows you mean a lot to me because *Mamma* tells him everything. I think he'll try to use you against me."

My brows furrowed. "Use me against you?"

He nodded. "Now that Fabiano's back, things might get out of control again. Antaro will want me to fix it."

"Why him nuh use waa hitman from the gang?"

"We can't kill Fabiano. *Mamma* would be heartbroken," he confessed solemnly, glaring at the headboard before looking at me. Standing more upright, he said casually, "Speaking of fucked up fathers, I'm killing yours."

I forced down a gulp. "M-my father?"

"*Sì.* You've seen that black guy with the nose?"

My eyes widened as his words slammed into me. A mi father that?

No. Nun cya go so. Him look too old fi Mommy, and mi nuh resemble him. We might have the same dark complexion, but look how much black smaddy ina the world.

"Why would he..." My throat tightened.

"He's an undercover police officer. He jeopardized his case to get between us."

Forcing down a lump, I focused on the ground. "How long yu know this?"

"The day I told you—" He paused. "Travis found out and told me," he said, and a tear fell from my eye.

Wow! Just... *wow*.

Sighing, Favio sat beside me. Him brush mi hair outta mi face, making me look pon him. Him try read mi eyes, but they're blurred by tears. "Do you still want to leave?"

I slowly shook my head.

Favio nodded, prying the bag off my shoulder. Him toss it to the furthest corner of the room, then try mek mi lay on the bed.

Mi push off him hands and run go tek up mi bag offa the grung. "Mama seh poverty will follow me," I whispered.

A small smile played on his lips as I walked toward him. I lay on the bed, and him pull me close by the waist. "Fuck him. He's not worth your tears."

I knew that, but it hurt knowing my father didn't want to be a part of my life.

A ten a.m., and we reach Steer Town waa hour ago. Me go check pon Mama, then Favi bring me back to him house cause mi still dissociated after the influx of information.

Honestly, if Favi kill the man, mi wudn care. Mi think mi finally understand why Yolo hate man.

Sighing, mi draw closer to Favi. Mi like being in his arms. His cologne and light breathing were comforting. Favi didn't know it, but he was my peace.

"Favi?" mi seh, and him stop type pon him phone.

"*Sì?*"

Me a sweat bullets and mi heart a pace. Three words deh pon the tip of mi tongue, but mi fraid fi tell him. What if him nuh feel the same? Me cya tek shame.

"What's wrong?" Him put the phone aside while mi clear mi throat.

"Nothing's wrong. Mi waa tell yu sum—"

A loud crash came from downstairs, startling me and making Favi tense.

"*Fratello!*" yelled a familiar voice. Now mi think bout it, mi remember seeing Fabiano around Steer Town when mi younger.

"Stay here," Favi ordered, and mi nod. Him grab him gun off the bedside table, and mi tell him fi put it down cause Diana would neva forgive him. Him leff the room, closing the door behind him.

Mi grab mi phone offa the bedside table. Favi did put it outta mi reach cause him seh a fi him time, not phone time. Him stay pon his cause him seh him have a business fi run. Mi really cya badda wid big man sometimes.

Chuckling, mi scroll through mi messages when mi hear sum drop and break. Alarmed, mi jump outta the bed and cautiously open the door. Mi walk toward the railing, peeking downstairs.

Fabiano was waving a pistol in the air while walking around a broken vase. Favi stand up a distance away wid one of him hands balled into a fist. Satisfied seh nun nuh dweem, mi about fi sneak back to the room. Mi nuh want him cuss seh mi stubborn and immature.

"Ah — *you!*" Fabiano exclaimed, and mi freeze as we eyes mek four. "Come here." He motioned the gun to weh dem deh.

Favi's jaw ticked, his eyes threatening to put me six feet under. "Go to the room."

Fabiano put the gun pon the table. "My gun's away. I won't hurt you, *bella*. But your boyfriend? Maybe."

Him will hurt Favi?! Mi fly down the stairs without a second thought.

Favi sighed heavily, using his body to block me from Fabiano. "*Perché sei qui?*"

"*Papà* told me you're in charge now."

"Oh, did he?"

Nodding, Fabiano looked at me, peeking from Favi's side. "Aren't you going to introduce me to your girlfriend?"

"Chayanne, Fabiano. Fabiano, Chayanne."

"My pleasure to meet you, *bella*," him seh, and as mi open mi mouth, him grab the gun and aim pon Favi.

Unimpressed, Favi stare pon him. Him cross him arms over him chest.

Pon the other hand, me? My heart wuda fly outta my chest soon.

"Put down the gun, *idiota*," Favi said calmly.

Fabiano paced the floor while waving the gun around. He was mindful of the broken glass. "Did you know your boyfriend's trying to take what's rightfully mine? My *brother* wants to betray me."

"Antaro said that?"

Fabiano stopped pacing.

They glared at each other, their eyes speaking a language I didn't understand nor wanted to.

Favi pushed me backward, and I stumbled over the sofa, hitting the floor. Dots filled my vision, taking a moment to fade.

Recovering, I stood, and my eyes widened.

Favi and Fabiano were tussling for the gun. Fabiano was bigger in body, but my man was more skilled. Fists met skin as they fought for dominance. Their groans filled the air.

Fabiano's nose bled, but he didn't give up. Not even as Favi grabbed his head and smashed it against the tile with a powerful force. A *crack* traveled through the room, and my insides turned.

"Favi!" I yelled, and him look over pon me, his eyes shrouded by darkness.

In that split second, Fabiano grabbed the gun inches away from his hand. He aimed at me and squeezed the trigger.

Pain seared through my abdomen.

Favi's eyes widened as a dark red blob formed quickly on my shirt.

Fabiano smirked.

Favi's horrified shout pierced my eardrums as my weightless body fell to the floor.

Favi got off Fabiano and tried rushing over, but Fabiano grabbed him by the ankle, yanking him to the floor.

Warmth poured out of my mouth while Favi's desperation grew.

Fabiano's evil laughter rang loudly while Favi struggled to get free.

I moved my hand from my abdomen, leaving a red trail on the tile as I stretched toward Favi.

He reached for me.

But he was too far.

And I was too weak.

Black dots blurred my vision, then my eyes fluttered shut. Favi's pleas for me to stay faded into a void as my life slipped away into nothingness.

Chapter Thirty-Seven

FAVIO

D ark crimson red.

That was the color of Chayanne's blood on my hands.

Staring at them now, I still felt the warm liquid gush between my fingers as I pressed against the wound. No matter how hard I tried, her blood wouldn't stop running.

She was unresponsive.

I was in a ghostlike state while I called her name. Shook her. Begged someone to grab my car keys so we could take her to the hospital.

No one helped me.

Instead, they tried to make me leave her here, as if she wasn't the center of my entire fucking world. My life had no meaning without her in it.

"Favio! We need to leave before the police get here," he urged while shaking me.

"Fuck off! Stay with me, fiore, please." My hand trembled as I grabbed my phone, trying to make an emergency call.

Antaro snatched the phone.

"Fratello, I-I'm sorry. I wasn't thinking. I—" said stupid fucking Fabiano.

Chayanne's breathing grew lighter.

I saw red.

Leaping to my feet, I searched my waist for my gun, then cursed. I knew I didn't have it, and that made me rage more. I blindly struck at Fabiano, hitting Antaro's face instead.

"Bloodclaat! Bwoy, watch weh yu deh do!" Antaro groaned while shielding Fabiano. "Figlio, step outside."

Fabiano left the room, and I rushed toward Chayanne. I stopped pressing the shirt against her wound, tightly wrapping it around her. I'd break the laws of time and this corrupt nation to get to the hospital within a second. Antaro halted my hand as I tried lifting her.

I slapped him away, sneering. "Antaro, mi swear pon mi mother if yu nuh call the fucking ambulance right fucking now! Or hold her so mi can drive—"

Antaro rolled his eyes. "I already dialed an ambulance. Rush is on his way, too."

That didn't ease my worry.

My jaw clenched as I looked at her. She was so still, like the most perfect figurine. I was restless and withering away as I helplessly watched her bleed out beneath me.

The door opened, and my head snapped up. I curled my fists as I saw Fabiano. I was going to gouge his eyes out, then feed them to my snakes. He didn't have the right to look at her.

Antaro stormed toward Fabiano, pushing him through the door. "You idiot! Favio and I had a new deal! He'd give everything to you when you came out of prison. Him never know seh yu come back, you fucking—" The blare of a siren interrupted his yell and my futile attempt to perform CPR. "Fuck, they're here. Grab Favio. We have to go."

I wasn't clear what happened after Antaro said that, but it led me to a dark room at a police station.

An officer entered the room. His eyes sparkled as he smirked at me. "The Top Dog a come fi tell yu exactly which hole him a go fling yu ina."

I made a mental note of this man's face, then looked at my hands, rubbing them against my sweatpants. I was going to kill him as soon as they took these cuffs off me. Not because he was jeering me, but because I didn't like how his voice sounded. It was annoying. After that, I couldn't care less about wherever the fuck they wanted to throw me. I'd dig that hole myself.

The door opened. "Leave," he ordered.

Officer Soon-Dead hurried out of the room, closing the door behind him.

The newcomer sat on the edge of the table before me, and I ignored him. He placed his pistol and badge on the table. "Favio Welsh, good evening. I am Warren Jones, Chief of Police, and I'd like to have a word."

Chapter Thirty-Eight

FAVIO

Smoking, I peered at Sicily. It was stunning in the day, but breathtaking at night. From my room on the hotel's top floor, I got a bird-eye view of orange and yellow hues streaming from buildings and cars, and people moving about.

Soft footsteps padded against the floor, approaching me from behind, then stopping before me. She placed a cooler on the glass-top table. Popping open a bottle of wine, she poured a glass for herself, then me. Sticking the bottle in the cooler, she rested her elbows on the railing behind her. Her silky robe swayed with the cool wind, giving me a peek at the near-perfect body that was free of underwear. My eyes trailed from the black strands framing her face and to her toned abdomen and long legs.

After a next sip of wine and a low hum of appreciation, she looked at me. "What's on your mind?"

"You." I took a sip of the red wine before placing the glass atop the table. It was good. Great, even. But it faded in comparison to the worst bottle of wine Welsh's could make. Not that I produced anything beneath the lines of perfection.

"You're not a good liar," she accused.

"Oh?"

"Mhm." She rested her glass atop the table, modeling toward me. She straddled me, and her pussy brushed against my boxers. "You've been tense lately, even after I do that thing you like..." She kissed along my jawline, slipping a hand into my

238

boxers. Placing a last kiss against my jawline, she dismounted me and kneeled between my legs. Looking at me through those doe eyes, she kissed my tip before sucking my dick into her mouth.

I looked toward the city, taking a drag from my spliff. The weed in Sicily was fuckry compared to the caliber in Jamaica, but I wasn't complaining. I had the sexiest woman in Italy on her knees, sucking me with a mouth like a vacuum. Except, I didn't like *that thing she did*. I never had.

Mi prefer fi fuck a gyal face to the point breathing a neevn waa option fi her. I'd never let this beauty know that, because I should be happy, but I was nowhere near. Not even after failing to convince myself that I wanted this.

Patrizia Moretti was gorgeous, but she had the personality of a dead log in a thick forest. She nuh back from buddy, but she too quick fi tap out and preferred things too vanilla. Maybe that explained why I spent most of our time silencing whatever she had to say by putting my dick in her mouth or between her thighs.

How could I tell a woman with many admirers that I wasn't interested in a serious relationship with her? How could I tell her the only time I came when we fucked, was when I thought of the only girl I imagined a future with?

Chayanne Arya Bailey.

Why my fucking fucked up life afi rip her from me?

Before she get fi mek a name fi herself ina this gamble called life?

Before mi get fi show her the world and change her last name?

Patrizia stopped sucking to look at me, her brows knitting. "Am I not doing it properly?"

Fuck! Did I forget to moan this time? "No."

She smiled before continuing. Her head bobbed up and down. Up and down. Too painfully slow.

Chayanne never had to question if she was doing it well enough. Not that she ever had the chance to. She was my likkle freak. My bad Indian, who only had to smile to get my dick hard.

Sometimes, I wondered if we would've lasted. What I'd give to have a coughing fit while she soaked herself in perfume. Her distinct fragrance was embedded in my memory. Whenever I caught a waft in public, my heart paced with hope.

Then, reality would crash into me, reminding me Chayanne was dead.

No one could replace her stubbornly annoying mouth, creamy pussy, or place in my heart. Mind. Soul.

I couldn't allow myself to move on.

Ever.

Chayanne haunted me in the worst and best ways.

Was it wrong to lust for a dead woman? Because I spent every waking second thinking about her — how I used to tie her up and force her fi tek rough fuck; and how she'd nyam mi hood like smaddy weh a dead fi hungry.

I could still imagine it.

No, fuck, I could still feel it.

I placed my hand on the back of her head, thrusting into her mouth while she gagged. *Sì*, like that, baby...

My abdomen tightened as I emptied inside her mouth, holding her head in place until I came down from the high.

She pulled back, licking her lips while my eyes widened. "Round two?"

Fuck. Patrizia.

I put away my dick and grabbed the wineglass, swallowing two large gulps. "Not tonight."

Not tonight when I was all you could think about, while a dead girl occupied my mind.

Not tonight when I wanted to risk throwing away all I built in Italy and return to Jamaica to trail a finger over Chayanne's headstone.

Not tonight when the dark sky wasn't as solemn as the weight on my heart because I killed the girl I loved.

Crossing my arms while leaning on the threshold, I watched her struggle to lift her weight on the pull-up bar. This was an eyesore, but I admired her effort. "You're doing it wrong."

Groaning after another failed attempt, she glared at me. "You do it since you know how to do everything!" she hissed in Italian.

"Why the attitude?" I asked, and she rolled her eyes as if she wasn't the one who asked me to help her workout.

"I don't have an attitude."

Pushing off the wall, I walked past the other equipment before standing behind her. I pointed at the bar. "Keep your hands shoulder-length apart."

"Like this?" she asked, and I nodded while releasing her. She made another sorry attempt. Her upper-body strength was lacking. I couldn't watch this anymore.

Sighing, I reached for the hem of my hoodie. I paused, glancing at the mirror. My jaw ticked, and I looked away to tug it off and rest it atop a table. Returning to Patrizia, I jumped in front of her and grabbed the bar. She wrapped her legs around my waist, then I lifted us.

Pulling up again, I met her face above the bar. "Better?"

We went low, and she giggled while rolling her hips. "Much better."

"Patrizia," I warned, pulling us up again.

"It's hard to concentrate like this."

No shit. My dick was hardening.

"Focus," I said firmly, and she pouted before following my order.

After a few more pull-ups, she said, "I can feel it poking me."

Cya do this shit right now. I dropped to my feet, grabbing my hoodie off the table and trying to tug it on. She halted my hand, evading the hoodie, because I ordered her never to touch it. I'd cut her fingers off if she did. I never told her that part, but she should know it was guaranteed.

"What's wrong?" she asked.

"Nothing." I walked away.

"You barely look at me these days. You don't even want to touch me anymore. Did I do something?" she asked, but I didn't reply. The door was a few feet away, and I yearned for more space between me and her. "Are you seeing someone else?"

I stopped walking to face her. "What? No."

She pouted, switching to English. "So, why are you pushing me away?"

My jaw ticked, and I marched over. I grabbed her by the waist, turning her around and bending her over the table. I pulled her shorts and panties to the side, surprised at how slick her pussy was. I wasn't horny, but exercising made my dick hard. Pulling my pants and boxers down to my thighs, I rubbed my tip along her pussy before sliding inside her.

Her pussy accepted me with ease, and she released a long moan. "Favio."

I gripped a fistful of her hair, tugging her head back so she could watch in the mirror as I slammed inside her.

She was crying. Moaning. Screaming my name while I fucked her hard.

But she wasn't loud enough to silence the raging thoughts that settled on my mind late last night. I looked at the ceiling, focusing on anything except her face.

"Ugh!" she groaned, tensing as she came all over me.

My thrusts halted, and I met her eyes in the mirror. She was a hot mess, brushing away loose strands of hair from her forehead. I believed Patrizia had a kink for getting fucked whenever I gave her the cold shoulder. This was the fifth time she came faster than I could snap my fingers.

Releasing my grip on her hair, I pulled out of her and fixed myself.

Patrizia faced me. "You didn't—"

"Don't worry about it," I said, then left. I couldn't come even if I wanted to.

Patrizia wasn't the problem.

It was me. It had always been me.

The emotions I tried to bury were forcing themselves to the surface.

Hate.

Anger.

Sadness.

Guilt.

They ate away at my conscience like termites.

Over time, I contemplated checking if they confused Chayanne with someone else. But I was too much of a pussy to seek more proof she reunited with Mikeila.

The crush of plastic jerked me from my thoughts. Looking down, I noticed I had a death grip on an empty water bottle. As I released it, I realized I was in

Patrizia's kitchen. When did I get here?

My phone rang, tearing me from a state of confusion. I gritted my teeth at the caller ID before I answered. "*Mamma*?"

"Hi..." she said.

"What is it?"

"Who are you talking to, *amore mio*?" Antaro asked from the background, and my jaw clenched tighter.

"Your son. Favio?"

"*Sì*?" I said.

"Been a while since yu call mi, so mi a check pon yu."

"Mi gov."

"Yu sure? I know her birthday's in a little over a month—"

"*Mamma*, I'm good. Later." I glanced at Patrizia, who entered the kitchen.

"Wait! Favio—" Her voice cut off as I hung up.

I didn't want to think about Chayanne because this always happened: my blood boiled, burning me from the inside out and leaving my skin scorched. I didn't care that Fabiano taught me how to drive, build my first spliff, and used to take the blame whenever I got in trouble. He needed to pay, but I couldn't leave the country. Antaro made Nikola put me on the no-fly list of every airport in Italy.

Gritting my teeth, I grabbed my new phone, calling in a favor I was advised eight years ago to use wisely.

Ending the call, I glanced at the woman standing on the other side of the island. "Patrizia."

She paused opening the dressing bottle for the salad she was making. "*Sì*?"

"I'm going on a trip." I walked toward the door.

Who the fuck was I trying to fool?

I was a Welsh. I wasn't a saint, and I'd never be.

"Where are you going?" Patrizia yelled.

I stopped walking to look over my shoulder, meeting her perplexed gaze. "Jamaica. Go live your life."

I didn't plan on making it out alive.

My will to live died two years ago.

243

Chapter Thirty-Nine

FAVIO

The last time I was at Steer Town Cemetery, there were two graves in this family plot. Only one had my focus — Mikeila Sharma's. Now, the newest one had my attention, and I was in a twist as I read the engraving...

I walked out of Sangster International at the pace of a man on a mission: visit her, find Fabiano, leave as quietly as I came. That plan flew out the window when I was greeted by Antaro. I knew it was risky calling in the favor with Nikola's son, but I never expected them to realize so soon that I left Italy.

My grip tightened around the handle of my carry-on. It was the only luggage I brought with me. "Why're you here?"

"Why're you here?" Antaro retorted, emphasis on 'you'.

"Answer me," I said tightly, and the corner of his mouth ticked upward as he leaned against the car.

"Why are you being difficult? Is it a crime to get my son from the airport?"

"Nago nuh weh wid you, big man." I walked past him, looking around for the escort I hired.

"I sent the car away."

An angry scowl twisted my lips, then I sighed. Loosening my grip on the suitcase, I walked toward the car. I placed it in the trunk while he went around the wheel.

"That wasn't so hard, was it?" he jeered after I entered the car.

I glanced around the blue interior of the BMW. "Why do you have my car?"

Shrugging, he drove off. "Figured you'd need a ride. How long are you staying?"

"How're you getting back to Kingston?" I asked, evading his question.

"Don't worry about it."

My fist curled atop my lap. Antaro angered me in unfathomable ways.

"Your mother has been worried," he added.

"She shouldn't be."

"Amore mio will always worry about her wash belly." Antaro chuckled. "Where are you staying?"

"You know where," I said, testing him.

"You're not staying in Kingston. You wouldn't land in Mo-Bay," he said, and I relaxed into the seat as I gave him the name of the hotel. "Oh..."

My eyes narrowed at him. He started growing his hair out again. The graying curls were well kept, as I knew it to be since I was a boy. Despite his age, he looked rather young — he always said that was what having a good woman did.

I looked out the window. Jamaica hadn't changed much. "Where's Mamma?"

"At home. She's sick."

I snapped around. "Sick?"

He nodded, sighing heavily. "Nauseous, vomiting, moody."

My brows raised. "Sounds pregnant..."

Antaro chuckled. "I hope not."

I hoped not, too. I didn't want another sibling. One crosses was enough for a lifetime.

Antaro and I played around with questions and answers until he dropped me at the hotel. As he left, I checked in and took medicine. I didn't want sickness impeding me from finding Fabiano.

After I got done, I bought roses and chartered a taxi to Steer Town. As I stood before the graves, remembering why I should be wary of la famiglia, another memory came to me...

He sighed as my eyes met his. Rush knew he couldn't send me to prison. Still, he had to play the role of Chief Commissioner. *"Wa happen, Slitta?"*

I looked at my hands, still feeling the blood. I was trapped in a nightmare with no escape.

Rush hissed his teeth. *"Look, youth, mi prefer yu ova yu bredda. But, if yu nuh help me, mi cya help you. If yu a go continue stay quiet, mi just a go fling yu ina prison—"*

"Dweet then, pussy," I challenged, wiping my hands on my sweatpants.

Rush chuckled. *"Yu know mi naa do dat, not after all yu father do fimi. But things nuh look good outta road. Mi cya let yu off the hook fi shooting that girl—"*

I slammed my fists against the table. "Me?! It was *fucking* Fabiano!"

Rush shrugged. *"You were the only one on the scene, so there's no escaping it. You're going to jail, but only for a week. Antaro will post your bail, and in a few months, I'll wipe your record."*

Bringing my fists to rest atop my lap, I muttered, *"Mi naa sleep ina nuh cell."*

"It wasn't a request. How it a go look if people think mi cya do mi job? Yu lucky yaa get off this easily," he said, and I hissed my teeth. *"Use your head, Slitta."*

I was.

I was thinking about how painfully slow I was going to kill Fabiano Eugenio Welsh once they released me.

Relaxing my fists, I nodded. Rush exhaled a breath, standing to leave.

"How... is she?" I asked when he was by the door.

"Still unresponsive."

I glanced at my wrist, my jaw clenching upon seeing it empty. They took away my watch before forcing me inside this room. If those fools thought I was going to leave this smelly station without it, they had another thing coming.

"It's been six hours," Rush said, and I tensed as he left.

I wasn't the most religious person, but that night while I tossed and turned on the sham of a bed in the cold cell, I prayed to whichever power would listen to the pleas of my corrupt soul.

When I got released, I hoped for a miracle as I headed to the hospital. Mamma stood outside the room with me. I couldn't go inside despite wanting to. I was frozen by the sight.

Chayanne was pale. She sweated a river. Her hair matted against her forehead. She was connected to tubes, and one was forced down her throat because she couldn't breathe on her own.

Kenzie sat on a chair beside Chayanne's bed. She held Chayanne's hand, her head lowered as she muttered incoherently. Kenzie was crying, and I was, too.

I wanted to enter and console her, but I couldn't. I hated seeing Chayanne like this. It was difficult standing outside the room. If I went inside, I'd be crippled. Chayanne was always full of life, and now she was—

Convulsing.

My eyes widened. I rushed toward the room, but the doctor and nurses pushed past me. A nurse escorted Kenzie out of the room. The door slammed shut in our faces, and we ran to the window.

Kenzie didn't see me. She was focused on Chayanne's heart monitor.

It flatlined.

I balled my hands into tight fists as I remembered what happened next. I should've fought instead of allowing *Mamma* to drag me outside to Antaro's vehicle because as I stood at the graves, rage blinded me while a question plagued my mind.

Why did this engraving say Saanvi Sharma instead of Chayanne Bailey?

247

Chapter Forty

CHAYANNE

If yu waa good, yu nose afi run.

Mi nuh too long clock ina the people dem work, but mi nehna expect fi have a table already. Grabbing my notepad, mi walk toward the table and greet the guest. Mi tek him drink order, then go put it in.

Fifteen minutes later, the drinks still nuh ready, despite us not being busy. Mi guest a get impatient, so mi go to the bar fi see waa gwan. The bartender rest mi drink aside when mi few steps away.

Mi smile at her and grab a tray. Balancing the tray in one hand, mi place the drink atop it with the next. Turning around, mi spot a guest, and mi freeze.

They looked like they saw a ghost.

"Chichi," someone said, making me jump.

The tray fell from my hand. The glass hit the floor with a loud crash, shattering into tens of pieces and making every eye in the restaurant settle on me.

Looking away from the guest at the bar, mi stoop fi clean the mess.

A second later, polished shoes stopped before me. Musky cologne filled the air, overpowering the scent of the spilled drink. He bent down, helping me to clean the broken glass despite Itanya telling him not to.

Slowly, mi drag mi eyes to his. Many emotions a swirl ina mi eyes, but not as much as his.

248

Slice!

Mi yelp and tear mi gaze away, my eyes widening at mi bleeding finger. Favio grab mi finger, applying pressure to it, and I winced. Him tek waa handkerchief from outta him pocket, pressing it against my cut. As the blood stained the material, I looked at him.

Favio dragged his gaze from my shaking hand, staring into my eyes. His eyes were as dark as I remembered. I didn't know if it was the blood lost making my world spin, but as I watched him, a thousand buried memories pushed past my barrier...

"Favi didn't shoot me."

"Are you sure, Miss?" the officer asked, and mi fight the urge fi roll mi eyes. Him deaf or wa? Cho, blousecup!

Swallowing the wit, mi repeat fi the umpteenth time, "Yes, officer. What did you say your name was? Jones? Officer Jones, Favi didn't shoot me. It was Fabiano."

Favi was sick in his head. Mi would admit to that fact any day. But to admit to a crime him neva commit? Especially one that involve harming me? I'd never.

The only thing me a go admit to a the anger, hurt and betrayal mi feel toward him. Mi deh ina the hospital fi a likkle over three weeks, and all now him nuh look fimi.

Diana look fimi, though. She seh Favi send him best wishes, but dat ano the same like from the horse's mouth.

Nothing nuh feel the same.

Especially my body.

It so foreign to me now.

Whenever mi shut me eye, me teleport outside mi body and watch miself get shot. Repeatedly.

Mi try stay awake fi nuh see the images, but the medicine make me drowsy. Aunty

Kenzie seh whenever mi fall asleep, mi start convulse cause mi body think mi a lose consciousness again.

Wa the officer a seh now? Him mouth a move but mi naa hear him.

Me a fall asleep again...

Mi jaw clench, and mi yank mi hand outta fi him.

Itanya run over, pulling me to my feet and making me realize seh a only a second pass, despite it feeling like an eternity. She pull me away from Favio, bringing me to the employee lounge. "You alright, Chichi?" Itanya ask, tending to the cut.

Mi open mi mouth, but no words formed. Mi nod instead, blocking out whatever she reply. Mi nuh waa go out there and risk seeing Favio, but mi cya hide ina the bathroom fi ever.

Putting on a brave face after Itanya finish, mi return to the dining hall. The tension loosen when mi nuh see Favio.

Disoriented for the rest of the shift, mi barely realize when night fall and mi ina the vehicle a head home.

Who that big foot bwoy feel him be fi show up outta nowhere and throw mi offa mi feet?! Pon top a dat, mi nearly lose the finger mi use play wid miself!

Him sick stomach bad, but my gosh! Bwoy still look fresh outta waa cologne commercial. Him still have a light stubble, him lips still nice, and him eyes—

No. Mi naa think bout him like dat.

Favio sick mi stomach. Whichever hole him crawl outta, him need fi crawl back in it.

Chapter Forty-One

Favio

I hated many things.

Things that angered me. Inconvenienced me. Lied to me.

I didn't come to Jamaica to play detective, yet here I was, staring at the picture *Mamma* made Lizard take at Chayanne's 'funeral'.

There was Chezandra.

There was Travis.

I didn't question the lack of Chayanne's face.

But as I zoomed in on the picture until it became pixelated, I saw new details. I could swear the girl with her head down and clinging to the arms of an older woman, was Chayanne.

Wa the fuck this, bredda? She alive? Dead? A duppy mi see yesterday?!

A car slowed before the curb, and I looked at it, hoping it was the man I hired to sweep my vehicle. It wasn't my car.

Scowling, I looked at the picture. It was hard to tell if this girl was really her. This girl had her hair up, and Chayanne always kept hers down. She was taller than Chayanne, but maybe that was because she was wearing heels. I couldn't see the length of the dress, but if it was something short, I wouldn't need more proof.

A familiar scent drifted toward me, and I looked up to see a woman fixing a kid in a car seat. I could've fooled myself that this wasn't the same person I saw yesterday, but I knew better.

My heart raced as the car drove off, and she turned around.

Those bright eyes were stumped, like mine.

Those full lips were agape from shock.

I wasn't seeing things. *Fiore mio* wasn't dead. She was alive and well, walking toward me.

I straightened myself while stuffing my phone in my pocket. She always complained about me being on my phone back then, and I wanted our encounter to be better than yesterday's.

She stomped past me. My hand shot out, locking around her wrist. She froze, chest heaving as she looked at where our skin touched, then dragged her eyes to mine.

I'd be lying if I said I didn't miss staring into the big, beautiful eyes that haunted me. They scorched my skin as they narrowed into slits, but I didn't dare to look away. I held her tighter, loving how soft her skin still felt.

"Take your hand off me, Favio," she venomously spat my name, melting the wall around my heart.

I didn't care if she wanted to hit me or scream. Whatever she gave, I'd accept. "Can we talk?"

"We nav nun fi talk bout."

I'd accept anything except that.

"Let me go," she added, and my grip tightened as my eyes narrowed. She knew I hated insolence, and she was already pissing me off.

"Chayanne..." I warned.

"Favio, don't. Please." Her eyes glazed over while she tried freeing her wrist.

I loosened my grip, swallowing a lump forming in my throat. "I can explain—"

"Save yu explanation fi smaddy else. I'm going to be late for work." She glanced at my pocket, which was vibrating. Shaking her head, she tugged herself away, scurrying away.

My eyes locked on her ass. She was more developed, the person I feared she would've never gotten the chance to become. Did she think I'd let her go?

I pulled my phone out, answering it. I rolled my shoulders, listening to the bullshit this woman spewed into the line.

A car pulled up, and I walked toward it. The man exited while giving me a thumbs up, and I paid him. Sitting behind the wheel, I drove to the hotel's car park and turned the car off.

"Diana," I cut her off.

"*Diana*?! Nuh feel seh because yu big yu can disrespect me, bwoy," *Mamma* hissed.

"Did you know?" I asked tightly, glaring at my windshield as she went into a congested coughing fit.

"Know what?" she asked after she got a hold of herself.

"That Chayanne was alive all this time I called and cried to you," I forced out the words, and her end went silent. "*Mamma*."

"Yes?" she muttered.

I angrily shook my head, my grip tightening around the wheel. "You and yu husband a fuckry—"

Mamma gasped. "Favio Matteo Welsh! Mi nuh care how vex yu waa be, yu nago disrespect me!" she exclaimed, and I hissed my teeth while someone sighed in her background.

"Favio, respect your mother!" Antaro hissed.

"Respect nav nun fi do with the fact seh unu a fuckry. Explain," I demanded through clenched teeth. I was one lie away from becoming an orphan.

"*Amore mio* has nothing to do with this. It was my idea. Mi tell yu from yu younger that you cannot kill Fabiano. That would kill *amore mio*, and I refuse for either of you to meddle in my marriage," Antaro said, and I pushed away a wave of flashbacks.

"But you could meddle in my relationship?" I asked, and he quieted, making me laugh humorlessly.

"Favio, if you stayed, you would've killed Fabiano. Please understand, I couldn't live with myself if one of you died," *Mamma* said through coughs.

"Since unu pickney dem precious to unu, as of today, May ninth at—" I looked at my watch. "—five thirty p.m., unu can start work pon a next set a youth."

Mamma gasped. "Yu nuh mean wa yaa imply—"

"I've never lied to you, Diana," I said slowly, my jaw clenching as she sobbed.

Ending the call, I blocked their numbers.

Dem love chat fuckry bout only *la famiglia* a go ina mi corner, but it was my fucking fault for believing them.

Smaddy a go dead ina dis fuck and mi neevn care if it a go be me, Fabiano, or our fucking parents.

Nothing would stand between me and Chayanne.

Not again.

Chapter Forty-Two

CHAYANNE

"Yu sure a him?"

Mi convince stick bruk ina Chezzy ears! Nodding, mi answer, "Yes."

"Who name Favio again?" Yolo ask.

"The man she did deh wid afta Dayshawn," Chezzy seh, and Yolo sigh.

Mi wince at the memory as mi look pon the baby beside me. Smiling, me place a long kiss against his forehead. Him have sleep apnea, so wi afi keep an eye pon him.

Zaveer a almost two. Chezzy had him the first time she go tek man.

"Chichi!" Chezzy yell, shoving me.

"Nuh frighten mi so! Wa yu seh?" mi ask.

"Him seh nun to yu?" She smile when mi shake mi head. "Good. Stay weh from him. Memba wa happen last— Wa kinda look dat, Chichi?" She slap Yolo foot. "Tell ar fi listen to me."

Yolo shrug. "Do what makes you happy, Number One. If ano me or S—"

"Oye, stop it!" mi exclaim, and dem chuckle. "Mek mi go get ready fi the people dem work."

"We will drop yu," Chezzy seh as mi walk toward the bathroom.

Yolo stand. "Me cya come. Mago check me gyal."

Stripping from my clothes, mi yell, "One-Shoes or Screw-Face?"

"One-Shoes," Yolo said, and me snicker.

Hopping in the shower, mi wince as mi run the cut under water.

His reappearance opened an old wound, but mi cya allow it fi fester. Favio Welsh belonged at the back of my mind — where him deh fi years, and where him a go stay.

After mi finish shower and get dressed, we leave. Zaveer sat on my lap during the ride.

Sighing, Chezzy meet my gaze in the rearview mirror. "Mi tell yu fi stop baby talk to him," she seh sternly.

"Sorry," mi seh, and she divert her focus to the road. She always a tell mi fi talk to him normally, cause a dat Aunty do to the twins, and dem start talk early. But look how Zaveer likkle and cute! Mi cya help miself sometimes.

Chezzy park before the hotel. We exchange goodbyes while mi exit the car and fix Zaveer ina him car seat.

"Aunty loves you." Mi kiss both him cheeks, and him grin. A waa nice black baby Chezzy get, but a waa pity him have him father big coconut head.

"Love Chi," Zaveer said, and mi smile widen.

Chezzy smiled at us. "Yu soon get one."

Mi scoff. This IUD naa come out until mi life deh pon track. Mi front goodly think mi dead and close like earring hole. Mi nuh use it since such man.

One thing me can seh bout me, Chayanne Arya Bailey? Mi nuh lucky. Why afta mi past the crosses outta door minutes ago, a him dis ina mi section now?

Mi vex seh running from a guest ano waa option. Withholding a sigh, mi grab the notepad and tek uneven steps toward him. "H-hello." Mi clear mi throat while him smirk. "How may I help you?" I asked, my voice was stronger than I felt.

"We need to talk." His voice was raspy, but my name sweetly rolled off his tongue.

Mi shuffle pon mi feet, refusing to melt like an icicle pon a hot day. "I-I can't talk right now. What can I get you?"

"Your number."

"No."

"Take mine."

A shaky breath escape me, knowing him nago drop this until mi give in. Against better judgment, mi give him the notepad.

Him jot him number down, then offer the notepad to me. Him nuh let it go when mi try tek it. "Call me when you get off."

"I'll think about it," I lied, and he loosened his grip on the notepad. "What can I get you?"

"You know what I drink." Him glance at the ringing phone atop the table. Before mi can see the contact name, him turn the phone pon its screen.

"I'll be back," I said, and him nod. Mi go get the Henny on the rocks, then place the glass before him.

As mi tek the first step away, him seh, "Take a seat."

Mi turn around, my eyes widening. "W-what?"

"Sit." He moved the glass to his mouth, staring through my soul above the rim.

Chapter Forty-Three

FAVIO

Chayanne sat on the chair across from me, her eyes flickering about. Was she scared of her boss? If they were a bother to her, I would kill them.

Placing the glass atop the table, I stared at her, recommitting all her features to my memory. I was in sheer disbelief that she was alive all this time.

We'd come too far in our relationship for it to be watered down to mere small talk. If she thought we'd be going back to that, she made a mistake.

"Cut the fuckry, Chayanne. I just want to talk," I said, and her eyes flashed anger as they snapped to me. "Please," I added softly, and she sighed.

"There isn't anything for us to talk about, Favio."

Favio.

I had yearned to hear her voice for many months now. I was scared I'd end up forgetting it, but I didn't, and she sounded the same.

Angelic.

"You don't want to know what happened?" I asked, and she nibbled on her bottom lip. Under normal circumstances, I would've snapped at her. I hated when she didn't understand I was at her mercy. "Chayanne..." I whispered, reaching over to lay my hand atop hers.

She stared at our hands. Her brows creased, then she tugged her hand away, concealing it beneath the table. "I do, but I can't."

"Can't or won't?"

"Favio…"

I grinned. "*Fiore*?"

"No. Call me Chayanne. And mi nuh waa hear wa yav fi seh. Yu swear yu did care bout me, but when mi did ina hospital, yu nuh look fimi! Yu deevn did have e decency fi contact mi from prison."

My brows crinkled. "*Prison*?"

Those bright eyes burned through me. "Nuh act clueless wid yu lyad self, Favio! Mi cuda lose mi life sake a fi a run backa yu like mi nav no sense. Mi need yu fi stay far from me cause mi nuh care boh wa yav fi seh."

Stay away? She expected me to fucking stay away when the sole purpose of my return was my fool's desperation of hoping to see her?

If she thought I was going to stay away because of whichever man she have a fuck her, shi must nuh know mi can kill that bwoy widout lifting a finger.

Chayanne belonged to me, and I refused to accept 'no' for an answer. Especially not after learning she got lied to, too.

"I wasn't in prison, Chayanne." I moved the glass to my mouth while confusion twisted her features. Taking a quick sip, I placed the glass on the table. "I was out of the country."

"Yu nuh sound sick," she said, and the corner of my mouth ticked upward. She glared. "Why were you out of the country?" She made air quotes around 'out of the country'.

"I don't have an answer for that." Not anymore.

"Favio, mi nuh ina the fuckry wid yu!" Her eyes widened as my brows flew up my forehead. "Sorry," she rushed out.

"You curse now?"

"No," she answered, and I hummed.

"You kept your hair how I like it," I complimented, and she froze, biting her cheeks while I smirked. I knew she missed me. "When do you get off?" I asked, realizing her hair was much longer than I thought. It was in a high ponytail, but once freed, it'd fall below her ass.

"Dat ano your business."

"I can bend you over the table and fuck the answer out of you—"

259

"Eleven. I get off at eleven."

Good girl.

"Give me your phone." I held my hand out.

"Yu already give me yu number."

"And I'm ensuring I have yours." My eyes drifted to my palm, then to her eyes.

Sighing, she handed me the phone. My grip tightened around it as I saw the wallpaper. It was a picture of her and that man's baby.

Mi neva plan fi be a step daddy to no man pickney.

Releasing an angry breath, I tapped the number in, called my phone, then handed her phone back. Pulling my wallet out, I dropped a few five-thousand-dollar bills on the table before leaving her with her mouth agape.

Soon give yu sum fi put in deh, baby.

"Yu drop a come in," said the person on the other line.

"When?" I asked.

"Uptown have e street a way..."

My grip tightened around the phone. "Wa go down?"

"Dem increase police presence close to the pier the other day. Warren a gwan like him waa run the wul Jamaica."

"That's never been an issue before."

"Yado dis behind yu father back. Things a go different," he said, and I gritted my teeth.

"Don't fuck with me, Fisha. Wa you and Antaro ina nav a fuck fi do wid mi."

"Things easier when him get shipments. Him mek Uptown turn a blind eye once dem get piece a food, too. Yu zimi?"

"Ah, weh your bwoy deh? Mi wi collect it miself."

"Ano waa good idea that... A so yu well want it?"

Sì. I was fucking desperate. I wanted an arsenal to tear down the wul a this bloodclaat until I found Fabiano wherever my fuck-ups of parents hid him.

"Just mek mi know when e thing reach, Fisha. And nuh call back mi fucking phone if ano the pier yu deh." I hung up. I walked toward Jelani, who was servicing my car. It wasn't running as smoothly as I'd like. "Bloodclaat, dawg! Why ina mi car so dutty?"

Jelani pushed himself from beneath the car. He stood, peering into my car. "A easy sum fi dat come off, Welsh. Start it and mek mi know how it feel."

Disgusted, I went inside. My BMW roared to life, and tears almost came to my eyes. No one understood how attached I was to this vehicle. It was time for an upgrade because Antaro put his hands on it, but this car had been here with me through almost everything. Exiting the car, I said to Jelani, "Get smaddy fi clean dat."

"Ano car wash yu come."

"Bro, do the thing. Mi afi go back a country soon." I glanced at my watch. It was six p.m.

Jelani called one of his workers over, and they drove my car away. "When yu come back? Deevn waa Irish Spring mi nuh see ino, dawg."

He didn't know about my second life. He was used to me going months with no contact, so he knew better than to question why I was away in Italy.

"Mi gi yu a thing when mi drop a yu foot."

"Yeah, but mi want Irish Spring. A wa? Mi nufi smell good, too?" he asked, and I chuckled.

How did I survive in Italy for that long? A dose of Chayanne and Jelani was working miracles to cure my homesickness, and I hated needing a dose of someone else to wash it all away.

She peered at me with drooping eyes, and my jaw ticked as I stepped past her. "Do you want anything to drink?" she asked, following me into the kitchen.

Opening the fridge, I searched for a bottle of water. "Relax."

"I didn't know you were in Kingston," she said.

I scoffed. Who was she trying to fool? She knew everything about me, so I hoped she knew how much restraint it took not to kill her.

Mamma sat on a chair around the island, holding her head low. "I'm sorry, Favio. I know how much you loved her."

"Love." I faced her, leaning on the fridge. "Why yu dweet?" I asked. Her silly logic about her firstborn was stupid. We weren't the most religious bunch, but *la famiglia* believed in sacrificing firstborns. "Where is Fabiano?" I asked before she could answer.

"I don't know."

I scoffed. "How does lying come so naturally to you?"

"Favio. Mi sick and a dead. Yu feel mi have the strength fi a lie right now?"

"Yu lie to mi every fucking—"

She grabbed her slipper. She threw it at me, and I dodged it. The slipper smacked against the fridge, falling to the floor. "Watch yu mouth, bwoy, and nuh mek mi watch it fi yu—" She sneezed.

"Do you need medicine?" I asked bitterly.

"*Amore mio* ran to the pharmacy to get medicine. Can you stay with me until he's back?"

"I don't want to see him. I already hate that I'm seeing you."

Her eyes watered as they met mine, and I couldn't tell if it was because she was sick or genuinely hurt. "I'm sorry, Favio."

"You're not." I pushed myself off the fridge to help her to her room.

I knew Chayanne wouldn't call me. It was foolish of me to expect her to do so.

So, I did what any lovesick man would do.

I drove to the hotel and parked in the darkness, waiting for eleven p.m. Thirty minutes passed before she exited, looking about as if she thought she could hide from me. A white Corolla slowed at the curb before her, and I glared. This was not the vehicle she placed her baby in.

Whoever this person was, I figured they would've come. Since she was their... woman, for the time being... I expected someone to drive her home, or she to drive herself.

My last search to find her house was a failure...

"Yu brave a show yu face round ya."

"Scare tactics don't work on me. Where's your sister?" I asked, disregarding his anger. If he wanted a fight, he had better try another day. I wouldn't allow anything to stand between me and Chayanne, and he had always proved to be an obstacle.

Stopping beside me, Travis looked at the house. A toy truck was in the yard. "She nuh deh boh."

"Who lives here?"

"Nago ansa dat, and mi nago tell yu weh shi deh, either. Mi respect yu, but a fuckry yu do. Yu know how mi did afi a collect work from Chez while Chichi lay dung ina hospital? Only Jah knows how she manage fi get eight Ones and two Twos."

My heart swelled with pride. I expected nothing less from her. I remembered how she'd have mental breakdowns with her studies, and how I'd stay up late to help her understand a challenging concept. "She's smart."

"Dunce, too," he said, and I looked at him for the first time. He got a teardrop tattoo.

"What?"

He was about to reply when his phone rang. His jaw ticked before he answered. "Yah, yu can come later," he said after a few seconds. Ending the call, he looked at me. "Stay weh from Chichi. She a do better without yu."

I flexed my fingers around the wheel, deciding not to follow her tonight. I'd probably cause unnecessary drama that wouldn't help me get her back.

If Chayanne was doing better without me, I'd make her life worse. There would be no such thing as 'better' if it wasn't a life with me.

Pulling my phone out, I snapped a picture of the car's license plate.

I would kill this man if needed.

I'd deal with the child later.

For now, that hooded figure closing the passenger door was the only person standing between me and the woman I should've never lost.

Chapter Forty-Four

FAVIO

"You can't keep showing up here."

"Are you kicking me out?"

"N-no," she said, and I smiled.

Cute.

"Weren't you supposed to call me?"

She looked away, her grip tightening around the pen pressed against the notepad. "I lost your number."

My eyes narrowed. "You know I hate when people lie to me."

She glared at me. "Mi neva waa call yu."

I smiled. "Now we're being honest. Sit."

"I'm working."

"I didn't ask. Sit," I said, and she sighed while complying. Tapping a finger against the table, I asked, "Who told you I was in prison?"

"That's what I heard."

I gestured at my face. "Does a face like this look like it would go to prison?"

She stared at me, rolling her eyes while looking away. Her brows furrowed as she looked around her empty section. I showed up minutes before her shift started, paying someone to take her guests.

Looking at me, she asked, "Yu know mi did ina hospital?"

My jaw clenched. "*Sì.*"

"You never visited..." she whispered.

I held my head low, my hand balling into a fist atop the table.

"Why—" She paused as my phone rang.

I declined the call without checking the ID. "You were saying?"

"Why—" Ringing cut her off again. She hissed her teeth, looking away.

"I'll be back." I walked out of the restaurant and answered the call. "Patrizia."

"I was so worried about you," Patrizia cried, and I didn't answer. "Favio?"

"*Sì?*"

"I miss you. I don't have any gigs right now, and I've never been to Jamaica—"

"No," I interrupted, then I let her down gently before returning to Chayanne.

She was smiling and laughing with a male guest, and though it aggravated me, I kept my cool. *My* woman was a beauty. She deserved to be shown off. As long as these idiots kept their hands to themselves, I didn't care if they gawked at her.

I returned to the table. Chayanne noticed me, sighing as she walked toward me. Despite ordering a drink I barely touched, I dropped a few dollars on the table, then slid my wallet into my pocket. "Give me your hand."

Sighing, she pocketed the money before giving me her hand. I locked my hand around her wrist, and she shivered. Meeting her eyes, I raised a brow, and she looked away. Grabbing the marker tucked into her pocket, I pressed it into her palm. She tried tugging away, but I kept her in place.

"Favio, wa yaa do?" Her eyes widened while watching me write in her palm.

"Nuh lose it this time." I released her hand.

She rubbed at the permanent ink, groaning when it didn't smudge. Smirking, I returned the marker. She dragged her eyes to mine, glaring while I grinned. It was fine if she hated me now. She'd learn to love me again. I'd ensure it.

"Have a good shift, *fiore*." I walked away while she burned holes in my back.

"Package a deliver Saturday," Fisha said into the line.

That was sooner than anticipated. I hadn't located Fabiano, but this early shipment would accelerate the timeline. Not that I was complaining. The sooner I got this shit over with, the better.

"How the pier look?" I walked around the house I rented at a Drax Hall housing scheme. I was making sure everything was as clean as I needed it to be.

"Easy fix dat. Put dem pon some likkle boat weh—"

"Fisha, wa kinda risky fuckry yado?" I gritted out.

"Easy nuh, Slitta. Memba Uptown have the place lock. Mi links a border patrol mek mi know the shift rotation, so we have time fi do the meetup."

I had years of service with Fisha. If he loved his life, he better not fall short now.

"Have sum else fi check yu pon," I said.

"Wa dat?"

"Yu know weh Fabiano lay him head?"

He paused. "Last me hear, Trelawny."

Trelawny? We didn't have a safe house there that was up to Fabiano's standards. Well, there was—

No. Fabiano cuda neva so fucking fool a day a him worthless life. And I doubted he knew much about *that* situation.

But snakes were my family, I could never be too sure.

Walking about this house and seeing the facade of a happy family made me sick. The last time I was here, I didn't realize she put up new family photos.

Ridding the unpleasant thoughts, I entered Antaro's office and sat before his desk. The office was decently sized and had necessities such as a bookshelf with a hidden safe Fabiano and I discovered as kids; a sofa *Mamma* rested until Antaro was ready for bed; file cabinets storing years of dirt and Welsh's assets.

I was here to discuss the latter.

"Are you sure about this?" Antaro sighed when I nodded. "You've done a lot for the company, even ran it remotely while you were away."

"I was being a good CEO."

"*Great* CEO. I'm proud of you. You ran the company better than I did. The student has become the master," he said, and I almost scoffed. He could keep his backhanded compliment.

"That's not why I'm here," I said. *La famiglia* overstepped too far last time. I couldn't turn a blind eye anymore.

"I think you should reconsider. This has been your dream."

"*Your* dream."

Antaro shrugged. "Regardless, you can't leave without due process—"

"Are you going to pretend you can't override my need to submit paperwork to the board?"

Antaro sighed, shuffling some papers on the desk. "I will temporarily fill your shoes while you give this more thought. I think this is a rash decision, and we know you always regret those."

I looked away, glaring at a spot on the carpet. I hated it when Antaro was right.

Loosening my grip on the duffle bag, I stuffed my phone into my pocket as I walked toward Fisha's office. We were at one of his safe houses. Fisha sold blue barrels people used to store water. It was his cover for his primary source of income.

Fisha trafficked guns and cocaine into Jamaica. Sometimes, he exported weed, but delivering quality marijuana was a tricky process, so he didn't do it unless he needed money.

Dropping the duffel bag beside my feet, I fixed my jacket before sitting on the chair before his desk. Fisha sat on the corner of the desk, offering me a drag from his spliff.

I shook my head. "Mi nuh smoke spliff mi nuh roll."

"Yu know mi nuh nyam nun weh nuh cook ina kitchen," he joked, but I didn't laugh. He was an idiot missing out on a good time.

"Thing cya come sooner than Saturday?"

"Feel man can control tide? Is a big risk maa tek fi yu. Uptown deh everywhere like fly pon shit."

I wished I could tell Rush about my shipment, but it wasn't worth the risk. He'd sing to Antaro like a canary, and Antaro would send Fabiano deeper into hiding. I didn't give a fuck what Antaro and *Mamma* said. I knew they were hiding him, just like they hid her.

"Anyway, mek wi talk dollars," Fisha added, and I tossed the duffle bag onto the table.

The man standing in the corner toward the table and grabbed the bag. He emptied it onto the table, then took a money counter machine out of a drawer.

I dragged my eyes away from him, narrowing them at Fisha. "Yaa try diss mi?"

Fisha blew a cloud toward the ceiling. "Cya be too trusting these days."

Chapter Forty-Five

CHAYANNE

M i lay pon mi bed, watching a vampire show Chezzy tell mi bout. The word dem a go over mi head. Realizing why, mi kiss mi teeth and glance pon mi hand middle. Mi use body wash, cake soap, bleach, and fab, but him number won't budge.

Groaning, mi grab mi phone from beside me.

Chiga toe fraid a trouble.

Sighing, mi put down the phone. Mi rest mi hands atop each other pon mi belly, staring at the ceiling and getting lost in thoughts...

"It's kind of pitiful you're the one who visits me," I said, and she waved me off.

"You're like a daughter to me. It's the least I can do." Diana smiled.

Mi look from her to the IV in my arm. "I miss him..."

Diana sighed. "I miss him, too."

The rawness in her tone hurt mi heart some more. Part of me blame her fi the current situation. If she did tell mi boh Fabiano, this cuda be avoided.

"He misses you a lot," Diana added, and mi deevn acknowledge her.
Mi tired fi hear dat overused line now.

Something sting mi palm, yanking me to reality. Unclenching my fist, mi glare at the nail print in my palm.

It did easy fi bury feelings when he wasn't around. Now he was back, and I... really wanted to hug him.

Sighing, mi grab mi ringing phone. "Yes, Aunty?"

"Chichi baby—" Aunty pause as crying interrupt her.

Mi smile and switch to video call. "Hi, Azera!" I cooed at the crying bundle in Aunty's arm.

"You can meet her when you come up August." Aunty's smile fell as I gulped. She glared. "Chayanne Arya, yu nuh fill out the application for the school and work program weh Tate send yu from how long?"

"No, Aunty..."

"Who have raw meat seek fire. You must know if yu waa serve table fi the rest of yu life," she seh, and mi fight the urge fi kiss mi teeth.

"Aunty, yu nafi say it so. Yu know mi tek time off school fi get mi mind back on track."

"I understand. But it's almost two years, and you said you'd do one. You need to figure yourself out. Yu naa get any younger."

"Alright, Aunty. Later. Tell Tate goodnight when him come from work," mi seh, and she nod, hanging up. Mi can barely think boh mi future. All deh pon mi mind a Favio this, Favio that.

Cho, blousecup! Mi sit up in a flash and dial the number. Mi nuh breathe while the phone ring.

Yu life long, but yu careless wid it.

"Chayanne," Favio's voice come ina mi ears as mi bout fi hang up.

I forgot how sexy his voice was over the phone! Exhaling a breath, I said, "Um, hello."

"Surprised you called," him seh, and mi roll mi eyes.

"Nuh flatter yourself. Mi only call cause yu number hard fi wash off."

"Have smaddy yu nuh waa see it?"

"No," I blurted, and he chuckled. I gulped.

"Did you want something?"

I curled my hand into a fist, covering his mark. "Mi waa know nuff things! Cause if a neva fi Diana, mi wudn know yu still alive!"

"*Fiore*, calm down."

Tears pricked my eyes, and mi shut dem. Mi nuh understand why mi a cry. "My name is Chayanne."

"Okay, *Chayanne*," he said mockingly. "This naa work. Let's talk face-to-face."

Remembering all those times at my work, mi open mi eyes and wipe weh the tears. "Not at my work. We can meet Saturday at a park in Ochi."

"I don't like to be kept waiting," him seh, and mi anger surge.

"Imagine being bedridden while waiting fi yu boyfriend show up!"

He quieted. The only thing between us a mi harsh breathing until him whisper, "It wasn't like that."

Mi scoff. "See you Saturday, Favio. And nuh show up back a mi workplace or else mi get a restraining order." Every time him show up, mi nav no table like him bathe ina people repellent.

"I was staying there," him seh, and mi kiss mi teeth.

Hanging up, mi toss the phone aside. Mi glance at Marshy, who stop play wid her ball fi bark at me. "Yeah, mi hate man, too," mi seh, and she bark again.

My ajar door opened and a head peeked inside. Mi sit up and smile.

"Hey, Pretty Girl. You good? Hear yaa shout," him seh, and mi fake a smile.

"Yeah, mi good," mi seh, and him sigh. "A wa?"

"I'm going away again," him seh, and mi frown as him sit beside me.

Mi draw closer, hugging him. Mi smile as him hug me back. "Me a go miss you."

"Going to miss you more, Pretty Girl."

CHEZANDRA

Sighing after I ended the call, I kissed atop Zaveer's head. I grabbed a blanket Chichi crocheted before returning to the living room. Apart from the television's low light, the room was dark. Chichi and Travis were whispering, and they stopped when they saw me.

"A wa?" I asked, sitting beside Travis. I didn't want to sit beside him, but there was nowhere else to go. Chichi was on the small sofa, and he sat on the long one.

"Nun. Yu still cold? Look how long mi turn off the fan." Chichi resumed the show we were watching.

"Mi still cold—" I almost screamed as Travis grabbed my legs, placing them across his lap. He pried my legs open, and I jolted.

Chichi looked at me. "Why yaa jump? Nuh you waa watch horror movie?"

"Yu friend fraidy fraidy," Travis said.

"Mi nuh fraid." I forced a laugh, gulping as he slipped my panties to the side and found my clit. I reached beneath the blanket and tried to stop him, but one look from him made me reconsider.

I bit into my lip, silencing a moan as he rubbed my clit. My traitorous body heated up while my pussy soaked his hand.

I glanced at Chichi. She was too hooked by the movie to realize what Travis was doing to me.

He eased a finger inside me, and I released a low breath. His finger felt so good, but I wanted him to stop. This was wrong. He was my best friend's brother, and I was in a relationship—

The movie changed to a different scene, drowning the room in a bright light. My eyes widened at Chichi, who was staring at me.

"You good?" she asked.

"Y-yes..." I nodded weakly, squeezing my thighs together as Travis slipped another finger inside my pussy. His slow thrusts were maddening.

"So why yaa sweat? Come from under the sheet."

"Can go for the fan?" I asked, and she nodded. After she left the room, I held his hand. "Stop. This wrong, and yu know it."

Travis glared, withdrawing his fingers. "So yaa seh, but when—"

"That different," I said through clenched teeth. A flash of hurt crossed his face, but it was too late to take my words back.

Chichi reentered the living room. While she fixed the fan, Travis stood, discreetly wiping his fingers on his shirt. "Weh yago, Mawga Boy?"

"Mi yaad," he said, and she frowned. "Have a thing fi deal wid. Mi will see yu when mi see yu."

Chichi nodded, looking away from him to turn the fan at me.

"Bye, Trav..." I said hesitantly.

He stopped pinching Chichi to look at me. His expression would be hard to decipher by Chichi, but to me, it was crystal clear.

Travis was getting tired of me.

Chapter Forty-Six

CHAYANNE

Sitting beside Trav, mi leg won't stop bouncing. A so me nuff? Maybe, mi shuda let things be. But dat hard fi do when Favio was approaching us now, looking sexy as ever.

Decked in a black shirt, black jeans, gold accessories and Clarks, the sight of this practically perfect man put my nerves at ease. My eyes locked on his thick arms. Both arms had half-sleeves with the same aesthetic as his old tattoos. He had a ring around a finger; it resembled the one Antaro had. Mi nuh know if a guard ring dem call it, but if a dat, mi need fi get one since crosses a seep ina mi life.

Him glance pon Trav. "Good evening, Chayanne. Is this necessary?"

"Yes." Mi sigh as dem glare pon each other. Dem try nuh badda wid the foolishness!

Shaking his head, Favio sidung. Him tap a simple black card against the table. "Are you going to stare at me or ask your questions?"

"Sorry." Mi clear mi throat. Oh gosh, why mi brain blank?! Him smell good, sexy body a distract mi. Mi cya stand him!

"Take your time."

"Where were you the past two years?" mi ask after a while.

"Italy," him seh, and mi brows knit.

"Why?"

"It was best I stayed away after what happened to you."

"Why yu wuda stay away when mi need yu?" mi ask, and him stop tap the card, jaws clenching as him look pon mi. Mi inch closer to Trav, and such man release a breath through him nose.

Tapping the card again, he looked away. "I thought you died, Chayanne. I mean, I saw you die..." He paused. "Everything happened so fast. I know I can't trust them, but I didn't know they'd lie to me like that."

"*Lied*? Mi nuh understand. I thought you were in prison—" Mi pause when him rest the card aside, pulling out him phone to show me a picture. My breath hitched. "That's Mama's funeral..."

He sighed, pocketing his phone. "I know that now."

As Trav lay a hand pon mi shoulder, mi ease him off. "I'm good," mi assure him, and him nod. Mi look at Favio. "Diana lie to we?" I asked, and him nod. Wow! What a conniving likkle—

"I'm sorry," he said, and Trav gasp. Favio glare pon Trav, who shut him mouth and glare back. "Yu cudn tell mi she straight?"

"Yu mek shi get hurt," Trav snapped.

"Trav, you spoke to him?" mi ask, my anger surging.

"One time. True yu deevn know how mi did waa fuck him up, Chichi. But mi hear fi easy miself, and be thankful mi nuh lose yu," Trav seh, and mi heart break.

Mi lay a hand pon him shoulder. "I understand, Trav."

Favio scoffed, standing. "Come here," he ordered, and mi nav a choice but fi go to him. Him tek mi hand ina fi him, and my fingers locked around his.

Mi drag mi eyes from wi hands to him face. Him a look pon mi. Mi look weh quick, hating how mi a fall back into stride wid him.

"Oye, nuh carry her go far." Trav glare at Favio as we walk away.

Favio mek we stop a short distance from my glowering brother, and mi release him hand. Mi cross mi arms beneath mi breasts, but him nuh look pon mi titty dem. Him eyes lock pon mine, a small smile on his lips.

"I want to make it up to you," he said after a while, and mi kiss mi teeth, looking away to a ripe mango hanging low on the tree we stood beneath. "We can take things slow," he added quickly, his desperation surprising me.

Mi think about it, then uncross mi arms. "Okay," mi seh, and his shoulders slackened. Giving him a tiny smile, mi bout fi walk weh when him grab mi wrist.

Favio step closer to me, and mi heart pace as him lean down to my height. Him place a feather-light kiss pon the corner of my mouth, and mi inhale a sharp breath. While my eyes widened, him pull away, smirking at me while his eyes glistened. "Baby steps."

Heart racing, mi quickly walk weh. Favio's eyes trail me, making mi steps uneven. Mi nuh waa drop and embarrass miself, so mi look pon the ground until mi reach Trav.

The silence stifling as we walk toward Trav car. Him disappointment a burn mi skin.

"Just say it," mi seh.

"Yu need fi stay weh from him," Trav advise.

"But I understand where him a come from."

Scoffing, Trav stop walk fi face mi. "The man leff yu fi near two years, Chichi! Yu forget that? Him and him lyad Mumma goodly a try weasel dem way back ina yu life fi fuck it up again."

"Favio isn't like his family..."

"Deevn you nuh sound like yu believe that, Jah knows." Shaking his head, him walk away. Him glance pon me when mi catch up to him. "Still a go Chez?" him ask, and mi nod while we enter the car.

The ride to Lime Hall feel longer than it usually be. When we reach, mi ask fimi godbaby, but Chezzy seh him father have him. Me and Trav sidung ina the sofa while Chezzy go the kitchen fi water fi we.

Mi sigh as Trav stand, walking toward the kitchen. Thankful fi the alone time, mi think bout the man. It nuh matter if him nuh good fi me. Nobody neva mek mi feel like how him mek mi feel, and me know me a the same fi him. No one understood us except ourselves.

"Here, Chichi." Chezzy hand tremble while she offer the glass to me.

Accepting the water, mi raise a brow. "Thanks. Yu good?"

"Y-yeah. Mi a go get ready fi work." She run go her room and slam the door shut, leaving me with my thoughts.

How me and Favio a go work when everybody hate him?

Chapter Forty-Seven

Favio

After I knocked on the door, I stepped back.

She peeked through the peephole before opening the door. "Favio baby!" She leaned against the threshold, smiling at me. Her too-short top rolled up a bit, exposing her under-boob. The belly ring dangling above her C-Section scar winked at me as I dragged my eyes to hers.

"Catty," I said.

"A the bwoy yu come look fa?"

"N—"

"Rajay, see Favio here!" Catty shouted, and the boy ran toward the door, smiling at me. He was eight now and had two missing front teeth.

I reached out, ruffling his curly hair, which all Welsh men had. "You good?"

"Yes," he replied, and I hummed before motioning for him to go away.

Catty smiled at him as he disappeared somewhere into the house. "He looks like you."

Catherine Tait.

My last girlfriend and the first woman I put my mouth on, in more ways than one. We had a long history, but the timeline was tricky. She wanted too much freedom, and I craved control. Really did rate her, but I had to let her go.

Not that I had a choice after she fucked me over.

"Wa yu been up to, Catty?" I entered the house and sat on the sofa, narrowing my eyes as she approached me.

"Missing you and that dick." She reached for my dick.

"Watch dem hand deh," I warned, and she pulled her hands to her side. I couldn't allow anyone to touch Chayanne's property. "When's the last time you talked to Fabiano?" I asked, and she tensed, making me glare. "Think carefully before you lie to me, Catty."

"I haven't seen him in a while—" She paused when the boy came into the room and said he was hungry. "I'll be back."

"No, it's fine. I'm leaving." I stood.

"Rajay, gwan ina the kitchen. Mi soon come," Catty said.

The boy waved while walking toward the kitchen. "Bye, Uncle."

Catty lowered her voice. "Can tell the big man I need money?"

I stared at her for a moment, then gave her every dollar in my wallet.

Later that night, I flashed the card to one of Fisha's men, Scotty. Afterward, we hopped in a nondescript vehicle, and he drove us to the pickup location. As Scotty and I checked the metal to make sure it was good, a small group of men approached us with their guns drawn.

"Yow, unu hand ova dem deh," one of them demanded.

"Who the fuck you, bredda? Go hand ova yu mada," a delivery guy said before he shot at them.

The newcomers returned fire, and I ducked behind Scotty's car, pressing my back against it while he did the same beside me. Scotty grabbed a rifle and tossed it to me. I quickly loaded it.

"Bomboclaat! Who dem deh?" Scotty whispered harshly, and I glanced toward the delivery car.

The delivery men were hiding too, clutching their guns ready to shoot once the gunfire ceased.

A moment passed before they stopped to reload, and we sent bullets flying. Three bodies fell, and one tried to run away.

Not a bloodclaat.

I stood and chased him. Once I had a clear shot, I shot him in his knee. He screamed, falling to the ground. I walked toward him, kicking his gun away, then turning him over with my foot. I pressed the heel of my shoe into his wound, and he groaned. Smirking wickedly, I yanked his mask off.

My smirk faded. Rage surged inside me. My grip tightened around the trigger as I aimed at his skull.

"S-slitta." He trembled while holding up a hand.

"Lizard," I spat, my eyes narrowing at him.

"Slitta, please. Look how much mi do fi yu—"

"Explain."

"Fisha—"

I squeezed the trigger. The close-up range made his brain splatter everywhere. I sneered at the blood leaking from his head, painting the dirt red.

Buonanima.

I marched back to the car, surprised to see Scotty lying in a pool of his blood. "Fuck!" I cursed.

"Put him ina the trunk. Quick," said one of the delivery men.

Another man walked toward us to help, but he froze as sirens blared in the distance. "We afi liff up." He backtracked to the car.

Throwing Scotty another glance, I hopped into the vehicle and blazed off in the opposite direction.

When I arrived at Fisha's hideout, my blood boiled as I kicked open the door of his office. I sneered at Fisha getting his dick sucked by a slut. I aimed the pistol at him while he fumbled to put away his pathetic excuse of a hood. The woman scurried away, plastering herself against a wall while screaming.

I shot next to her head, and her screams died off. "Shut up," I hissed, and she nodded frantically while clutching her wig to her chest.

"Slitta! Wa the fuck yaa do?!" Fisha exclaimed.

My body shook as I aimed at him. "Wa the fuck *me* a do?! Pier. Talk fast."

"Wa yaa chat boh?!" His eyes darted to the door as three of his men ran into the room.

They aimed their rifles at me, but I didn't flinch. If they wanted a war with the Italian mafia, they should shoot me.

"Why Lizard did deh the drop?" I asked coldly, hoping he knew better than to lie to me. The only reason I gave him a small fucking chance to come clean, was because of his years of loyalty to me.

Or so I fucking thought.

Recognition dawned on Fisha as he stood more upright, telling his men to lower their weapons. "Antaro—"

"Antaro?!" I squeezed the trigger. The bullet barely missed his head as he ducked, causing the slug to lodge into the wall behind him.

He put a hand to his ear, pulling it back with a gasp. Blood dotted his fingertips as he stared at me through petrified eyes. "Antaro call and seh fi mek him know if yu try buy metal from me."

"And you agreed?"

"The money did good!"

"Fuck wid mi again, and maa kill yu," I promised, lowering the gun while he nodded. "Do you have anything to drink?"

Releasing a breath, he motioned for his men to leave the room. The woman ran out of the room with them. We walked toward the minibar, and I fixed my drink.

Glass in hand, I sat on the chair in front of the desk. My arm hung off the armrest while I swirled the glass. I glared as Fisha sat on the edge of the desk. "Your loyalty is swaying. You're either with me or against me."

"Me wid you, Slitta. This naa happen again. The money did just too good fi deny."

I paused bringing the glass to my mouth, deciding against drinking. "How yago explain Scotty death to him wife and youth?"

"Scotty knew what he signed up for. Me will ensure him get a good funeral."

Nodding, I stood and walked toward the desk. As I rested the glass on the table, my eyes zoned in on his hand which was laid flat against the table.

I wished I could've said I wasn't thinking clearly about my next actions, but

I was. I'd been seeing clear as fucking crystals since I found out my woman was alive.

Grabbing my gun from out my waist, I pressed it on the second knuckle of Fisha's index finger. I held him tight as he struggled to get free, then I pulled the trigger. His scream pierced my ear, his eyes widening as he looked at what was left of two of his fingers. I grabbed him by the shirt, ensuring we were eye-to-eye as I threatened in a whisper, "Next time, it will be your life. Fuck with me again, Fisha."

"E naa happen again," he groaned out.

I smirked as I released him, using my hand to smoothen the ruffles in his shirt. "Glad we could come to an understanding."

He curled his good hand around his injured finger. Blood oozed through the creases between his fingers, trailing down his hand.

Shaking my head, I wiped my gun against his shirt. Once, then twice.

I hated people's blood.

As I walked out of the room, I realized there was something I hated more — men who screamed like pussies.

"Chayanne."

It took a ring too long for her to answer. "Favio?"

"I want to see you."

"Favio, it's one a.m., I was sleeping."

"Oh, really?" I leaned against my car, crossing my feet at the ankles while her silhouette froze.

She marched toward the window. Pushing the curtain aside, she gasped. "Favio," she gritted out, and I imagined her glaring despite not being able to see her clearly. "How yu know where mi live?"

"Do you really want to know?" I asked, and she didn't reply. "I'm coming in."

"No! Mi have a knife!" She ran away.

"I have a gun."

She stopped shuffling about, and I smirked as she returned to the front. Gravel crunched beneath my feet as I approached the house. The door was open by the time I got there. I hummed from approval as I slipped my phone in my pocket, looking at her. She was in a dress so short and tight, my dick was stirring to life. Her nipples pressed against the material, and my eyes locked on them.

"Favio, yu cya start do dis again," Chayanne complained, stepping aside so I could enter — backward with my right foot first. She closed the door, facing me with her arms crossed. "Things are diff— Why blood deh pon yu?"

Fuck.

I wiped the blood off my cheek with my hoodie's sleeve. I must have missed it in my haste to get here.

Since we met, seeing her was the only thing that could sate me whenever I was angry. I'd planned on breaking in, but I tried a saner approach after I saw her moving about the house.

Chayanne stepped closer, lifting my hoodie. Her mouth gaped, and I smirked, causing her to blush and look away.

"Still shy?"

"No."

"Look at me," I ordered, and she did for a second before looking away. I laughed, and she hissed her teeth.

"Whatever, Favio. Stay yaso."

I hummed, watching her ass sway as she walked into another room. How long did she expect me to wait before fucking her? I hoped she didn't plan on punishing me for too long.

A moment later, she returned and handed me a hoodie. My grip tightened around the green material while she tipped to clean my face with a wipe.

"You kept it..."

She hummed and pulled away, motioning to the one I wore. "Give it."

I gave it to her, and she took it to the kitchen. As I slipped the clean hoodie on, something burning filled the air. I smirked as I lowered myself onto the sofa.

She returned a moment later with a glass of Hennessy, and I raised a brow as she offered it to me. "What? Mi nuh know wa yu drink?"

"Why yu have Hennessy lying around?" I looked around the room, my eyes narrowing on the game console beside the TV. "Which man—"

"Mi naa do this wid yu tonight, Favio."

I looked at her, struggling to keep my anger at bay. "Who a fuck you?"

She rolled her eyes. "Mi naa sex nobody."

"Don't lie to me, Chayanne," I warned, and her eyes flickered away before settling on mine.

"Believe wa yu want. Mi nuh know why it matter—"

"It matters because I'm killing who was fucking you for me."

She hissed her teeth. "Yu cya behave fi once, Favio?"

My jaw ticked, and I looked at the console while taking a swig. Why did I insist on taking things slowly? I wanted her now, but I had to wait.

I hated waiting when she was so close, yet so far.

Chapter Forty-Eight

CHAYANNE

Waa loud knocking wake me up. Groaning, mi about fi get up, but mi freeze. My head was on Favio's chest, and my arm and leg were thrown over his body. His arm was around my waist, his fingers splayed across my abdomen.

Memories from last night return to mi, and mi smile while watching him sleep. Him look so at peace when him a sleep. That was how me feel when wi did stay up a talk bout any and everything.

The knock come again, and mi carefully come outta Favio hold. Mi go wash mi face and gargle likkle mouthwash, then run toward the door. A must me and dem own the house mek dem a knock the door so.

Mi hope ano such man, cause mi nuh know how me wuda explain this.

Relief fill me when mi see seh a big head Lamar. "Morning, Lamar." Mi cover a yawn as him tell mi seh him come collect sum fi Zaveer. "Soon come."

Lamar stop the door when mi try close it. "When since mi cya come in?"

"The house nuh tidy." Mi lock the door and run go the kitchen. Mi grab the bunch of banana, then return to the door. As mi open it, waa presence come behind me.

"Who you?" Favio hissed, and mi stiffen.

"A who dis, Chichi?" Lamar asked, and Favio step forward.

Mi step before Favio. "Bye, Lamar. Kiss mi baby fimi." Mi shut the door,

285

turning fi glare pon Favio.

"Yav a baby, Chayanne?" him ask coldly.

"Yu know seh mi nago ansa yu, though." Mi try step past him, but him grab mi wrist. Mi look weh from weh him hold me, meeting his glare as mi try pull free.

"The least you can do is answer. I doubt you were..."

Mi stop fight against him, raising a brow. "Doubt mi what?"

"I doubt you were keeping your legs shut."

Mi heart stop beat as him words slice through me.

"Chayanne, I'm sorry," he rushed out, and mi yank mi hand free.

"Lamar is Chezzy's babyfather," I spat, not finding pleasure in the regret that rushed to his eyes. A really so him think bout me? Shaking my head, mi step past him.

Him follow mi into the bedroom. "*Fiore...*"

Mi face him in a flash. "Yu cya just come back and feel seh everything back to normal, Favio! It nuh work dat way! Mi still hurt ova you leaving, and this isn't taking it slow!"

"I already explained that to you. Why're you bringing it up again?"

"It nuh matter wa yu explain! Yu cuda find a way come a mi so-called funeral, just like yu find a way fi do everything else! But no, all yu do a hide ina Italy like a fucking pussy!" Mi grit mi teeth as him eyes widen. This man always know how fi bring out the worst in me. "Please leave, Favio," mi seh, exasperated while pointing at the door.

"Ah." Him exit.

Mi kiss mi teeth, then go let out Marshy. Mi past Favio a search the living room, and mi roll mi eyes as mi continue walk toward the back door. Long as him nuh buck up ina Al things, mi nuh care wa him waa do.

"Wa yu do wid mi car key?" Favio ask.

"Mi look like mi want yu piece a key?" mi ask, and him glare at me and Marshy, who run back ina the house. Mi kiss mi teeth, then go get ready fi the people dem work.

Moments later, mi exit mi bedroom. Favio still a search fi him piece of key. Mi grudgingly help him find it.

We find it ina Marshy cage...

Favio tell her waa long string of Italian bad word, but mi deevn have the energy fi defend mi puppy pride.

We leave the house together. Mi walk past him car go down the road. Seconds later, him slow beside mi. Him exit the car and open the door, and mi look ina the opposite direction.

"Chayanne. Come in and don't let me have to put you in myself."

Weighing my options, mi enter. Mi hope him nuh feel like mi waa drive ina him piece of car. Mi only come in ya cause the sun hot and mi clean skin can use the likkle AC.

The car ride to Ochi from Exchange long and awkward. Mi waa open the door and jump out! Mi put mi hand pon the door handle, about fi yank it open when him mumble sum. Thinking him a try be slick, mi nearly bruk mi neck fi look pon him. "Wa yu seh?" mi hiss.

"I need a new car," him reply without looking pon me.

Mi look round him piece of car, realizing a him favorite BMW. "Surprised you still have this."

"Follow me to buy a new one," him seh, and mi mouth drop. Typical Favio! Him unfazed while mi a beat mi chest and froth up.

Mi clear mi throat, nodding. "Okay. Next Saturday."

"It's a date."

"It's not," I hissed, and he smirked.

CHEZANDRA

"Yu cya serious, Chichi." I glared while she watched the food spin in the microwave. She got in from work a few minutes ago, and I was sleeping over because I didn't want to be by myself.

"Tell Lamar fi stay outta mi bizniz," she replied calmly, and I hissed my teeth.

"Him nuh good fi yu! Mi cya believe yaa mek him fool yu so!"

She snapped her head around, giving me the first reaction since I started my rant. "Are you jealous mi can be happy with Favio while yu ina waa relationship wid a man yu cya stand?!"

My shoulders loosened as I stepped backward, my mouth gaping. Her eyes widened as she reached for me, but I took another step away.

Her angry eyes softened. "Chezzy—"

"Wow." I laughed while shaking my head.

"I'm sorry. I didn't mean it like that—"

"No, mi hear yu loud and clear." I left the kitchen and went to her room, where Zaveer slept.

"Chezzy, please doh leave. It late and yu nuh know where Lamar deh—" She grabbed my arm, and I shrugged her off.

With my son over my shoulder, I made a beeline out of her house. Tears pricked my eyes, but I couldn't tell if it was from hurt, anger, or both. I ignored all her pleas as I fixed Zaveer into his seat, then entered my car. I drove away without looking back.

My lips trembled as I journeyed from Exchange to Lime Hall. It was almost midnight; the road wasn't very busy. I wanted to pull over and cry this heavy weight off my heart and mind, but I couldn't with Zaveer in the car. I couldn't drive too fast either.

As I parked in the driveway, I got a text from Chichi. Ignoring her apology, I bit my cheeks to stifle a scream and repeatedly slapped the wheel.

I didn't feel any better by the end.

Wiping away my tears, I brought Zaveer inside and laid him on his bed. I went to my bedroom, looking at the space everyone thought Lamar and I shared. I was ashamed to let them know I slept alone every night while he warmed the sofa.

The quietness of the house taunted me as I dialed the person who most likely didn't want to talk to me.

"Pree?" he answered within the first ring, and a sad smile crossed my face. His voice got deeper over the years, and I loved it.

I lay on the bed, staring at the ceiling. "Uh, hi."

"Yu nuh usually call dem time ya. Sum happen between you and him again?"

"No."

"Surprising..."

"How?"

"Yu only check mi when unu ina things," he said, amplifying my guilt.

I couldn't bear the emotions in his voice, so I changed the topic. "It's Chichi. Yu know seh she and Favio a talk again?"

"Nuh stress yuself ova Chichi."

"Why yu sound like yu nuh approve either?"

"I don't, Jah knows."

"Then why yu nuh tell her fi lowe him before him mek she get hurt again?" I asked, sadness and anger filling me. Chichi was my other half; I knew her from diaper days to me changing diapers. I wouldn't be able to live with myself if she got hurt again.

"Ano just now Chichi love have ar own way. She afi experience things pon ar own fi learn. Lowe her."

Sighing, I rolled onto my belly. "How are you?"

"Yu know," he said plainly, and I frowned.

"Trav... I..."

"Can't or don't want to?" he asked, and I chewed my bottom lip.

"Goodnight, Trav." I hung up before he could reply, then crawled beneath the sheet. Trailing my hand across the cold space beside me, I sighed heavily.

Chapter Forty-Nine

Favio

Ending the business call, I slowed before Ocean Village, taking a second to appreciate my woman. She was eating a blue snow cone. She was in a sexy, short yellow dress, and swapped her go-to Crocs for sandals. Her hair was in a high ponytail. Recognizing my vehicle, she strolled over while looking at her feet. I exited to open the door. Her perfume suffocated me as she passed by to sit, and she laughed while I coughed. Shaking my head, I closed the door, before returning to my seat.

"Hi!" She smiled at me before she continued sucking the life out of the straw.

Fuck. To be a straw...

Blood rushed to my dick, and I drove off before it could harden more. "You look beautiful."

"Thanks..." she whispered, and I glanced at her. She was blushing, making me realize how much I missed seeing that beautiful smile. She broke the trance when she offered the cup to me. "Yu waa sum?"

"No."

"Oh... Tru mi see how yaa watch it."

I didn't reply.

She filled the silence in true Chayanne fashion by talking the entire journey to the car dealership. While I listened and gave my input here and there, I realized two things.

One, she missed me.

Two, she was hesitant about us.

It didn't bother me. I didn't mind working on getting her to trust me again because this moment confirmed that just as I was waiting for her, she'd been waiting for me.

"Then a so car expensive?" Chayanne tried her best not to gawk at the vehicles.

"These are next year models, Chayanne." I trailed behind her. The way her ass sidung ina the dress have mi a way.

She stopped walking to glare at me. "Why yaa walk so slow?"

"I like the view back here," I said, and her eyes widened before she resumed walking, her steps uneven. Grinning, I caught up to her within a few long strides.

Her eyes lingered on an SUV before they dragged to a four-door coupe. "I like this for you."

She had great taste; I had to admit.

After I bought it and told them my mechanic would pick it up to handle the interior at his shop, we returned to St. Ann. Chayanne fell asleep, so I drove her to the house I rented. I was taking her out of the vehicle when she stirred awake.

Yawning, she looked around while I helped her to stand. "Weh we deh?"

"My house." I watched as she grabbed her bag before following me to the house. I entered after her and offered something to eat or drink, but she declined. My brow raised. "You good?"

She nodded. "Why?"

"You don't ever turn down food," I said, and she chuckled before sighing. "Come here." I pulled her to the living area and made her sit beside me on the sofa. "I'm listening."

She played with her fingers. "Me and Chezzy have waa argument. She nuh waa mi talk to yu."

"Thought she liked me?"

Chayanne scoffed. "Like yu care boh if people like yu or not."

I smirked. "You're right, but it's surprising because you used to say she'd always tell you to fuck me."

She gasped. "Mi cya believe yu memba dat!"

"I remember everything you've told me."

Smiling, she scooted closer to me. As she curled into my side, I threw my arm over her shoulder. "Everybody waa mi stay weh from yu, but I..."

"You?"

She leaned off me, searching my eyes for a moment. "I don't want to." She pressed her lips against mine.

Shocked, it took a second longer for me to kiss her back with all the force she kissed me with. Her lips were softer than I remembered. My dick throbbed at how she sexily moaned into my mouth. She straddled me, and as I pulled her closer by the ass, I was more at peace than I'd been for a long while.

Moving my hands from her ass, I trailed them upward, lifting her dress inch by inch. I passed the waistband of her panties and grazed her abdomen. As I reached for her right breast, she pulled away.

Panting, she climbed off me and fixed her clothes. "Sorry. I'm not ready yet."

I covered my lap with a cushion. "Don't apologize."

"Can we take things slower?" she asked, and I nodded at the same time her phone rang. "I have to take this." She walked outside.

I should clone—

No. I needed to put more trust in her. Chayanne knew better than to fuck with me. After my last wild accusation, I needed to be better.

I wanted us to be better this time.

Tossing the cushion aside, I grabbed a bag of weed and went to the backyard. I left the door ajar.

While I smoked, I answered business messages from a wise old man. I met him at a bar in Naples on one of the many nights I was drowning my sorrows.

Minutes later, Chayanne was approaching the door. "Mi nuh know, Al," she whispered.

I narrowed my eyes, then shook my head to rid the absurd thoughts.

She ended the call before walking through the door. She placed her phone atop the table beside the lighter, then straddled me. I released her hair from the tie, watching it fall below her ass as I ran my fingers through it.

Weed and my woman were the perfect blend.

"Surprised yu still love smoke," she said as I blew fumes away from her.

"Surprised yu still love chat."

She rolled her eyes, and I chuckled. "Mek mi try it."

"Come offa mi, Chayanne."

"Please nuh," she begged, and I stared at her for a moment.

Taking the spliff from my mouth, I put it in hers and watched her lips curl around it. "Inhale." I withdrew it after she did. "Hold."

She erupted into a coughing fit. "Mi chest!"

I roared with laughter while she furiously rubbed her chest. "Too fucking nuff."

Chapter Fifty

CHAYANNE

I woke up in an empty bed, dressed in Favio's shirt. Mi go use the bathroom, then go downstairs. Mi find him in the gym, and mi smile at him. His golden-brown skin glistened with sweat. I loved how his muscles flexed while he bench-pressed. God really spend an extra day or two fi sculpt him from the finest stone! Mi waa lock him ina the house so no gyal cya look pon him.

"Good morning." Mi step further into the room.

"Thought you weren't going to come in," he said, and I chuckled.

"I was enjoying the view." Mi raise a brow as him put dung the weights and call mi over. Mi walk toward him. "Wa yaa do?"

"Bench press you."

Mi stiffen as him hoist mi ina the air. "Nuh drop mi!"

"Relax."

Him effortlessly push me up and down, and mi relax a bit. After mi think the likkle batty mi put on a weigh mi down, him prove mi only weighty ina mi imagination. Four minutes later, him put me down.

Mi grin. "Mi did trust you!"

"*Bugiardo*," he said, and I chuckled while watching him stand.

"Go shower. I'll make breakfast," I said, and he nodded before going upstairs. Mi enter the kitchen in search of ingredients. Him nav much food, so mi mek do wid wa him have.

By the time mi done cook and plate the food, him enter the dining room. Him shirtless, making it hard for me to focus on placing the plates on the table. Him hold the phone to him ear while a laptop in the other hand.

"Yu cudn put on a shirt?" mi ask as him sit opposite me.

"Nothing you haven't seen before, Chayanne," he said, and I dragged my eyes from his pecs to my food.

"You need groceries," mi murmur.

"We'll go later," him seh before focusing on the call. Based pon what likkle Italian mi understand, him a talk to Sergio, the man who a help him build a new wine company from scratch.

Moments later, we done eat, and mi start wash the plate dem. Him sneak behind me, wrapping his arms around my waist and kissing my cheek. A shiver ran beneath my skin as I blushed, about to face him.

Tek time mash ants, yu find him belly.

My smile faded, and mi ease him off me.

Sighing, him step backward. "I have to go to Italy for a week."

Mi frown. "Why?"

"Work. Do you want to come?"

"No," I blurted, and him brows furrow. "I have work and... stuff."

"My woman shouldn't work."

"Me ano nobody woman." Not his. Not such man. Nor tha youth deh.

Favio scoffed. "I can pay you double to come."

Mi chuckle and walk toward him. Throwing my arms over his shoulders, mi pull him down to mi height. Mi smile when him arms wrap around my waist. "It's okay. Go work, but... please don't take forever to come back."

"I'll never leave you like that again, *fiore.*"

Chezzy cut her eye afta me, then go back ina her house. Sighing, mi enter and close the door. She walk toward the kitchen while me go to Zaveer, who ina the playpen.

Him notice me and stand up, smiling brightly. "Chi!"

"Hi, Aunty's baby!" I lifted him, kissing both his cheeks. "Missed me?"

He nodded. "Yes!"

Mi reveal the toy mi did hide behind mi back, shaking it in front of his face. "What's this?"

"Banana!" Zaveer accepted the banana plushie, making me chuckle as we enter the kitchen.

"What should you say?" Chezzy ask while checking her pot pon the stove.

"Tank you!" Zaveer held my cheek and kissed it.

"*Thank*," Chezzy seh while me kiss Zaveer.

Smiling, mi sit at the table, watching Chezzy stir the pot. "Chezzy..."

"Yes?" she asked coldly, and mi sigh.

"I'm sorry for what I said... Mi understand why yu stay with him, but if you naa leff, yu nufi try dictate who me—" I paused as she glared. "I know you don't approve of Favio, but he's my boyfriend. I'd really love it if you'd at least try to give him a chance."

"Yu too forgiving, Chichi. Yu deserve better."

"I don't want better. I want him."

Chezzy sigh, covering the pot and facing me. "Mi nuh like wa yu seh boh Lamar either, but me will mek it slide. And for Favio, mi naa mek no promises, but me will try be cordial with him."

Smiling, mi jump to mi feet and go hug her while being mindful of Zaveer. When mi pull away, mi go put him ina him playpen. Him start cry.

Chezzy shake her head as mi reenter the kitchen. "Mi tell yu fi stop liff him up so much. A you spoil him."

"Lies!" Mi return to Zaveer and put him to sleep. Mi return to the kitchen fi help Chezzy cook we Sunday dinner. "How's work?"

She smiled. "Good."

Chezzy have waa associate's degree in phlebotomy, but she only work pon weekends. She wish she cuda work more, but she afi stay wid the baby cause Lamar work during the week and him nuh waa Zaveer get a babysitter.

"Good to hear. Anyway, yu can go get ready fi work. Mi will done cook, so yu can eat before yu leave," mi seh, and she smile while hugging me.

"Thanks, Chichi. Not just for this, but fi keeping Zaveer, too. Lamar seh him busy this weekend, so mi nuh know how mi wuda manage widout yu."

"Stop the foolishness. Yu know Zaveer a mi baby. Gwan go bathe," mi seh, and she chuckle while walking away.

An hour after Chezzy leave, me and my godson have a full day. By the time Chezzy come home, the two a wi sleepy. Chezzy beg mi fi sleep over, but mi decline cause mi nuh waa see dutty Lamar, who should've taken over from me two hours ago.

Mi tck a taxi go home. Mi lay pon mi bed and talk to Favio pon the phone until mi drop asleep.

By the morning, mi ina pain cause mi sleep terribly. Fi mek matters worse, mi a run behind schedule and smaddy a knock pon mi door. Mi almost trip over Marshy while running fi go open the door.

The man clear him throat as mi pull down mi dress, covering my panties. "Chayanne Bailey?" him ask, and mi nod, focusing on the bouquet of roses in his hands.

Smiling, mi sign fi it, then accept them. "Thank you," mi seh as mi heart float to Cloud Nine. Mi go the kitchen, leaving Chezzy to shut the door. Mi rest the bouquet atop the counter, then read the handwritten note.

Have a good day, fiore.

"Aww," I swooned, and Chezzy peek over mi shoulder, then scoff. Mi sigh as mi tuck the note between two of the thornless red roses. "Good morning to you too, Chezandra Hope Tomlinson."

"Realize mi nuh seh nun to yu?" she retort, and mi roll mi eyes.

"Weh mi baby?"

"Him father have him," she seh while mi smile at her outfit. She ina waa tight-fitting green blouse, and a skirt weh sidung proper pon her big batty.

Mi squeeze her ass. "Yaa waa nice piece a gyal ino, no sah! A weh yago?"

She slap weh mi hand. "Mi parents."

Maybe Lamar upset her this morning or she deh pon her period... Sighing, mi return to mi room fi finish getting ready fi the people dem work. After mi done, mi give Marshy a treat, then leave wid Chezzy.

We reach Aunty ina quick time. Chezzy drive senseless like Trav, who teach wi fi drive the summer after we graduate high school.

"Morning," Aunty seh to me, giving Chezzy a head-to-toe before she go inside the house.

Chezzy roll her eyes before looking at me. "Tell Mommy mi soon come help unu put Daddy's files in the new office."

Mi nod and go inside. "Chezzy seh shi soon come back," I told Aunty while grabbing a box of files.

"Ah doh know wa wrong with her," Aunty grumbled while we enter Uncle office.

"Wa yu mean?" mi ask, glancing at the twins, who a sit pon the floor while shredding a box of paper.

"Chezandra think because she a tek man now, she nuh supposed to still answer to me."

Mi purse mi lips instead of seh nun. Aunty Kenzie and Aunty Simone must think seh me and Chezzy a still baby.

Chezzy return waa hour later. Me and Aunty done sort the files minutes ago.

"Bye, Aunty. And tell yu son dem fi stop stay up late a play game," I said while hugging Aunty pon the veranda.

Aunty sighed. "Mi tired fi talk to dem, Chichi. Mi waa hear seh dem a fail waa class so mi can handle them. Later." Aunty waved at Chezzy, who blew the horn.

Mi stroll toward the car, pausing when mi phone ring. Checking the caller ID, mi gulp. Mi cya deal wid next man right now. Favio will kill me and him. Mi nuh know wa mi wuda tell Yolo if Favio kill ar favorite cousin.

Shane five years older than me, and we met at graduation. Mi did only entertain him cause Chezzy seh mi fi try move on.

Declining the call, mi enter the car. A strong aroma fly dung mi throat, and mi choke. "Sas Crise, Chezzy! A the wul perfume bottle yu use pon yuself?" Mi bring down the window.

Chuckling, Chezzy pinched my cheek. "I want to smell good like you."

Mi slap her hand away, and she laugh before driving away. The entire journey, mi look through the window and think about Favio while Chezzy sing along to the radio.

Oh, God, mi a go come!

Been so long since mi use mi rose, and all the alcohol I did earlier with Yolo and Shane, go right between my legs.

Parting my legs wider, I massaged my breast as I pressed the toy harder against my clit. The flick of its tongue made me miss Favio more, but there was nothing I could do when he was miles away and my mind was full of images of him.

Naked.

Between my legs.

Sucking me.

Touching me.

Making me scream.

Repeatedly hitting new highs.

I shut my eyes tighter, arching off the bed as my orgasm drew closer. "*Favi*," I moaned. I was so, so close now. My legs shook as the toy brought tears to my eyes. Its mechanical whir added to my pleasure. I was going to come harder than I did lately.

And I would've.

If the light fi the room neva flick on.

Screaming, mi snap mi legs shut. Mi eyes fly open fi meet... Favio?

He burst out laughing. A big, dutty laugh weh him throw him head back and wipe tears outta him eyes.

"Stop!" Embarrassed, mi jump outta the bed. Mi cover the toy with mi sheet, then slip on mi big shirt. "How did you get in here?" I hissed, crossing my arms when him nuh stop laugh. "Favio!"

"I'm sorry—" He bit his lips, bursting into another fit of laughter seconds later.

Mi roll mi eyes, looking away. Mi afi go bag mi head afta today.

"Where's your bathroom?" him ask, and mi give him the directions. His loud laughs faded as he exited.

Deciding I'd clean the toy later because mi too on edge fi think properly, mi throw it ina mi drawer of toys.

Favio reappeared, closing the door as Marshy ran toward the room. "Give me it." He extended a hand that had a water droplet on it.

"Why?"

"I'll show you," he said, and my brows furrowed as I took it out of the drawer, handing it to him. He pulled a chair near the edge of the bed, then sat. "Come skin out yu pussy fimi."

Mi choke. "W-what?"

A mischievous smirk stretched across his face, pulling me toward him. I lay before him, keeping my legs pressed together. "I'm not shaved..." That was the only thing mi cuda think of nufi jump Favio's bones before time.

"I don't care." He tried prying my legs open, and I tightened them.

"But—"

"It's just hair, Chayanne. Am I twelve?" he asked, and I shook my head. "Exactly. Open your legs, cause mi nuh know who yu think fraid of hair."

A shiver ran down my spine as I opened my legs. He grabbed my ankles, tugging me closer and resting my feet on either handle of the armrest. A rush of cold air hit my clit as he lifted my shirt over my head. His eyes trailed my body, settling on my pussy.

Sas Crise! The man must a wonder wa kinda forest this him a come explore after so many years.

Favio reached forward to grip my chin, making me look at him. "The shyness."

"S-sorry..." I tensed as he parted my folds, pressing his thumb against my clit.

"Do you want me to stop?"

"N-no," I said, and he smirked, releasing my chin.

Leaning back, he stopped rubbing my clit to turn on the toy. A hum filled the room, and his eyes widened. "Mi bloodclaat!"

Mi sit up. "A wa?"

"Never knew it was this fast," he said, and I chuckled. "Lay down."

"Okay." I obeyed his command, laughs becoming moans as Favio pressed the toy against my clit. It licked me hard and fast, making me writhe.

He slipped a finger inside me, thrusting and curling it. "Like that?"

"Yes. Faster," I begged, and he narrowed his eyes.

"No."

"Favi," I groaned, tightening my legs as my orgasm rushed forward. "I'm—"

"Not yet." He turned the toy off, tossing it onto the bed. Dropping to his knees, he slipped another finger inside me and brought his face closer.

His eyes hooked onto mine as his hot mouth closed around my clit, sucking it into his mouth. Weakened, my leg fell over his shoulder. His fingers sank into my thighs, preventing me from running from his talented tongue.

"Mm, faster, Favio." I panted toward the ceiling, my eyes closing as I tossed my head back and grabbed at the sheets. My back arched off the bed and my lips parted wide, no sound escaping as my orgasm took full control.

Pleasure shot through my body, making me tremble. I buried my fingers in his hair, tugging at the long strands as his tongue amplified my powerful climax.

I rode out the throes of ecstasy on his face, weakened as I regained control of my limbs. My chest heaved as I released his hair.

Favio pulled back, smirking as he wiped the back of his hand across his mouth. "Still loud."

"Stop," I groaned, blushing as I covered my face with the pillow.

"Why are you hiding? I'm not finished with you yet." He pried the pillow off my face, and my eyes locked onto his dick that saluted me.

Kiss mi neckstring! A dat mi used to tek ina mi young age?!

"Are you scared?" He chuckled as he crawled over me. His naked chest brushed my sensitive nipples, making a breathy sigh escape me.

I shook my head. "Do you have a condom?"

He gripped his dick, looking between us as he rubbed the tip along my wet slit. "No."

I laid a hand on his arm. "Wait—"

He stopped rubbing and met my eyes. "I'm clean, and you're clean, right? You said you weren't fucking anyone."

Jesam peace, watch how mi lie dem a ketch up to mi! I smiled, hoping him never see how mi eyes widen briefly. "Yeah... I'm clean, but don't come in me."

He stared at me, then shook his head. He released his dick, resting his hands on either side of my body. "Put it in."

Looking into his eyes, I reached between us and grabbed his dick. The veins pressed into my palm as I found my entrance. A breath passed our lips as he slowly entered me. I bit into my lip, silencing a scream as he pushed in further. He paused, closing his eyes while turning his head toward the ceiling.

"*Fuck.*" His eyes fluttered open to look at me. "Yu nehna fuck fi real?"

"Favio," I groaned, trying to relax. Sex fi so hot?

"Relax."

"I am. You're too big," I cried, and he smirked.

"You took it before," he said, and I glared while he grinned. Pulling out, he stood at the side of the bed. "Come here."

Mi smile and go over there fast.

He chuckled as I arched. "A demon alone nuh fraid of backshot ino, Chayanne."

"I'm your demon."

Humming, his fingers sank into my waist as he moved his waist around. My eyes widened as his dick brushed my ass.

"Favio!" I screamed, pulling away.

He pulled me back. "I'm not fucking you in your ass, Chayanne. Relax," he said, and I sighed. Chuckling, he lined his dick with my pussy.

I pushed back onto him, gripping the sheets at the intrusion.

"*Stai bene?*" His voice was strained. He wanted to sex me into the sheets, but he was holding back.

"Yeah," I said before I started throwing it back at him.

"Slow down before mi come quick," he complained despite matching my pace. His entire length was deep inside me, but it felt too good to run away from.

I whined.

Squinted my pussy.

Moaned at the top of my voice while he thrust into me so sweetly.

Yet so hard.

It was a mix of pain and pleasure, and I loved it because it was from him.

He grabbed a handful of my hair, tugging it hard. My scalp burned as he craned my neck. My heart raced as I looked at him.

"How me do without yu pussy?" He kissed my forehead before pushing my head onto the sheets.

Our slapping skin filled the room as Marshy scratched at the door, but I ignored her by moaning louder. I screamed into the sheets as I fell flat, and he followed me down. His thighs slapped against me as his dick touched me at an angle that made me see stars.

"Tek time, mi a go dead."

"Do you want me to fuck you faster, Chayanne?" Favio taunted, and I nodded eagerly as tears filled my eyes.

"Yes... Yes," I cried while he moaned in my ear. My abdomen tightened, and I bit into the sheets to muffle my screams.

His breathing was heavy against my skin as he showered my neck with kisses. My skin tingled and my soul was about to leave my body, but my phone rang.

I glanced at it. "Favio—"

"No." He pulled out, flipping me over and slamming into me.

My legs wrapped around his waist, locking him in place while his mouth covered mine. He slowed his pace as his tongue slipped inside my mouth, making my eyes roll back. I didn't fight for dominance. I was his, and I wanted him to control me.

He broke away, leaving me in a daze as he kissed from my neck to my breasts. His tongue swirled around my right nipple as he sucked it into his mouth, making me pant heavily at the ceiling.

After he showered my left breast with a little affection, he kissed to my mouth.

His lips tenderly grazed mine. "Come with me, *fiore*."

I nodded, eager to please him. "I'm close."

He lifted his body off mine, staring at me while maintaining his pace. "I know."

"Come in me," I coaxed, clenching my walls tighter around him. I couldn't hold this anymore.

Neither could he.

Tremors shook my body as Favio released inside me while I came.

The high was beautiful, an out-of-world experience that left me with aftershocks even as he pulled out of me.

Breathing heavily, he lay beside me. We stayed in silence for a while, catching our breaths. Mi need fi go pee, but mi too tired. Rolling over onto my side, I threw an arm and leg over him. Cum crawled out of me, seeping into the sheet.

"Let me get the rag—"

I held him closer. "It's fine. Let's sleep."

"Okay." He rubbed my shoulders and kissed my forehead, making me smile as I drifted off to sleep...

That sleep only lasted a few minutes because my phone rang.

Groggy, mi lean off Favi. He was asleep. I loved seeing him sleep. He was always relaxed. Mi wish him cuda look like this all the time.

The phone ring again, and mi sigh as mi answer it. "Chezandra?" mi snap, realizing Favi cleaned the mess between my thighs. He didn't redress me, though. By the look of it, him naked, too.

"Chichi?" Chezzy sobbed, and mi sit up.

"Yu alright?"

What she said next made me spring into action.

Slapping Favi out of his sleep, tears brimmed in my eyes as I rushed out, "Carry me to the hospital. Chezzy baby naa breathe."

Chapter Fifty-One

FAVIO

Hospitals. I abhorred them.

There was something about the rush and disorder that amplified the hate I had for these places. The stench of blood slipped through the barrier of disinfectants and disarrayed my senses. I never went to these places unless I had to. Even then, I stayed outside.

Yet here I was — being hauled by Chayanne through a horde of sick people in search of the front desk. Her nails dug into my palm, but I held it like a man. She was going through a lot. She almost ran out of the house naked after she woke me up. I had to throw on the first clothing I saw on her. The dress had a tear on the neckline and the Crocs were mismatched, but it was better than her running around with her pussy facing the world.

Arriving at the front desk, Chayanne rushed out, "Miss, morning. Where—"

The lady scrunched her nose. "Sorry, can you speak louder?"

"Where can I find—"

"Chichi!" came a yell from behind us.

Chayanne and I spun around, and she released my hand to run toward Chezandra, who stood beside Travis. Chezandra's body shook from loud sobs as Chayanne pulled her into a hug. Rubbing my palm, I walked toward them.

"Me—" Chezandra sniffled. "Me still cya get Lamar!"

Chayanne rubbed Chezandra's back. "Maybe him on him way?"

Chezandra shook her head. "N-no. All mi a call him, mi naa get him. Y-yu can follow me back to the room, please?" she asked, and Chayanne glanced at me before they walked away.

Travis and I put space between us.

It was bittersweet watching Chayanne with Chezandra, but it made me smile a little. Their relationship reminded me of the one I had with Fabiano, back when he was my brother.

The smile faded when Chayanne returned moments later.

Travis walked toward us. "Him a breathe?" he asked, and Chayanne nodded as she wrapped her arms around me and laid her head on my chest.

"Chezzy ina the room with him. Thanks fi come through fi her cause mi never hear mi phone."

"Dat good, Chichi." He looked behind us, clenching his jaw. "Mi afi shove out now. Tell ar fi shout mi if she need anything." He took long strides away.

Chayanne looked at me. "Sorry for bringing you here. I know how much blood bothers— Nuh stinking Lamar dat? Lamar! Lamar!" Chayanne pulled away to wave her hands in the air, and the man ran toward us.

Mi bloodclaat! A wa kinda big head dis? Man head look like it grow since the last time mi see him.

Chayanne crossed her arms. "Weh yu did deh?! Yu know how Chezzy worried?!"

He dragged a hand down his face. "Mi did a deal with sum so mi phone deh pon silent," he said, and she hissed her teeth. "Weh dem deh?"

She laced her hand in mine, leading us to a room. Through the window, I saw Chezandra sitting at her son's bedside, clinging to his small hand. One of the many monitors displayed a steady heart rate. Lamar rushed into the room. He hugged Chezandra, who didn't release their son's hand to hug him back.

Chayanne smiled at them. It warmed my heart how much she cared for this little boy. She'd make an exceptional mother.

She dragged her eyes to mine, looking away with a small smile when she realized I was staring at her. "Ready?"

"Been," I said, and she snorted.

I woke up too early in the fucking morning because a phone wouldn't stop ringing. I nudged Chayanne. "Your phone."

Still half-asleep, she shoved my body. "It's yours."

Groaning, I found the phone buried somewhere in the mess of sheets. When I found it, I answered without checking the ID. "*Sí?*"

"Yu can come get we, please?" cried a woman.

Moving the phone from my ear, I looked at the ID and clenched my jaw. Getting out of bed, I tugged my boxers on and walked toward the balcony. "Speak," I said after I closed the door behind me.

"Him find me and Rajay."

"What the fuck does that have to do with me?"

"Him beat mi and seh him soon come back."

"Where are you now?" I returned inside. Passing by the bed, I glanced at Chayanne, who was in a deep sleep.

Good fuck do that.

"I'm somewhere in Albert Town," she forced out.

I stopped tugging on a hoodie to raise a brow. "Nuh Stetin yu live?"

"Mi just tek up Rajay and run. Come, please. Mi already tell the big man, and him seh mi fi mek you come cause you closer," she said, and I dragged a hand down my face. How did she have this much energy at five in the morning?

Mi nuh like when nobody except my woman stress mi.

Scratch dat.

Mi nuh like when nobody fucking stress mi.

"Where are your bodyguards?" I asked, and she told me he sent them away. "Soon fawud." Hanging up, I finished getting dressed and returned to the room. I glanced at my woman.

The white sheets were lazily thrown below her round, perfect ass. Her hands were tucked beneath the pillow, displaying a teasing side view of her right breast that I tried swallowing whole a few hours ago. One of her legs was bent at that ninety-degree angle women seemed fond of, giving me a peek at her pussy.

I should wake her for a quick fuck.

No, I couldn't. Not right now. She needed to rest.

I walked closer to the bed and kissed her head. "I'll be back," I whispered, bringing the sheet up to her waist before leaving.

A little over an hour later, I parked before a bus stop. I exited the car, nodding at the boy as he entered. Grabbing his mother by the hand, I hauled her a short distance away.

"Favio baby—" She hugged me, and I released her hand to push her off.

"Don't fucking start, Catty. Yu good now?"

"Yeah." She smiled through tears.

My jaw clenched, hating how she still looked so pretty. "You can drop the act."

"What act? Yu think mi do this to miself?" She pointed at the red palm print on her face.

"I never said you did."

She pouted. "So why don't you believe me, Favio baby?"

"He has no way of finding you unless you reached out to him."

"I—"

"Don't lie to me, Catty."

Looking away, she gulped. "I get lonely sometimes... The big man seh mi nav permission fi deh with anybody else because I'm a part of *la famiglia*. And Miss D said if I wanted to leave, I could, but not with Rajay." She dragged her eyes to mine, her lips trembling as she sought pity.

I showed her none. I knew how my parents were.

"Yu naa fuck the man again a wa yaa seh?" I asked, and she sighed.

"Okay, fine... I am. Mi find him about two years ago, and mi tell him bout Rajay. Him did upset, but him neva act up cause him seh him need a place fi stay. Mi beg the guards nufi seh nun to the big man because we did a do good, and him nuh put him hand pon mi until today. Him very antsy since yu come to the house—"

I raised a brow. "How did he know I was there?"

She stepped backward. "Mi neva know seh him put camera pon the house, Favio baby. Please doh hurt me."

"Mi eva put mi hand pon yu, Catty?" I asked, and she shook her head. "He did this to you because of me?"

Her shoulders slumped as she wiped away tears. "I-I don't know. Him only ask if mi tell yu weh him deh, and I said no. Mi deevn know where Ambi deh most of the time unless him want sex or food. A me afi beg him fi bond with Rajay."

Her trembling body weakened my resolve. Sighing, I walked away. She followed me to the car, and I drove to St. Ann. The boy kept talking to me, but I couldn't look at him.

I'd thought the boy was mine until I found out why Fabiano almost beat Catty to death. They were fucking behind my back, and she didn't want to abort it.

My grip tightened around the wheel as I parked on Runaway Bay's highway, then exited the car. I made some calls trying to find a hotel for her, but they were all full. *Mamma* hadn't booked a room for her. They left her in my care as if I was the one who was supposed to clean up their bastard's messes.

I dialed my last option. "Chayanne."

"Yes?" she answered within the first ring, and I smirked. She was learning. Good.

I sat on the bonnet. "Are you still at the rental?"

"Yes, but mi about fi go to the hospital cause a soon visiting hours. Weh yu deh? Mi did a call yu, but it go voicemail."

"I had to do something." I looked over my shoulder at Catty, who was watching the boy relieve himself in the bushes.

Chayanne's voice lowered. "You good?"

"*Sì*. Drive my car—" I pulled the phone from my ear as she squealed loudly. "Yu sure?!"

"Don't crash it," I warned. Jelani brought it from Kingston while I was away. I wanted to double-check the interior detail, so I had yet to drive it.

"I won't!" she promised, hanging up.

"Who was that?" Catty asked as I walked toward them.

"Why the fuck yu feel yu can question me?" I hissed, and she winced.

"Can you not curse around him?" She squeezed the boy's shoulders while he looked at me.

He was a Welsh. He'd be another fuck-up.

I entered the car, and they entered after me. I drove them to the rental and got them settled in a guestroom. "You can stay here for the time being. I'll find somewhere for you guys to stay this evening."

"Thanks, Favio b—"

"Catty," I warned, and she sighed. I looked at the boy. "Food is downstairs if you're hungry."

"Thanks, Uncle," he said, and I nodded.

I went to the room I shared with Chayanne, chuckling at the new sheets. I unblocked Antaro, and we discussed new housing arrangements for Catty.

Afterward, Antaro asked, "You heard that Lizard died?"

My brow raised. "Really?"

"Yeah. Do you know anything about that?"

"No." I moved the phone from my ear to see that my woman was calling. Without so much as a goodbye, I ended Antaro's call to answer her.

She told me she needed me, and I got there as fast as possible. She was sitting near the front desk. When she saw me, she ran over with tears in her eyes. She jumped into my arms, and I held her close. "Favi," she cried.

"*Stai bene*?" I asked, hoping her godson hadn't gotten worse.

"Can we talk outside?" she asked, and I allowed her to take me outside. Releasing my hand, she glared at me.

Why me always attracted to the mad gyal dem? I gulped as I stared at her. Did I do something? I didn't leave the toilet seat up, and I didn't fuck her hard enough to bruise her.

"Where were you this morning?! I had a breakdown, and I needed you!" she whisper-yelled.

"Sorry. I was—" I paused, unsure how to tell her I was with my ex.

"Yaa gimi bun?" she asked, and my brows knitted.

"I don't get hard for anyone except you."

She hissed her teeth. "That the wul a unu man always seh! Mi hope when mi start gi yu back bun, yu can wul dat!"

Wa the fuck this? "Chayanne, careful wa yu talk round me, yere dat?"

She rolled her eyes. "Whatever. Mi park far from yaso, so yu can carry mi go Exchange, please?"

"Mek whichever man yu waa fuck carry yu," I said, and she opened her mouth to argue. Gyal ya ago mad mi. Shaking my head, I walked toward my car and opened the door.

She stared at me for a moment before she walked toward me and entered. She crossed her arms as I closed the door.

I got behind the wheel and drove away. "Are you okay now?"

"Like yu care?"

"Watch yu mouth before mi crash this fuck with the two a wi."

"So yu nuh crash it then!" she barked, and I floored the gas. Her eyes widened and her hands darted out to press against the dashboard. "Favio, stop!"

Rum chat.

I slowed down.

She fumed quietly for the rest of the journey, but I was thankful. Chayanne knew how to bring out the worst in me, and she insisted on testing me.

When we arrived at the house, I sat on the sofa and played on her console. She searched for something for her godson.

After she found it, she stomped toward the door. "Mi ready."

I turned the game off, trailing behind her as the doorknob rattled. Chayanne's eyes widened. She tried pushing me toward her bedroom, but I stood my ground and pulled out my gun. Mek a man come in ya see if mi nuh kill him, then she.

The door swung open, and I smirked.

Chapter Fifty-Two

CHAYANNE

"Chayanne, wa dis bwoy a do ina mi house?!" Al yelled.

"Chayanne, move," Favio stated calmly.

Mi heart a beat so fast. Mi can hear it ina mi ears while cold sweat form pon mi farid. "Unu put down the gun dem, please!" mi beg, on the verge of crying.

Them ignore my pleas. Both men too focused pon trying to kill each other without shooting me. Mi know mi need fi move, but mi rooted in place — standing at an angle where I could see the both of them. I couldn't imagine losing either of them. They meant everything to me.

"Favi, put down the gun, please," I begged, but he kept his icy glare on Al. "Yu cya kill mi father, Favi."

Favi scowled. "A this yaa call father, Chayanne?"

"*This*?! Yu almost kill mi pickney! Yu lucky yu even a walk right now!" Al exclaimed, and Favi laughed humorlessly.

A chill ran down my spine.

Goosebumps rose on my skin.

I glanced at Favi, then gulped. I'd never seen Favi look so cold before...

Even when he looked at his father.

This wasn't my Favi. This was Slitta.

If this situation a go cool, mi need fi start wid him first. Swallowing my fear and trusting Al not to shoot, mi face Favi. Mi try gently lowering his gun, but mi get pushed to the side from behind.

My body slammed into the wall, and I groaned as pain seared through me. Everything went dark while my head thrummed painfully. Blinking to clear my dazed vision, I held my head as I sat up and leaned against the wall.

Two deafening shots filled the room.

My eyes widened as a body dropped to the floor.

A blood-curdling shriek tore from my mouth.

"No!" I screamed, trembling as I crawled over. Uncontrollable tears blurred my vision as I pressed my hands against his abdomen. I couldn't tell if he was breathing. "Wake up!" I begged, but he didn't budge.

God, please. Yu cya tek him away from me...

Chapter Fifty-Three

Favio

"Chayanne."

She shrugged off my hands. "What did you do?" she mumbled repeatedly, clutching the pig to her chest.

I sneered at her. What about me? He shot at me, too. "He's not dead." Man just dramatic nuh fuck.

She perked up. "Really?"

Stooping beside them, I prodded him with my gun. "See? Bulletproof vest."

She sighed, then glared at me. "How yu fi try kill mi father?!"

"How him fi try kill me?" I asked, slapping his cheek with the pistol.

Chayanne's gasp got cut short by his groaning. His eyes fluttered open, and I scowled. Fucking pretender.

I stood, stepping backward while Chayanne helped him stand. Leaning against the wall, I placed a foot on it and traced a finger along the hot barrel of my gun.

"Yu alright, Al?" she asked, and I scoffed.

"Yes." The pig glared at me while reaching for his gun on the floor.

She yanked it from him, then marched toward me. She extended her hand.

"No." I didn't take my eyes off her *stronzo* of a father. If he so much as blinked in a way I didn't like, I'd kill him. I'd deal with Chayanne's backlash later. Already know the remedy fi she.

"Favio," she hissed through clenched teeth, and I unwillingly placed the gun in

314

her palm. She flicked on the safety, her hands curling around both guns. My eyes widened while Alphonso's shined.

She glared at us. "Unu calm down?"

"Calm down?!" Alphonso yelled.

"Yow, watch how yu talk to her." I leaned off the wall, stepping forward. I clenched my jaw, stilling as Chayanne stepped before me.

"Why yu have this man ina mi house?!" Alphonso asked.

"Your house? You gave it to me..." Chayanne whispered, and he glared.

"Nuh carry back dat bwoy ina mi yard!"

"If him nuh allowed in ya, then mi nuh allowed in ya either!" She walked toward him, shoving his gun in his hand before pulling me toward her room. Fury radiated off her in hot waves, and I hated admitting to this, but Chayanne fucking scared me.

While I stood by the dresser, she stomped around the room and packed as much as she could into bags. She handed the heaviest bags to me, then reached for something on the dresser, which fell. We stooped, our fingers brushing as we reached for it.

It was the conch shell I gave her years ago...

I looked from it to her. She looked at me, and I smirked.

"Doh say it, Favi," she rushed out. She grabbed the shell, then we left the room. She leashed her dog, and I grabbed the console.

Alphonso fumed by the door. His eyes softened as they settled on her. "You nafi leave—"

"Yu put yu hands pon me. Mommy neva put her hands pon mi a day a her life."

Cazzo. I'd been so caught up in watching this man for any sudden action that I forgot the whole reason for shooting him.

I scanned Chayanne. She didn't look hurt. I released a quiet breath. If I still had my gun, I'd kill him.

"Yu neevn a go apologize? Any day mi buck yu outta road, a dirt," I promised.

"Nobody naa kill nobody! Goodnight, Al," she said in a clipped tone, walking through the door.

I smirked as I walked past him, and he gritted his teeth. I helped her pack the car, then we drove away in a tense silence.

When we were approaching Ochi, she put my gun in the glove compartment. "Pull over."

I did as told, and she exited. Chayanne glared at me through the windshield, and I sighed before exiting. Leaning against the bonnet, I looked at her. She was cute when angry.

"Don't look at me like that," she hissed, and I smiled.

"How?"

"Like yu want sex. Mi deevn a go ask right now why yu have a gun when you told me you stopped, so what was that, Favio?"

I looked behind her, admiring the silhouettes of dancing trees. They were a perfect backdrop to the star-filled sky. "*Che cosa?*"

"English, please. Mi too angry fi memba wa that mean."

I looked at her. "What?"

"Why would you shoot my father?"

"Him put him hand pon yu before?" I wanted to know how many bullets to fill him with. Plus more, until I became satisfied, though I doubted I'd ever be.

She shook her head. "Al has been good to me. If you do anything to him, Favio, mi a leff yu."

My mouth dropped. What the fuck did he do to her while I was gone? "Bredda, yu cya serious."

"Me look like me a laugh? Al might not be the best father, but he is a trying father. I'd appreciate if yu nuh tek him from me when he's the only parent I have... *Please*, Favio."

"Ah," I said, though I didn't intend to keep my promise. If he fucked with her again, a dirt.

"Thank you." Her shoulders slackened as she walked toward me. She tipped, and I leaned down to accept the quick kiss.

"How's your head?"

She squeezed my hand. "It's okay. Mi never get hit bad."

I ran my thumb over her knuckles. Bringing her hand to my mouth, I placed a kiss on each knuckle, then her forehead. When I pulled back, she smiled, and I

316

was more at ease. We re-entered the car and drove away.

"Mi kinda hungry. Mi nuh know if nobody waa feed mi," Chayanne said while we were passing by KFC.

I chuckled. "Look how much healthy food yu buy the other day, and every time we deh pon the road, a pay junk food yu eat."

She rolled her eyes. "Leff mi alone, big foot! Park here so. I'll go inside because the drive-thru line too long."

I complied, giving her my card. "0727," I said, and she blushed.

That smile. What I'd give to see it for the rest of my life.

For the second time today, I parked before the hospital. Chayanne didn't wait for me to open the door before she jumped out of the car. She ran toward Chezandra and Zaveer, who were waiting outside. Leaning against the car, the corner of my mouth quirked upward as I watched Chayanne shower the kid in kisses.

My ringing phone interrupted the moment. It was Sergio. He never called unless it was important. I walked away to answer the call. After a few minutes, the call ended, and I checked my emails.

Chezandra approached me with a scowl. "Favio."

"Chezandra," I said, my tone flat.

"Mi nago beat round the bush, so dis a wa mi have fi seh. Chichi a one hefty piece of yam fi you, and yu can neva do wrong ina her eyes, so please treat her good this time. Whenever yu hurt her, a me always afi pick up the pieces. She deserves better, and mi hate see her wid you."

She needed to close her eyes then, the fuck.

"Are you done?" I slid my phone into my pocket.

"Mi nuh done! If yu mek Chichi come to mi a cry again, me a go to police boh yu. Nuh think mi nuh know who yu be!"

"If you know who I am, why are you speaking to me like this?" I always knew

Chayanne's friends were annoying, but I didn't know they were stupid, too.

"Because if yu mek nun do me, she a go leff yu. Yu either mek her happy or she leff, either works fine with me." She smirked.

"I didn't know you were this feisty, Chezandra," I taunted, regressing my former thoughts. I liked Chezandra's sass and bluntness. I could see why Chayanne kept this little nuisance around.

"You bet. I can make her love you more or hate you to the point yu hate yuself. I told you, one way or the other — I win."

Before I could tell this gyal to stay the fuck out of our business, Chayanne walked toward us.

"Here, Chezzy. Dem neva have soda." Chayanne handed Chezandra a bottle of orange juice while balancing Zaveer on the other hand.

As Chezandra accepted the drink, Lamar approached us. "Yu ready, Chezzy?"

Chezandra nodded. She took her baby from Chayanne, subtly glaring at me before walking ahead of Lamar.

"Chayanne..." I paused as she faced me. I was taken aback by her beauty and those eyes that always reeled me in, seeing into the depths of my soul no one else reached. "I have something to tell you."

Yawning, she rubbed her eye. "Can it wait until tomorrow? I'm tired and me afi go drive."

I shook my head, and she gave me her full attention. "I'm going to Italy."

"Fi wa? A the one likkle argument mek yaa run weh again, Favio?"

"No. It's my—"

She held her hand up. "Mi nuh waa hear it. Gwan weh yago." Hissing her teeth, she took out her phone and started walking away.

I grabbed her wrist, forcing her to stop. "Yow, easy yuself." I released her hand, not wanting to be rough on her after what happened earlier. "Gwan ina the car."

"No. I'm staying with Chezzy. Mi nuh waa drive yu piece of car anymore, either." She tossed the key to me, and I caught it. She was as crazy as her silly friends if she thought I would let her drive after admitting she was sleepy. I'd get someone to drive my car home.

"Gwan ina the car, Chayanne."

"No. Safe flight." She brought her phone to her ear, walking a distance away.

A moment later, a vehicle slowed at her feet. She didn't look at me before entering the car. Shaking my head, I entered my car. Today was one of the worst days I had in a while. It worsened when I arrived at the rental and didn't see Catty and the boy. The only thing I saw was a note atop the bed. The ink was faint, making it hard to read.

favio bboy

ambi call mhi n say fin cum bk bu him kill mhi n Raj

fin d 1st mhi scared

mhi nun wan nuuhn dun mhi bboy

thx fi cum through fin mhi n Raj doe

mhi owe u d worl n mhi biggest mistake a losing u
buh mhi c sen u nuve different gyul now
a black one

dat ano ur type favio bboy buh as long as u happy

mhi hope she gud 2 u n mhi hope u gud 2 her

mhi nun wan caz nun chubble between u n she suh a dass y mhi leff
2

mhi can manage u bredda but it wudan nice if u visit more caz Raj look
up 2 u

thx again favio bboy

catty <3

Swear she a go mek dat bwoy kill her one day. Shaking my head, I called Antaro and told him to ensure Catty's new security detail had eyes on her. Cya worry boh next gyal right now.

Mine had me fucked up in more ways than one.

It was eight a.m. I didn't want to be at this house, but I had no other choice. I needed to know if she was okay before I moved on to the important tasks I had to do before leaving for Italy tomorrow.

After a minute of waiting, the door creaked open, revealing the antagonizing woman. She rolled her eyes at me. "Chichi nuh deh here."

Chayanne was fucking here. I knew where she was at all times. She couldn't breathe without me knowing so. Currently, she was in the kitchen. The aroma of one of her favorite breakfast foods — omelets with a lot of bell peppers — wafted in the air.

I didn't have time for their childish antics. I reached into my pocket, then stretched my hand toward her. "Ah. Give this to her when she comes."

Chezandra eyed it, her brows furrowing. "Wa this fa?"

I dropped it into her hand. "The key to my house."

She better give it to Chayanne. Knowing how the gyal hate mi, she goodly fling weh the key. She can dweet still if she wanted her child to become an orphan.

I'd just stuffed the last piece of clothing into my suitcase when Chayanne entered the room. I raised a brow at her. "Why are you here?"

She held up the key I dropped off hours ago. "I guess I live here now."

Chuckling a bit, I leaned on the dresser and curled a finger. "Come here."

She walked toward me, stopping between my legs.

I grabbed a handful of her ass, pulling her closer. "Still vex?"

"Yes."

"Do you want to come?"

"I would, but... it's not a good time. I want to be here for Chezzy if anything happen to Zaveer again," she said, and I nodded. "Why yafi leave again? Yu just come back."

"I need to sort out something with my company. And I need to get my snakes. I'm coming back to you, *fiore*. I promise."

Sighing, she wrapped her arms around me and laid her head on my chest. We stayed like that for a while, but Chayanne being Chayanne, the quietness was short-lived. "When yaa come back?"

"Two weeks to a month."

"No sex fi a month?" she asked, and I chuckled.

"Mi cocky always ready fi yu. Just say the word."

She leaned off me, looking into my eyes. "I want you..."

Fucking minx.

She pulled away, dropping to her knees. Running her hands up my thighs, she didn't break the stare as she laced her fingers in the waistband of my shorts and tugged it down. She kissed me through the boxers, and my dick jerked, making her giggle. "Yu want me that bad, Favi?"

"Don't play with me, Chayanne."

She chuckled, lowering the boxers. My dick was soft. This was the first time she saw me in this state, but I was getting too fucking horny to care. I wanted her mouth around me. Now.

As if she could read my mind, she took my dick in her hands. She placed kisses on the tip and shaft, then got it wet. Her tongue swirled around my tip. She sucked on it, getting me hard as I gripped the dresser behind me.

"*Fuck*, Chayanne, your mouth." As she took my entire dick into her mouth without using her hands, I looked at the ceiling with a long sigh. "Demon," I hissed, and a vibration ran through her throat, making my dick throb harder.

She bobbed her head up and down. My dick was at its full length and hitting the back of her throat, but she didn't stop pleasing me.

I looked at her, then took her cheeks in my hands. She moved her hands off my thighs, resting them on hers.

"*Brava ragazza.*" Smirking, I slowly bucked inside her mouth. "Wider," I commanded, and her mouth stretched more. I fucked her throat hard and fast, exactly how we both liked it.

Tears were in her eyes as she looked at me, and all I could think was my woman was so fucking beautiful.

With spit dribbling down her chin.

Choking on my dick.

Choosing to swallow me whole instead of breathing.

"*Fuck*, Chayanne. Stop squeeze mi balls like that." I moaned like a bitch while smugness shined in her eyes. She had me trapped in this tight little mouth, and she knew it.

My abdomen tightened. I was close, but I wouldn't allow her to make me come this quick. I pulled out.

"I wanted you to come in my mouth." She pouted as I lifted her onto the dresser.

"Yu waa suck mi soul out of me?" I asked, and she giggled, wiping away the spit.

"Yes."

"Shut up and mek mi fuck yu." I tugged her dress off in a swift pull. I was about to rip her panties apart when she stopped my hand.

"I like these." Chayanne tried getting off the dresser to take it off.

"Sit down."

She obeyed, pouting. Smirking at her obedience, I ripped the panties off and hauled her toward me while she lay back. I threw her legs over the crook of my elbows, then drove inside her in one powerful thrust.

"Ah!" she screamed.

"Chay... Anne..." I groaned after each thrust.

She was so wet.

Tight.

Blessed as fuck.

And she was all mine.

"If yu fuck pon mi, mi kill yu," I promised, fucking her harder and faster.

"I'm... yours," she cried, tossing her head back and moaning at me. She put a hand between us as her walls clamped so hard on my dick, I had to look at my reflection in the mirror to not come before she did.

Sweat poured off me.

Hair stuck to my forehead.

My muscles flexed while Chayanne's legs bounced on either side of me.

"Favio!" she screamed, her nails sinking into my abs.

I looked at her. "Move your hand."

322

She did.

I fucked her faster. I gave her every inch of me until I was balls deep, but I didn't stop. I was angry. She deserved this.

"Faster, Favi, please," she begged.

I slowed to grab a ripped material of her panties, stuffing it into her mouth. It wasn't time for that mouth.

I only wanted to fuck her. Harder and faster until she remembered who she belonged to.

Throwing her legs over my shoulders, I squeezed her neck. Not too lightly, but tight enough that she couldn't breathe if I didn't allow it.

"Mhm," she groaned into the gag while tears poured down the sides of her face.

"Yu blessed, Chayanne," I praised, watching my dick slide in and out of her pussy. Her cream coated my dick, but I couldn't stop to wipe it away. "Play with your pussy."

As she moved a hand between her thighs, a loud crack rang through the room. Thrown off balance, we stilled and glanced at the broken leg of the dresser.

"You good?" I asked, and she nodded while spitting out the gag.

We burst out laughing. The way our bodies shook while we laughed, still connected, our orgasms took us seconds after the other. It was nothing like I ever experienced before.

I was laughing.

Smiling.

On a high while I filled my woman with cum.

Chayanne was on this high, too.

Fuck, she was so beautiful.

Her smile was mesmerizing.

I could listen to her laugh all day.

Chayanne was everything, and I never wanted to let her go.

We climbed down from our high a moment later, and I pulled out of her pussy. Cum leaked out, running down the front of the dresser.

"Yago mad mi, Favi," she laughed, wiping tears from her eyes.

If only she knew I was already beyond the point of no return.

Chapter Fifty-Four

CHAYANNE

Slipping out of Favi's hold, mi tiptoe downstairs before answering the call. "Goodnight, Al," mi seh while making a sandwich.

"Dat bwoy do yu sum? How mi a call yu from last night and cya get yu?"

Mi roll mi eyes. "Nuh you run mi outta yu house?"

Him sigh. "Mi neva run yu. Yu leave pon yu own."

"Well... yu give mi the house, and now yaa come tell mi who mi can and cannot keep there. Mi nuh waa stay there anymore if yu kindness only go so far."

"Yu naa see mi point. He's too old for you—"

"Yu did ten years older than Mommy," mi seh, and him go quiet for a while.

"That's different," him seh defensively, and mi scoff as mi sidung round the island and start Maths up mi two peanut butter sandwich dem.

"Me nuh care how it waa different. None a unu cya mek mi leff him."

Al sighed. "Yu neva have fi tek him up back, Chay..."

Mi tired fi hear dis now! If Favi waa be crosses, him a my crosses! "Goodnight, Alphonso." Mi hang up the phone. Mi lock screen catch mi attention, and mi pause taking another bite.

A waa picture of me and Mommy when I was in primary school. It was my first day in grade one, and she neva feel well, but she drag herself outta bed fi walk me to school. She walk wid mi every single day until—

Mi wipe weh tears before they could fall.

Mi know yu do it all by yourself, but Alphonso's here now, Mommy...

"Dis a the reason mi neva waa yu round that good fi nun bwoy."

If smaddy did tell mi months a go seh my sperm donor wuda scold me every day while me ina hospital because mi man brother put me here, mi wuda laugh till mi ketch stitches.

But see me ya — housed in a private hospital room with all my expenses paid in full by Alphonso Bailey.

Mi wudan a lie if mi seh mi nuh skeptic boh him. But, mi neva have much energy fi run him. Mi too tired fi argue with anybody about anything. So, I remained in the hospital for weeks, gradually getting closer to my father.

He told me he wanted Mommy to abort me. Him did about fi get ina waa comfortable spot ina him career, weh him wuda be able fi maintain their potential future family, so he didn't want to put it on pause. He also thought having me was a bad idea because she was getting sickly and doctors cudn figure out wa do her.

Mommy disagreed. She told him she fling mi weh, then she leff him and focus pon herself.

Few months after me born, Al link back Mommy. Dem start deal again, and a so comes mi name change from Chayanne Sharma to Chayanne Bailey.

When I turned one, Al get an opportunity fi work toward waa big promotion, so him abandon we. Him never get it, but him never show up back until Mommy dead. He was at the funeral and wanted to reconcile with me, but Mama and Aunty neva allow him to. Though him did still attached to work more than me, him seh Mommy death was a wake-up call. It mek him watch over me from a distance...

He was at my primary and high school graduation.

Him put money from all his paychecks ina waa account fi give me when mi turn eighteen, along with the stolen exams fees. Now, mi have five million sitting in my bank account. Mi a wait pon a rainy day fi use it.

Al risked his career by trying to keep me away from Favi. Him witness too many incidents of young girls getting caught up with gangsters, and it never end well for the girl. Him seh him regret robbing me, but it was the only thing him cuda think of fi protect me from Favi afta mi never tek him warning.

Him love undercover jobs, but him tek desk duty for the entirety of my stay in the hospital. Him visit mi every day with home-cooked meals and keep me company whenever days seemed to drag on with no end. The days did tense sometimes when him and Aunty visit at the same time, but dem behave fi me.

Al gave me one of his houses to stay in, and him cover all the bills. Him understand seh mi neva waa stay ina Mama house after she died from the heart attack, because Fass Paul tell her mi get shot. Mi rent out Mama house, but after this lease end, mi a lock up the house and mek it rotten dung. Mi think dat a wa Grandpa wuda want.

Sighing heavily, mi look pon mi wallpaper. A waa professionally edited picture of me, Mommy, Mama, and Aunty Kenzie. "What should I do?"

Dog wid too much master sleep without supper.

CHEZANDRA

I crossed my arms as I watched him storm out of the living room to enter the bedroom. "You a go walk weh while mi a talk to yu, Lamar?"

Grabbing his suitcase, he hissed his teeth and shouted, "Mi afi pack, Chezzy!"

"Yu can keep down yu voice? Zaveer is sleeping," I scolded, and he ignored me as he continued packing. "Yu go get VISA and deevn did mek mi know seh yaa think bout migrating. Yu think that right, Lamar? The apnea a bother we son again, and I don't have anyone to babysit while I'm at work."

"Carry him to mi mother."

"Mi think you nufi go right now."

He stopped packing to look at me. His eyes swirled with anger, but it didn't faze me because I was used to it. "I'm leaving for him. Jamaica a wul dung. Mi can get better opportunities in America fi ensure him straight."

Sighing, I sat on the edge of the bed and dropped my head in my hands. The bed shook from the force he used to toss his clothes into the suitcase, and it brought tears to my eyes. "Mi understand dat, but yu nuh go about this the right way. Mi cya do this by miself, Lamar."

I loved being Zaveer's mom, but I never got me time anymore. I was with him most of the time, while Lamar always found excuses. This time, it'd be work. Another time, he had to help a friend.

It wasn't convenient to bring Zaveer to Lamar's mom. She lived in Annotto Bay. I had Chichi and Mommy, but Mommy was tricky, and I felt guilty every time I had to ask Chichi despite her never complaining.

If I knew one drunk fuck would bring me here, I wouldn't have gone out with Chichi, Yolanda, and Eltham that night. When I found out I was pregnant, Lamar treated me so well. That was how we started dating. We had the perfect relationship until Zaveer started walking a year into our living together.

"Mi give yu solutions and yu naa listen. Weh yaa complain fa?" Hissing his teeth, Lamar grabbed the suitcase and his clothes, then left the room.

Wiping away tears, I stood and went to Zaveer's room. I put my finger beneath his nose to check if he was breathing. He was a wild sleeper, and the apnea didn't bother him as much as it used to, so his doctor recommended not using the CPAP machine anymore.

A puff of air grazed my finger, and I smiled as I lowered myself onto the floor beside his bed. I brushed back his wild twists, then kissed his forehead.

"Everything I do is for you..." I whispered into the darkness.

CHAYANNE

Favio Welsh a go be the death of me. Sometimes, mi waa vex till mi buss when it come to him, then him do things weh mek mi waa curl up and gwan like kitten a get pet. Imagine, afta mi plan fi vex until him come back, the man arrange fi roses get delivered to mi every morning.

Today, me a cheese like crazy! The bouquet of a hundred had fifty roses wrapped in US hundred-dollar bills, paired with a card that read '*Best Pussy*'.

Texting him thanks even though him ina waa meeting, mi grab him new BMW key, then drive go meet mi father. Al shake him head as mi walk toward him.

"Nuh start, Al," mi seh as mi enter the building before him.

"Fine, but we can talk bout it later," him seh sternly.

"Mi nuh waa talk bout it later either." Mi a go support mi bredda later, mi nav time fi Al foolishness.

"You are associating with a criminal," he whispered like ano we alone ina the gun range.

I raised a brow. "Who?"

Al glared. "Don't act coy, Chay."

"If him a criminal, why yu nuh arrest him?"

"We never can find anything solid to tie him to anything."

"Yaa build a case against mi boyfriend, Al?" Mi narrow mi eyes when him shake him head. "You'd tell me, right?"

"No."

"Even if it keeps me happy? Remember, you said you'd do anything for me."

"We're not building a case against him. Like I said, there's never anything solid,

328

and we stop investigate Blood Paw after the war dem cooldown. Regardless, I don't like that you're involved with a gangster—"

I grabbed the earmuffs and put them on. "Mi cya hear yu."

Sighing, him hand me a rifle. Him seh mi good with handguns, but mi need fi learn fi handle the recoil from rifles.

This was how my father and I bonded. Whenever him return from undercover cases, him teach mi self-defense. Him seh the violence a get too out of hand in Jamaica, and him will sleep better if him one pickney know how fi protect herself.

Al signal fi mi begin, and I went straight for the kill shot. He taught me to never aim for anything less.

Trav deh pon the come-up! When we were younger, him seh smaddy offer him an opportunity fi pursue him passions. He took it, and now he was a music producer.

Him still live a Steer town, but him give back to the community every chance him get. Him host the occasional fish fry, party, or giveaway. Today a waa big fish fry pon the football field, and Trav got an upcoming artiste to perform. The place full a vibes bad!

Mi wudan a enjoy miself if such man nehna text mi, and if Chezzy nehna nyam off mi ears. Mi happy she deh here, but shi supposed to deh a work. Mi feel like she call out fi lecture mi.

"You never listen. I told you not to fuck him," Chezzy scolded.

Mi swallow the last of my fish. "Yu nuh understand. Mi hate him, and the sex neva all that, but mi neva waa give mi body to nobody new," I said, and Chezzy chuckled. "Weh yaa laugh fa? Any day yu leff big head Lamar and get some good dick ina yu life, yu a go see how horny yu be when the good dick leff yu."

"I'm not leaving Lamar," she said firmly, and I sighed.

"Him call yu from him go up?" I asked, and she nodded before suddenly turning around. Mi lean to the side, smiling at Trav, who a approach.

Nodding at Chezzy while him step past her, him sidung beside mi pon the step of the old post office. "Yu good?"

Mi nod. "Mi like tha chef ya. Hire him fi the next fish fry."

Him look pon the two fish bone. "Yu want a next one?" him ask, and mi nod, making him chuckle as him look at Chezzy. "Yu want one or yu good?"

She pick at the half-eaten fish in the foil paper. "I'm good, thanks."

"Remember Lyrica seh shi want fish," mi seh to Trav, and him clench him jaw as him nod. "Mi a go look fi mi people. Mi want mi fish when mi come back."

"Need mi fi come wid yu?" Trav ask, and mi shake mi head.

After the short walk to the cemetery, mi smile at the fresh bundles of roses in the three vases. Over the years, Favi still sent them. It bothered me at first, but mi learn fi accept it. Him have it pon autopay, mi doubt the chump change noticeable ina him bank account.

Sitting at the foot of Mommy's grave, mi brush off the dirt. "Mi wish the breeze wuda calm down so yu can stop dirty up," I muttered, glancing at Mama. "At least unu together now," I choked on the last word, then started crying. I dropped my head on top of my lap as sobs shook my body.

I was tired of questioning God. Mi know everybody afi die one day, but *why*? Why did everyone around me die abruptly?

I wasn't sure how long I cried for, but the crunching of dirt made me sit up and dry my tears. Looking over my shoulder, mi eyes widen before mi stand and run over. Jumping into his arms, my legs wrapped around his waist. He stepped backward while his arms tightened around me. The gun tucked in his waist pressed into my skin while I smiled into his neck.

"When yu come back?" I asked.

"Today." Chuckling, he lowered me to the ground. Him cough into him elbow, and mi frown. "I'm not drinking any of your poison again. I have an icy mint." Him tek it outta him pocket, unwrapping it before placing it in his mouth.

"Dat nago work, but you'll see," mi seh, already thinking of which bush tea mi a go give him.

Him scoff, then glanced at my family. "*Stai bene?*"

"Yeah. Just one of those days. You ever lose someone close to you?"

His eyes showed a flash of emotion before returning to their normal state. "Once."

Mi smile sadly. "Mi waa seh yu lucky, but mi know yu nuh believe ina luck." Mi stand beside him, laying my head on him while he threw an arm over my shoulder. Cya imagine life without this man. "Favi?"

"*Sì?*"

"Nuh matter how anybody waa feel about our relationship, I want you to know I love you."

Favi stiffened, and I looked at him. His expression of shock, relief, and happiness was comical. "You love *me*?"

I nodded. "Yes, I love *you*, Favio Big-Foot Welsh." I never got the chance to tell him my feelings because I was waiting for the 'right time'. The other day, I realized that any time with him was the right time because he was my person.

"*Ti amo.*" He leaned down to kiss my forehead, then my mouth.

I was a smiling bomb into the kiss. When him try deepen the kiss, mi pull away with a short laugh. "Behave before Mommy grab yu foot," I said, and he scoffed while looking at the grave. "I wish you could've met her. I think she would've loved you."

"What was she like?"

I dug into my memories of Mommy. I had to remind myself of them every day because I didn't want to forget them. As they played at the front of my mind like a movie, I smiled. "Mommy was... kind. Forgiving. The sweetest person ever. She always put other people's needs before her own, even if it was at her expense. She was suffering here, so I know this is selfish to say, but I wish I got to spend more time with her."

Favi held me tighter. He didn't have to say anything; I understood him completely.

"Anyway." I wiped away a tear before it could fall. "How was work?"

"Stressing," him seh after a fit of coughs.

"Tell me about it after yu drink some tea." I turned, walking toward the exit while he held my hand.

"I'll tell you after you fuck me."

"Look who neva waa sex mi ina car," mi tease.

"I'd do it right here, but I know you're superstitious about fucking in a cemetery," him seh, and mi buss out a laugh.

People really waa mi leave this man? Must be joking!

I was whole with or without a man, but Favi made my life more complete. We were locked in for life. I loved him more than words could ever explain, and I dared anybody to try getting between us again.

Chapter Fifty-Five

TRAVIS

Chez wanted to use the bathroom, but she neva waa use the one pon the ball ground. So, I brought her to my house. I was lying on the bed when she exited. I watched as she straddled me, showering my face with kisses while I focused on my phone.

"*Travis.*" She took my phone, tossing it aside before kissing my mouth. Deevn kiss her back, so she pull away with a pout. "I missed you."

Mi halt her hand when she try grab mi hood. "Yu cya keep do this, Chez."

"Do what?" She innocently bat her eyelashes, making my dick stir beneath her.

"Fuck me and the man."

"We don't have sex..."

"Nuh mek a difference. Mi tired a the bunna man bizniz, Chez. Near two year now yav mi a wait fi treat yu right." Mi shake mi head as she crawl off me, hanging her head low. "See wa mi a talk bout?"

She nuh look pon me. "What?"

"Yu get vex once mi show yu a pree. Yu cya waa mi and still deh wid the man—"

"We nuh deh."

"But yu live wid him?" Mi grab her wrist as she get up, pulling her to sit. "And whenever mi try talk to smaddy else, yu get vex and jealous."

She free herself from mi hold. Wiping beneath her eyes, she stood.

Mi stand and try hold her again, but she step outta mi reach. "Chez—"

"I'll leave you alone." She hurry outta the room, almost bumping into mi mother. "Sorry," she mumbled, bolting down the stairs.

Mommy look pon mi. "A wa do she?"

"Go put on a shirt." Mi scowl at her, and she rolled her eyes before walking away. Mi look at Chez, shaking my head as she slam the front door shut.

Mi return to mi room. Mi do well fi miself over the years. Mi add on pon the house, and mi get Mommy fi stop sell her body. All she do now a spend off mi money and frowsy up the house wid the smoking, but that better than knowing she a walk the road. Cudn spend another day a hear man run joke bout which position dem set mi madda ina.

Sighing, mi go pon the balcony, watching Chez rush off Godsto with her head held low. Mi cya tek fuckry, and a dat alone she deh pon...

It grieve mi fi see mi likkle sister ina hospital, Jah knows. Foolish of me fi think Slitta a waa top shotta weh wudn mek nun do her. Mi glad a neva nun worse cause Chichi a recover day by day. Chelsea ask mi fi drive her to the hospital every evening so she can drop off the homework Chichi get a school. This keep up fi weeks until me and Ceychelle turn friends. Mi even help her study fi exams cause Chichi beg fi her. These evenings a sum mi look forward to—

"Weh yu go, Trav?" Chole laughed while she snap her fingers before mi face.

Mi glance from her lips to the study papers. "Nowhere."

"Lie! Yu did a look pon me again," she teased.

Mi look pon her. "Is that a bad thing?"

Smiling, she shook her head. She a smile more these days. "Mi look good. Yu free fi look pon mi."

"Eeh?" I raised a brow, and she blush then look away, making me chuckle. Sometimes when mi ketch miself a stare pon her, guilt tek mi. Asia death still fresh, I shouldn't move on yet. Mi nuh believe ina bun, and this feel like cheating.

334

With Sandra— Mi mean Chez, time move so fast. Whenever she leave, all deh pon mi mind a when mi a go see her again. Whenever we naa argue, mi like her laughs, smiles, and complaints seh shi cold while mi a sweat dung the place. 'A the crosses ina yu a try escape through yu bird chest,' she'd always say, and now mi cya sweat without think bout her.

Asia mother always tell mi seh mi ano no good. I didn't want to taint Chez, especially cause her mother stay like Miss Olive, but mi know mi can do better with her. So, when mi mek the first move, tek the virginity, treat her like a Queen, and carry her out whenever her mother get pon her nerves, I never thought she'd leave as soon as Chichi got discharged. I already went through enough leff and deh back with Asia, now mi just waa smaddy solid ina mi corner.

Chez a neva that person.

B avoid mi fi months. When she reappear, she have a baby and a live with a man, weh mek mi sorry fi him madda hole.

Asia fuck mi up. No jokes. But Chez? Jah knows. She affect mi worse than anybody else.

FAVIO

Chayanne was the bane of my existence. We'd been doing good since I came back, now she start her fuckry.

"Yu cya stay ina the yard, bredda?" I glared as she stepped into the shortest fucking dress I ever saw. I bought it in Italy because I knew she'd look sexy in it, but she was wearing it to piss me off more than she already did.

"Me stay ina the house wul day wid yu yesterday, Favio!" she yelled.

"Every fucking week yu gone a party."

"And me a party this week, too! Yu can come if a mi crochiz yu waa watch."

"Fuck pon mi if a waa shallow grave yu waa dem find yu ina," I warned, and she paused zipping up the dress to glance at me.

"Mi cya stomach yu behavior, Favio! Yu just come back ina mi life, and is like yu expect mi fi put everything pon pause fi yu! It nuh work dat way, and mi too young and pretty fi lock up ina house like furniture! Yu nago rule mi!"

I chuckled. "Ah." I walked onto the balcony and sat on a chair. Taking the spliff from behind my ear, I lit it and blew the fumes into the air while relaxing.

Footsteps padded toward the balcony, stopping at the door. "Favio..."

Another drag.

She sighed. "Mi nuh waa we argue tonight. Mi just waa go out go have fun with Yolo cause since she move back a Portland, mi nuh see her as often."

Still not looking at her, I took another pull.

She stood before me, and I closed my eyes. "*Seriously*?" She yanked the spliff from my hand before I could take another drag, and my eyes snapped open. She held it at a scornful distance, and I glared at her.

"You think now's the time to fuck with me?" I asked, and she sighed, placing the spliff on the tray. I reached for it, and she swatted my hand away as she kneeled before me.

"Do you want head?" she asked shyly.

I reached for the spliff as she tied her hair in a high ponytail. "Do your thing."

I blew the fumes away from me while watching the car slow in front of the gate.

336

Chayanne hopped out, still in the dress from last night, and glanced at the house. Sighing, she looked at her friend Yolanda — another crosses red gyal.

"Yu can come wid mi?" Chayanne asked.

Yolanda choked. "*Me*?"

"Please nuh. Him a go kill mi," Chayanne pleaded, and I smirked while moving the spliff from my mouth.

"Gweh from mi, afta we ano Juliet and Juliet! Plus, mi cya stay. The sun so hot cause a man—"

"How mi reach ina this?" Josiah asked. His voice was distant.

"Mi forget you deh pon the phone. Bye." Yolanda ended the call, looking at Chayanne. "Drapers deh far, and mi hate deh from Mommy fi too long. Just go suck him hood fi friend him up."

"I did, but mi still leave after him tell mi not to," Chayanne said.

"Try suck him toe this time," Yolanda said, and I raised a brow. I couldn't see what look Chayanne gave her, but it made Yolanda shrug. "Mi nuh know wa unu straight people do ina unu bedroom. Bye, Number One." She winked at Chayanne before driving away.

Turning around, Chayanne sighed, oblivious to the camera hidden in the wall. When I bought this house and got a room fitted for my snakes, I ensured everything was equipped with the latest technology so I could keep a closer eye on her. As she walked toward the house, I went downstairs. I opened the door, and her eyes widened.

"Favi," she said, and I looked at her. "Good morning..."

I stepped past her, heading toward my car.

Hours later, I parked before the house. There were two other cars here. I walked toward the front door, pausing as chatter drifted through the door.

"Never have I ever ignored someone over foolishness," Chezandra said, and I turned around.

"Never have I ever led someone on," Travis snapped, and I paused.

"Never have I ever been so stubborn, mi cya see weh smaddy a come from!" Chezandra yelled over Chayanne, who was trying to get a word in.

"Never have I ever stopped being selfish, and fi once think boh other people feelings!" Travis retorted, and the house quieted. Even Chayanne's annoying dog stopped barking.

"Um... We can play a different game?" Chayanne asked, and Josiah agreed.

Turning around, I walked toward the back of the house. I slipped through a door and made my way to the kitchen. I heard the tail end of Travis telling Chayanne 'bye' before the door slammed shut. Two more sets of footsteps left, then Chayanne entered the kitchen after I washed my hands and poured myself a drink.

She glared at me. "Weh yaa come from?"

"Don't question me," I said, and her glare deepened.

"Oh! Me cya question you while you afi know everything when yaa try lock mi up ina house?!"

I paused moving the glass to my mouth. "Nuh you waa yu freedom, so mi leff the house gi yu?"

She hissed her teeth. "Yu know wa mi mean, Favio! Every time mi waa go nowhere, yu have a problem."

"Dat past and gone, so just do yu thing, bredda."

"Stop call mi dat! Mi ano yu bredda!"

"Okay, *Chayanne*."

"Nuh seh mi name like that."

"Wa more yu want from mi?"

"Yaa talk to mi like mi a waa burden to yu," she said, and I didn't answer. Tears filled her eyes. "Wow... Mi a burden to yu, Favio?"

"I didn't say that."

"But a dat yaa imply..." Her voice cracked at the end, and guilt took me over.

I walked toward her and lifted her onto the counter. She threw her arms over my shoulders, and I held her close as her tears soaked my shirt. "What's wrong?"

"Yu nuh love mi," she cried.

I pulled away, holding her chin. "I love you, *fiore*. You just get on my nerves sometimes."

She chuckled. "Sorry about leaving..."

I clenched my jaw. "Nuh fuck up mi medz again, Chayanne."

"Sorry," she mumbled, wiping away tears before kissing me.

I kissed her while she lay back, pulling me down atop her and hooking her legs around my waist. My hand crawled beneath her dress, trailing to her panties. I rubbed her through it, and she moaned into my mouth.

"Favi, I need you," she said. Her voice was breathy.

"Patience," I said, burning with anger and need.

Pulling away, I slipped the straps off her shoulder, exposing her round breasts. "Fucking beautiful," I said, and hairs rose on her skin. I inhaled an uneven breath before taking her right nipple into my mouth. She must have showered not too long ago because she tasted like body wash.

Tongue circling her nipple while she writhed beneath me, I slipped her panties to the side. My finger trailed her slit, and a shiver ran through her that made me smirk. I always loved how responsive her body was to my touch. Shifting my focus to her other breast, I thrust a finger inside her.

"Mm," she moaned, arching off the counter.

Watching her every action while I sucked her nipple, I slipped another finger inside her and pleased her in the way she liked.

I curled my fingers.

Pulled out to the first knuckle, then sank my entire finger inside her tight pussy.

"Faster," she begged, and I gave her what she craved.

Picking up my pace, I broke away from her breast to suck on her neck. She craned it, giving me better access, and I smirked against her skin. Her pussy soaked my fingers; it was dripping into my hand.

Fuck, she was too wet.

I broke away. Slipping my fingers out of her, her brows furrowed as she looked at me through hooded eyes.

"Why'd you stop?" she drawled.

"Yu soon see yu period?" I raised a brow at my fingers despite blood not being on them.

She glanced at my finger, relaxing as she looked at me. "Mi nuh know. Probably. How yu know that?"

She was ovulating? It was the right time to come in her.

"I know how you're supposed to feel." I wiped my fingers on my shirt, and she chuckled.

"It's irregular since I came off the pills and got an IUD," she explained, knocking the wind out of me.

"Wa the fuck yu mean yu have an IUD?"

Her brows knitted as she sat up, fixing the straps on her shoulder. "I thought I told you..."

Neevn a go say nun bout that because mi know how her brain work. "Take it out," I stated calmly.

"Wa? No. Mi nuh ready fi nuh pickney."

"I have money, and I love you."

"I know, but what about wa mi waa fi miself?"

"My love isn't enough?"

"It is, but mi nuh want nuh baby until mi get mi life pon track."

My brows pulled together as I looked away, glaring at the floor for a few seconds. I did my best to reel in the anger before I returned my focus to her. "Stand and turn round."

She smiled and complied. I would've laughed at how excited she got for backshots, but I didn't. Nothing was funny. What the fuck did she mean by she had an IUD? She was going to have my kids sooner rather than later, and I was going to make sure of it.

Chapter Fifty-Six

CHAYANNE

Me get off early, so mi ina the lobby a wait fi my man. Days ago when the man sex the attitude outta mi, him tell mi seh him family a have a get-together and him a carry me. Him seh mi nuh suppose to have nuh complaints cause mi love road like red plate taxi. Mi cya stand him—

Mi phone ring. Jesam peace! Him a read mi mind? Mi chuckle nervously as mi ansa. "Hey, babe."

"Chayanne, how big yu pussy be?" Favi asked.

Mi choke pon mi spit. "Excuse me?!" Mi know him live ina mi hole, but afta it nuh stretch out like old scrunchy.

"I don't see extra small or less than that, so I don't know..."

Mi furrow mi brows. "Wa yaa talk bout?"

Him clear him throat. "Well... because it's almost your... time of the month, and you said you forgot to pack them... I'm... buying sanitary items for you..."

Mi buss out a big dutty laugh, not caring how guests stare pon mi. "Pad nuh sell by vagina size."

"Yu sure? This says size five, and look like the long rag dem weh sell a market back," him seh, and mi a laugh so hard now, mi belly a cramp up. "Chayanne," he said through clenched teeth.

Chuckling, mi wipe tears outta mi eyes. "I use tampons."

"A me alone fi ina yu, Chayanne."

Mi laugh, biting my bottom lip when mi sense him anger. "Tell me what you see," mi seh, and him list the different types. "Yes, buy that pack. Get wings, too."

Him sigh. "Spicy or barbeque?"

"Favi! Pads, not food."

"Later, Chayanne." Him quickly hang up.

Chuckling, mi move the phone from mi ear and scroll through mi pictures. As a person whofa navel string cut by a seaside, the last person who mi expect fi see, approach mi. Mi eyes widen as mi skim ova him security uniform. "Yaa stalk mi?!"

Dayshawn scoff. "No. Mi get tha work here the other day. Deevn did know yu still work yaso. A dis yu did a do mek yu stop link mi?"

"Mi tell yu from wappy seh we done." Before mi start talk to Shane, mi did go back to this crosses.

Dayshawn smirk. "Yu soon come back."

"Why's that?"

Him look out the window before shifting his focus to me. "A the brown bwoy yaa fuck again?" him ask, and mi gasp. A cya mi big hood man him a class as bwoy! Before mi can tell him bout wa mek him up, him add, "Yu need a strong black man a fuck out yu hole—"

Mi hold up a hand. "Just stop. Yu sick mi stomach, and yu cya walk ina mi man shoes nuh day. Seh sum bad bout him again and see if me nuh squeeze the trigger this time."

Him laugh, thinking mi a ramp. Mi remain stoic, and him laughter fade.

"That's a promise, Dayshawn," mi add before walking outside.

Favi already have the door open, but him nuh kiss mi like him usually do. Him stare at Dayshawn's departing back. "Who that?"

"Nobody." Mi tip and kiss him cheek, then we enter the car. "You brought Marshy to Chezzy?" mi ask as him motion to the backseat. Him get both spicy and barbeque wings fi me, and mi smile and thank him before digging in.

Favi scowl as him drive off. "Sì."

Taking a bite from a wing, mi raise a brow. "A wa do you?"

"Yu fucking dog piss pon mi Clarks."

Mi eyes widen as mi heart stop beat. "I'm sorry."

"It good. I got rid of the problem."

"Wa?!" Mi grab mi phone, calling Chezzy. She show mi Marshy, and relief flood mi as mi hang up the phone while Favi kiss him teeth. "A you mek she hate yu."

Him deevn answer, and mi chuckle.

While we drive, mi scroll through mi messages. Mi neva get fi read dem cause of how busy mi did be today. Mi sigh when mi see a new message from Aunty and Tate. Mi still nuh send in the application, and the deadline a end of month.

"Favi, what career yu think wuda fit me?" I asked.

"A lawyer," him seh, and mi smile because him think highly of me.

"Really?" Mi smile stretch when him nod.

"*Sì*, cause yu chat too much."

Mi smile wash weh, and mi kiss mi teeth. Mi look through the window while him laugh mi to scorn. "Mi cya stand yu," mi seh, and him laugh louder, making me laugh, too. Him laughter always contagious.

Hours later, we reach Cherry Gardens. Him give me a tour of his half-built three-storey.

"Surprised yu stay this close to them," mi seh.

"Why is it surprising?" Favi asked after we enter the vehicle.

"Because you always wanted independence from them."

He gripped the wheel tighter. "It's not that simple when it comes to *la famiglia*, Chayanne. Italy's culture is a bit more family-oriented than Jamaica's, so we usually live close to each other. It's been like this since my—"

Mi raise a brow when him nuh finish. "Since?"

"Family stuff," he said, and mi nod, knowing him nago say nuh more.

We park in the driveway, then enter the house. Him parents a sleep, and me thankful. Mi nuh ready fi bury the hatchet yet, but mi a go play hypocrite tomorrow fi Favi's sake. We go to his room, and mi bathe before joining him pon the balcony.

"Yu cya stop smoke?" Mi glare while him take a pull from the spliff.

"No. Come here." Him eyes trail up mi body, which was hidden beneath the fluffy white robe.

343

Mi walk toward him, and him put the spliff pon the table. Him stand, stepping closer toward me. My back pressed against the railing as mi look at him.

"Ever got fucked over a balcony?" he asked, and my breathing quickened. He smirked. "Scared?"

"S-suppose someone hears?"

He kissed my lips. "Let." Kiss. "Them." Kiss. "Hear."

CHEZANDRA

I stood from the sofa. "Mommy, mi soon come back."

She glanced at the clock. "It's almost ten. Weh you a go?"

"Mago drop off sum at one a mi friend dem." I glanced at my brothers, who were fighting for the game controller. I had to babysit them today because Mommy had to handle some business.

"Alright. Drive like yu have some sense," Mommy warned, and I chuckled before going to the car. Things were better between us since Daddy visited last week. I knew it wouldn't last, so I was treasuring it.

Parking before the house, I swallowed my anxiety when I saw movement behind a curtain. I grabbed the jacket, rubbing my thumb over the soft material. He gave me it a long time ago. It was one of those rare days I didn't wear a jacket to his house. Travis said he liked to look at me, and I wanted to give him easier access. He made fun of me when I was shivering, then gave me this jacket.

Smiling at the memory, I looked toward the house. He'd been avoiding me since our row at Favio's house, and I wanted to apologize. I was out of line. Maybe finding his jacket in my closet was a sign for me to be here.

Fixing my hair and adding a splash of perfume, I tightened my grip on the jacket as I walked before walking toward the house. I knocked on the door and held my breath while waiting. I wanted to wear something prettier, but it was hard to change in the car with Zaveer's car seat. I couldn't change at Mommy's; she'd ask too many questions, and I didn't want to lie to her more than I was already.

The door opened, and my smile washed away as my heart dropped to my feet. Who was this bitch?!

She was in one of his old shirts — the one he used to clean cum off me the second time we had sex. I'd promised myself to never let it happen again, but it happened a third time. Fourth. Too many to count.

"Goodnight." She gave me a head-to-toe while I scowled.

"Who yu be?" I asked through gritted teeth.

"Who deh the door—" Travis quieted as he saw me. His eyes widened before returning to normal, making me seethe more. He walked toward the door while saying to the girl, "Go wait in the room."

"Okay," she said, giggling. Travis eyed her ass while she sashayed to his old room. Her ass wasn't round. It was broad and flat, like a big pancake.

Crossing his arms, he leaned on the threshold and raised a brow. "Yu man nuh fuck yu good tonight?"

I blinked rapidly, unable to find my voice as my grip on his jacket loosened.

He looked at it, his eyes widening. "You still have that?" He leaned off the door and reached for it.

Despite my grip being slack, I couldn't let go. I couldn't even find my voice to scream how disgusted I was by him.

As his finger brushed mine, I found a last bit of strength. I shoved it in his hands and stormed off. I vaguely heard him say something, but maybe that was my broken heart imagining things.

Entering the dark house, I felt along the wall until I found the light switch. I flicked it on, and the room drowned in brightness. Closing the door behind me,

I released Marshy's leash so she could roam the house. I walked toward Zaveer's room while forcing myself to text Chichi.

WIFE: We just reach a town.

Thanks fi dogsit fimi and mek sure yu kiss mi baby goodnight.

Okay.

Yu good?

Yeah, just tired. Goodnight.

Alright. Gwan go rest fi the people dem work tomorrow.

Mi just done bathe so mago head to bed if the people dem son nuh try cripple me.

Exiting the chat, I placed the phone aside. I lay Zaveer on the bed, smiling sadly as he stirred. Wiping underneath my eyes, I went to the kitchen for a drink of water. Lime Hall's humidity amplified the heat. It added to the range of emotions I felt.

Anger.

Hurt.

Betrayal.

Sadness...

Diverting my attention to the phone while I chugged the water, I sighed heavily when I realized there was still no response from Lamar. Gritting my teeth, I called him. My anger surged when he answered after the third call. "Yu nuh see mi call yu from morning, Lamar?!"

"Mi did busy." His background was quiet. If a pin fell, it would've echoed.

"So yu cudn send mi a text or sum?"

"Weh Zaveer? Him a sleep?"

"Him nuh must a sleep! Yu nuh see seh a afta eleven?!"

"A after eight fi me," he said, and I looked at the ceiling, pursing my lips while blinking away tears.

"Which is why you should've called. Yu know that's when he goes to sleep."

"Chezzy—" he began, and I hung up because yelling at him didn't make me feel better.

I wanted to know if he was good with me hiring a sitter for Zaveer. We were yet to discuss this new arrangement, but I'd ask him tomorrow when he called... If he did. I'd probably have to call out from work tomorrow despite it being the only thing I looked forward to all week.

Sighing, I moved to the bedroom and lay on the cold bed. Bringing the blanket to my neck, I stared at the space beside me. This wasn't the life I imagined for myself, but it was what I had now.

I was stuck with Lamar while the man who owned my heart moved on.

Chapter Fifty-Seven

FAVIO

"Yav on panties?"

"Yes." She grabbed a perfume bottle off the dresser and sprayed herself.

I moved to the open balcony door. "Take them off."

Her eyes widened. "Mago deh round yu family wul day!"

"So?"

"Suppose me period come?"

"If it didn't come after how I fucked you last night, it's not going to come now," I said, and she blushed, looking away. "Off. Now."

Resting the bottle on the dresser, she hooked her fingers beneath her dress. She avoided my gaze as she slowly lowered the panties down her legs, making my dick harden. I smirked as she stepped out of it, tossing it toward me.

"Good girl," I praised as I caught it, and she blushed, turning away to grab the perfume bottle. "Ready now or yu nuh done drown yuself yet?" I asked while looking at the panties. They were black and lacy. I bought it for her in Italy. I needed to see her in it again before shredding it. Smirking, I tossed it onto the bed.

"Yes, mi ready now cause mi deevn eat mi lunch yet." She was still upset that I didn't allow her to leave the room this morning. Instead, I got breakfast for her and brought it to our room.

348

Taking her hand in mine, I led us downstairs. As we went into the backyard, chatter drifted from every angle and added to my unease. Chayanne couldn't take her eyes off the foam machine, the colorful bounce houses filled with kids jumping around, and the chefs and servers bustling about. I always found it amusing how everything intrigued her. She thought I didn't realize, but I made it my duty to know everything about this woman.

I loved her.

I enjoyed looking at her.

Until *Mamma* appeared, breaking my focus from Chayanne, who was eating her food plus the food she insisted I should have.

"Favio, I thought you changed your mind and left." *Mamma* offered me a smile I didn't return. Sighing, she looked at my woman. "Hey, Chichi."

My woman faked a smile. "It's Chayanne."

Mamma gulped. "Is it okay if I sit here? I want to talk to you," she said, and Chayanne nodded while I rested an arm on the back of her chair.

What the fuck did *Mamma* want? It was bad enough that I showed up at this annual cook out she begged me to come. Now she wanted to be in my presence when she knew she was still on thin ice? The audacity of *Mamma* baffled me.

"I want to start by apologizing for keeping you two apart," *Mamma* said, and I scoffed.

"What did you have to gain?" Chayanne asked, not hiding her anger.

Mamma sighed. "You wouldn't understand, Chi— I mean, Chayanne. It nuh matter if dem a big man now, they're still my babies. I brought them here, and I tried my best to make them love each other, but all they did was fight." She glared at me, and I returned it. "I thought keeping them in different countries would ensure they're safe."

"Yu cuda at least tell him mi nuh dead! Yu know how much him did a go through, and yu lie to him!" Chayanne yelled, garnering a glance from those around us while I clenched my jaw.

I needed to bring her inside before her attitude came out. Antaro didn't take lightly to anyone disrespecting his wife. I'd hate to put aside my love for *Mamma* and kill Antaro if he touched a hair on Chayanne's head.

Mamma glanced at my finger tracing Chayanne's shoulder. "I could have, but it was safer to send him away instead of Fabiano. Your relationship was collateral damage, but I'm happy you worked things out. You bring out the best in him."

"Apology not accepted," Chayanne snarled.

Mamma was about to reply when someone called her name from elsewhere. I looked in that direction, glaring at Antaro while Catty stood beside him.

"Why's she here?" I asked *Mamma*, and she gave me a look.

"I'll speak to you later, Chayanne," *Mamma* said, and I clenched my jaw as she left, disappearing into the house.

"Who's that?" Chayanne asked.

"Fabiano's girl." I scanned the area. He couldn't be here, could he? *La famiglia* knew better than to break *omertà*, but my parents still banned Catty and the boy from events. It wasn't worth the risk of anyone slipping up to Fabiano that they survived. "I'll be back—"

"Wait," Chayanne said, and I paused getting up. "Let's leave—"

"No." I couldn't see the guards in the mingling group of *la famiglia*, but I knew they were there.

Chayanne sighed. "*Shame ano load, but it bruk neck.* Please don't do anything you'll regret. You're better than them."

I wasn't.

"Get up. You're going back to the room."

I clenched my jaw as he took the gun from me, adding it to his collection. He exited the room, leaving me trapped with these people.

Nikola. Luca. Antaro. Fabiano, who hid behind Antaro while I skimmed the office for something to bash his head in with. My fists curled at my side as I realized they cleared the room of sharp objects and anything heavy. There was nothing in here except me and my anger.

350

"You are late," Nikola said, but I didn't look away from Fabiano.

Fabiano chuckled nervously. "The show can't start without the star, right?"

"Fabiano, don't upset your brother," Antaro hissed, and he nodded quickly.

"Or me," Luca added. "I don't know why I'm here. I'm not the one involved in whatever shit these two are in... again."

"This concerns all the men of *la famiglia*." Nikola sat on the chair behind the desk.

I tore my gaze away from Fabiano to settle it on my eldest uncle. "Where's Alessio and Romeo?"

"They don't need to be here." Nikola shrugged, and my jaw clenched as I glanced at Antaro.

Antaro was the youngest of three sons. If anything happened to Nikola or his son, Antaro would oversee the Welsh mafia. Things were this way because Alessio expressed disinterest in becoming the next godfather.

I relaxed my jaw as I leaned on the wall beside Luca. "Mediator like old times?" I asked Nikola in Sicilian, and he nodded.

"They probably think I'm going to play Russian Roulette with you again," Fabiano said in Sicilian, and I had a vivid memory of when he got his initiation at thirteen.

I was eleven at the time, and my life was hell since then. Fear gripped me after every empty click and made me pray for death. If *Mamma* hadn't barged into the room and snatched the gun Antaro left lying around, I would've died on the next spin.

"Fabiano," Nikola said, and everyone quieted to listen to him. "I trusted my brother to get you under control, yet you still insist on your childish behavior. Do you know how much restraint I used to not allow Favio to come to Jamaica and kill you? Do you think you'd be alive if it wasn't for my respect for Antaro?"

Fabiano glanced at me, his eyes lowering as he looked away.

"Really, *fratello*? You're speaking as if I didn't raise them exactly how *Papà* raised us," Antaro said.

"No. You focused only on Favio because he reminds you of yourself and how *Papà* treated you," Nikola said, and Antaro clenched his jaw. "Favio has no

351

interest in the mafia, just like Alessio and Romeo, but they are still *famiglia*. You're the root of your own problems, and if your marriage fails, it's because you don't know when to give up."

Luca yawned, and Nikola glared at him. "And you're a disappointment. Have you ever seen me yawn in a meeting?" he asked, and Luca stood more upright, shaking his head. Nikola scoffed, looking at me while switching to English. "I wish you had an interest in being the next godfather. You'd be better than these two combined, but when this mafia was made, we had principles not to force anyone to lead if they didn't want to. It's how we remained strong all these years. Favio, if Fabiano bothers you again, you have my permission to kill him."

Fabiano gasped, and I smirked as I looked at him.

"Leave," Nikola demanded, his eyes locking on everyone before settling on me.

They left, and I sat on the chair before the desk. He poured us a drink, swaying in the chair as I took the first sip.

"If Fabiano doesn't bother you and you try to kill him, I won't step in if there's a war between you two. If you die, you know she no longer gets protection, right?" Nikola asked.

My eyes widened. "*Che cosa?*"

Nikola looked at a stack of documents atop the desk, his eyes settling on the one with 'Welsh's' stamped on it. It was the paperwork for regressing Antaro's role as interim CEO. "I'm using resources to protect a girlfriend, but that's as far as my kindness will stretch. Fabiano can risk a war. If he dies, Catherine's protected because she gave birth to a Welsh, but your girl has no connection to us. So, it's up to you what you want — peace with your brother or your girlfriend's death?" Grabbing the file, he slid it across the desk to me. "The future is in your hands, Favio. Show me you can be the man I made."

Chapter Fifty-Eight

CHAYANNE

Laughing, mi throw mi head back. "Yolo, mi hate yu!"

Yolo roll her eyes. "Cause me in love? Look how long yu cuda have me to yuself."

Chezzy chuckle. "Mi happy fi yu."

Mi nod. "Tell me more about how yu meet her."

Yolo blushed. "I was in a supermarket while me deh pon the clock, and me accidentally bump ina her. Me compliment her blouse cause me dee like how her titty dem stand up ina it, and she start blush out hell—"

"Wait, she gay?" Chezzy ask, and Yolo nod, making me and Chezzy gasp.

"Me never waa say nun yet cause me dee waa see how it go, but it's nice having a girlfriend. Me hope me rastaman neighbor nuh try kill mi or nun. From wa day, me hear him a play 'Chi Chi Man' by T.O.K every day. Him deevn know seh all me and me girl do a fuck to it."

"Then watch how she fall in love and a drop off the map," mi seh, and Chezzy chuckle.

"Like you ano the same whenever your man call you," Yolo said, and Chezzy hummed. "You a the next one! A long time yu deevn call me, and me know yu naa work much."

Chezzy clear her throat. "I, um—"

Mi look toward the window when mi hear a loud engine.

"A the man dat, don't?" Yolo ask, and mi blush. "Wa me just seh, Chezzy?"

"Whatever, bye! Mago try convince my man fi come the beach." Mi hang up the phone, walking toward the window fi look pon him.

Him look so good! Him ina waa white shirt and dark jeans, looking at his phone while walking toward the house. Him a come from somewhere wid Matt. Smiling, mi run go open the door fi him. Him pause with the key in midair.

"Come here! I have a surprise for you!" Mi grab him hand, hauling him upstairs.

"Yu neevn wait fi mi walk in back way," he said, and I chuckled as we neared the room. Him enter the bedroom before mi.

Mi chew mi bottom lip, watching him look pon the arrangement on the bed: three pairs of Clarks, a few colognes for his collection, and a new watch from his favorite brand. "Do you like it?" I asked, watching his lips part slightly.

Him look at me, a smile gracing him face. "*Grazie mille.*"

"You're welcome!" Mi hold mi breath as him tek up the watch. Mi know him wuda look pon it first. "I know it's not a lot, but it's a little gift for being the best boyfriend."

"*Little*? I was thinking about adding this watch to my collection," he said while swapping it with the one around his wrist. He held his arm out, admiring the watch from all angles. "Yu rich nuh fuck."

Chuckling, mi sidung pon the bed while him smile at the watch. "Try on the shoes. Mi waa mek sure it can fit yu big foot." The other day, Trav follow mi go buy dem cause mi neva waa buy nun fake. Trav did a gwan like mi a bother him, but mi figure a because him and Favi nuh close like one time.

Scoffing, Favi sit beside me and try on the shoes. Looking away from the shoes, Favi kiss mi forehead. Mi eyes flutter close, and mi heart beat wildly as mi forehead tingle. Mi love him!

Him pull away, smiling at me. "It fits perfectly. Yu know yu man."

"Who else fi know yu?"

"Nuh start wid yu fuckry," him seh, and mi roll mi eyes. "Mago be yu house husband now, so there's one thing left."

"What's that?" Mi hope ano pumpum him want. Him nuh stop come ina mi, and mi keep on a forget fi buy Plan B.

"A baby," him seh, and mi sigh.

"Favi... We talked about this and my period started," I said, and him happiness fade.

Him phone ring, and him look at it. Without a word to me, him stand and walk toward the balcony. "Sergio?"

Sighing, mi bring his gifts to his section of the closet. While mi put dem away, mi think bout mi future. Mi send in the late application, but mi nuh tell Favi yet because mi might not get in. Mi know him will find a way fi mi get in, but me waa do this by miself.

He paid for my exams, giving me the opportunity fi come this far in life. Mi need fi carry the torch the rest of the way. If mi get accepted, mago gwan do Interdisciplinary Studies fi the time being. I wanted to do something in the medical field like Chezzy, in honor of Mommy, but that ano mi dream anymore.

Patient man ride donkey.

Mi look pon Favi as him enter the closet, and mi frown. "You have to leave?"

"This weekend," him seh, and mi sigh. Him glance at me while taking off the shoes. "Why are you sighing?"

"Might as well yu go live a Italy," mi grumble, and him raise a brow.

"You're coming with me."

Mi eyes widen. "Huh?"

"You said the next time I'm going to Italy, you'd want to come. It's almost your birthday, don't you want to see new places?"

Mi smile and start jump up and down. Him stop wa him a do fi watch mi. Mi waa stop jump and act like mi used to things, but mi too excited!

"Oh my God! Mi nehna think!"

"You never do."

Rolling my eyes, mi prance round the room. The doll a go abroad! "Mi deevn ask fi time yet!"

"You don't need their permission."

Laughing, I ran out of the closet. Mago call work and tell them seh mi Granny dead. Mi sure Mama and the one mi neva know, won't mind.

Beach day was well-spent! Minus when wi cudn find Trav and Chezzy, and mi did afi listen to Eltham complain bout staying with Zaveer. Also, when Favi try teach mi fi float, and him nearly mek mi drown cause him seh mi chat too much fi a person weh cya doggy paddle.

Mi about fi cut mi eye afta him when we server approach the table. She place the cheque before Trav, who a treat we to dinner.

"Have a good rest of your evening." She smiled at Trav.

Trav flash him nice smile at her. Him dark skin always make him teeth look whiter.

"Oops!" Chezzy seh, and mi look pon her. She a roughly wipe the cheque with waa napkin.

"A weh Yolanda deh fi blame woman clumsiness pon man?" Eltham ask, and mi chuckle, stopping when Favi glare pon me.

"It good." Trav tek the glass off his lap, resting it on the table.

"I'll go ask our server for another cheque," Chezzy seh.

"Yu nafi do that."

"I insist. The numbers pon tha one ya neva look right anyway." She smile at him before leaving the table.

Him kiss mi forehead as mi lay mi head pon him shoulder. "*Stai bene?*"

I nodded. "Yeah, just sleepy."

"We can go to Exchange tomorrow instead."

"No. Exchange deh right up the road." Mi lean off him as Chezzy return and slap Trav card pon the table.

Shaking his head, Trav tek up him card and slip it ina him wallet.

Favi stand and hold out him hand toward me while saying to Trav and Eltham, "Ina the lates."

"Yah," Trav seh while Eltham ding off Favi fist.

Mi kiss Zaveer farid, then go Exchange wid Favi. "Favi, yu can take down the suitcase for me, please?" mi ask, and him rest the laptop aside.

Him follow me ina the room and reach the top of the closet without a fuss. As him put the suitcase pon the floor, waa cockroach jump off it.

"Ahh!" Mi run around the room while the roach crawl up the wall.

Favi brows furrow. "Mi bloodclaat. A first yaa see waa roach, Chayanne?"

Mi point a shaking finger toward it. "Kill it! Kill it right now!"

Favi burst out laughing and grab mi slippers. Him approach it.

"Nuh wid mi slippers!" mi hiss while him wipe tears from him eyes.

Him grab one of Marshy toys and fling it at the roach, and it fly off the wall!

"Murda!" Mi lick up ina the door as mi run outta the room.

Favi's loud laughing travel through the house. Tears blind mi vision as mi haste ina the bathroom. Mi chest heave while mi slam the door shut, pressing mi back against it. Sas Crise, roach cuda fly all this time?!

Seconds later, Favi knock the door. "It's dead."

My hero! Exhaling a big breath, mi open the door. A loud scream tear from my mouth when mi see Favi a grin while holding the roach by its antennas. Him step toward mi, and mi hold out a hand while tears fill mi eyes.

"Favio, stop! Mi naa ramp wid yu!" mi scream.

Him stretch it toward me. "It wants to be your friend."

"Favio!" Mi hop ina the shower while him wave it at mi. The likkle crawny foot dem a sick mi stomach! Mi think mago— Mi gag, covering mi mouth.

"Sorry," him seh quickly, throwing it ina the toilet and flushing it. Him wash him hands, then take me outta the shower. "*Mi dispiace.*"

"Mi hate yu, Favio!" Mi push past him when him try kiss mi.

Him grab mi arm, making me stop. "I didn't know you're afraid of roaches."

"Yu shuda know from the first time yu carry waa live rat round me and seh yago feed yu snake dem!"

Him brows furrow. "That's different."

Mi kiss mi teeth, exiting the bathroom. Look how mi afi go bun dung the house now! Mi go the kitchen fi a drink of water. While me calm mi nerves, him stand at the other side of the island, watching me. Mi cut mi eyes afta him and toss the empty bottle ina the trash. Mi long, coffin-shaped nails catch mi attention, and mi smile.

Before we went to the beach, I had a girl's day with Chezzy. Mi did ask Favi what color to do my nails, and him suggest black. The black did too bland, so mi add a golden glitter topcoat to it. Waa 'F' deh pon my left ring finger, while two conjoined hearts deh pon the right ring finger.

"I forgot to ask if you like them?" Mi walk toward him, holding mi hand before him face. Mi know him nuh care; mi think him only care boh mi appearance if mi cut mi hair. It deh a mi tailbone now, and him nuh wrong fi haul mi to him like when goat a try run weh.

Him take mi left hand in his. A small smile came on his face as his gaze lingered on his initial. "*Sì*."

"They're special."

Him brush him thumb below the first knuckle of my ring finger. "How?"

"They glow in the dark." Mi pull away, turning the light off and flooding the kitchen dark. Mi walk toward him and show him mi hands. "See?"

"I didn't know it could do that," him seh, surprised.

Mi chuckle. "Yes, Favi. Mi get them because mi waa show yu sum."

"What's that?"

I kneeled, tilting my head to look at him. "Use my mouth however you want."

Chapter Fifty-Nine

FAVIO

Taking a sip from the bottle, afi thank fuck Chayanne brought water for us. Place hot nuh fuck and dem man ya deh yaso a drink liquor.

I glanced at Travis, my brows furrowing while he stared into space. As Josiah walked away, heading toward the sea, I asked Travis if he was good. We didn't speak like we used to, but apart from Jelani, he was the only person I considered a friend.

"Yah. Mi gov." He nodded, his eyes drifting toward the shore.

I narrowed my eyes because it looked like he was staring at Chayanne, then I realized who had his attention — Chezandra. He looked at her like she was something he wanted but couldn't have.

Chezandra glanced in our direction, her gaze finding Travis. Her eyes widened, lowering as she looked at Chayanne and forced a smile.

Travis looked at me. "Yu mek ar happy. Nuh mess up dis time."

I didn't plan on messing up, but even if I did, Chayanne knew she couldn't leave. Any man afta me, a must God she gone to.

"I won't," I said, and Travis hummed, offering a bag of weed to me. "Mi good."

He raised a brow. "When since you nuh smoke?"

I wasn't telling him Chayanne refused to kiss me whenever I tasted like weed, so I told him to fuck off. Travis chuckled, and I scoffed as I stood. I walked toward the women and Zaveer, who were building sandcastles.

"Travis needs you," I said to Chezandra, and she left with Zaveer.

Chayanne smiled as she looked at me. I smiled back. I loved her smile. Her eyes. Her.

"See something you like?" I teased.

"I see something I love." She tipped to kiss me, and I grabbed a handful of her ass, tugging her closer. She broke the kiss, chuckling. "Behave. We ina public."

I smirked, holding her hand and leading her further into the water. "Let me teach you how to swim." It was an eyesore watching her all afternoon. She never allowed the water to past her waist.

"Mi fraid."

I stopped walking, looking at her. The water was below her breasts. "Do you trust me?" I asked, and she nodded, making me smile. I didn't believe in luck, but *que sera, sera*. Chayanne was everything I could ask for and more.

Fiore mio.

Chayanne partied too much.

Sometimes, it bothered me. Other times, I loved how she enjoyed her life. She'd been working too hard lately.

We were at Tavern, a nightclub in Steer Town. Travis was hosting a party. Chayanne insisted on coming because we were going overseas soon. I'd rather relax at home after such a long beach day, but here I was.

I sat in a corner, nursing a Hennessy and my second spliff while watching her. She was on the dance floor with the red gyal, moving her hips like she was auditioning to be dancehall's next top dancer. A so Chayanne behave whenever she go parties? And I allowed her to wear pay short and revealing clothes like mi nuh know how some man stay?

I never had a problem with what she wore. I admired her confidence — she was sexy and beautiful. I liked looking at her, and I didn't care if other men did. I had

a gun, and I enjoyed peeling skin down to the flesh.

Relaxing into the booth, I blew fumes into the air. It joined the mix of sweat and alcohol while someone sat beside me.

"Slitta," they said, and I glanced at him.

One of his hands was in a cast. He used the other to place a Hennessy bottle beside mine.

"Pree?" I looked at Chayanne. What the fuck was she doing now? I didn't know she could bend like that. I was going to fuck her like that tonight, and she better not complain.

"A touch base."

"Hm..." I took another pull.

"Neva see you a Scotty funeral."

"Wasn't here."

Why the fuck that red gyal have her hands all over Chayanne? She a fuck mi woman? I needed to investigate her. As a matter of fact, I needed to hurry and get Chayanne pregnant so she could stop partying this much. That fucking IUD was working overtime, and I hated it.

"Weh yu did gone?"

"My business isn't your concern."

The wicked red gyal whispered into Chayanne's ear, then motioned her head toward me. Chayanne glanced at me. Her eyes widened as they met mine. She blushed and looked at her friend, shaking her head.

"Wudn have my woman outta road dressed like that."

"I didn't ask." I put the spliff in my mouth, my eyes trailing down Chayanne's legs. She was in the shortest dress I could find in Italy, and I told her to wear it. My dick was hardening from thinking about undressing her.

Fisha huffed, and I spared him a glance. He struggled to pour the liquid into a cup, and I watched him for a second before helping. "Bless."

I nodded toward the cast. "How's that?"

He glared. "Good. No thanks to you."

"If I sign your cast, will it make it better?"

Fisha's glare deepened. "Yaa one sick rass, yu know?"

Taking the spliff from my mouth, a small smirk stretched on my face as Chayanne took hesitant steps toward me. "I've been told."

I had to bring out the private jet. Cya carry mi woman a foreign and have her on a commercial flight.

She sat across from me, staring through the window at the boring view of the runway. She was dressed in a tight-fitting dress, which stopped above her knees, a denim jacket, and white sneakers. Even when dressed simply, she was still beautiful.

"*Fiore,*" I said, and she looked at me. I patted the seat beside me, and she came over, then buckled in.

"Mr. and Mrs. Welsh, we will be en route to Italy in about fifteen minutes. Do you have questions for me?" asked the flight attendant.

Chayanne smiled. "No. Thank you, Kitania."

Kitania nodded, walking away to finish pre-flight preparations.

"Mrs. Welsh, huh?" Chayanne teased.

"Like that?" I asked, and her smile stretched.

"It has a nice ring to it."

Hours after we took off, Chayanne was a yawning mess. We'd switched seats so she could stare through the window while I occupied myself with my laptop. I had a lot of business to do when we landed, so I needed to get a head start. Chayanne would want to go everywhere and see everything, and I needed to make myself available for her.

"Go to sleep, *fiore,*" I said, still typing.

"Mi nuh waa sleep. Mi waa see everything."

"There's nothing to see except water. I'll let you know when we're over land."

"Okay..." She curled into the seat, closing her eyes.

"Go to the cabin, Chayanne."

We were three hours out of Italy. She'd be uncomfortable by the time we arrived, and I'd be on the receiving end of her complaints. Cya tek the nagging.

She sat up. "You have a bed in here?" she asked, and I nodded. "No sah, Favi! How much money yu have so?"

"Legally or illegally?" I asked, despite knowing I couldn't tell her everything unless she was my wife.

She thought for a moment. "Never mind! Me goodly ketch stroke if yu tell me. Where's the bed?"

Kitania was passing by, so I asked her to bring Chayanne to the cabin. Now that Chayanne was gone, I could focus on working and breathing freely.

We landed an hour ago, and we went to a restaurant. Chayanne's hands shook while she held the menu.

"Do you understand what you're reading?" I asked.

Chayanne rolled her eyes. "Mek mi gwan like mi used to things nuh! Where are the prices? How mi supposed to know what to take?"

"Have I ever made you pay for anything?"

"No, but— Never mind, big foot," she said, and I chuckled.

This restaurant didn't give women menus with prices, and I liked that. The first time I brought Chayanne to a restaurant, she asked me, 'We cudn go somewhere cheaper?' Long time she a test mi, but I'd been getting her more accustomed to wealth. Whenever she figured out what she wanted for herself in the future, I'd be right by her side, ensuring she attained her own wealth.

"Do you want pizza?" I asked, and she scowled.

"Mi can come a foreign and eat pizza? Get me what you a have— Wait, no. Mi want some of this! The name look like it taste good! And mi want some of this, this, and—"

Amused, I cleared my throat, and she looked at me. "The food nago anywhere,"

I joked, and she blushed, looking away.

We ordered our food, and it came minutes later. During our meal, Chayanne asked about my upbringing, Sicily, and my upcoming event. She talked all the way to the house. Afi wonder how her mouth nuh get tired. Not even when she a suck dick her jaw nuh lock up.

"Why yaa smirk? Yu even did a listen to me?" She frowned when I nodded. "Wa mi seh?"

"People here don't steal streetlights like they do in Jamaica," I said, and she huffed, slumping into the seat. I chuckled as I exited to open the door for her. Why did she think I wasn't listening?

As a single child, she didn't have anyone to talk to. Whenever she got comfortable around someone, she talked a lot. It worked for me because I was taught to observe and listen.

She pulled her head back while I loosened my grip on her hair. She wiped tears out of her eyes. "Maybe I ate something bad."

"Maybe..." I agreed, and she sighed. I helped her to her feet, standing close as she brushed her teeth. I was going to get that restaurant shut down. She'd been vomiting nonstop since last night.

Finished, she faced me. "Okay, we can go—"

"No."

"Favi, today's your day. Mi naa take that from yu. I'll chew a piece of ginger, and mi nago get worse." She knocked her fist against the threshold. "Let's go, please?"

My jaw ticked, but I gave in. The second she looked uneasy, I'd bring her home. She smiled, and I led her to the kitchen for the ginger. After she cut a small piece, we went to the car and drove to the first test launch of my unnamed company.

It was an evening gala, and Sergio handled the guest lists. Everyone important in the wine industry was here. Sergio did most of the talking while I stuck to Chayanne's side. She had yet to throw up again, so I allowed her to drink a glass of wine when she asked for my permission. When I got a break from all the formal conversations, I whisked us away from the crowd.

"*Tanto di cappello* to you," Chayanne said in her best accent.

I smiled, impressed that she had learned a new term in only a few hours. "*Grazie mille.*" I took her hand in mine, kissing it.

She smiled when I pulled away, taking a big sip from the wineglass while her eyes darted around the room.

"You should slow down on this." I took the glass from her, placing it on the nearby table. "Do you like it?"

"Like? I love! And yu know mi nuh really drink wine. You did your thing, Favi." Smiling, she tipped to kiss my cheek.

"*Grazie.*" I stopped a passing server to grab finger food for her. "It's Arancini," I said while she opened her mouth. Her lips closed around my fingers, sucking on my thumb while I pulled out of her mouth. I narrowed my eyes. "Behave."

She innocently batted her eyelashes while chewing. "Or what?"

"I'll fuck you on this table for everyone to see."

Her eyes widened, and she stepped backward. I smirked as I stepped forward and wrapped my arm around her waist. I pulled her closer.

She gulped, her chest heaving as she met my eyes. She pulled against me a little, and I tightened my grip. "Favi, we're in public—"

My eyes locked on her bottom lip as she wetted it. "So?"

Blushing, she looked away, and her eyes widened. "Mi blousecup! A Patrizia Moretti that?" she asked, and my world stilled.

I snapped my head in that direction.

Fuck! It was Patrizia. She looked stunning in her all-white attire, disregarding all the looks of admiration being thrown her way. She was speaking to Renata, too occupied to notice me.

Buono. Let me take Chayanne elsewhere before these two cross paths.

"She look prettier ina real life." Chayanne stepped out of my hold that had loosened around her.

365

I stepped before her, blocking her view of Patrizia. "How do you know her?" I asked, my tone not giving anything away.

"Mi nuh live under a rock! She always ina perfume commercials," Chayanne said, and I gulped. What a small fucking world. "Yu know her?"

I debated lying, then realized I couldn't. Renata and Patrizia were joined at the fucking hip. There was no easy way out of this. "*Sì...*" I confessed, and her eyes brightened.

"Introduce we!" she begged, and I almost shat myself. "Please! Mi really—" She moved a hand to her mouth.

I jumped into action, grabbing her hand. I took long strides toward the bathroom in the opposite direction of Patrizia, exhaling a quiet breath.

What a close fucking save.

Chapter Sixty

FAVIO

Despite being twenty-seven, Renata was the best tour guide in the entire Sicily. Today was her day off, but she brought Chayanne on a tour of Palermo. I trailed behind them while listening to what Renata was saying. She told *fiore* about how she, Romeo, Fabiano, Luca, and I were the biggest headaches to her father when we were growing up. She joked that men were scared to hit on her when we went clubbing because we were very protective of her, despite her not liking men.

Renata led us street after street until she stopped at one that was full of different stalls. Some were decorated nicely, others had little to no effort. Shopkeepers stood before steaming pots or ice coolers, while children weaved through them with smiles on their faces. The potent mixture of foods made Chayanne's belly growl loud enough for us to hear, and I laughed.

"Gweh nuh, before mi step pon yu big foot!" she hissed at me, then glared at Renata, who hid her smile behind her hand.

"Are you vegetarian, *bella*? Pescatarian? Vegan?" Renata asked.

"She eats everything except beef, Ren." I glanced at Chayanne. "Italy's street food is better than Jamaica's."

"Nuh weh nuh better than yard," Chayanne said, and I couldn't disagree because both were my home.

"Know unu naa leff yaso fi now, so mago check yu bredda," I said to Renata, and she hummed. I kissed Chayanne's head. "Behave."

"Afta mi nuh give trouble," Chayanne said, and I scoffed as I glanced at Renata, who nodded subtly.

After yesterday's close encounter, I spoke to her about not bringing Chayanne around Patrizia. She better not mess up and mek my woman give me blue balls.

Hours later, Renata dropped Chayanne at my office. Chayanne lounged on the sofa, smiling at her phone while Sergio and I talked business. Nuh know who have she a smile so; she try nuh fuck wid mi.

I tore my eyes off her, focusing on Sergio. The test launch was a success, and I was going ahead with starting the company.

"Why don't you use the unnamed company as a new line of Welsh's wine?" Chayanne said, surprising me because I thought she was busy with a man.

I was taking back control of Welsh's by the end of the summer, so this made sense. Why didn't I think of that? I translated what Chayanne said to Sergio, and he nodded. We thanked Chayanne, who smiled before returning to her phone. I should clone her phone—

No. I promised myself I'd give her privacy.

Pushing away the thoughts, I devoted myself to work until Sergio left. I brought Chayanne home, and now we were standing in the garage.

Chayanne gasped. "Yu serious?"

A so me love give joke? "I'm serious." I handed her the Ferrari's key.

Squealing, she ran to sit in the driver's seat. I entered after her, watching as she looked at everything with a big smile.

She ran her hand along the wheel. "Can it go that fast?!"

"One way to find out," I answered. There was a bridge nearby. Romeo and I used to race our hypercars there, and I was going to show it to Chayanne.

"Sas Crise! Weh the gear stick deh?" Chayanne exclaimed, and I chuckled before giving her another rundown of the car's mechanisms. "See why mi stay far from rich people things? Anyway, yu ready fi the drive of yu life?"

"Are you comfortable?" I eyed how close she was to the wheel. Was she blind? She better not scratch my fucking car.

"Yes! Can I rev it?" she asked, and I nodded. She squealed as the car roared, and I smirked. "Mi in love! I need one."

"No," I said, and she pouted. "There's something else you should know. The brakes are sharper than you're used to, so shadow the breaks wid yu heavy foot."

"Mi a big driver!" she declared.

"Ah. Do road," I said, and the vehicle jolted forward before coming to a sudden halt. I glared at her, and she smiled sheepishly.

"Sorry..."

I shook my head while double-checking our seatbelts. Sending the Man Above a quick prayer, I told Chayanne to drive and not kill us.

"The driver always live. A yago dead," she joked, and I tensed as she drove off, only relaxing after she parked in the garage moments later. Turning the car off, she smiled at me. "How did I do?"

"Never again." I exited the car, my legs wobbling while she laughed. Chayanne took three years off my lifespan. I needed a glass of water, a bottle of Hennessy, and two spliffs.

Chayanne might have food poisoning. She'd been vomiting up everything she ate. Earlier, I smoked off my trauma while Aunt Ludovica — Alessio's wife — made Chayanne soup. It was the only thing she kept down.

I released Chayanne's hand as we arrived at the secluded area Renata reserved for us, and I smiled at the arrangement. A red plaid blanket laid on the sand, and a thin white curtain raised around it in the shape of a circular tent, shielding the food basket atop the blanket. Strings of LED lights crawled up the tent, meeting the four lanterns hanging off the roof. Red rose petals decorated the white sand path leading inside.

Sobbing came from beside me, and my eyes widened at Chayanne. "You don't like it?"

"No, I love it. You keep doing all these nice things for me and I—" She threw her arms around my waist, crying against my chest.

Smiling, I wrapped my arms around her. "You deserve it, *fiore*." I kissed the top of her head, then pulled away. I led her into the tent, and after she took pictures of everything, she started eating. The gentle crash of the waves became a background noise in our conversation.

"What caused you to be fascinated with the sky?" Chayanne rested her bowl aside, laying beside me. Stars winked at us through the roof's small opening.

"I liked science when I was in school."

"Yet you ended up in business." She threw an arm over my waist, snuggling closer to me. Her sweet rose fragrance drifted up my nostrils, and I inhaled deeply.

"Yu know how dat go already."

"Yeah... Can you name any of the constellations?"

I searched the sky, pointing at a cluster. "There's the Big Dipper."

"Yu so smart!"

"You are, too."

"Me?" She laughed sadly. "I'm turning twenty in almost two weeks, and I haven't accomplished much. Mama would say *tek wa yu get until yu get wa yu want*. I'm trying, but I don't know what I want anymore."

"You'll figure it out, *fiore*. We can brainstorm—"

"*No*." She sat up, pressing her index against my lips. "Me deh pon vacation. Let's live in the moment and figure that out another day."

I chuckled. "Okay."

She smiled, moving her finger. "Let's go release the lanterns."

I groaned, and she pouted.

My jaw ticked, and she smiled.

Sighing, I stood. The power Chayanne had over me should be criminal.

After we released the lanterns, we went into the water. I tried teaching her how to float, but it was a failure. We ended up fondling each other. Her legs wrapped around my waist, and I grabbed her ass. She kissed me hard while the water sloshed against our bodies.

She broke the kiss, turning her head to the sky while I kissed her neck. "Put in the tip," she begged.

"I can't fuck you in the sea," I said, despite how my dick ached for her.

She moaned, rolling her waist against me. "I need you so bad."

"Are you okay out there?!" someone yelled, shining a light toward us.

Chayanne squealed, burying her face in my neck.

I held her close, hiding her naked chest as I turned her away from the man. "We're good," I yelled to the late-night lifeguard, and he gave me a thumbs up before leaving.

"Mi so embarrassed," Chayanne said into my neck, and I sighed. She wasn't letting me fuck her on the sand now. We might as well call it an early night.

TRAVIS

Mi park before such girl house. Deevn waa deh yaso, Jah knows. Chichi lucky mi will do anything fi ar. Mi kiss mi teeth, then tek out the bag of dog food from the trunk. Mi walk toward the big head man house and knock the door.

She open the door and her radiant face saddened by the sight of me. Mi nuh believe ina sadness pon Chez face, but my days a playing comforter done. She pick ar side. She need fi tan ova deh.

"H-hi..." she said.

"Pree?" I asked.

"Nothing." She glanced at the bag in my hand. "That's the food for Marshy?"

"No, me."

Her brows furrowed as she looked at me. "Stop that, Travis."

"Stop what?" I asked, and she was about to answer when her baby ran over.

"Drav!" Zaveer said, and mi chuckle as mi drop the bag fi liff him.

"Wahm, boss?" mi ask, and him show me waa piece of paper him a scribble green lines pon.

"You drew that?"

"Yes. And those." Zaveer pointed at the papers scattered on the living room's floor, and mi smile. Youth smart and him deevn touch three yet. Chez and the man do a good job wid him, Jah knows...

Mi chest tighten, and mi put dung Zaveer. Him run toward the papers.

Chez look pon mi. "I can show you where to put it."

"No, me have somewhere fi go." Mi use mi foot fi push the bag closer to hers. Mi turn fi leave, and she grab mi hand.

"We can't be friends, Travis?"

Mi face her. "Me cya be friends with yu, Chez." Mi try be friends when she hide we from Chichi, and when she tell mi nufi come ina her, but she mek a next man breed her. Jah knows, mi tired fi try now. Mi waa sum real.

Releasing mi hand, she sigh. "Mi cya leave him... We have a baby. Yu know it hard fi mi watch children grow up in separate homes because I wasn't."

"Some of us were," I said. Deevn know if mi bredda and father alive.

"I know, but—"

"Yu good. Do yu thing." I returned to the car.

"Ting gov?" Eltham ask, and mi nod.

"Mek wi touch the studio," I said, and he cheered.

Mi chuckle as mi drive off. Glancing in the rear-view mirror, mi grip tighten around the wheel as the house get smaller. Cya even focus pon the music now, Jah knows. A go call Niyah and tell her link up later.

Chapter Sixty-One

CHAYANNE

A soon midnight. Mi so excited, mi cuda scream! Tomorrow a mi birthday!

Favi give mi the best pre-birthday fi the past two weeks. We visit several European countries, and minus the vomiting whenever we eat at restaurants in Italy, mi enjoy miself!

Mi come back Sunday, but him neva come wid mi. Him busy wid work, which a why mago tease him so him can get a sample of what him a miss. Earlier today, mi go out by miself fi buy lingerie. Chezzy ina her feelings, so shi neva waa come wid mi. Mi video call Yolo, and she tell mi fi get this one. It purple, cute, and sexy.

Mi phone ring from in the bedroom. Mi run outta the bathroom fi ansa it.

"Chayanne."

"*Fiore.*" Mi glare at his abs, hating how him shirtless in bed without me.

"Nuh start wid yu fuckry."

Mi roll mi eyes, reaching for the necklace around my neck. A waa simple gold necklace with waa heart locket. Him buy it fimi ina Paris, and print mi phone wallpaper put ina it.

"You good?" him ask, and mi nod.

"How was work?"

"Good. What are you doing?"

"Thinking about the fish fry Trav is hosting Saturday—" Mi pause as him kiss him teeth.

"Yu cya stay a yu yard, bredda?" him ask, and mi laugh.

"Nope! Mi a enjoy mi young life," mi seh, and him glare.

"Mi soon breed yu bloodclaat."

Mi smile fade. "Favio, nuh threaten me like that."

Him laugh, and mi scoff. "I can't see you properly. Fix the phone."

Inhaling a deep breath, mi lean the phone against the pillow. Mi kneel, resting my ass on my heels.

Favi's eyes widened. "Chayanne, wa the fuck dat yu have on? Weh yu deh?"

"In our room," mi answer, toying with the hooks connecting the thigh straps to the panties.

"Let me see you," he ordered, and I obeyed.

Leaning in, I gave him a close-up view of the lacy material clinging to my body. I ran my hands over my breasts, squeezing a nipple and biting my lips when he inhaled a sharp breath. "Do you like it?" I whispered.

"I love it."

Smiling shyly, I turned to the side, trailing my hands over the curve of my ass. "I bought it for you." I faced the camera. Laying on the pillow pressed against the headboard, I parted my legs, showing him my pussy. The panties were crotchless, and he watched closely as I spread my pussy with two fingers. "Look how wet I am for you, Favi."

Favi released an uneven breath. I smirked, loving how I affected him.

Sticking a finger into my mouth, I released it with a pop before sliding it between my folds, tracing my hardening clit. "I want you, Favi..." I moaned as moisture coated my fingers.

"Stop playing with me."

My fingers paused. "I'm not playing with you." I inserted the first knuckle into my opening, releasing a soft moan. "I'm playing with myself."

"Take off the bra. I need to see all of you," Favi demanded.

Eager to please him, I removed my finger, sucking it off before slowly undoing the bra. His eyes narrowed, and I winked, loving how riled up he was.

"Wish you were here?" I teased as my breasts sprang free, and his eyes hooked onto them.

"*Sì*." His gruff voice made the hair rise on my skin.

"But you're not here..." I trailed off, and his eyes snapped to mine. I wetted my lips, and his eyes followed the action too. My hand crawled between my thighs, grazing my pussy. "What do you want to do to me?"

"I want to fuck you," he said, and I released an uneven breath. "Don't move." He turned the phone on its screen. There was nothing but darkness until his devilishly handsome face filled the screen again. There was a bottle of oil in his hand, and he doused his palm in a considerable amount. "Camera on your pussy."

Biting into my lip as a smile grew, I followed his order. I looked between my legs at him. I couldn't see his dick, but I saw him moving his hand.

Up and down.

So painfully slow, it felt like I was punishing myself instead of him.

"Play with yourself," he said, and my fingers found my clit, trying to mimic how he always pleased me. Favi knew my body better than I did, and my clit throbbed out of a need for him.

"Favi..." I whined.

He smirked. "Two fingers, baby."

I inserted another finger into my pussy, thrusting in and out while he stroked his dick.

"Rub your clit with your thumb. Slow, just like that."

I followed his orders like a doll — I couldn't move or breathe unless he ordered me to. My thumb felt so good against my clit. I needed him now more than ever, especially because of how he watched me with so much need and unfiltered passion. My orgasm was drawing closer already, and I wasn't ashamed. My body was in heat for him, and the low moans exchanged between us drove me crazy.

"You're so fucking sexy, *fiore*. Fuck yourself faster for me," Favi said.

I did, staring into his eyes while his focus was between my legs, watching my fingers slip in and out how he ordered me to. My juices were soaking into the sheet, making such a mess I wish he was here to lick clean.

Then he'd kiss me. Roughly. Passionately.

My lips tingled from imagining it.

I ran my free hand up my abdomen, cupping a breast, tightening around my neck until my thumb brushed my lips. "Favi..."

"Fuck, Chayanne," Favi hissed, his hands moving faster. "Spread your legs wider. I need to see your pretty pussy."

I spread my legs as wide as I could go, showing him everything.

He made me finger myself fast. Slow. Made me remove my fingers and suck them clean before putting them inside again.

It was sweet torture. I never wanted it to stop.

"Go for your favorite toy," he ordered, and I stopped fingering myself to grab the toy.

I lay before him. "What do you want me to do?"

"Put it on the highest setting. Don't move it unless I tell you to. I don't care if you start trembling."

My eyes widened while my lips parted. "Favi, you're torturing me."

His eyes dragged from between my thighs to settle on mine. They darkened as he smirked. "I know."

Pouting, I pressed the toy against my clit. "Oh," I moaned, my back arching off the bed. My clit was swollen and sensitive. Sweat dotted my forehead as my legs tightened.

"Keep your legs open, Chayanne. You don't come until I tell you to."

"I c-can't," I stated breathlessly. Hot tension built in my middle. All the edging was going to make me come so hard, that I might pass out.

"You can." His eyes locked on mine, daring me to come without his permission. "Remove the toy. Use your finger— One, Chayanne. Curl it. Good girl. Feels good?"

I nodded, panting as I tried my hardest to hold back my orgasm. "Favi..."

"Do you want to come?"

"Yes!" I screamed, my fingers weren't good enough anymore. I needed his dick. Him. All of him.

And there he was... smirking at me. He wasn't stroking himself anymore; he'd given me his full attention during his sweet torture. "Stop," he commanded, and my actions halted because, at that moment, he was my master.

I groaned. "Please don't do this to me right now... I'm on edge, and it hurts."

Favi's smirk stretched. "Relax. You're getting fucked like my slut when I'm back."

"Favi, me cya hold this until yu come back next week."

"You can." He glanced at his watch before looking at me. "Happy birthday, *fiore*."

On special days in movies, a girl always wake with her hair not messy, the sun glowing, and a smile on her face. That ano how me wake pon my birthday. Mi wake with mi hair in knots, an ache between my thighs, and a miserable scowl pon mi face. Mi cya sleep without Favi, and mi vex wid him. But mi nago mek that spoil mi day! Me a big bad twenty! Today, me waa get so drunk, me deevn memba mi name!

Squealing, mi hurry and go bathe, then get dressed. Mi a go have brunch wid my friends. Mi have so much new clothes courtesy of my man, and mi a go wear a dress him pick out fimi last night. This cute, white mini dress a probably the only thing mi have from Favi weh nuh tight and revealing. Mi pair it with nude stilettos, gold accessories, and comb mi hair into waa nice updo. By the time mi done get dressed, check pon Favi snakes with the strict rules him gimi, then head downstairs, Trav arrive with Eltham, Chezzy, and Yolo.

"Happy birthday, best bitch!" Chezzy pull me into a tight hug.

"Thank you!" Mi grin as Yolo join the hug, showering me with kisses.

Trav hugged me after they pulled away. "Happy birthday, Chichi. Nuh feel yu too big now."

"Gweh." Mi roll mi eyes playfully, accepting the quick one-arm hug from Eltham.

Yolo wipe away fake tears. "Me cya believe yaa turn big woman pon me."

"Girl, please." Mi laugh as mi accept the gift bags from them. "Thank you so much," I said while realizing sum. "Weh mi baby?" mi ask Chezzy, and she sigh. Mi tell mi other guests fi go to the living room. When me and Chezzy alone, mi stare expectantly.

"Him deh wid Lamar mother." She shrug, and mi brows furrow.

"Yu sure yu good? Sum off with yu lately—"

"Mi good."

"Yu sure? Mi understand if yu miss—"

"You don't understand!" she snap, and mi mouth drop, making her sigh. "Sorry. Mi nuh waa argue wid yu today, Chichi. It's your birthday. Mi good. Leave it alone, please?"

Mi nod, and she smile before pulling me toward the living room. Trav shake him head as we step past him.

Mi open their gifts, and mi cudn stop the waterworks. Trav got me a camera and a bottle of liquor because mi been a say mi waa get wasted. Mi unsure wa Chezzy get me, she seh fi open it later. Yolo got me another dildo.

"Thanks, Yolo. *You shouldn't have*," I said while she snickered.

Trav try peek ina the bag. "A wa?"

"Mind yu bizniz, Mawga Bwoy." Mi pull the bag away from him, and Chezzy chuckle.

"Chichi a gwan like is a dildo or sum," Eltham seh, and mi choke pon air.

"Shut up, Josiah Eltham," mi snap, and him sigh.

"Why you and your man love use mi government?"

"Bo'claat. A Joseph yu name, dawg? Wul time mi think Eltham a yu real name," Trav seh, and Chezzy shake her head.

"Dawg, we a roll from high school, and yu just a learn mi name?" Eltham kiss him teeth when Trav scratch the back of him head.

"And him deevn get it right. Man fool ino," Yolo seh.

"Very fool," Chezzy mutter, but a mi alone hear her.

"Mi agree wid yu fi the first," Eltham seh. Him bump Yolo fist with his, and she grin.

"Anyway! Unu ready?" mi ask, and dem nod. Mi give Marshy a treat before we leave. In the car, mi answer the well wishes from my friends and family. Shane wish me a happy birthday, and mi tell him thanks, then block him. Mi nuh waa Favi find out bout him; mi know how him get bout next man round mi.

After a short drive, we reach the restaurant in Ochi. Chezzy give them her name for the reservations, and the host lead we to wi seat.

Me? Hungry bad. Since mi come from foreign, mi a nyam dung the place. It nice fi eat without worrying seh mago throw up.

We server tek wi order, and Yolo flirt with her until she leave fi put dem in.

"A go tell Gabby yaa give her bun," Eltham seh, and Yolo scoff.

"Nuh gyal cya leff me, so go ahead. Besides, me nehna go bun her. Me loyal now." Yolo smile, and mi chuckle.

A moment later, the server make her way to our table. Favi was beside her. Gasping, mi run outta the seat and jump into his arms. My feet raised off the ground as him hug mi tight with one arm, making his gun press against me. Smiling, mi pull away fi kiss him.

"Happy birthday, baby," him seh after breaking the kiss. Him hand me the bouquet of roses that was in his other hand.

To how me a blush, mi cya even find the words fi thank him. So, mi kiss him again, and everybody swoon as we settled into our seats. The server tek Favi order, then leave.

"Unu did know seh Favi come back?" mi ask Trav and Eltham, and dem nod. Mi gasp, facing Favi. "You liar. You were here last night?"

Him nod, and mi smile widen. I was happy before, but now me a the happiest girl alive!

Mi bring mi hand to mi hair, and Favi halt me.

"Leave it. You look beautiful," him seh, and mi blush.

"Me heart a hurt me," Yolo sing, and Trav knock a beat pon the table fi her off-key notes.

Favi glare at her, wrapping him arm round mi waist and pulling me closer.

Minutes later, wi order arrive. The food sell-off, our server was amazing, and a waa nice likkle vibe. It made me sad when we leave. We a go back a Favi house fi chill likkle. Waa beach party a keep later weh mi did plan fi go, but now that Favi come back, mi might stay inside wid him. Him owe mi birthday buddy.

Favi park behind Trav car, and mi brows furrow when mi see another car parked in the driveway. Placing my hand in Favi's so him can help mi outta his car, mi gasp when mi look pon the strange car good. It was a BMW SUV with a big red bow atop it.

"A so Chichi pussy pension dee expensive? A must pregnant pussy she have," Yolo seh, and Eltham raise a brow.

"Wa yu know boh pregnant pussy?" Eltham ask, and Yolo smirk.

Tears spring to mi eyes as Favi jingle the key before mi face, taking me away from my state of shock.

"Favi! Mi tell yu mi love yu from morning?!" I exclaimed, and Yolo sigh loudly in the background.

"*Sì*, but tell me again," Favi said in Italian.

"I love you!" I smiled as I hugged him. Mi love the big foot brown bwoy isi!

"That's not all." Him lead mi inside, and mi almost faint!

The house was transformed into a garden of red roses. Petals covered the floor, mi cudn see no trace of the tiles. Flower vases led up the staircase with some roses wrapped in money while others had cards tucked between them.

Favi led me into the living room, and my lips trembled. An arrangement of large floral letters that read 'HBD' deh before the media wall. The mountain of gifts beside the 'H' and 'D' made it hard to see anything else in the room.

"I-I don't know what to say," I cried, fanning my face while Chezzy record me and Favi.

"Thank him! Him love yu more than me fi true," Yolo said, and we laughed.

Mi wipe weh tears fi look at Favi. Mi know mi look a mess, but mi nuh care. How did I get so lucky? "Thank you, Favi. I love you," I said through sobs.

He smiled, making my knees weaken. "*Ti amo.*"

"Yu sista turn him ina simp," Eltham whispered.

"From younger days him rate her," Trav seh, and smaddy sigh.

"Okay, let's give them some space! Unu know me cya stay weh love deh fi too long. It will act up me sinus," Yolo seh.

Favi chuckle, leading me to the sofa while our guests left.

"Yu go all out ino, babe," mi seh as him hand mi a jewelry box.

"Do you deserve less?" him ask.

"Never." My man mek it feel like every day a mi birthday! Favi gave me the world, and I couldn't wait to get my life together so I could give him the clouds, stars, and moon.

"Exactly," him seh, and mi chuckle.

Mi look from him fi open the jewelry box, and mi gasp. A gold custom-made necklace glistened at me. The chains met at a pendant of red diamond studded letters that read 'FIORE'.

"Oh my God," I said in awe. "Look how yu have mi a bawl like mi nav no sense!"

He chuckled. "Do you like it?"

"I love it, Favi!" I kissed his cheek, pulling away with a smile. "Put it on for me, please?" I asked, and he did. I held the pendant between my fingers after he pulled away. "It's so beautiful."

"Sì," he said, and I looked at him, blushing because he was looking at me. I was about to look away when he gripped beneath my chin. "You're twenty now, Chayanne. The shyness cya work."

"You make me nervous..." I murmured, trying my best not to look away as my heart raced.

A small smirk played on his lips. "I do?"

"You know you do. Nuh act smart."

"One of us has to be." He chuckled as I gasped. "Nuh badda vex up yuself."

"Mi nehna go vex," mi seh, and him scoff, releasing mi chin.

Him reach toward the basket which was resting atop the table. It was full of all my favorite fragrances. Freeing a card tucked between two bottles, him hand the card to me. "I wanted you to read this later, but I want to see your face now."

Mi trace my name on the front of the card. Him have good penmanship for a man. Everything about Favi perfect! That was why mi love him wid alla mi belly!

"Read it to me." I tried handing it to him, but him gwan like him nuh see it. "It's my birthday."

Him glare at me, snatching it while mi grin. "Midnight needs to hurry and get here."

"No cause yu nuh cook fimi yet."

"Only thing a go down yu throat tonight a mi cocky."

Mi eyes widen as mi look round. "Behave!" mi hiss, and him chuckle.

"Everyone is outside, including your dog. Relax." Making himself comfortable, him throw an arm over mi shoulder while mi curl into him side. Him sneeze, and mi lean off him. Him did seh him tek medicine before him come a the brunch, which I believed cause him neva sneeze until now.

"Mi ago mek yu sum tea."

He shook his head. "Mi good."

Tears rush to mi eyes. "Favi, no. I hate when people are sick. Mago mek the tea. Soon come."

Him sigh before me go to the kitchen. While mi mek the tea, mi eavesdrop ina the conversation that drifted from outside.

"Tell wi bout the pregnant pussy," Eltham seh, and Yolo chuckle.

"Me tonguematize this girl me dee a deal wid one time, and shi leff ar man fimi," Yolo seh, and Eltham laugh dryly.

"A woman leff ar man fi plastic hood?"

"Nuh know why yaa gwan like if yu have a gyal me cya tek her," Yolo seh, and Eltham kiss him teeth. "Yu lucky me loyal now! Tell him, Chezzy!"

"Mhm," Chezzy seh, and mi sigh, knowing big head Lamar goodly upset her.

"Yu alright?" Yolo ask.

"Yeah. Mi a go round a the front, mi need fi call Daddy."

"A longtime she emo ino," Eltham whisper as Chezzy's footsteps fade, and Yolo kiss ar teeth.

"Shut up, crosses man. Listen to the voice note her man send me. Him bawl fimi leave him woman alone cause dem deh from high school and him really love her." Yolo play the voice note.

Eltham ina tears by the time the voice note done. "Wa kinda mahma man this?" him ask, and Yolo laugh.

"Yaa ask me? Every man a mahma man except Chichi own. That's why mi waa mi own Favio ina the shape of a likkle titty woman," Yolo seh, and mi chuckle while Eltham kiss him teeth.

"Yow, Trav, yu can use the voice note as waa intro to a song— A weh him gone?"

"Me nuh know. Me nuh watch man. Go look fi him and give me space because yaa act up me sinus," Yolo seh, and Eltham kiss him teeth.

Steam rise from the pot, and mi turn off the stove. Mi strain the bush tea ina waa cup, then bring it to Favi. "Mi a go fi waa sweater fi yu." Mi walk away before him can protest. Mi go ina fi him portion of the closet, freezing as mi see the knitted hoodie mi give him fi him twenty-fourth birthday. Smiling, mi bring it downstairs. "I didn't know you still had this," I said, and him look from him phone to me.

He smiled at the hoodie, then coughed. Him tek a sip from the tea, gagging as him rest the cup atop the table. "Why did you think I wouldn't keep it?" he asked as him put it on. The hoodie was black with red details on the left crest plate — a snake with a watch around the end of its tail; Trav drew it for me.

"Maybe for the same reason you thought I wouldn't keep the shell." Mi smile as him chuckle. "Are you feeling better?"

"You gave me poison to drink, why would I feel better?" him ask, and mi roll mi eyes. "I don't feel well enough to read."

"Mi cya stand yu!" mi hiss, and him grin while mi curl ina him side. "Before I start, can I ask you a question?"

He freed my hair from the updo, running his fingers through it. "You're asking for permission to talk now?"

"You don't have to answer if you don't want to..." I cleared my throat. "The way you go all out fi me makes me curious why you hate your birthday."

Him sigh. "I don't hate it. I just don't celebrate it."

"Why?"

"I had my initiation at thirteen."

"Huh?!" mi fly up fi look pon him, and him pull mi back pon him.

"You ask too many questions, *fiore*. Get to reading," he said, and I pouted at the letter.

Fiore mio,

I know you're beyond elated by all the love and well wishes you've received today. You're probably smiling right now, but can you make that smile wider for me?

Ti amo, Chayanne. So fucking much. I might have been a fucked up man to you in the past, but I'm trying to be a better man to you for all our tomorrows.

Until then, we have today.

A stubborn person once told me "You only turn 24 once, you know?" I know you're not there as yet, but I still hope you have an amazing day and celebrate this milestone to the fullest.

I hope you like your gifts. And no, the car nua send back, so don't start yu fuckry.

I only get the best for the best woman, because she only turns 20 once.

Buoncompleanno,
Your Favi.

A fresh stream of tears run down my cheeks as mi reach the end. Favi kiss me atop the head, and mi heart do somersaults while mi smile.

What a fi yu, cya be un-fi yu.

Chapter Sixty-Two

CHAYANNE

C ause summer soon done, people a frequent the hotel more. Mi hours longer, but today mi get off a likkle earlier. Mi thankful Favi got me this car. Him come for me most nights, but me prefer fi drive home cause him busy with launching the new line of Welsh's.

Sometimes, mi nuh feel good enough fi him. Mi young a try figure out life while him very accomplished. Him tek care of mi while all mi have fi offer a pussy, attitude, and love. Mi waa spoil him, too.

Sighing, mi clock out. Mi step outta the cool AC into the hot air. Sweat form pon mi farid as mi walk through the empty employee's parking lot. Mi jingle mi keys while texting Favi that mi on mi way. Him tell mi fi drive safe, and mi smile.

Mi cya wait fi go home! Mi hungry, but mago sex him first. The bwoy buddy nice bad! Me a try be more outgoing for him, so mi sex him pon the poolside under the stars pon mi birthday. Mi did scared, but it was nice being more explorative.

"Breed me," I moaned, watching his dick slide in and out of my pussy. I was lying

on the side of the pool. My ankles were behind my head, and my hands were holding my thighs, spreading me wider.

"Mm," he groaned out. The water splashed around his legs louder than our moans and my wet pussy.

"I'm close," I announced, my walls fluttering around his dick.

"I know, baby. Marry me," he said, and my eyes widened as they snapped to his. Favi turned his head to the sky, his lips parting as he came deep inside me.

Him nuh seh back nun bout marriage, and mi nuh bring it up either. A so good sex mek people seh anything weh come to them mouth.

Chuckling, mi about fi reach mi vehicle when mi remember mi leff the tumbler Ren buy fimi. Jesam peace! Mi run toward the hotel and search inside the employee's lounge, but mi nuh see it. Sighing, mi a walk toward the front when mi buck up ina Dayshawn.

"Chichi, yu good?" him ask, and mi shake mi head, wiping away tears.

"Mi cya find my tumbler," mi seh.

Him scowl. "A waa tumbler yaa cry over?"

"It's special!"

"Mi will see if mi can find it fi yu. How it look?" him ask, and mi describe it.

"Thanks," mi seh, and him nod as mi leave. Mi still cya stand him, but we afi be cordial with each other. Now by the car, me a fumble with the keys when smaddy sneak behind me. Before mi cuda turn fi acknowledge the person, them slap waa large, calloused hand over mi mouth. My reflexes kicked in, and mi flail against them, freezing as them press something into my side.

A gun.

"If yu scream, mi kill yu," a scratchy male voice warned, sending shivers down my spine as tears flooded my eyes.

I wasn't sure if my heart was beating as cold bumps rose on my skin.

His slimy, oddly shaped lips grazed the side of my face. His tongue jutted out and licked my cheek. Disgust ran down my spine, and he chuckled. "Yago enjoy it. I fuck good," he promised.

My chest heaved.

I desperately tried to remember what Al taught me.

Scream.

Fight.

Anything to save me.

But my body was crippled by fear.

"Yu body firm and sexy," he whispered in my ear, making bile sting my throat as he squeezed my breasts and ass. His rancid breath fanned my face as he opened the back door of my car, shoving me face-first onto the back seat. "Turn over," he ordered, kicking away my keys that slipped out of my hands onto the paved ground.

I rolled over, and he positioned himself between my legs. My body shook as he pushed my dress to my waist, yanking my panties to my ankles. He lowered his jeans, and his engorged erection sprang free, leaking pre-cum. He took my hand and made me palm it. It throbbed beneath my fingertips.

Grinning, he moved my hand toward my mouth. "Open."

I shook my head, pursing my lips while turning my head away from him. My eyes landed on the wheel. Even if I stretched toward it, I wouldn't reach the horn.

"I said open," he hissed, pressing the gun against my forehead.

An uneven breath passed my trembling lips as they parted. He forced my index into my mouth, and bitterness seeped into my tastebuds.

"Love when unu listen," he commended, laughing as he released me.

I yanked my finger out of my mouth, turning to the side to spit on the floor.

I was disgusted.

Ashamed.

I tightly shut my eyes. Tears rolled down my cheeks as I heard the rip of a condom.

As he shuffled about while putting it on, I was hit with the realization that a cya Slitta woman and Al daughter this.

The thought fueled me with the strength this man was taking from me. With all the energy I could muster, I opened my eyes. I balled my hand into a tight fist and punched him square in the nose. A satisfying *crack* rang out into the night, and he screamed as he backed away.

"Ow!" I cried, shaking my hands to rid the sting. My adrenaline pumped as he approached me, and I kicked him in his face, sending him flying. As he fell a short distance away, I sat up, panting at the hideous face and jagged lips that kissed me everywhere.

"Aye, bloodclaat gyal, yu bruk mi fucking nose! Mi did a go mek dis nice fi yu, but fuck the deal, mago kill yu rass!" He moved his hand from his bloody nose, reaching for the gun that fell from his hand.

Eyes widening, I hauled my feet inside and slammed the door shut. My panties got caught in the door, and I kicked them off in a rush. I felt around the car for my fob. My fingers smeared the blob of spit. "No, no," I cried, frantically searching the floor.

Blousecup! They were outside, and my car couldn't start unless it was inside. Heart racing, I searched for my phone instead. As I found it in my bag, a voice came from outside.

"Pussy, drop yu gun now!" he barked.

Releasing an uneven breath, I pressed my face against the tinted windows, watching as my savior pointed a gun toward Ugly, who trembled like a coward. Slowly, he turned around, then shot at my rescuer. Missing the shot, Ugly's eyes widened before he escaped into the nearby bushes.

I dropped onto the seat with a loud breath. Waves of relief washed over my racing heart, trying to soothe it, but all it did was make me cry more. Something knocked on the window, and I shot up, startled. Spotting my rescuer, I exhaled an uneven breath before opening the door.

Noticing my half-naked state, Dayshawn grabbed my panties, offering them to me while looking away. Trembling, I redressed, shooting Mama a silent thanks cause mi always wear mi good panties pon the road.

"Him touch yu, Chichi?" Dayshawn asked, and I opened my mouth, but I couldn't find my voice, so I shook my head. Him sigh, handing me the tumbler while putting away the gun.

Mi toss it into the trunk. Mi nuh want it anymore.

Him tek out him phone. "Mago call the police—"

"Please don't," mi seh quickly, and him brows knit.

"I need to report it, Chichi."

I knew that, but... I couldn't. Not right now. I couldn't breathe properly. I could still feel his heavy body atop me, his breath fanning my face while his rough hands forced off my panties. What did I do to deserve this?

"I'll report it when I'm ready... Thank you," I whispered, and he smiled gently.

"Nafi thank mi fi dat. Really sorry this happen to yu. Mi know wi nuh deh pon the best of terms, but nuh fraid fi link mi if yu need to, zeen?"

Unsure what else to do, mi nod. Him smile, grabbing mi key off the ground. Mi accept it with trembling fingers and settled behind the wheel. I was unsure how I reached home, but I did. As soon as I entered the house, I made a beeline to the bathroom. Tears ran down my face as I rubbed my skin raw. I still felt dirty as I went into bed, hiding beneath the covers.

Favi entered with a tray of food moments later, and I pushed it around the plate. "Yu nuh hungry?" him ask, and mi think mi shake mi head. "*Stai bene?*" him ask, and I blocked him out.

I could still feel the seat leather pressing against my face while Ugly turned my face to the side, kissing up and down my neck. His hands as they covered my mouth. How aroused he was at the thought of—

Mi cover mi mouth, placing the tray beside me on the bed. It turned over as mi bolt toward the bathroom. I dropped to the floor before the toilet, dry heaving into it. Something touched me, and I screamed, plastering myself on the wall farthest from it.

A face stared at me in worry. His mouth was moving, but I couldn't hear what he was saying. He approached me, and I decided not to submit to him this time.

So, I fought back.

Scratching.

Slapping.

Pushing.

Kicking.

If I had a gun, I would've emptied it into him.

"Chayanne! Chayanne!" the sick, disgusting man shouted, and I hated my name on his tongue. He grabbed my hand, and I continued my blind fit of rage until he restrained me.

Drained, I surrendered.

I didn't have the energy to fight.

I tried, but I failed.

Just like in the car.

I was a disappointment to Al and Favi.

I was helpless, and he was going to rape me at my home.

"*Fiore?*" came a gentler voice.

I froze, blinking away tears to clear the haze.

Favi. My Favi. He had the most perfect face, and the deepest yet most soothing voice. He was the owner of my heart, who had powerful arms of comfort wrapped around me.

"Fuck," he cursed, heaving a tired breath. "*Calmati*. It's me," he said, and I threw my arms around his shoulders. He held me close, and I cried into his neck. "What's wrong?" he asked, trying to pull away to look at me. He sighed as I tightened my grip around him, then he stroked my back. "I'm here, *fiore*." He kissed me atop the head, and I inhaled a deep waft of his familiar scent.

Favi held me close for the next few minutes. I cried in his arms while he whispered that everything would be okay.

"If my cooking disgusts you, you should've said that instead of being dramatic," he joked, but I didn't laugh.

I was incapable.

The only thing I knew how to do was think about how I wanted him to kill the man in the most gruesome, inhumane way. But I didn't want him to fall back into his old ways because of me. He worked hard to separate himself from that life. He was always elevating. I knew how much a normal life meant to him. I didn't want to drag him down when my life was stagnant. Even if it meant I had to suffer in silence, I wanted nothing but the best for Favi.

By the morning, mi tears dry and mi numb. Mi lay a look at the ceiling. Favi must have brought me to bed last night. Mi sit up when him enter the room, carrying a tray of food that had a mouth-watering aroma.

"Frittatas," him seh. It was the only food I didn't throw up in Italy. "Go brush your teeth."

Like a zombie, me do wa him seh. Returning to bed, mi accept the food.

Him watch me eat in silence. After me swallow the last drop of tea, him ask, "What happened to you last night?"

Mi look weh from him, unsure how fi answer.

Him hold my chin, making me face him. "What happened last night? Smaddy fuck with yu?" he asked, and tears pricked my eyes. "Ah, doh ansa." He jumped to his feet, taking his pistol off the nightstand. He muttered Italian in such a dark tone, it chilled me to the core.

"Favio!" mi yell, resting the tray aside to grab him. "Mi nuh feel comfortable a talk about it right now."

Him brush weh mi hand. Anger burned in his eyes as he looked at me. "Chayanne, nuh tell mi fuckry. Wa happen to yu last night?"

Sighing, I released him. "Favi... Please. Mi will talk to yu when mi ready."

"Okay," him seh after a while, placing the gun on the nightstand. He sat on the bed, making me straddle him while I tensed.

This strong chest was Favi's.

These hands were Favi's.

This man was Favi.

He loved me. He wouldn't hurt me, right?

Mi pull away from his hug and stand, not meeting his gaze as him stare pon me wid furrowed brows. "I'm going to Al. Mi need a little space."

I'd been eating away my sadness. Not even food a help the ache in my chest and disgust mi feel by my skin. Mi shower about four times since mi come here, but mi still feel dirty. Mi ina Favi hoodie, him sweatpants, and Chezzy tights, but mi still feel naked.

"You should tell him, Chichi," Chezzy say.

Mi sigh, taking another bite from my sandwich. "I'm not ready to."

"I understand that, but him worried about yu. The man doh like me, and me worse nuh like him, but him reach out to mi cause yaa push him away."

Guilt gnawed at me even though it nuh as simple as them a mek it seem. Unless a dem get pinned down at gunpoint in their own car, dem cya tell mi how fi feel or who mi fi share the story with.

Bile rise to mi throat and mi rush toward the bathroom. Mi hunch over the toilet, throwing up everything mi eat in the past few hours.

My eyes stung.

My throat ached.

Everywhere hurt.

When mi done, mi flush the toilet and gargle mouthwash. Chezzy lead me back to bed, being mindful of Zaveer, who fell asleep pon the floor minutes ago. Mi thankful she deh here, but mi waa she leave. I hated that someone was seeing me like this when I couldn't stand to look at myself in the mirror.

"Thought it was the Italian food making you vomit." She wrapped us in my blanket as the door knock.

Yolo enter. She crawl beneath the sheet, and we lay in silence fi a while. Mi nuh tell Yolo wa happen, but Chezzy did invite her over when Favi call her.

"A wa do Chichi? The man a act up again?" Yolo ask.

"No," mi seh.

"Oh, alright. Cause me dee a go tell yu fi give him bun. A wa do yu?"

Chezzy tighten her grip around my waist. "Nuh ask her dat right now."

"Okay... Yu waa hear boh wa happen to me?" Yolo ask, and mi nod weakly. Yolo smile. "The other day me carry Gabby go hotel, and ina the night me feel sum a drip pon me face. Me wake up ready fi cuss seh the people dem ceiling a leak, only fi see the gyal a chant waa language nobody nuh use since fifteen BC, while she fling sum outta waa black bottle pon me."

Chezzy burst out laughing. "Wa yaa seh to me?"

"The gyal obea me!" Yolo shriek. "A river me dee deh when yu call. That's why me tek so long fi come."

Chezzy ask Yolo more bout it, and mi block dem out. Mi appreciate dem trying to mek mi feel better, but I'd never be the same person again.

Favi could read mi like a book. In times like these, mi neva like it. Him visit mi this morning, and mi brush him off until him sigh and leave, giving me the space mi ask fa.

Suppose him think mi damaged? Suppose him nuh attracted to me anymore? Him always seh nufi mek nobody touch mi, and I wasn't strong enough to defend myself when another man tried to.

Sighing, mi walk toward the lobby. Mi come tell mi boss mi need time off, and he granted it. Arriving in the lobby, mi stumble ina Dayshawn and Itanya.

"Chichi, how are you?" Dayshawn ask.

"Okay," I lied, glancing at mi car, weh park at the front. "I have to go—"

Itanya put a hand pon mi shoulder, and I tensed. She quickly retract her hand, apologizing. "Can I hug you?" She give me a look of pity, and mi glare at Dayshawn. "Chichi, him neva directly tell mi wa happen," Itanya state, and mi look at her. "A me find yu tumbler and did a carry it come give yu. When mi see wa did a happen, mi run come call the first person mi see. I'm so sorry, girl. If you need a friend or anything, call me."

Dayshawn nodded. "Know mi always deh ya fi yu, Chichi."

Mi look at the ground, blinking away tears. "Okay... Thanks," I muttered, taking brisk steps toward mi car as the tears break past mi resistance. Hopping in the car, mi drive fast like Chezzy until me reach Exchange. Mi stay by miself until night come.

The door knock, and mi jump up. Remembering Favi seh him a come check mi, mi sigh and run to the kitchen fi hide the liquor bottle. Mi pop a gum into mi mouth before opening the door. Mi eyes widen at Dayshawn. He brought me chocolate, and it made me smile. My first smile since—

Mi smile wash away, and mi raise a brow.

"Just come offa work and a check if yu straight. Mi cya stop think boh yu, and mi nuh waa yu deh by yuself. I'm willing to be a listening ear," him seh.

Mi look from him to the chocolate. I needed someone to talk to, and I felt safe around Dayshawn...

Safer than I felt around Favi.

But Favi a come over soon, and mi nuh want him see Dayshawn deh here. Mi about fi decline him company when mi phone vibrate.

FAVI: I have an emergency meeting with Sergio. I'll come over a little later. Make sure you eat.

Swallowing to dampen mi dry throat, mi step aside. Dayshawn entered, smiling brightly.

Chapter Sixty-Three

CHAYANNE

Dayshawn just leff Al house. Fi the past two weeks, him and Itanya come check pon mi. Mostly Dayshawn, though. Dem understand mi better than my other friends. Chezzy busy a stress bout if Lamar a sex white gyal fi green card. Trav busy a the studio with him tail. Yolo busy a go river every day pon the people dem clock. And Favi...

He was slowing before my house now. Why was he here? Mi tell him mi a come home tomorrow. These video calls and brief physical interactions nehna cut it.

Mi feel likkle bit more comfortable ina mi skin. Mi hope being around him more can give mi the courage mi need fi tell him about wa happen, even though mi waa heal completely so mi nafi tell him and mek him get ina trouble.

Him exit the car, holding a bag of food in one hand and twirling the car key in his next. Stopping before mi, him stop twirl the key round him finger and ask calmly, "Who dat?"

"A friend from work." Mi tek the bag from him. Mi nuh know how mi neva realize before how mi hungry, cause mi can feel the movement ina mi belly now.

We enter the house, and Favi kick the door shut. The noise startle Marshy, who did curl ina the sofa a sleep. She bark and growl at Favi.

"*Zitto*," Favi snapped, and Marshy whine before she run toward mi bedroom.

Mi shake mi head as mi sit round the island, picking around the food.

"*Fiore*, we talked about this. I won't force you to talk, but you're going to eat whether you like it or not," he said softly.

This a wi routine fi the past days: him get food delivered, then video call and watch mi eat it; or, him carry it come, and stuff it dung mi throat until him satisfied.

Mi dweet miself today fi spare miself the hassle. Taking a bite, mi gag and push the plate away. "Mi nuh like how it smell."

Him glance at the food, then walk toward the pantry. Him tek out ingredients, and mi smile a little. Mi walk toward the stove, wanting to help him make the pasta. Mi about fi break it above the pot when him halt mi.

"Chayanne, what the fuck?" Favi yanked the pasta from my hand.

Mi brows furrow, my heart thrumming because his change in attitude was scary. "Wa mi do?" I whispered, stepping backward.

"Don't ever break pasta. That's bad luck," he said, and my nerves calmed.

"When since yu believe ina luck, Favi?" mi ask, and him chuckle.

"Don't worry about that. Go sit down. I'll cook."

Mi smile and comply. The two layers of clothes mi ina a mek mi hot, so mi go fi the fan. Mi wait patiently fi him done cook, then mi eat the pasta while him eat the box food him did bring. While eating, me scroll through my emails. Mi still nuh hear from the school yet. Aunty call mi since week and cuss seh a my fault if mi nuh get in.

After we finish eat, Favi did the dishes, then walk toward me. He was too close.

Remembering Dayshawn's words that not all men were the same, and mi afi put miself out there if mi waa tek back mi power, mi force miself fi relax.

Favi spin round the stool, standing between my thighs and resting him hands pon mi waist. "Can I get a kiss today?"

This was Favi.

Favi wouldn't hurt me.

Mi nod slowly.

He kissed me hard, which I missed a lot. When him break away, him look pon mi wid a expression mi cudn read. Him brush back mi hair, placing a long kiss atop my head. "You said you're going back to work tomorrow?"

"Yes."

"I'll pick you up. And nuh carry back nuh coworker over here. I don't give a fuck if it's your friend. If I can't be around you, nuh next man cya round yu."

"Mi never seh a waa man—"

Him pause. "Mi seh wa mi seh, Chayanne."

I sighed. "Okay, Favi…"

"What's the attitude for?" him ask, and mi nuh ansa. "Yu lucky mi nuh run red light, cause mi wuda fuck tha attitude deh outta yu right now."

Mi tense briefly. All mi lies a catch up to mi. When Favi visit yesterday and ask fi sex, mi lie seh mi deh pon mi period. Just like mi lie seh mi use some of mi vacation days cause dem a expire. "Goodnight, Favi," mi seh, and him give mi lips a last kiss before leaving.

I had one condition when returning to work: mi naa do night shift. Mi man rich, mi nuh need money. The slow pace of morning shift a exactly wa mi need. Mi clock out at five pon the dot. Mi a walk toward the lobby fi meet Favi when mi buck ina Dayshawn.

"Evening, Chichi," him greet, smiling.

Mi return the smile. "Hey. Mi cya talk right now—"

"That good. Mi just have a likkle question fi yu," him seh, his tone serious.

"What question?"

"Why yaa gimi mixed signals?" him ask, and mi brows knit.

"Wa yu mean?"

"You been a spend every night wid mi fi the past weeks, and now yu gone back to tha man deh? Yu deevn trust him enough fi mek him know wa do you."

"I'm going to tell him…" I whispered. Mago tell him tonight so him understand fi be more patient than how him already be.

"Whatever yu seh, Chichi. Mi only want wa best fi yu," he said, and mi scoff.

"Wa best fi me? *You*?"

"If it means me a someone you trust fi share everything wid? Yes. Mi have mi life together now. Mi can give yu everything mi neva gi yu when wi young," he said, and my mouth dropped.

"Stay away from me, Dayshawn," I warned before stomping outside. Mi eyes narrow pon Itanya, who a talk to my man. Why mi mek dem jancro ya feel like hummingbird?

Chapter Sixty-Four

FAVIO

"*S*litta," *Travis said, and I shifted my focus to him. "Yu gov? A the second time yaa play off-side."*

Cazzo.

My jaw ticked, and Travis motioned his head for Josiah to leave the room. As soon as he was out of earshot, I asked Travis, *"Yu think sum do Chayanne?"* I still couldn't make sense of why she acted like that last night. I moved a hand to my jaw, working it as I remembered the *deafaz* she gave me. My skin was still flaming red, but not as hot as my anger.

The guards assigned to her couldn't give me any answers about what happened. They said she always left at eleven. If not, then one. Her schedule was like clockwork, and they went to grab a drink during the hours of twelve.

"Wa yu mean?" Travis asked, and I explained. *"Dat nuh sound like Chichi fi real. Knowing how Chichi mad head can tek ar morewhile, she goodly up ina her feelings bout the likkle argument dem yu seh unu did a have..."*

Knowing that look all too well, I chuckled. I still hated how close he was to my woman, but I was becoming more accepting of him in her life. No one could care for *fiore mio* more than I did, but Travis was a close second. "We weren't arguing about anything serious. It was petty *fuckry,* like me forgetting to put down the toilet seat," I said, and he hummed.

"Maybe a work. Need mi fi check it?" he asked, and I shook my head.

"I went there when she went to Alphonso's house, but I didn't find anything."

"Mi still a go see wa mi can do. Anybody fuck with her afi get dirt," he said, and I smirked. "Wait. Yu leff her by herself deh a Elder? Yu know mi nuh believe—"

"She's with Chezandra," I said, and his eyelids lowered as he looked away, grabbing the controller.

"Oh... Mek wi run tha match ya," he said, and I smirked as he pressed resume. How did fiore not realize they were fucking?

Women never seemed to understand the concept of time. I texted Chayanne five minutes ago, yet she still wasn't outside. Clearly, she was fucking lost. Gritting my teeth, I exited the vehicle and walked toward the hotel's entrance.

I hated that she worked here. Something happened to my woman in this fucking place, and I wasn't going to let it slide. No matter how much money I waved and threats I promised, they couldn't get me the footage I needed because most of the exterior cameras weren't working. They could only show me Chayanne leaving, reentering a few minutes later, then exiting again. She was home within the usual timeframe of an hour.

Maybe I was overreacting, but I knew Chayanne. The problem was here.

If her boss was competent, I could've gotten a list of employees who worked that night, but the hotel was so disorganized that they couldn't get me a calendar with today's date if I pointed at it. I didn't want her working here anymore, and I would discuss this with her.

A familiar face approached me as I neared the front door. "Evening, sir."

I ignored her. I wasn't interested in anything she had to say. I wasn't obligated to listen to women who weren't Chayanne and *Mamma*.

"Mi have sum fi tell yu boh yu woman," she yelled, and I stopped walking.

I turned around, giving this woman — Itanya, according to the nametag — my full attention. "Get on with it."

Fidgeting, Itanya reiterated all the events of *that* night, then cleared her throat. "Mi neva waa say anything because she nuh waa tell anybody, but she need someone. Mi try be there fi her, but yaa her man, she need you regardless of wa she think."

Anger.

Red, fiery anger boiled in my veins.

My hands balled at my side. My finger twitched to shoot something.

Punch.

Or cut.

Whatever it took until who dared to touch my woman paid with their life.

Footsteps approached us, and I looked in that direction. I could smell Chayanne from anywhere.

She stopped beside us, curling her fingers around my biceps. "Bye, Itanya," Chayanne said with faux sweetness before she forced me to walk away. "Favi, can we stop at the supermarket, please? Mi feel fi likkle tomato juice."

"Tomato juice?" I asked. Someone tried to take advantage of her and she a come tell mi bout fucking tomato juice?

"Yeah. Mama used to mek mi drink it all the time."

How could she sound so normal when she was hiding such a secret from me? I unclenched my fists and opened the door. My fingers gripped the door so tightly, the color drained from my knuckles. "Get in, Chayanne."

We drove home in a stifling silence. She sensed something was off with me, but she didn't question me. She knew I wasn't in the mood to talk or argue. I was too occupied thinking about how slowly and painfully I was going to kill whoever thought they could hurt her.

"Chayanne," I said as the door closed behind me.

She placed her annoying dog on the ground, looking over her shoulder at me.

"Yes?"

I motioned my head toward the living room, and she followed me there. "Sit," I ordered.

Her brows furrowed as she sat, uncapping the tomato juice. "Yago want any?"

I shook my head, and she moved the bottle to her mouth. I needed a spliff or two, but I didn't want her out of my sight again.

How should I approach the situation? How could I miss the signs? Why didn't I do more to protect her?

Jaw clenching, I sat on the sofa across from her. I rested my arms on the armrest, asking calmly, "*Fiore*, what happened that night?"

She tensed, relaxing as she moved the bottle from her mouth. "I don't want to talk about it righ—"

I sat out, lacing my fingers between my thighs. "How yu nufi waa talk boh how a man force demself pon yu?"

Her eyes widened, her shoulders slumping as she looked away to mumble, "I-I didn't want you to find out like this..."

"Didn't want me to find out?" My voice raised as I continued. "Wa sense yu have me as yu man if yu neevn a go tell mi when man try assault yu?!"

"W-why yaa get upset with m-me?! Mi neva ask fi it!"

"I didn't say you did! I'm upset because you thought you couldn't talk to me!"

"I was going to tell you, Favi... I just didn't want you to do anything to anybody."

"Stop talking." I leaned back, staring at the ceiling before closing my eyes. Thinking of torture methods calmed my mind.

Penectomy.

Rat torture.

Flaying.

Sniffles disrupted me, and I looked at her. Chayanne hung her head low as she cried, and I kneeled before her within seconds. I removed the bottle from her shaking hands, taking them in mine. "Do you trust me, Chayanne?"

Nodding, she met my eyes with her watery ones. "I do."

I brought her hands to my mouth and kissed each knuckle. I didn't wipe her tears away. I hated seeing her like this, but I needed her to feel it.

Not hurt. Nor disgust. But to express herself because she thought she had to hide this from me.

She wrapped her arms around my neck, crying hard like that night. Her tears seeped through my shirt, settling on my skin. Not breaking the hug, I sat beside her and pulled her onto my lap. Her body shook violently against me as she sobbed.

My chest was tight. Minus the time she got shot, I never felt this way before.

Fuck! Did this happen to her because of me, too?

I was trying to be a good man and give her the world plus more, but all I brought her was pain.

I was determined to change that.

Someone had to die for this. I wouldn't rest until they did.

We'd been lying on the sofa for the past few hours, facing each other. She drew circles on my bare chest while I held her, scared of letting go.

I wasn't fond of therapy, but Chayanne loved to talk. Maybe it'd be good for her. No, never mind. She couldn't talk to me; it'd be hard for her to talk to anyone else. All I could do for now was to be there for her in any way she allowed me to.

"Chayanne," I said after a while.

"*Sí?*" she replied, and for the first time in hours, I smiled for a few seconds.

"I want to talk about it," I said, and she sighed.

"Okay..."

"I know you don't want to talk about it, but I can't rest knowing there's someone out there that hurt you."

She smiled weakly. "I know."

"If anything becomes too much, let me know," I said, and she nodded. "How did he look?"

"Ugly."

"*Ugly*?" I asked, and she nodded.

"Mi cudn see him face good, but it disfigured."

"Can you give me more details than this, baby?" I asked gently, and she nodded.

She stopped tracing my chest, turning around in my arms. She laced a hand with mine.

"You're safe," I said, grazing her skin with my thumb.

"I know, Favi..." She inhaled a deep breath. "He had a scar. Yu know when yu open fish belly fi clean it? A so him face look. Waa long cut run from the side a him mouth to the tip of him ear, and it nuh stitch up good."

Cazzo, that didn't ring a bell. I kissed the back of her head. "That helps a lot."

"I... I remember something else. Him talk waa way. Mi deevn know how fi describe it, *but it sound like this,*" she said, her voice sounding deep and raspy like something from those supernatural dramas she always watched.

The situation wasn't funny, but I laughed. "Chayanne, wa dat?"

"Gweh nuh, big foot! Mi cya do it like him, but a so it sound like chalk pon metal." She chuckled, making me smile. *Sì,* come back to me.

"Last question, okay?" I asked, and she nodded. "What did he say?"

She shrugged. "I was trying to block out everything."

"I'm sorry you had to go through that, *fiore*. It won't happen again," I promised, and she sighed.

An eerie silence fell over us for a few minutes until she bolted up, looking at me with wide eyes. "Mi remember sum else! He said someone paid him."

Sealah.

I got Chayanne to sleep half an hour ago, and I was smoking on the balcony now. I needed to stop; I knew that, but I couldn't always fuck away my problems. Especially not now.

I moved the spliff from my mouth with a sigh, resting it on the tray. I needed to stop. Right now. Chayanne hated the taste of weed, and I had a lot of work to do until she felt like herself again. I didn't need any hindrances.

My phone beeped, and I stood. I walked into the bedroom and checked on Chayanne. She was still sleeping. I swiped her phone off the bedside table before exiting the room. I didn't want to leave her, but I needed to check on my snakes.

Night was pregnant. Whenever she gave birth and her eggs hatched, I would sell the snakelets. I never bred my snakes, but Chayanne caused it to happen the last time I went to Italy. I didn't blame her, but she called crying when she walked in on them. She thought she accidentally allowed my black-headed python to free-roam with the others. Ink was a good boy, but I kept him isolated because he was cannibalistic.

Stopping by Night's terrarium, I kept my distance to feed her a thawed rat. This was her first pregnancy since I had her, and it made her snappy toward me.

While I watched her devour the rat, I opened Chayanne's phone and scrolled through her contacts. The first contact was the one I needed. I hated asking a pig for help, but I was desperate to hurt who hurt my woman.

"Hey, Pretty Girl," he answered.

My eyes narrowed on Night. "This is not Chayanne."

Silence came before the unmistakable ring of the dial tone.

Ketch this big, stinking pussy.

I called back.

"Mi nuh ina no talking with you, bwoy," he snarled.

"Watch yu mouth, pussy."

"And wa yu can do?"

"Find out," I warned. This pig was on his third strike. I *wanted* him to pass his dirty place with me. "Mi neevn call fi argue wid yu. This is about Chayanne."

"Anyhow yu mek nun do mi pickney—"

I gulped. "She almost got raped…"

"W-wa?" he forced out, and I sighed.

"I found out today, and I… need you to do something for me." I asked, wanting to rip my tongue out.

"Anything yu need, consider it done, mi boss."

"Look out for my call." I ended the call and pocketed Chayanne's phone. I checked on my other snakes. By the time I was done, Night finished eating. After washing my hands, I walked toward the bedroom while answering the new message that came in the group chat of *la famiglia*.

"Favi," came a sleepy mumble a few feet away, and I looked up from my phone.

"What are you doing up?" Pocketing my phone, I rushed toward her.

"I woke up and didn't see you—"

"I went to check on Night," I said, and she nodded as I helped her into bed.

She didn't want me holding her in bed, so we faced each other with a lot of space between us. She was sweating despite the AC, but she refused to take off my hoodie and sweatpants.

"Go to sleep. I'm right here," I said.

"Can we go to Italy?" she asked, and my brows furrowed. Whenever Chayanne was hungry or sleepy, she chat fuckry. She wasn't shaking, so it wasn't the former.

"Why do you want to go to Italy?"

"I don't want to be in Jamaica right now."

Fucking same.

Chapter Sixty-Five

CHAYANNE

Since we come Italy two days ago, all me do a sleep out mi likkle life. Jetlag sidung pon mi this time around. Meanwhile, when Favi naa treat mi like a figurine, him deh all over Italy, overseeing his business.

Being away from Jamaica a mek mi feel better already. There was no scarred face man, workplace, or bad vibes. Just me, my man, and the occasional breakdown or nausea from random flashbacks.

Plus, Dayshawn. Him sick mi stomach! Him won't stop text and call mi. Mi need fi block him before him mek my man vex wid mi.

Like the jancro know me a think boh him, mi phone ring while Favi place a plate of food before mi. Mi eyes widen and mi bout fi flip the phone over, but Favi stop me.

"Answer it," him seh.

Mi look pon him. "W-wa?"

"Matter of fact, let me talk to him."

Mi pull the phone to mi chest. Its vibrations ran through my body. "Fi wa?"

"Mi naa do the youth nun, Chayanne." Him tek the phone and sit across from me. Him answer the call.

Dayshawn said, "Hey, Chichi—"

"A her man this," Favi said calmly, and mi gulp.

"Oh—" Dayshawn clear him throat, deepening him voice. "Wahm, mi g?"

"I'm not your g." Favi glared. "Rate wa yu do fi Chayanne," he said, and some tension leave mi body. When I told Favi about what happened, him get vex seh mi confide ina mi ex. The only reason him neva rage, a cause him glad mi did have smaddy fi help mi.

"A the least mi can do. Some man nuh deserve woman," Dayshawn said, and mi choke.

Favi glance pon mi, then direct him focus to the phone. "Don't call her again."

Mi sigh as him hang up and hand mi the phone. "Yu cya behave, Favi?"

Him scoff. "Bout yaa find comfort ina next man. Block him, and nuh mek mi ketch yu round him again."

Mi roll mi eyes and comply. "Mi tell yu mi hate when yu talk to mi like that."

Him open him mouth fi seh sum, deciding against it as him look at the food. It was takeout from a nearby restaurant, weh mi neva get fi try the last time. "Eat."

Mi nod and obey. Afterward, we go to the living room. Favi sat beside me, tapping on his phone while football reruns play pon the TV. Him have one arm thrown over mi shoulder, his hand tucked in my hoodie while him play wid mi right nipple. This a the only way him touch mi since the incident. Him neva waa touch mi at first, but mi beg him fi treat mi normal until mi feel like miself again.

During this, Yolo call. "Like how me a work so hard fi buy Mommy the big house pon the hill, me treat meself to a likkle sum. Look here! Mago call tha one ya Buss Belly!"

Mi eyes widen. "Weh yu get dat fi buy?! Favi, look pon wa she have—"

Him look pon the big strap-on Yolo a wave in front of the screen before she cuda move it, and him narrow him eyes.

She chuckle nervously. "Favio... How are you?"

"Good," he replied.

"I'm good, too. Thanks for asking."

"I didn't—"

Mi move the phone outta him face. "Sorry, ignore him."

Yolo laugh. "Me know him nuh talk to nobody except you."

"He talks." Especially round him older cousins.

She wave mi off, showing me the toy again. "You like it?"

"It look like it can gwan. Mi think yu did a tek a break from woman?"

"I am. Me buy it cause Eltham seh me plastic hood dem nuh all dat. Me a show him seh at least mine can be any size while him stuck with a teelee. Plus, me need fi prepare meself fi when me start chat to dem wicked gyal ya again."

"Nobody nuh more wicked than you," mi seh, and she roll her eyes.

"This a why me like talk to Chezzy instead! She entertain me."

"Cause she like hear people sex story. And she a ruler, so stop it."

Yolo smirk. "Girls are spaghetti, Number One. If she neva have the baby, me wuda tek her from tha bwoy deh," Yolo seh, and mi frown.

Mi hate big head, black body Lamar! Day and day Chezzy more up ina her feelings, and mi hate see her like this. "Later mi call yu back, Yolo."

"Weh yaa run me offa the phone fa? Yu nuh love me again?"

"Mi always a go love yu," mi seh, and Favi sigh heavily. Mi glance pon him, then look at Yolo, who a smile. "Mago call Ch—" My mouth watered and my throat stung. Mi rest mi phone aside, rushing toward the nearby half-bath.

Favi watch as mi hunch over the toilet, throwing up everything mi eat. He held my hair back, and my eyes watered. They weren't watering only because I was vomiting my soul out, but because Favi was always there for me no matter what. I really loved him.

The dry heaving slowed, and mi wait a few seconds before flushing the toilet. Mi walk toward the sink, gargling while meeting his gaze in the mirror.

"You're going to the doctor tomorrow," he deadpanned.

The last time I was here and vomiting up every Italian food mi eat, him seh him a go bring me to the doctor if it happen again. Maybe mi have a food allergy mi nuh know bout.

Sighing, mi nod. "Okay."

"Congratulations!"

Mi draw back mi head. "Excuse me?" A must language barrier this! Favi neva seh the woman fluent ina English? Why mi sick and she a come talk boh congratulations?

The doctor chuckled. "Congratulations. You're nine weeks pregnant."

Mi freeze.

Pregnant?

"No. That can't be right. I have an IUD." I shook my head while she smiled.

"No form of contraceptive is a hundred percent effective," she said, and I gasped as mi move mi hand to mi belly. The doctor's smile washed away. "Unplanned?" she asked, and I nodded.

Mi life nuh ina no order fi waa baby. Moving my hand from my belly, mi cover mi face and cry.

"Would you like to discuss your options?" she asked.

Options? *As in?*

Mi shake mi head. Mi move mi hand from mi face and wipe weh the tears. "No. I'm not going to kill... it." Mommy neva fling me weh. Why would I do the same?

Favi can easily mind a baby. Him wuda be a good father cause him been a look forward to dis. On the other hand, mi barely comfortable ina mi skin. Lately, all mi do a drink, stress, and nuh eat unless Favi force mi to.

"Is the baby okay?" Mi look at mi belly. She sure mi pregnant? Mi belly too flat.

She tapped her pen against the chart in her hands. "We'll have to run more tests and an ultrasound to determine that. You'll also have to remove the IUD to lessen pregnancy complications."

I nodded. "Of course. Anything." I lay back, and she moved between my legs.

Wow! Nine weeks with many years to come. Mi smile at the ceiling. Mi need fi get mi life together fast. I had a little human who'd be depending on me soon.

After she removed the IUD and ran the tests, we talked about habits I'd have to change and adapt. She answer all mi questions with a smile, making this surprise less harsh on me.

"*Grazie mille*," mi seh to her as mi leave the room, and she smile. Mi walk outside to Favi's waiting car.

"What happened?" Favi ask as him settle himself around the wheel.

"It was the food."

"I'll try to find somewhere that sells Jamaican food. Maybe it'll make a difference."

"Or maybe you can cook for me," I suggested, and him sigh as him drive off. Mi nuh know why him hate cook. Him can cook better than mi, and that seh a lot fi smaddy whofa granny raise dem.

"Do you need to stop at the pharmacy?"

"No." Mi get waa prescription fi help with the nausea, but mi nuh ready fi fill it cause mi nuh know how fi tell him mi pregnant. Should I blurt it out? Draw arrow pon mi belly? Wait till him dream see fish? Mek lizard jump pon mi?

"*Fiore*, yu hear mi?" Favi ask, and mi stop smile outta space fi look pon him.

"No, sorry. Wa yu seh?"

"Ludovica wants to know if you're well enough to go to the party next week."

Mi nod. "Yu know yu nafi ask dat!"

"Love party too fucking much," Favi mutter, switching to Sicilian to speak to Ludovica.

Oh, mi know! Like how Ren super busy right now with her tours, mi can wait until the party fi ask her fi a place. She know every cribble and corner ina Palermo. She can suggest someweh nice and romantic fi surprise Favi with the picture of the ultrasound. Mi need fi make this moment as special as possible for him because him been a wait pon this. Mi so excited!

Mi poke mi belly while looking in the mirror. "Favi."

While fixing his tie, him walk toward me. Him stop behind me, and we eye meet ina the mirror before mi look at mi belly.

"Yu think me a get fat?" mi ask, wondering when mi a go start show.

Him trail him eye down me body — I was only in my bra and panties; the dress mi a wear still ina the closet — then shake him head. "No. You're gaining healthy weight because you're eating again."

Finished with his tie, him grab mi hips and pull me on him. His mouth trailed from my cheek to my neck, making me shiver as he placed a feather-light kiss on the crook of my neck. "I prefer this on you." He trailed the curve of my ass and gave it a hard slap, making me flinch.

"Favio! Dat hot!" Mi push him away fi rub mi batty jaw.

Him chuckle. "Hurry and finish getting ready. You're going to make us late."

Mi eyes widen as mi look pon the clock. Sas Crise, ketch the time! A eight-thirty, and wi fi reach thirty minutes ago! Mi hurry and finish get ready. Favi drive wi to the party.

Entering the building, mi gasp. Mi know seh Favi family rich, but this gala exceeded my expectations! It looked like something straight out of a movie. The room was decorated with chandeliers, an ice sculpture of Renata and Romeo as children, and a live jazz band.

"*Bella!*" someone yelled from across the room, and mi look in the direction fi see Romeo a dance toward us.

Mi smile. "*Buoncompleanno!*"

"*Grazie.* Look who's getting better at *l'italiano.*" Romeo hug mi.

Favi wait two seconds before him tug mi to him side. "Nuh fuck yuself."

"Behave," mi hiss, and him scoff while Romeo chuckle.

"Is that Sergio?" Favi ask while scanning the crowd, and Romeo hum. Favi look at me. "I need to talk to him. I'll be back soon, okay?"

"I'll take care of her," Romeo said, and Favi give him a warning glare before walking away. Romeo allow me fi chat off him ears fi the next few minutes. "Ren is fashionably late as always," him seh when mi ask fi her. "She's probably with Patrizia."

"Patrizia Moretti?" mi ask.

Him nod as we exit the elevator, walking into the garage. "Yes. She's our good friend."

"Favi's too?" mi ask, my brow raising. Mi know him and the twins a peas in a pod, but how him fi have waa gyal as a good friend and nuh tell mi?

"No, they're not friends like *that*." Him clear him throat. "Anyway, this is her."

Brushing off him odd behavior, mi look pon the car and gasp. "This is yours?!"

"Yes. This is Lucia, my baby." Romeo smiled lovingly at the cobalt-red car.

"Wow," I said in awe. Mi never see a Maserati before!

"Do you want to go for a spin?" he asked, and I shook my head.

"I can't... I'm pregnant," mi seh, and him eyes widen. Favi wuda kill mi if mi go ina waa sports car while mi a breed.

"Pregnant?" he asked in Italian, and I nodded with a small smile.

"Please don't tell Favi. I want to surprise him. That's why I want to see Ren."

Romeo smiled, leaning against the car. "Hopefully, you'll see her soon. Congrats to you and Favio. How far along are you?"

"Ten weeks." I looked at my belly hidden beneath the little black dress Favi bought for me.

"Why did you say it like that?" Romeo asked, and mi look at him. His brows were knitted. "You're not planning on *aborting* it, are you? It would break Favio."

"I'm not," I said, and him shoulders sag.

"Good. My cousin loves you, and he'd do anything for you and the baby."

"I know, but... I'm just twenty, you know? I told him before that I'm not ready for children. Now I have to carry it for nine months." I sighed. "I don't have a family to fall back on like he does, and I'm thinking about quitting my job when I go back to Jamaica. I'm stressed because I haven't heard from the school I want to get into. I don't think I'll be a good mother right now, but I'm trying."

"I understand, *bella*. God doesn't give us anything we can't handle or are not yet ready for. Suppose my nieces or nephews help you to find your calling?"

Mi chuckle. "Niece or nephew, Romeo."

He smirked. "I mean... you may be having a twin. It runs in our family. *Mamma* thought she was having only one baby, then my sister popped out after me. Imagine hiding for eight months. I should've eaten her."

Mi buss out a market laugh. "Romeo!"

Him laugh as him ansa him phone. Him talk in Sicilian fi a minute, then hang up and lean off the car. "Well, my other half is here, and Favio is looking for you. Let's head back before he bursts a blood vessel."

Mi chuckle as we return to the party. The elevator *ding*, and the first thing mi see as the doors open, a waa Melchizedek-sized display bottle of the new Welsh's wine in the middle of the room. Smaller bottles circle it, and wine glasses were stacked into a triangle beside them.

"*Wow.*" Tears rushed to my eyes as I focused on the label. It read 'FIORE'.

"Do you like it? This is Favio's surprise for you," Romeo said.

"I love it!" My eyes scanned the room, landing on Favi and Patrizia, who were exiting the hallway that had the bathrooms.

Favi a straighten him jacket.

Patrizia lipstick smeared.

Mi smile fade. Mi try nufi overthink, but as Romeo lead me through the crowd toward Favi, the world close in pon me.

A red stain was on the white of Favio's collar.

I didn't wear lipstick.

"Favio, what's that on your collar?" I pointed at my neck.

"What's what?" He looked away from Romeo and Patrizia as dem disappear into the crowd.

"Yaa cheat pon mi, Favio?" I asked, scared of his answer.

"Cheat?" he asked, then his eyes flashed something.

Regret.

Mi lips tremble, and mi shake mi head as mi walk weh. My feet took me toward the balcony, and him catch up to me.

"I can explain." He made me face him.

"So explain! It betta be a good explanation, too!" mi shout, not caring about the patrons on the balcony.

"She came on to me."

Mi yank mi hand outta fi him, balling it at my sides. "You're a grown man, Favio! Yu deevn talk to people like dat fi some gyal feel bold enough fi come onto—" Mi pause, my memory drifting to Romeo's odd behavior. Shaking from rage, I asked, "Y-yu have sex with her, Favio?"

"*Sì.*"

The word crashed into me like a powerful gust of wind, almost knocking me off my feet as I took a step back. Then another, and another. "W-what?"

"When I was—"

Him voice fade as mi move mi hand to mi belly. Mi heart a beat loud ina mi ear, but it nuh as loud as the sound of it breaking.

Piece by piece.

Until nothing but a sore shell remained.

"I'm pregnant," I blurted, and he shut up. Mi deevn look pon him. Mi nuh waa see if him happy, shocked, or hate mi fi getting pregnant while him ina dealings wid a gorgeous model.

"You're pregnant?"

I closed my eyes, tears rolling down my cheeks.

"*Fiore*—"

I sensed him step closer, and mi step back. My back hit the railing, its coldness seeping into my body. There was nowhere to run now, but mi nehna go mek Favio Welsh trap mi.

Mi open mi eyes. Despite being blurred by tears to see him, they burned into him. "*Was* pregnant. Mago fling weh this fu—"

"Wa?" His anger surged as him step forward. His quick breaths fanned my face. "What the fuck is wrong with you?"

"Me?! Wa wrong wid *me*?! The only thing weh wrong with mi is that mi only open mi legs fi you while you stick yu hood everywhere!" Mi push him chest, and him grab mi wrists, but mi nuh stop hit him. "Yu probably give mi sum wid yu nasty self! Mi hate yu, Favio! Mi hate yu!" My screams died off into loud sobs.

He didn't let me go. He held me tighter. "Stop making a scene."

Mi look pon him wid wild eyes. "Scene?!" mi yell, not caring who watched us. The wul world fi see wa kinda lying, whoring man Favio Matteo Welsh be! "Leggo me and go hands up yu gyal!"

His glare deepened. He released my hands to grip my neck. "A you a mi gyal, and me a tell yu fi calm down."

My hands balled into fists at my side as I glared at him, not daring to back down.

"Patrizia is an old fling. I would never cheat on you."

"Yaa lie to me, Favio."

Him release mi neck and straighten him suit. "I don't have a reason to lie to you. You're acting as if you've never kept secrets."

"Mi nuh keep secret about anybody mi sex from yu."

"You know better."

My fists tightened, my nails piercing my skin. "I want to go."

Him raise a brow. "Go where? You don't want to keep it?"

I'd never been surer of anything when I looked him dead in the eyes and gave a firm answer. "No."

"Yu naa go no-fucking-where fi kill wi youth!"

"Yu cya keep mi here! Yu did a think boh me when yaa push yu hood ina next woman?!" mi scream at him stupid face, and him glare. The two a we inches away from each other, raging like wild animals.

"We stop fuck long time, Chayanne! Why the fuck are you still upset?!"

"Because yu gyal shudn a hands yu up when yu have a woman!"

Favio kiss him teeth, walking outta the bedroom into the closet. Him unbutton him cuffs. "You're not going to Jamaica. Get that out of your mind right now," he said calmly.

"I'm going back whether yu like it or not!" Mi push past him and grab mi suitcase, stuffing mi clothes into it.

Him nuh pay mi nuh mind. Him continue undo the buttons, and it anger mi further.

"And wi done," I spat.

He paused, facing me. The tip of his ears reddened as he asked through clenched teeth, "What did you say?"

"I'm breaking up with you. I'm done!"

"Chayanne, come outta mi fucking sight before mi do yu sum mi will regret."

Mi draw back mi head, my brows raising. "Like wa? Any day yu put yu hands pon mi, mi father a go kill yu!"

Favio's jaw ticked before him stomp toward me, making me take several steps back until mi hit the wall. Him hand reach round mi neck faster than mi brain could process, squeezing so tight, mi struggle fi breathe. "Do you think I'm afraid of your fucking father? A yuself yu fi worry bout cause if yu kill wi youth, mi a bury yu beside yu mother."

"F-Favio—" I choked, scratching at his hand. "Stop. Yaa h-hurt me."

Him eyes widen and him retract him hands, taking two steps backward while I swallowed a big gulp of air. He looked at his hand like it was a foreign object. "Sorry. Fuck. Sorry."

Mi sniffle, turning away fi grab mi suitcase.

"Weh yago?" him ask.

"Mi a find mi way home miself." Mi rub mi throat while walking away. By the time mi reach the threshold, mi surprise him nuh seh nun to mi yet. Mi look pon him. "Yu deevn a go ask mi fi stay?"

"Gwan yu fucking ways, Chayanne," he said calmly, shrugging off his shirt. The movement of his snake tattoo seemed mocking.

The urge fi cry nearly stifle mi, but mi wudn mek him see mi cry again. Mi straighten mi shoulders, holding mi head high as mi haul mi suitcase outside. I paused before the tall gate as it crackled with electricity.

Mi scream, then stomp inside the house, leaving my suitcase by the front door. Favio was in the kitchen, pouring Henny into a glass while him phone rest pon the counter.

"Turn off the gate," mi hiss, and him pause fi look pon mi.

"Yu nuh reach Jamaica yet?"

"Favio," I said through clenched teeth, and him eyes narrow pon mi.

"Sit," he ordered.

"No! Mi seh turn—"

"One."

Mi cross mi arms.

Him chuckle before taking a sip from the glass. Him slam it down pon the counter, his grip tightening around it. "Two."

Mi tap mi foot pon the tile.

Him tek another sip, slowly placing the glass down as his eyes locked on mine. "Thr—"

Mi sidung pon the stool.

A devious smirk twisted his lips, but it disappeared quickly. "Yu ready fi talk like an adult or yago keep up yu childish fuckry?"

Mi open mi mouth fi ask him if mi a pickney then him a wa, but mi decide against it. Pursing my lips, mi look weh. "I didn't want a baby in the first place."

"You're having it," he said, and I gasped as I looked at him.

"Yu cya force—"

"Don't think for a second that I won't lock you inside this house for the entirety of your pregnancy," he said coldly, and I gulped.

"I-it's my choice..."

"It's *our* fucking choice!" him yell, and mi jump. "You're not going to kill our child over something that isn't there."

Mi swallow a lump, trying my hardest not to cry. "Why yaa treat mi like this, Favio?" I asked, and he scowled.

"You made me this way."

I shook my head. "If yu want waa baby so bad, go to yu gyal. She eager fi open up fi yu regardless a if we deh or not."

He released a long sigh. "Chayanne, listen closely because I hate repeating myself. There is no one but you. I am incapable of getting hard for anyone but you. She came on to me, and I pushed her away. I love you, and I will love our child. Please, go to bed and talk to me in the morning when you're not being too fucking stubborn to see reason."

"Me nav a choice over mi body? Yu call that love, Favio?"

"When I give you freedom, you do fuckry. When I control you, I'm the worst. What more do you want from me, Chayanne?"

"I want to have a choice! Mi doh trust yu, and mi nuh waa deh round yu after—" Mi move mi hand to mi neck. The skin was tender. Favio never touched me like this before... It scared me and brought me back to how weak I was that night.

"Fine," Favio said after a while, and mi look at him. "Pack your bags. You'll leave first thing tomorrow."

"Okay... Thank you." Fighting the urge fi smile, mi hop off the stool.

"Nuh thank me," he said, and I paused. "Because if yu kill we youth, yago see who a this lie and wicked man yu cya trust, yere?"

Trembling, I looked over my shoulder at him. His face was void of emotion, and it made my throat dry as fear gripped me.

I couldn't swallow.

I couldn't breathe.

I could only change my mantra.

This was not my Favi. Slitta would hurt me.

Chapter Sixty-Six

Favio

My face was a calm facade. I buried my hands in my pockets as I stood above her, watching as she looked everywhere in the jet except at me. "I apologize for last night." My anger got the best of me. The mere thought of her killing our child made me angry again, but I forced away the feeling.

I wasn't Fabiano, and I didn't want to become him.

I saw how she was with Zaveer; she loved children. I understood she wasn't ready, but our child was here now. She better get her fucking self ready. If she thought I was sending her back because I 'respected her choices', then she made a stupid mistake. I was sending her back because it would've been cruel to keep her in a foreign country, pregnant and feeling trapped after what she'd been through.

"Have a safe flight, *fiore. Ti amo*," I added.

She shifted about the seat, still not looking at me, and it made bitterness fill me. "Can you go..."

I unclenched my fists, walking away. I stopped by the door to speak to Kitania. "Ensure she gets whatever she needs."

"Of course, Mr. Welsh," she said, and I nodded out of respect. Kitania wasn't an average air hostess. She'd been in *la famiglia* since I was in my early teens. She was trained to serve and protect in case anything was to happen in the air.

"And ensure she sleeps. She needs the rest." I looked at Chayanne, sighing as she stared through the window with puffy eyes.

Last night, I slept on the sofa while she had the bed to herself, but she didn't sleep at all. She stayed up all night crying. I wanted to comfort her, but I couldn't. The door was locked, and she had to learn to face the consequences of her actions.

When I returned home from the private airport, the past hours hit me like a truck.

Chayanne was pregnant.

We were going to be parents.

She didn't want the baby.

Sighing, I grabbed the Hennessy bottle off the sofa, taking a large chug. It burned going down, but I craved it. I needed something else to focus on other than these emotions.

I didn't know if I did the wrong or right thing.

She didn't answer my calls last night. I knew she landed safely, though. It pained me she was so far away. Today would've been the day I asked her to marry me...

Why we happiness cya last long?

I sighed, deciding to try her phone again.

Her fucking best friend answered. "Wa yu want?"

"Give her the phone."

"No. Why she come dung a cry?! She just cut off the wul of her hair, and all now she deevn tell mi wa do her!" the gyal yelled.

"You need to stay the fuck out of our business."

Chezandra gasped. "Excuse me?! A bet yu neva hear from her again!"

"Bet."

"Chezzy, please," said Chayanne's distant voice. There was shuffling until her soothing voice came in my ear. "Yes, Favio?" She was still upset, and she sounded tired and hoarse.

"Let me talk. Don't interrupt until I'm finished, okay?"

"Okay," she said, and I cleared my throat.

"You have all right to be upset about Patrizia, but she came on to me, and I pushed her away. I know I should've told you about her earlier, and I apologize about that, but there isn't anything there. I swear to you."

She took a long pause. "I hate when you keep secrets."

"I hate when you do, too," I said, and she sighed.

"Why we cya ever be good, Favio?"

"Because you're miserable, and I'm ignorant."

"Dark and fool," she corrected.

"Selfish and childish," I countered, and she hissed her teeth.

We quieted for a while, and I heaved a sigh before saying what I should've done last night. "I can't say I'm sorry for getting you pregnant. You knew this would've happened, so don't do anything stupid."

"Already made the appointment," she replied without missing a beat.

My world stopped.

How should I get through to her?

Aggression: she bawl.

Being nice: she did fuckry.

Chayanne a go mek mi fuck her up.

"I'm going to pretend I didn't hear that, Chayanne."

She didn't reply.

"Chayanne," I drawled.

"I'm upset because I feel like you're forcing me to go through with something I told you I'm not ready for."

"If you want to be angry, take it out on me. Not our innocent baby."

"I wasn't going to... I wanted to surprise you, but this is too much right now. Mi nuh believe yu about the Patrizia situation. No gyal shudn comfortable fi feel like dem can still sex yu," she said, and I sighed.

"I know, I'm sorry. I think she misinterpreted the situation. She told me her father died, then hugged me. I was pulling away when she tried to kiss me—"

"Mi nuh waa hear bout it," she said with a trace of attitude.

"What do you want to hear? Anything you want, I'll give it to you—"

"I want space," she said, and I was stupefied. "I'm trying not to hate you, Favio. I just need time to clear my head, okay?"

"Okay…" I sighed as the dial tone filled my ear. *Que sera, sera.*

The following day, Romeo urged me to slow down on all the alcohol I'd been drinking since last night. "Stop fretting. *Bella* won't kill the baby," he said in Sicilian.

I wasn't worried about her killing our baby. She couldn't visit a clinic without me knowing when, why, and where. But I knew my woman. Her granny raised her. She goodly know how fi look six months pregnant even when a drop a cum nuh blow pon her fat front.

Plus, her security detail increased. She was pregnant with a Welsh baby. Her safety was the top priority of *la famiglia* now.

I told them not to tell me anything about her unless there was a threat to her life or our child. I was going to give her fucking space. I even logged out of all the cameras in and out of the house, except the one in my snakes' room.

"You should've seen how her eyes lit up when she told me she was pregnant. *Bella* already loves the child," Romeo said, and Luca hummed while nodding.

Two ladies walked into the kitchen, and my grip around the Hennessy bottle tightened. I wanted to strangle Patrizia until her trachea crushed beneath my fingers.

Renata's eyes widened at me. "I didn't know you were still here."

I didn't reply. Instead, I went to the balcony.

Footsteps trailed behind me. "Favio."

"Patrizia, go away." I took a swig from the bottle.

"No," she said, and my nostrils flared. "You're a good man. She's lucky to have you, and I'm sorry for the trouble I caused... All the best in life, Favio."

I didn't answer. How could I have the best in life when my sole reason for breathing was miles away?

Chapter Sixty-Seven

FAVIO

Placing my right foot into the house, I paused when delicious cooking wafted from the kitchen. Releasing an uneven breath, I closed the door behind me. I left the suitcase by the door before walking toward the kitchen.

Wow! There she was — sauntering about the kitchen in a dress. In the two months we'd been apart, she gained a bit more weight, but she was glowing. She looked even more beautiful and was just as surprised to see me.

"Hey!" Smiling, Chayanne covered the pot before walking toward me. She hugged me.

My mouth dried as I wrapped an arm around her. I used my other hand to feel her forehead. "*Stai bene?*"

"Yes." Laughing, she swatted my hand away. She broke the hug and walked toward the cupboards, grabbing a plate while her hair swayed a few inches below her shoulders. "Are you hungry?"

"Sure..." I watched closely as she approached the stove. I washed my hands in the sink, then sat on a stool by the island.

She plated a large portion of rice and stew peas, then placed it before me with an expectant stare.

I dragged my eyes from the food, narrowing them at her. "Yaa try tie me?"

She hissed her teeth. "If mi did waa tie yu, mi wuda dweet already."

That was true, but I was still wary. "Did you poison it?"

Her eyes widened. "Wa? No!" she exclaimed, then tasted the rice.

"Taste the peas, too."

She did, then sighed when I still didn't eat. "I didn't poison it, Favi. Yu waa some tea? Yu eye dem red, and yu probably soon start sneeze."

I looked at the food, forking some into my mouth. A burst of flavor washed over my tastebuds, and I hummed while swallowing. I would've said Chayanne was the wife type, but now I was unsure. "I'm good. Why are you here?"

"Yu waa me leave?"

"No. You were mad at me, so I thought..." I looked at her belly. She was four months pregnant, but she wasn't showing much.

Her hand moved to the small bump, her eyelids lowering. "I'm sorry, Favi. I wouldn't kill our baby. I was emotional and overreacted, but I'm doing better."

"Better?"

"I've been going to therapy," she said, and I paused moving the fork to my mouth. "Can we talk after you finish eating?"

"No. Talk."

Sighing, she hopped onto the stool beside me. Her dress rolled up, exposing the hem of her shorts. She fixed the dress, then propped her elbow on the counter. She rested her head in her hand while looking at me. "Yu still waa deh wid me?"

"Nuh you seh wi leff?" I asked, and she looked away, making me scoff. "I try my best to keep you happy, but you keep testing my patience."

"How? Yu nuh seem fi understand seh me used to do what I want when I want. You're trying to change me—"

"Stop talking," I said, and she shook her head, looking away. Sighing, I dropped the fork onto the plate and faced her. I took her hand in mine, and she looked at them. "I don't want to change you, *fiore*. I love you how you are, so I don't try to control you like I do everything else in my life. But I have a lot of enemies, and I couldn't live with myself if anything happened to you, so you need to listen."

"I understand..."

"You don't," I hissed, and she looked at me.

"Sometimes yu too much, but me will try fi listen more. I want this to work, especially for him." She pulled a hand away to rub her belly.

Smiling, I laid my hand atop hers. "We're having a son?"

She shrugged. "Mi nuh know. Mi waa be surprised, but mi feel like a waa boy cause mi right titty bigger."

"It's always been bigger. And it's a girl."

"How yu know that?" she asked, and I smirked.

"When mi set yu pon tha position deh, mi know wa mi put ina yu," I said, and she chuckled.

"We'll see when him get here! Mi already start pick out names." She released my hand to grab her phone, and I continued eating. "First on the list... Favio."

"Fuck no, Chayanne. My son won't be a junior," I stated, and she rolled her eyes as I finished eating.

"How about Zidan?" she suggested as she shared a second plate.

"Soon seh Maradona and Lionel," I said sarcastically.

"I like Lionel!" she said, and I scoffed as she placed the plate before me. "What? Nuh you want a football team?"

I swallowed a bite. "We're not naming him any of those. And it's a girl, though they are tricky to raise."

"Why are girls tricky to raise?"

"I won't trust anyone with her. I don't want her around men until she's twenty-six," I said, and her mouth dropped.

"Yu look me when mi a seventeen, Favi. Now me think bout it, yu shuda deh prison," she said, and I scoffed.

"I had good intentions with you," I said, and she hummed.

"How yu know her boyfriend won't be good?"

"I said what I said, Chayanne," I dismissed, and she rolled her eyes. My phone vibrated atop the counter, and I glanced at it. It was Sergio. I'd answer him later.

"Mi nuh tell nobody mi pregnant," Chayanne said, and I looked at her.

"Not even Chezandra?" I raised a brow as she shook her head. "Why are you so secretive?"

"It's how I avoided people being disappointed in me," she said solemnly, then gave me a small smile. "Anyway, now that yu come back, mi can have a baby shower?"

"Why are you asking me?" I asked, and she glared.

"Mi tell yu mi a try do better! Mi ask because mi know how yu feel bout party and dem thing deh!" she yelled, and I winced, almost forgetting how loud she could be.

"You have my card. Do whatever you want," I said, and she smiled. "When did you start therapy?" I diverted the topic as I considered asking for a third plate. What did she put in this food? It made me insatiable.

"Like a week after mi come down... Mi first therapist quit her job, so mi a see somebody else. Anyway, the time apart did good fimi. Mi get accepted into college and mi a do online classes!" she said, and I smiled at her child-like excitement.

"I'm proud of you," I said, and her smile brightened. I wished I could've said the time apart was good for me too, but I couldn't. I missed her every day, and I could barely eat or sleep. The only thing that kept me grounded was what happened a week ago.

Chayanne grabbed the empty plate, taking it to the sink to wash it. She told me about therapy and school as we moved to our bedroom. While I showered, she sat atop the toilet and told me how excited she was for the baby to arrive. Minutes later, we were curled in bed.

"I want you to get tested," she said as I slapped away her hand that was playing with my nipple.

"Tested?"

"For STDs..." she said, and I hissed my teeth. Sighing, she leaned off me. "Please? Mi tell yu mi a try do better fi wi baby. You have to, too."

"What does that have to do with our baby? I don't have any diseases."

"Mi nuh forget bout Patrizia..." she said, and I stared at her.

"Okay," I said grudgingly, and she smiled before lying on my chest.

She trailed her hand to the waistband of my shorts, making my dick stir. "I want to start... doing it again."

"Are you sure? I don't want you to rush your healing process because I'm back," I said gently, despite having blue balls. If she so much as showed me her pussy, I'd come prematurely, like a pubescent boy.

"I'm sure. The toys naa cut it anymore," she said.

"Nuh use it again next thing wi youth come out a stammer."

Laughing off my complaint, she straddled me, making me groan. Her eyes widened. "Wa happen? Yu sick?"

"No. Yu just a get heavy nuh f—" I paused as tears rushed to her eyes. "Chayanne, I'm sorry."

"How yago call mi fat when a you mek mi like this?!" she sobbed, trying to escape my tight grip on her waist.

"I'm sorry..." I said over and over, sighing when she calmed down. Fuck... I'd have to deal with this for five months? Plus, the other five times I planned on getting her pregnant? I'd probably need therapy, too. "Are you sure we can do this? Suppose I hit the baby?" I asked, grazing her belly with my thumbs.

"I'm only sixteen weeks. It's safe," she said, but I was still wary. Leaning to the right, she reached into the bedside table and grabbed a condom.

My brow raised. Before I could ask her why she readily had condoms, Chayanne sheathed my dick and fucked the life out of me. She never had this much energy before.

Chapter Sixty-Eight

CHAYANNE

My gold and white themed baby shower a gwan wid itself! The mount a congrats mi get, cya done! Everybody happy fi mi, except mi nephew. Chuckling, mi wipe weh him tears. "You're always going to be Aunty's baby."

"Pwomise?" Zaveer asked, and I nodded. Him smile, throwing him arm dem round mi neck. "Love Chi."

"I love you more." Breaking the hug, mi shower him face with kisses until him start laugh.

"Chayanne," someone said, and mi stop kiss Zaveer fi look pon Favi, who a stretch waa glass of tomato juice toward me.

"Thanks!" Smiling, mi move the glass to my mouth.

Favi scowled. "Of all the things in the world, tomato juice?"

"The baby likes it," mi seh, and him shake him head.

"Did you call your Aunt?" him ask, and mi eyes lower as mi look away. "*Fiore,* we talked about this."

Mi finish the last of the drink, then hand the glass to him. "Mago call her now," mi seh, and him nod before leaving. "Let's go find Mommy," mi tell Zaveer.

Nodding, him grab him banana plushie, holding it to him chest as mi liff up the two a wi. Mi belly barely a show! Mi look two months pregnant instead of four. Mi naa complain still, mi nuh waa swell up like how Chezzy was.

Passing by a tower of gifts, mi smile. Mi tell everybody fi bring pampas if dem think a waa girl, and wipes if dem think a waa boy. Jelani brought a truckload of wipes, like him think seh a the wul world me a carry ina mi belly. Him a the only person Favi invite. Him parents nuh get invited. According to him, them too blasted fass. He said it more colorfully, though.

Reaching outside, mi spot Yolo beside Eltham and Favi. Favi sidung pon him car bonnet, tapping pon him phone. Eltham sidung beside him, a skin up him face afta wa Yolo a seh.

Mi walk toward them, and Favi narrow him eyes pon mi. "Mi soon go back in," mi seh quickly. Mi nuh know why him a gwan like the scorching sun a go melt the baby outta mi.

"Still cya believe Favio tek me friend outta the game!" Yolo exclaim, and Eltham chuckle.

"About time," Favi murmur, not looking away from his phone.

"A by buck ups," mi seh, and him glare pon mi. Grinning, mi look at Yolo. "Weh Chezzy?"

"She deh ova—" Yolo point toward the chef pon the grill, her brows furrowing.

"Chezzy a must Avatar to blood—" Eltham pause as him look pon Zaveer, who fascinated by wi conversation.

"Mago check ina the house." Mi go inside and check all of downstairs, but mi nuh see her. Mi bout fi go ina the backyard when Zaveer yawn. "Sleepy?" mi ask, and him nod. Mi bring him upstairs to a guest bedroom. A long time apnea nuh bother him, but mago mek Chezzy know him a go sleep. "Do you want a blanket?" mi ask Zaveer while mi lay him on the bed, and him shake him head. Mi tek mi phone outta mi pocket, calling Chezzy.

Ringing come from the bathroom, followed by shuffling.

"Chezzy?" mi call out.

Seconds later, she step outta the bathroom, closing the door behind her. Taking quick steps toward me, she brush back her messy ponytail. "Never hear when yu come in here. Mi did run come use the bathroom." She tek up Zaveer, whose eyes were drooping. "Mi a go carry him home. It a get late, plus Daddy a come from Barbados tonight, so Mommy a go waa mi watch mi brother dem while she go the airport."

"Bye, baby." Mi blow Zaveer a kiss, smiling when him catch it. Mi walk outta the room backa them, closing the door behind mi. "Yu still vex?" mi ask, and Chezzy sigh.

"Yes. When yago stop give him so much chances?"

"When me dead."

She glance at me, shaking her head while looking away. "Mi hope him pull up him socks fi yu."

"We a go do better fi the baby."

"Me know you will do better. The problem a him. Later." Chezzy walk down the stairs.

Sighing, mi continue down the hallway. Mi enter the snake room and check pon Favi snakes. Satisfied everything was as it should be, mi exit the room while making the call. Trav a walk down the stairs, pulling him pants up. Mi bout fi yell him name, but the call connect.

"Chichi baby!" Aunty seh, and mi smile as mi walk toward mi bedroom.

"Hi, Aunty," mi seh while mi go pon the balcony. Mi see Jelani ina the pool, nervous while Yolo flirt wid him.

"Yu call fi see Azera?" Aunty switch to video while walking to Azera's room.

"No, Aunty... Mi call fi talk to you."

Her brows furrow, and she stop walk. "What happened?"

"I'm pregnant..."

Her brows fly up to her hairline. "Wa yu seh, Chayanne Arya?" she ask, and mi show her the likkle bump pressing against my dress. "Who give yu belly?"

"My boyfriend..."

"*Boyfriend*?! How yu mek him put a baby inside you before him put a ring pon yu finger? Ano one day monkey waa wife."

Mi throat tighten. This a why mi neva waa tell her nun. Al tek it better when mi did tell him. Him neva surprised, but him did very disappointed. "Mi know, Aunty... But mi love him, and him love me. Him a go take care of the baby."

"What about you? Yu ina school, yu waa quit yu work, and yu mother nav no dead leff fi give you—"

Mi phone get snatched outta mi hand. A screech almost tear from mi mouth until mi see a who.

"I respect you, Mrs. Kenzie, so I'm only saying this once. I told you years ago I would take care of Chayanne, why would our baby be any different?" Him voice nav no emotion, it send chills down mi spine while Aunty quieted. "Chayanne doesn't need a ring to prove I love her. She doesn't need a job because I'm rich. And she doesn't need you to accept our baby because I've got them."

Mi gasp. "Favi—"

Him glare pon Aunty. "She's her own big woman. I don't rule her, and neither will you. If you ever make her cry again... Do you understand where I'm going?" he slowly said the last words.

"Favio," mi hiss, and him nostrils flare as him give me the phone.

"Mi hope yu know wa yaa do, Chayanne Arya," Aunty warned, and mi shoulders sag.

"Hang up," Favi hissed, and I did.

Mi sigh as mi tighten mi grip round the phone. Mi step toward him, and him nuh hesitate fi wrap him arms round mi. "Yu shudn do that. She nago unvex wid mi fi now."

"She'll get over it," he said, and mi sigh as mi pull away from him.

"Mi neva try stand up to her before..."

"You don't have to stand up to anyone. I told you, I'm here."

"*Ti amo*, Favi," I said, and Favi did something he rarely did.

He smiled.

"Wow..." Dayshawn drawled, shaking his head.

Mi roll mi eyes and cross mi arms. "Yu can come outta mi way, please?" mi ask, hating every second mi spend at this hotel that involved being in his presence. Favi hate seh mi a work while me pregnant. Even though mi waa work up to six months, mi put in waa three weeks' notice fi give him peace of mind.

"Yu know mi want yu back and yugo breed fi the man?"

"Yago mek mi disrespect—" Mi pause. "Give me thousand dolla."

Him raise a brow. "Why?"

"Yu waa woman but cya give mi a grand when mi need it?" mi ask, and him stare pon mi before going ina him wallet.

Him place him last thousand ina mi hand. "Weh yu want it fa?"

"Mi deevn a go ansa yu." Mi kiss mi teeth, walking outta the hotel. Mago put it toward the fish fry ticket dem weh mi a sell fi Trav, then actually sell the ticket dem to smaddy else, so Trav can mek more money.

Eltham bring down the front window as mi stop outside the car. Him raise a brow. "Yu naa come in?"

"My man doesn't make mc touch doors."

"Mi ano yu man."

"True, but yu already a walk a thin line wid him cause you won't stop mek mi laugh. Imagine if him find out seh—" Mi smirk as Eltham hop outta the car, opening the door. "Thanks, Josiah Eltham."

Him close the door behind me, then sit behind the wheel. Him drive off. "Yago straight home?"

"No. Carry mi go Trav studio," mi seh, and him nod.

Minutes later, wi park before the studio. Trav come outside to wi.

"Wahm, Chichi?" Trav ask, dapping up Eltham through the window.

"Nun. Mi just come drop off sum fi yu." Mi rest mi tomato juice aside fi go ina mi bag. Mi grab the money fi the fish fry ticket dem, making sure the gold napkin deh pon top of it. "Here." Mi hand it to him.

Trav's eyes widened as him look pon the napkin, which had notes for a beat scribbled on it. Mi eyes shine, waiting fi him confirm mi suspicions.

Clearing him throat, him slip the money and napkin ina him pocket. Him expressionless as him look pon me. "Thanks, Chichi. Carry her home," him seh to Eltham, and Eltham nod.

Mi sigh. Maybe me a imagine things from last week.

Eltham drop me home, then switch from my car to his. Mi shake mi head as Eltham drive outta the yaad while cussing Yolo pon the phone. Mi a watch as the gate close, when waa police car stop before mi gate. A lanky man exited the car, slipping through the gate before it closed.

"Can I help you?" mi ask.

"Is this Favio Welsh's residence?" the man ask.

"Credentials?" mi ask, and him flash a badge.

"Junior detective Kyle White. My partner is on sick leave. This is Favio Welsh's residence?" him ask, and mi nod. "Who are you to him?"

"His girlfriend, Chayanne. What do you want with him?"

"We're investigating an abduction," the man seh, and mi eyes widen.

"W-wa?" I asked while him tek him phone outta him pocket.

Kyle show me the phone screen. "Is this Favio Welsh?"

Mi narrow mi eyes pon the picture. It blurry and dark, like a mi old banga tek it. Mi cuda mek out a few details: a man's hand rested on the back door of a vehicle; his hoodie was pulled up, but he held his head low. Regardless, mi wuda recognize the person anywhere.

Because of the ring pon him finger.

Mi drag mi eyes from the picture to the detective. "No. I've never seen that man a day of my life."

Him sigh, slipping the phone ina him pocket. "Are you sure, Chayanne?" him ask, and mi nod. "Okay. I have a few more questions for you. Can you provide an alibi for him on September twenty-eight?"

"He was here, watching my favorite shows with me. Favio is a reputable businessman and citizen, not a low-life thug," mi seh, but him unmoved. "I'm disgusted and appalled by your justice system to accuse—" I winced, my lips twisting into a grimace as my hand moved to my belly. "Oh, God."

Kyle stepped forward, laying a hand on my shoulder. "Are you okay?"

Mi shake mi head, hunching over and glimpsing the neighbor a walk around his yard. "My baby—" I groaned, rubbing my belly. "I need to call my doctor."

"Okay. Please call the station if you remember anything else."

Nodding, mi waddle inside the house. As the door close behind me, mi straighten miself and release a big breath. Ignoring Marshy, mi run go the kitchen. Mi find mi tomato juice and swallow large gulps while dialing Favi.

Him answer the phone, breathing heavily while sweat dotted his forehead. "Chayanne."

"Where are you?" Mi cya see his background because of the phone's angle, but it was eerily quiet.

"Came to look for Catty's son," he said, and mi chuckle. "What happened?"

"Nun, Favio. See you later." Mi hang up. Mi busy miself until him come home late ina the evening, freshly showered and with a haircut, too.

Laying behind me, him pull me close by the waist and shower me wid kisses. Since wi start sex again, mi front cya rest. Mi push him off and stand at the side of the bed. Him brows furrow while me cross mi arms, glaring at him.

"*Stai bene?*" him ask.

"Where yaa come from?" mi ask, and him tell mi the same lie. "Stop lic to mi, Favio!" mi yell, and him face go blank as him sit up fi look pon mi.

"Who are you raising your voice at?"

"You! Yu know seh police come here today?"

"*What?*"

"Stop gwan like yu nuh know!"

"How am I supposed to know, Chayanne?"

"Yu nav man a follow mi?" mi ask, and him eyes widen before returning to normal.

"How do you know that?"

"Mi realize since mi come from Italy."

"They're for your protection, and I don't want to talk about that. Who is the officer?" him ask, and mi tell him. "What did you tell him?"

"Wa yu mean wa mi tell him? Mi lie fi yu! Who yu kidnap, Favio?" mi ask, and him jaw tick as him look away. "Yu deevn ago ansa? Yu deevn ago tell mi seh yu deh a Jamaica long before the day yu come home?"

Him look pon mi, then walk toward me.

Mi step back. "Yu think mi fool, don't?!"

"Relax. You're putting stress on the baby," he said calmly.

"A you a cause mi fi work up miself! Yu deh here fi two weeks, and mi nuh know weh yu go a nighttime! Yu think mi nuh realize seh since yu come back, yu nuh sleep ina the bed, but always have breakfast ready by the time mi wake?" mi ask, and him open him mouth. "I swear if yu lie to me, mi a walk outta the house, and mi naa come back."

Exhaling a heavy breath, him tell mi everything.

How him and Al find the person weh try rape mi.

How dem a torture the man every day.

By the time him done, mi heart a race and tears a prick mi eyes.

"You're the reason Zip tried to rape me?" mi force out, holding my bump. It feel like mi belly bottom a drop out.

Him drag him eyes from mi belly to my eyes. Him eyes a swirl with so much emotion, mostly regret. "*Sì*," he said, and I slapped him across the face.

Huffing, mi retract mi throbbing hand.

Favio slowly turn him head fi face mi. Him cheek a redden, but him nuh get angry. "Let that be the last time you put your hands on me."

I backed away, hitting the wall as him step forward. Mi hold mi hand out toward him, grabbing at the neck of my nightie with the next. "You... You..."

Yu cya ketch Quako, ketch him shut.

Favio ease mi hand away, bringing me toward the bed and rubbing my back while we sat. "Breathe with me, *fiore*. Deep breaths... One... Two... Good, like that," he coached, breathing with me until mi calm down.

Mi free mi hand from his hold. "Sorry," mi mutter, glancing at my fingerprints on his red cheek while wiping tears from mine.

"I deserved it." He took his arm off me. "I wasn't lying to you."

"Omission is lying."

"I didn't tell you because I didn't want you to get triggered and relapse."

"I get that, but that wasn't your choice to make, Favio," mi seh, and him sigh. "Yaa hide anything else from me? Nuh lie, else mi swell up the next jaw."

Favio chuckled. "Aren't you in therapy, Chayanne?"

Mi roll mi eyes. "You need it more than me."

"I don't need fucking therapy," him seh aggressively, and mi lay a hand atop his. Him look pon it, then take it in his. Moving my hand to his mouth, him kiss each knuckle, lingering on the ring finger while him stare into mi eyes.

Mi heart feel full, but mi still a gwan like mi vex. Him deserve fi feel mi anger!

Favio pulled away. "Let's get some sleep."

Nodding, mi lay down. Him pull me close by my waist, grazing my belly with his thumb.

"Can I see where you're keeping him?" mi ask.

"No."

"Please? I want to see that he can't hurt me anymore," mi seh, and him go silent fi a while until him sigh.

"Okay. Tomorrow after work," him seh, and mi nod.

"Please be more careful. We have a son on the way, and mi cya imagine life without you," I whispered, scared of my own words. Mama always tell mi bout the power in the tongue.

"It's a girl," him seh in Italian.

"Boy," mi correct, and him scoff.

"We need a nickname for her," him seh in English.

"Plum," mi seh, and him kiss him teeth.

"Yu love yu belly too much, Chayanne."

"Not more than I love you." I faced him, smiling.

Him nuh smile back, but his eyes softened as they met mine. Resting a hand on his cheek, mi kiss him. Slowly. Passionately.

As he pulled away, he murmured against my lips, "Yu waa fuck?"

Chapter Sixty-Nine

CHAYANNE

Favi park before waa dilapidated building, weh deep ina Brown's Town bush, then face me. "Do you know what *omertà* means?" him ask, and mi shake mi head. "It's a code of silence."

"Favi, I knew who you were from the beginning, and mi never consider selling you out before. Me nuh bout fi do it now, cause it's deevn about us anymore. We have Plum," I said.

He stared at me for a while then looked away. Him grab sum off the backseat. "Put this on." Him hand waa black hoodie to me. A the same one him have on ina the picture Kyle show mi.

"Why mi afi wear this?" mi ask as mi put it on.

"Not everyone has to know we're pregnant." Him exit the car, strolling around to my side fi open the door. When mi exit, him hold both sides of mi face, craning my head fi meet him eyes. "I know why you want to be here, but you don't have to stay to see it. The moment I sense you're uncomfortable, you're leaving."

"I understand," mi seh, and him sigh before placing a long kiss pon mi farid.

Releasing me, him tek a kerchief outta him pocket. Him fold it into waa triangle, wrapping it around the bridge of mi nose and covering the lower half of mi face.

"Wa dis fa?" mi ask.

"It stinks in there." Him tek mi hand ina his. Him lead wi into the building,

439

and mi wrap mi other hand round him arm, plastering myself to his side.

The interior contrast the exterior. It dimly lit, but the place well taken care of. Big, burly men were stationed before each metal door. Cameras ina every corner of the ceilings.

Favi approach waa door. A guard nod at we before opening it. Favi lift mi up, carrying mi down the stairs. The air get colder as we descend underground. Reaching the bottom, him place mi to mi feet, then lead we into waa room. The room full of expensive technology, and me cya put a name to most of them. Two men sat on chairs before waa wall of monitors, watching the cameras' live feed.

"Is he patched up?" Favi ask ina Italian, and the men nodded. "Wake him up."

A bald man grabbed a walkie-talkie, speaking Italian while focusing pon a screen. Upon closer inspection, mi realize a Salvatore. Him a mi chief bodyguard, who pose as mi neighbor. Looking away from Salvatore, mi focus pon the screen him a stare pon. Waa completely white room — from the ceiling to the floors — weh have no furniture nor a window, have waa blinding light bulb ina the ceiling. It have one door being used as the enter and exit. Mi almost neva see it cause it painted white, too. The door open, and three man enter the room.

Trav?!

Favi look in my direction. Mi give him a reassuring smile before looking at the screen.

Trav walk toward waa body pon the ground. The person only have on a brief, and dem curled ina waa ball. Trav nudge dem wid him foot, but the person nuh move. Shaking him head, Trav look pon Eltham and open him mouth.

"Turn off the sound," Favi seh in Italian, and Salvatore complied.

Eltham and the other man exit, returning wid a big bucket. Water spilled over the sides, splashing onto the floor. Dem throw it pon the sleeping man, and him jolt up, screaming. His wide, bloodshot eyes darted around the room while terror seized him. A mix of dirt and blood washed away in the water beneath him, running toward Trav, who laughed.

Eltham and the man drop the bucket pon the ground. Them march toward the cowering man, grabbing him by the arms and hauling him outta the room.

Favi look pon me. "Still want to see more?" him ask, and me nod.

Salvatore look pon mi, saying sum to Favi ina Sicilian. Favi nod, leading me outta the room. Mi waa ask him wa dat bout, but mi know better than fi question him in front of certain people.

Instead of going above ground, Favi lead we down waa other hallway. We stop in front waa enormous iron door, weh tek two man fi open. We enter the room. As the door slam shut, all eyes focus pon we.

Specifically... me.

"Wa she a do here?" Al snarled, stomping toward us.

Favi put him hands ina him sweatpants. "She's free to go wherever she wants."

Al angrily shake him head, glaring at me. "Yu nuh belong here!"

"I know..." mi whisper, looking past him and scanning the room.

In here stink! Blood and dirt stained the walls and floor. Chains and whips hung from the ceiling. Mechanical torture devices were stationed around the room. The room a waa psychopathic serial killer's wet dream, and Favi was smirking while watching the center of attention.

Zip strapped to waa metal chair at the front of the room, his head hanging low. Him body bruised and swollen. Even standing on the opposite side of the room with a mask pon mi face, the rancid mix of vomit, blood, pee, and doodoo a burn mi nose. Zip slowly lift him head, his soulless eyes finding mine. Mi try gulp, but mi throat dry. Mi step closer to Favi, grabbing handfuls of his hoodie.

Favi looked at me. "He can't hurt you."

"Him won't ever get the chance fi hurt yu again," Trav seh, but mi cya look away from Zip, who smirked at me.

"Travis, stay with her," Favi seh, and Trav walk toward us, shielding my body with his. Favi walk away, his shoes padding against the iron floor.

Mi look at mi feet, trying not to panic. Waa blood stain deh beneath mi foot, so mi close mi eyes.

If yu nuh waa leaf drop pon yu, tan from under tree.

"The moment you tried to touch my woman, I became your God. You don't eat, breathe, or shit unless I want you to. Do you know what I want today? An apology. To her—" Favi seh, and mi sense Trav step aside.

Lifting my head, mi eyes snap open and settle pon Favi. Him motion him head

441

toward me while Zip look pon him.

"That's all I'm asking for, and maybe I'll hold your special surprise until tomorrow," Favi seh.

Zip look pon mi, and mi inhale a breath as mi heart beat faster. "Mi naa apologize to nuh bitch," him snarl, spitting a big blob pon Favi's shoes.

Mi eyes widen, then narrow pon Zip.

Mi fist curl at mi side.

My breathing shortened.

Wa him really just do?

Favi chuckle, and dat mek mi angrier. Zip disrespect him, and him a laugh?! Anger about fi propel mi forward when Favi's words mek mi freeze.

"Bring him in," Favi order.

Eltham run toward the iron door, knocking a pattern against it. Seconds later, the door open, and a tall man entered. Him have rings pon every finger, and him body muscular like him feed pon steroids.

Muscle Man walk toward Favi while everybody ina the room leave, except me, Trav, and Al. The iron door nuh shut behind dem, causing their chatter to drift into the room.

Favi yet fi move a muscle. Deevn him shoes with the spit nuh move an inch. Staring at Zip, who a stare pon me with lust-filled eyes and a devious smirk, Favi asked, "*Fiore*, do you remember where he touched you?"

I nodded, glancing at Trav, who tense. The assault nuh bother mi as much cause therapy and Favi helped. But mi never know seh Trav know. It weird with him witnessing this.

"Where?" Favi asked, still looking at Zip, who furrow him brows.

"My... face. Breasts. E-everywhere," I forced out the last word, and Favi inhale a deep breath. In my peripheral, mi see Al curl him fists.

"You got that?" Favi asked, and Muscle Man nodded excitedly. "I want you to make it ten times worse. When he's bleeding, don't stop. When he's crying, don't stop. Don't stop until he's begging for death. Even then, don't stop."

Zip's eyes widened.

Mine, too.

Favi turn, walking toward me. While Trav and Al exit, Favi offer me a hand, which mi nuh hesitate fi take. Favi lead me through the door while mi look over mi shoulder. Muscle Man a walk toward Zip while undoing his belt.

"B-bossy, w-wait nuh! Mi sorry!" Zip yelled at our departing backs.

Before the iron door slam shut, a petrified scream bounced off the walls.

Thirty minutes later, Al a scold me while we stand beside Favi's car. "I can't believe he has you here."

"I want to be here," I whispered, and him sigh.

"He's not a good influence."

"Mama wuda say *finger never say 'look here', it say 'look yonder'.*"

"My situation's different. You're pregnant. Why would you bring the baby around this?"

"Maybe fi the same reason yu neva tell mi you and Favi a work together," mi hiss, and him about fi reply when him phone ring.

Him look pon the screen, sighing. "I have to go. This conversation isn't over."

"Alright, Al." Mi hug him before him walk away.

Trav walk toward me, leaning against Favi's car. "How's Plum?" him ask, and mi resist the urge fi touch mi belly.

"Good, but mi nuh waa talk bout him right now," mi seh, and him sigh.

"A facts Elder a talk, Chichi. Yu nuh belong here so. Cya believe the man bring yu, Jah knows."

"Mi have mi reasons, just like you have yu reasons fi nuh tell mi boh you and Chezzy," mi seh, and him eyes widen. "How long unu a sneak round?"

Trav sigh, looking away. "Since yu ina hospital," him seh, and mi gasp.

"We nuh usually keep secrets, Trav," mi seh, and him sigh.

"I wanted to tell you, but mi nuh believe ina playing brain games anymore. Mi a breeze her."

"Breeze her crochiz ina mi house?"

"Mi did a breeze her throat," him seh, and mi fake a gag, making him chuckle.

"Mi think unu wuda mek a good couple, but unu tek unu time. *Que sera, sera*."

"Mi ano yu man, Chichi. Talk to mi straight." Him kiss him teeth, and mi chuckle.

"People who belong together always find dem way to each other. Just look pon me and Favi." Mi smile at Favi, who deh a few feet away, talking pon the phone with Sergio.

"Why yu sound sad?" Trav ask, and mi blink away tears.

"I hate myself because Favi doesn't want this life, but what happened to me dragged him back into it. Mi feel like him waa grow, and mi a hold him back."

"Nuh seh that. The man rate yu. Mi neva see him do half a wa him do fi you fi anybody else, Jah knows," Trav seh, and mi smile.

"You think so?"

"Me know so. Come here," him seh, and mi scoot closer. Trav throw him arm over mi shoulder, and Favi look ina our direction, glaring. Trav grin and pinch mi cheek. "See how you and the man connected?"

Chuckling, mi elbow him while motioning for Favi to focus pon him call. "Whatever. Tell me about you and Chezzy. Mi nuh waa think about waa happen in there so..." Mi glance at the building.

"Ah. Mek mi tell yu how she a fuck up mi medz," Trav seh, and mi listen keenly.

We talk until Favi join we, then we head inside. Zip lay down fixed in the fetal position, staring wide-eyed at the wall before him. Trembling, him murmur something incoherent to himself.

"My money?" Muscle Man asked Favi.

"Come collect it." Trav walk outta the room, and Muscle Man follow him with a pep ina him step. Seconds later, a loud gunshot drifted into the room.

Favi slowly shook his head. "Can't stand rapists."

Mi neva flinch as another shot go off. Staring at Zip a mek me see red. "Favi," mi seh, and him look at me. "Give me your gun."

His eyes widened. "*What?*"

"Give me your gun. I want to kill him."

Chapter Seventy

Favio

"Repeat wa yu seh, Chichi," Travis said, reentering the room. He stopped beside Chayanne, wiggling a finger in his ear. "Mi ears give problem sometimes, and mi nuh believe ina hearing aid."

Chayanne's jaw ticked, her eyes narrowing on Zip. Her face drained of the warmth I was used to. She... looked like me.

I stepped before her, and her darkened eyes dragged to mine. "*Fiore*, you can't come back from this."

"I know, but I want him dead. He disrespected you," she said.

My brows furrowed. "Disrespected?"

She glanced at my shoe, then at my eyes. She held her hand out. "You already have too much blood on your hands because of me. Give me your gun."

"Fuck no, Chayanne," I hissed.

"Mi tell yu fi send her home!" Travis exclaimed, and Chayanne shot him a glare that shut him up.

I grabbed her hand, bringing it to my mouth and kissing each knuckle while I held her stare. "I don't care how bloody my hands are if yours are clean."

She moved her hand from my mouth, lowering it to grab my other hand. She laced our fingers. "I want to kill him. This man tek weh nuff peaceful night from me, and he made me disgusted with myself. He almost made me lose you because I was losing myself. I know nothing can bring back all he took from us, but I want

445

to take something he can't get back, either."

Fuck.

I stayed out of her therapy, but I didn't know this was the extent of her trauma.

I released her hand, turning my back to her and focusing on Zip. He was a shell of himself, and I imagined him as Chayanne on that night. She was defeated as she cried herself to sleep. Her sobs pained me. I wished I could've taken her hurt and carried the burden myself.

My jaw clenched as I looked away from Zip, pulling my gun out.

"Slitta—" Travis warned.

"You can stay or leave." I handed the gun to Chayanne, pocketing my hands. She walked toward Zip. "Trav, pull him up."

Sighing, Travis tucked his gun into his waist. He shook his head as he walked toward them. Zip didn't react as Travis settled him on his ass, but he winced as he brought his knees up to his chest and wrapped his arms around them. Blood trickled from between his legs. His flaccid dick rubbed in it while he rocked back and forth.

Chayanne stooped before him. She dug her boot's heel into his left foot, but Zip didn't react. I didn't know if it was because my woman was too tiny to do actual damage, or if it was because Zip was still in shock. She flicked off the safety, moving the gun to his mouth. "Open," she said coldly, and Zip continued rocking instead of obeying. "You're going to love it. I said open," she taunted, but he still didn't move.

Travis nudged Zip with his foot. "Oye, listen to wa she seh before mi bring in the torch again."

Zip stopped rocking, his eyes settling on Chayanne while opening his mouth. Grinning, her eyes sparkled. "Suck it."

Zip sucked the barrel into his mouth. His eyes snapped shut as more tears broke his defense.

"Love when unu listen," Chayanne taunted before squeezing the trigger.

Pieces of teeth clattered onto the floor as Chayanne pulled the gun out of his mouth. Zip's body fell to the floor, his life draining from his eyes as they stared ahead. Blood poured out of his mouth, forming a puddle on the floor.

Chayanne wiped the gun against his abdomen twice, leaving a bloody 'X' on his dirty body. Satisfied, she stood and faced me while handing the gun to Travis. Blood streaked her face. "Can we go home now? I miss sleeping with you."

Travis' mouth dropped, and I smirked.

We'd been at home for two hours, and I had yet to take my eyes off Chayanne. She sat around the island while eating, acting as if she didn't kill someone in cold blood with our kid inside her.

"*Stai bene*?" I asked.

"Yes," she answered, her voice cheery.

I walked behind her and spun the stool around. Stepping between her thighs, I rested a hand on her waist, using the other to tuck her hair behind her ear. I showered her at the safe house, and again when we got home. I could still imagine all the blood in her hair and on her face as it washed down her growing belly. Chayanne was unphased through it all.

I looked in her eyes. "I don't want you to get tied to this life—"

"But I have to keep up with you."

"Fuck no. I became a killer because I didn't have a choice. You know better."

"Favi, mi born and raise a Steer Town when violence rampant. Mi know yu nuh like when mi call yu badman, but that's who I met you as, so mi nuh new to this. I know you'll do whatever it takes to protect our family, and I will, too. It's called ours for a reason. I didn't mind doing it because him disrespect you," she angrily said the last part.

What the fuck did I do to her? She was a killer now, but it made me love her more. Killing someone so I didn't have to do it was the nicest thing a person ever did for me.

Gulping, I carefully chose my next words. "Chayanne, you're an angel. You give your dog massages, crochet tiny socks for Plum, and cuss me if mi get sick. I

447

don't want you like this, *fiore*—"

"Then why did you choose me?" she asked, and my brows furrowed.

"*Che cosa?*"

"I was young, from a different tax bracket, and based pon yu browning or white ex dem, mi ano yu type—"

"You're everything I want," I said. "I chose you because the first night I met you, I knew you could hold your own."

"And that's what I'm doing." There was no remorse or sadness in her eyes. Nothing like when I got my first kill.

"You're the one perfect thing in my life. I don't want you tainted like the rest. Promise me you won't do anything like this again, especially not when Plum's in here." I trailed her belly with my fingertips.

"I promise." She kissed me, pulling away with a smile.

"Finish eating. I need to talk to your brother." I went outside.

"She good?" Josiah asked, leaning off his car.

"She's more than good," I said, glancing at Travis, who hung up his phone and walked toward us.

"So why yu sound so?" Travis asked.

I had so much to say, but I wouldn't discuss it with them. "Now that's dealt with, Elder will handle the prison situation," I said, and Travis sighed.

"Cya believe the man wuda do that, Jah knows," Travis said, and Josiah nodded.

I shrugged. "Can't be too trusting."

"Kill wi fi kill him! Fuck Elder promotion cause him shuda dead long time, too," Josiah said.

"Easy yuself. We naa kill mi sister father," Travis said, and Josiah grumbled.

"Yago back a Brown's Town tonight?" I asked Travis, and he nodded.

"Afta the man nav no woman fi warm him bed," Josiah joked.

Travis glared. "You have one?"

"No, dawg. Woman a wicked," Josiah said, and Travis hummed.

"Unu done the fuckry?" I asked, and they quieted. "Nobody nago miss Zip, so cut him up and leff him someweh ina Ochi. Him deh pon the Most Wanted list, so that's the most help wi a go give the pigs."

"And the next one?" Travis asked.

"Bout him waa passport fi flee country. Mi nuh know how man force demself pon woman... Or man," Josiah said, chuckling with Travis.

"Cut him up, feed him to the pigs, then kill dem and burn dem. Also, take her old security out of the white room. Tell them they've been in there for a year," I said, and Travis nodded.

"But a barely two months," Josiah said, and I smirked.

"They don't need to know that." My favorite torture method was white rooms. I woke them at random intervals, tortured them, then patched them up. I loved the power of them not knowing when I'd strike next, but I was done having fun with them. Chayanne's new guards were doing a better job. "And tell them I said *buonanima*," I added.

"Slitta waa Trav bite him tongue," Josiah joked.

"Jah knows, mi deevn a go try seh that. Chichi wuda say idle dog fuck sheep," Travis said, and Josiah laughed.

"Chayanne doesn't curse," I said. Though by her behavior tonight, her actions shouldn't surprise me anymore.

Chapter Seventy-One

CHAYANNE

"I can't do this," Favi curse, and mi glare.

"Yu do it before. *Please* nuh," mi beg.

"You're showing more now. It's weird fucking a pregnant woman. Suppose I hit the baby?" him ask, and mi kiss mi teeth.

"You're not going to. Just go slow," mi seh with a bright smile, and him wearily eye the bump. "Cho, come offa mi!" Mi do my best fi push him from above me. Him move, and mi slap weh him hand when him try help mi offa the bed.

"Yago vex with me over sex?" Favi ask, and mi nuh ansa. "*Fiore*, it's weird."

Mi turn round in a flash, wiping away the tears from mi eyes. Mi clit a burn mi to how mi horny, and him nuh waa sex mi! Mi hate man, and mi hate him! "Yu neva know it weird all the other time dem yu push yu hood ina me?!"

"That's different. You're pregnant and want sex every minute—"

Mi kiss mi teeth and finally manage fi get up. Mi grab mi phone offa the dresser, calling the doctor on speaker. "Doc, please tell my boyfriend it's safe for us to have sex," mi seh, and Favi choke.

Doc chuckled. "You're experiencing an increase in libido?"

"Yes." Mi glare at Favi, who look like him waa the Earth swallow him.

"Mr. Welsh, Miss Bailey is healthy, and Plum is, too. Give her what she wants," Doc said, and mi end the call with a victorious smile.

Favi look at mi belly, groaning while him look weh. Mi kiss mi teeth, waddling to the bathroom. Mi have work in a few hours, maybe a nice shower will wash weh the horniness. While the water gwan warm a likkle bit, mi stand naked before the mirror, admiring mi bump.

Life been going great since Zip dead weeks ago. Aunty nuh ina her feelings anymore, so she happy bout Plum. Mi complain to her seh as mi approach six months, pay stretch mark a tek mi over. She tell me seh when Mama did pregnant with Mommy, she rub olive oil mixed with a bush pon her belly, so me dweet, too. Except for this belly growing every day, mi nuh see a difference.

Al come offa waa undercover case last week, but him gone again. Him and Favi a get along likkle bit better. Mi think him come to terms seh Favi a go always ina mi life.

"Bring the pussy to me, Chayanne," Favi drawled, and mi meet him eyes ina the mirror. Him look tired from the four rounds mi beg fa throughout the night.

Smiling, mi turn off the shower. Mi run over as fast as mi can, and Favi's eyes widened.

"Stop shake up wi youth!" him hiss, and mi giggle as him liff mi onto the counter with a huff. Him tek little wormy out and spit on it, stroking while looking between my parted legs. "I should've made you suck me."

"I would, but mi nuh like how it and yu cum taste these days," mi seh, and him stop stroking fi glare at me.

"Wa the fuck yaa try seh?" him ask, and mi chuckle.

"Not like that, big foot. The last time I did, it tasted funny. I think it's the baby."

"When mi start seh yu pussy taste funny—" Favi paused as I spread my legs wider, his eyes locking on my pussy.

"Put it in and make it grow inside me."

"Tek care of yuself, and safe delivery." Itanya hug me, and mi smile.

"Thanks, Itanya." Mi pull away fi accept the hug from another coworker.

"Where's mine?" waa male voice asked, and mi stiffen. Dayshawn grinned as mi face him.

Mi force a smile cause it wuda rude fi nuh hug him when mi hug everybody else. Withholding a sigh, mi give him waa one-arm hug. Mi try pull away after a second, but him wrap him next arm around me, trapping me in place.

"Should've been ours," he whispered while we coworkers walk weh.

Mi yank free from his hold, glaring while insults brew pon the tip a mi tongue. *When yu fan fly, yu hot up sore.*

Straightening mi shoulders, mi adjust mi bag and turn round. Mi freeze when mi see Favi, taking long strides toward the building. Blousecup! Mi forget seh a him a come fimi today cause Eltham ask fi a day off fi handle some business. Gulping, mi rush outside before him can enter the hotel. With each step closer, it feel like me a walk toward waa bloodthirsty lion.

"Fav—" Mi pause as him return to the car and open the door. Sighing, mi sit down. Mi deevn try explain as him drive off cause mi know wa Favi silence mean.

Minutes later, we park at home and enter the house.

"What the fuck was that?" he spat, his eyes swirling with anger while his hands clenched at his side.

"Nothing. Dem just did a hug me cause a mi last day—"

"Which fucking man can hands up mi woman so? Get fi realize mi mek yu tek mi too lightly," him seethe, and mi sigh as mi rest mi handbag pon the nearby table.

"Wa yaa talk boh? A waa hug. Yu nafi gwan so."

"Wa kinda hug that yaa give your ex, Chayanne?! Yu goodly did a fuck him all this time and a gwan like a trauma him a help yu wid," Favi yell, stunning me.

"Wow... Mi naa do this wid yu right now." Mi try step past him.

Him hand shoot out, grabbing me by the neck and pushing me against the door. Pain ran up mi spine, and I cried out.

"I've told you before not to walk away when I'm speaking to you," he said calmly.

"Favio, I'm pregnant! How yufi—"

"Are you fucking him?" he asked coldly, his grip tightening and making my feet rise off the floor by a fraction.

My breathing shortened as I struggled to shake my head. "No, Favio," I forced out, and he laughed as a tear fell from my eye, dropping onto his hand.

"Do you take me for an idiot, Chayanne?"

"No." Choking, I scratched at his hand. "B-but you tek mi fi a wh-ore."

"You're acting like a whore."

My hands went limp.

I forgot how to breathe as I stopped fighting against him.

His nostrils flared as he released me. Choking, I inhaled a big gulp of air while he stepped backward.

"I want a paternity test," he said, and I froze.

"W-what? All this over a hug? Yu know mi wuda neva—"

Him tuck him hands ina him pockets. "I don't know anything. I want it done."

Mi stare at him back as him walk weh from mi.

Blinking away tears while rubbing my neck, mi tek up mi handbag. Favi act senselessly when him angry, so mi a go give him space fi cool off. Until then, mi a go eat a snack and do mi homework. Mi have waa therapy session later, and mi doh waa late. Cya wait fi tell her seh with work out of the way, mi can focus pon my man and our family!

Chapter Seventy-Two

CHAYANNE

Favi step past me, stopping at the sink. Alcohol hit mi nose, and mi sigh.

Mi stop try reach fi the flour pon the top shelf, facing him. "Yu cya cut down pon the drinking, Favi?" I asked, and him ignore mi as him continue wash him hand. "Do you want fried chicken or something else?"

Ignoring me, him grab a glass and Henny bottle. Deciding against pouring it, him turn the bottle to him head. Mi lost count how much bottle him go through ina the past two weeks. Him deevn breathe pon mi since wi argument.

Sighing, mi go grab a chair. Mi bout fi climb pon it, but him walk over and take down the flour. As he handed it to me, our eyes met.

"T-thanks," I said.

Him nuh ansa. Him grab the chair, returning it to the table. Grabbing the Henny bottle, him walk toward the exit.

"Favi, why yu still upset? Ano my fault him won't leave mi alone!" mi yell at him back, and him pause. Mi stand more upright, hoping him wuda talk to me.

The hope crumbled as him walk outta the kitchen. Angrily wiping away mi tears, mi start pon dinner. Mi sure a pay tears drop ina the pot, but it deevn matter. Favi nuh eat none a mi cooking since we argue. Mi nuh know if him a eat, mi only see him a drink.

A few hours later, mi finish cook the rice and peas with fried chicken. Mi did consider going to the supermarket fi buy beef, but dat wuda mek him angrier. Mi settle wid making wul heap a Mama's potato salad.

Mi try eat, but it hard fi swallow ina the tension of this house. Defeated, mi grab mi phone. "Eltham, yu can come for mi please?" mi ask, and him seh him soon come.

Mi go to the downstairs bedroom Favi did wordlessly move mi into. Mi think a because a mi back pain, but mi nuh waa get a head of miself. Through sobs, mi pack a bag. When Eltham reach, mi go outside. Him know better than fi ask wa do mi, so him quietly help mi ina the car.

Mi scream when sum move ina mi belly. "Eltham, the baby!"

Him eyes widen while mi grab mi belly. "It a come? Please say no because mi will faint!"

Mi laugh, grabbing his hand and placing it where mi feel the kick. "That was his first— Ah! Yu feel that?" mi ask, and him smile.

"That nuh hurt?" him ask, and mi shake mi head while him move him hand.

This a the most exciting thing fi happen to mi ina forever! Mi cya wait fi tell Fav— Mi smile wash weh.

Eltham sighed. "Where to?"

"Chezzy," I answered, and him flash mi a look of pity before him shut the door, walking toward the front.

Mi cup mi hands beneath mi belly fi the entire ride, but Plum never move again. Eltham park, helping mi outta the vehicle toward the veranda where Chezzy stood. She sighed, hugging me before bringing me to her room.

"Where's Zaveer?" mi ask through hiccups while we lay pon the bed.

"Him a sleep." She wipe weh my tears, and more replaced them. "Him still naa talk to yu?"

"No, but mi a try nufi vex cause mi know a my fault," mi seh, and Chezzy sigh.

"Yu shuda tell Dayshawn fi leave yu alone. Yu know how yu man stay."

"I do, but mi indebted to Dayshawn. Mi nuh know why Favi a gwan so—"

Alligator lay egg, but him nuh fowl.

Mi sigh, angrily wiping away the tears. "Maybe this a mi karma fi Italy."

"Yu still nuh tell mi wa happen ina Italy."

Mi stop tell her alla wi business. Chezzy too wishy-washy, and mi nuh like when nobody bad mouth Favi. A me alone fi cuss him, but mi nuh waa argue right now. Mi therapist seh when we have problems, a 'us versus it', not 'me versus him'. It hard fi fix the problem when Favi a treat mi like mi thief him white fowl.

"It nuh matter." Mi smile when Plum kick again. "The baby's moving."

Squealing, Chezzy feel mi belly. "Mi nephew fi go turn footballer!"

Mi cya wait until the next two week come. It a go be mi six-month checkup, and mago give him the stupid paternity test. Wi cudn do it earlier cause the doctor seh mi pressure high.

"Everything a happen at such a bad time. Yu birthday a come up, and mi waa carry yu go Slovenia fi the week, but it nuh look like that a go happen. Mi cya travel right now, and mi fraid fi ask him fi the jet," mi seh, on the verge of crying.

"It good. Ano like Zaveer have a passport fi mi carry him go anywhere," Chezzy seh, and mi sigh. If me and Favi did good, him wuda sort out everything fi dem.

A my fault this, too. Mi did keep on a forget fi settle all the preparations cause mi did a study fi waa exam. Now, this situation with Favi and Plum a the only thing mi can focus pon.

"No. Mago sort it out. Mi waa yu enjoy yu birthday, even if mi cya come. Maybe yu can go with Trav," mi seh, and she choke.

"T-Trav? I mean, why?" she ask, chuckling nervously.

"Yolo fraid a plane, so him a the best option. Him did tell mi him want a break from the studio cause him finish work pon waa album. Yu can go ask him," mi seh, and her eyes widened. Mi bite back mi smile. "*Go*. Mi think him deh home. Mi will watch the baby fi yu."

"O-okay." Nodding, Chezzy stood and exhaled a long breath.

Two hours later, I was at Al's house. Chezzy nuh come back yet; she seh Aunty call her fi do sum. Mi neva believe her, so mi text Trav, and him seh shi deh him house. Mi waa see how long her big batty baxide a go keep this up fa!

Chuckling, mi finish mi homework, then hop in the shower. While the water run down mi belly, mi smile. "I hope you don't have anger issues like Daddy."

Waa door close someweh ina the house.

"Zaveer?" mi yell, but him nuh ansa. Turning off the shower, mi drag on mi towel and go to my bedroom. Seeing Zaveer sleeping on my bed, I furrowed my brows. "Mi know mi naa mad. Maybe mi leave waa window open." Mi walk toward the living room, and a bloodcurdling scream tore from my mouth.

Dayshawn's severed head rested atop the TV stand. His cheeks were chubby, and upon closer inspection, I spotted a knuckle partially visible in his mouth. Blood leaked from his neck, splattering onto the floor.

Mi step back, staring wide eyed at what was left of Dayshawn.

"Favio," mi curse, hurrying to the bathroom fimi phone. Mi call him, but him nuh answer. Seething, mi go pon the veranda and yell into the darkness, "Salvatore!"

Wind whistling through trees was the only answer.

"Come out right now, else mi tell Favio yu mek somebody hurt me!" mi hiss, and six men emerged from the shadows. They stood before me, keeping their attention above my neck. "Who put the head in my house?" Mi cross my arms atop mi belly, glaring when them nuh ansa. "Salvatore, call Favio right now."

"We're not supposed to call him unless you're in danger," Salvatore stated.

"I don't care. Bring him here. Now," mi demand, and him remain unmoved. Mi glare pon another man, and him gulp, pulling out him phone.

Salvatore glare pon the man, who spoke Sicilian into the phone. Mi smile as him move the phone from him ear.

"He'll be here," him assure, but mi neva satisfy.

"Who's your boss?" mi ask, and them glance between each other. "Don't lie to me. I know it isn't Favio because he isn't involved in *that* anymore."

"We're not at liberty to say," Salvatore stated.

"Mi a go drop pon mi belly and roll—"

"Nikola," the one who made the call rushed out, and Salvatore glared.

"Give me Nikola's number," mi seh sweetly, and he complied. "*Grazie.*"

Flashing them a smile, mi go inside to the kitchen. After making the call, mi rest the phone pon the island and swallow large chugs of water while staring at Dayshawn's head. Mi nuh worried about Zaveer seeing it cause him usually sleep long.

Movement come from the front door, and mi look toward it.

Favio frantic as him search the room. When his eyes landed on me, he scanned my appearance before relaxing and giving me a piercing glare.

Mi return the glare as mi march toward him. "Wa wrong wid yu, Favio?! Yu hate mi that much?"

"I don't hate you," him seh, and mi laugh humorlessly.

"*Really*? So, why yu kill Dayshawn? See, yu cya even ansa! Mi tired fi tell yu mi nuh lay dung wid nobody but you!"

"He told me he fucked you," he said, and mi gulp hard. "I hate being lied to, Chayanne."

Mi lick mi dry lips. "That was when you were gone... And you did a sex other people too, so yu nav no right fi be angry or kill him."

Favio look at Dayshawn's head, a small smirk on the corner of his lips.

"Look how happy yu be. Mi fi believe seh yu nuh hate mi?"

Him look pon me. "You said he was bothering you."

"A that it tek fi get yu attention? Not me telling you Plum is yours? Not me telling you I'm horny?"

His eyes drifted to my lips, then to my eyes. Him step forward, but mi nuh move. He smirked, taking another step forward. Gulping, I stepped back until I hit the wall. His hand wrapped around my neck, tight enough to make my pussy throb while he rubbed my vein with his thumb. I turned my head to the side, my chest heaving.

"If the baby isn't mine..."

"I'm not scared of you."

"Good." He leaned in to kiss me. Hard.

My eyes snapped shut. Mi throw mi arms round him shoulders, kissing him back with passion. We fumbled toward the sofa, but he swiped the things off the coffee table and placed me there instead. I unwrapped my towel while he tugged down his jeans and boxers.

"Ah, God!" I screamed as he slammed inside me. The wetness of my pussy filled the room, my clit throbbing with need as he pounded into me relentlessly. My wet body made strange noises against the glass tabletop.

"Favio." His fingers wrapped around my neck, squeezing tightly.

I was only allowed to breathe whenever he loosened his grip, but I loved it because he knew how to heighten my senses. I threw my head back, staring at Dayshawn's head while I moaned louder. Even in death, I wanted him to know that he could never amount to half the man Favio was.

"Faster," I begged, and Favio's fingers dug into my thigh as he picked up the pace. I bit into my lips to stifle my moans because this — getting the best sex I had in a long while, while my ex's severed head watched me — was so wrong.

But it felt so good.

Too good.

"When yago stop fuck with me, Chayanne?" Favio asked harshly.

"I don't," I cried, tears springing to my eyes as my abdomen tightened. This orgasm was going to be explosive; I could feel it in how sensitive everywhere on my body was.

"You're a fucking headache," Favio cursed, and I looked away from Dayshawn to him. His hair hung low in his face as he thrust into me harder each time. He could kill me with his dick and I wouldn't care. He turned his head toward the ceiling, his lips parting slightly.

I tightened at will around him. My pussy ached as I moved a hand between us, rubbing my clit and pulling my orgasm closer.

"*Fuck*!" Favio cursed, thrusting sloppily as we reached our orgasm. His darkened eyes settled on mine as we rode out our high, not looking away until the bliss passed over us. His grip loosened around my neck and thigh as the feeling passed, and I released a long breath. "Don't ask me for sex again until I know it's not another man's child in you," he said coldly, and mi glare while sitting up and wrapping the towel around myself.

"Yu just kill mi so-called baby father," mi seh, and him glare pon mi while standing, wiping the cream off his dick before putting it away. "Yu can mek one of them tek the head outta here, please?"

"No. Let it stay there and rot until you understand what will happen if you give another man your pussy."

Mi kiss mi teeth. "I don't want my nephew to see it," I said, and he looked at the head, debating. "Yu sick ina yu head—"

The door flew open, and Favio shielded my body with his. Salvatore and another bodyguard were frantic. The other ran further into the house while Salvatore rushed out something in Sicilian to Favio. Favio sprang into action. While grabbing the gun he'd tossed onto the sofa in our haste to undress, he helped me stand.

"What's happening?" Mi glance at Salvatore, who have a pistol ina him hand while peeping through the window.

"I need to get you to a safe house," Favio seh, and my heart raced while the hairs rose on my skin.

"My nephew—"

"Down!" Salvatore yelled seconds before bullets sprayed the house.

The glass windows shattered, pieces clattering against the floor as Favio yanked me to the floor. Pain seared through my back. I groaned while moving a hand to my bump. Favio propped his hands on either side of my body, shielding me while being mindful of my belly. Salvatore screamed Sicilian phrases into his earpiece while returning fire.

"Favio! Mi nephew!" I screamed, trying to get from beneath him despite the throbbing pain in my body, but he wouldn't let me move. I wasn't sure if he heard me. Warmth was soaking my towel, and one look at his grimace confirmed my worst fear.

Favi got shot.

Chapter Seventy-Three

TRAVIS

Mi lean pon the wall, watching a gruesome scene unfold before mi. Naa seh mi can stand the man, but alladis cause Chichi coworker dem gi her a hug? Slitta a get fucking outrageous.

Mi lean off the wall and walk toward him, stopping him from working on Deshaun's left arm. Him already bruk the man right elbow, and each finger at the knuckle. "Yu do enough, Slitta," mi seh, and him glare pon mi. One time mi used to fraid a tha man ya, until mi tek fass go step to him boh mi sister. Since then, mi nuh fraid. Mi tek the branding iron outta him hand, looking at the skin sticking on it. The ting stink nuh fuck! "Weh yu get this?"

"Antaro used it to mark special edition wine labels during a press run," Slitta seh, not looking away from Dawson. Now dem brand people wid it? What a crazy fucking family.

"Come go home to Chichi, dawg. She pregnant, and it a get late."

Him sigh. "She left..."

Dobson breathing labored, and him have deep lacerations pon him farid. Blood crawled over him eye, weh swollen shut. Him lip busted, and him jaws swollen from the teeth extractions him get with some pliers.

Mi brows pull together. "She leff yu fi him?" Mi nuh believe this. Chichi mad fi deh wid a man like Slitta fi so long, but she nuh so fool fi go back to tha bwoy ya. Mi look pon the branding iron, debating killing him miself.

"No," Slitta seh, and mi look pon him. Him tek the branding iron from mi, walking away. Him place it beside the torture equipment on a table. "Tell Josiah to drop him at his house. He knows if he speaks, he dies."

"Ah." Mi leave the room, going above ground fi give Eltham the instructions. Then, mi go home, wul a fresh, and go to the kitchen. "Wa yu cook?"

"Mi neva cook nun. A waa box food mi buy a Tavern," Mommy seh, and mi shake mi head.

"Wa yu do wul day?"

She stop clean the counter fi stare pon mi. "Mi ano yu pickney, bwoy."

"And mi ano yu parent! Mi deh road wul day a work hard fi ensure yu good, and deevn a hot meal mi cya get!"

"I was working..."

"And me did waa betta fi yu!" mi shout, and she stomp outta the kitchen. Mi kiss mi teeth and grab ingredients fi mek some white rice wid curry chicken. Sometimes, mi wish Chichi did still live a Steer Town. Mi wuda have a proper meal fi nyam yanow.

After mi Maths up dat, mi call ova a b and do the damage downstairs.

Brushing my teeth while tapping on my phone, mi exit the bathroom with a towel wrap round mi waist. Mi raise a brow when mi see Niyah sprawl pon mi bed. Mi tap ar leg. "Yafi shove."

"Thought you wanted me to spend the night," she seh.

"Mi ever mek yu spend the night?" mi ask, and she sigh, getting outta the bed fi put on her clothes. Grabbing mi wallet, mi give her waa five grand pon the food mi gi her already. Mi follow her to the door, watching as she walk through the gate toward her house, weh three houses away. Once she inside, mi look at mi phone, my grip tightening as mi reread Chichi text.

Mi lean back ina the chair, watching as she sidung pon the edge of the bed. She run her hands down her thick thighs, and mi swallow hard. Jah knows.

"I..." She cleared her throat. "Chichi wants me to go to Slovenia for my birthday, but she cya come anymore. *She* waa yu come with me."

"Mi a Chichi send out bwoy?" mi ask, and Chez sigh.

"This was a bad idea." She stand, and mi scoff. She glanced at me, then sat.

"Chichi need mi fi show yu to the door, too?"

She sighed heavily, looking away for a moment before giving me a stare I couldn't look away from. "I want you, Travis, but you naa mek this easy fimi."

"Because mi stop run yu dung?"

"Because yu stop ansa mi texts and calls," she hissed.

"Changed my number."

"And nuh give me?"

"Why should I?" mi ask, and she sigh. "Exactly."

"Well... I... I'm going to leave Lamar. I just need to get approved for a loan so I can buy a house. I want you, Travis... I miss you," she said.

Mi scoff. Chichi wuda seh mi mada nuh shit mi out.

Chez stand, walking toward me. She straddle me, and mi keep mi hands at mi side while she throw her arms round mi shoulder. She lean in, her eyes flickering to my lips before she pulled back, sighing. The hurt in her eyes pain mi, but mi afi firm up mi heart when it come to Chez.

"Just give me time, please. As soon as mi get the house, mi a go make you love me again," she seh, and mi raise a brow.

"When mi tell yu mi love yu?"

"You don't have to tell me. I know. I feel it every time you look at me, and every time you try not to," she said, and mi look away. She placed a hand on the side of my face, turning it to her. "I..." She paused, her eyes darting away before settling on mine. "I want us to do this the right way. When I leave tonight, I won't hide from Chichi, and you won't see other people."

I raised a brow. "Mi nuh have two eye fi see other people?"

She scowled. "Yu know wa mi mean. And yu only use that much cologne when yu round next gyal. You had her in here?"

"You're the only one I brought up here," I said, and she smiled.

"Give me time, please?" she begged, but mi neva have fi think when mi nod.

Chez know mi weak to her. If she fuck it up this time, deevn Chichi likkle matchmaking nago mek mi pree Chez the same ever again.

We spend the next hour sitting on the floor, talking and joking like we used to. It was refreshing. Mi neva realize how much time passed until mi get a call.

"Slitta get shot," Eltham rush out, and mi sit more upright.

"*Wa?*" mi ask, listening while Eltham talk. "Him good?" Mi glance at Chez, whose eyes were watery; she heard everything cause mi phone loud.

"W-wa do mi baby?" she sobbed, scared of the answer.

"The man naa mek nuh sense." Mi get up, helping her to to her feet. "Fawud."

We run downstairs and hop ina the car. Mi blaze go Slitta house, and Chez gasp. The wul a the shadow bodyguards dem out, and the normal ones, too. Every man a wul a rifle with a military-grade bulletproof vest over them chest. Dem on high alert while walking around the yard.

Chez's trembling body clung to my side, tears streaming down her cheeks as mi hold her. Mi push through the defense, carrying her into the house. It loud nuh fuck. One bagga confusion as people come and go.

"*Mek one jackass bray!*" Chichi yell, and the place quiet down likkle as me and Chez run toward the dining hall.

Mi eyes widen at Slitta pon the table. Two doctors and a nurse a patch him up. Chichi deh by him side, clutching him hand while him seem annoyed.

"Chichi, weh mi baby?!" Chez ask as she rush over, but Chichi cudn ansa.

"Him upstairs," Eltham seh, and mi allow him fi tek Chez.

Waa follow her, but mi know nun cya mek her feel better other than seeing Zaveer. Mi divert mi focus to mi sista. Mi rest mi hand pon her shoulder, and she drag her eyes away from Slitta fi look pon mi. "Yu good?" mi ask, fixing the strap pon her shoulder while sitting on the chair beside her.

"Y-yeah," she said.

"Wa happen?" mi ask, and she tell mi everything. To how Chichi head far gone, she nearly tell mi which position the man set her pon. Mi skin up mi face as the sex scent box mi. "Nuh need fi know alladat," mi seh, looking away to Chez.

Chez have Zaveer ina her hand, who a hold a banana plushie while looking around the kitchen. "Aye, gyal, yu crazy?!" Chez yell, glaring at Chichi while the doctor help Slitta offa the table.

"Sorry..." Chichi mumbled.

"Yow, watch how yu talk to her," Slitta said at the same time.

"You watch how you talk to her," mi seh, and him glare pon mi.

Holding her lower back, Chichi sighed while standing. "Favi, go upstairs, please."

"That's all yav fi seh?! *Sorry*?!" Chez screamed.

"Wa else yu waa mi seh, Chezandra?! Nuh come in ya come gwan holier-than-thou when yu have yu own dolly house fi play ina!"

Chez gulped, then her anger flared. "Doh go deso right now, Chichi! Mi son cuda lose him life, and yaa gwan like yu doh care!"

"Him good while Favi isn't—"

"Mi nuh care bout Favio!" Chez snarl, and everything happen so fast after.

Mi nuh know if a me throw the first punch or if a Slitta. All me know was that the two a we attack each other.

Punching.

Kicking.

Fighting off everybody while our women screamed for us to stop.

Zaveer was crying, but we were in a haze.

Deevn know who manage fi part we, but when they did, we did a huff. Blood drip from mi nose into mi mouth while a doctor lead Slitta toward the table. He ripped his stitches. Fucka.

"Dawg, fawud. Unu better than this." Eltham tugged me outside.

Chezzy ran toward me, holding my face and scanning me with her teary eyes and soft hands. "Are you okay?"

"Mi good, see?" Mi move my hand from my nose. Blood rushed out, and she pinched my nostrils.

"Travis!" she hiss, hauling me toward the house while saying over her shoulder, "Eltham, stay with Zaveer."

"Now mi see why Yolanda hate man," Eltham mutter while him walk toward mi car, which had the doors closed, and the windows rolled up.

Chez mek mi sidung ina the dining room. She tell waa nurse fi bring a first aid kit. The lady try tend to mi, but Chez give her a tight smile. "I'll do it myself," she seh, and the nurse nod, returning to Slitta.

The man glare pon mi from across the room, and mi do the same. Fuck him feel like?

Chichi sigh before saying sum to him. Him jaw tick, then him look weh from mi. Pussy whipped.

Chichi walk toward we, stopping behind Chez. "Mi sorry, Chezzy..." she seh, but Chez pretended not to hear. Sighing, Chichi look pon me. "Yu good?"

"Him good. No thanks to you or yu man," Chez snapped.

Chichi glare. "Yu check if me good, Chezandra? Or yu too busy a gwan like yu perfect?"

Chez stopped tending to mi, returning Chichi's glare. "Gwan run backa him and mek him lead yu astray. If Zaveer tell mi seh sum dweem, mi a go to the police bout yu man."

Chichi glanced at one of the many men in the room. "Grab her." Her eyes narrowed into slits as a man restrained Chez by the elbows, making her gasp.

"Chichi, wa the fuck yaa do?!" Mi jump to mi feet, about fi pry the man's hands off Chez when another guard held me. Mi flail against him, but dem Italian man ya must feed pon steroids to bloodcleet.

"Let me go!" Chez demanded while Chichi scowled.

"Chezandra, you have all right to be angry, but Zaveer didn't see anything. *You're* the one who took him from my room, where he was reading a book, then brought him downstairs with all the guns," she said, and Chez froze. "Yu nuh know how mi drop and hurt mi back. Yu nuh know how mi tear weh miself from Favi when he was bleeding out, just so I could get to Zaveer and protect him. So, nuh tell mi seh mi nuh care when mi cuda l-lose mi boyfriend and baby just fi ensure you nuh get your happiness taken away. A-and yu waa seh m-me nuh c-care?" Tears streamed down Chichi's face as she forced out the last sentence, pointing at her chest. "*Me*, Chezandra?"

Chez eyes widen. "I-I didn't know... Are you okay?"

Scoffing, Chichi wiped away her tears. Her face blanked. "Let them go," she ordered, and the guards released us. She walked toward Slitta with them on either side of her.

I held Chez's trembling body and made her sit. "Nuh blame yuself. None of us were thinking clearly."

"Chichi was..." Chez said, and I sighed because mi wudn pick sides between dem. Wiping away her tears, she grab a cotton ball and tend to me minor cuts and bruises. She tell me to hold my head forward so the blood nuh flow down mi throat, but mi nuh comply cause me cya look away from her.

"Tell me what you wanted to say earlier," mi seh, my hands getting clammy.

Disposing of the bloody cotton ball, she raised her brow. "Huh?"

"When we were in my room," mi seh, and her eyes flashed recognition.

"It's not the right time..." she whispered.

"Now or never, Chez," I said, and she looked at me, her eyes shining.

"I love you."

Chapter Seventy-Four

FAVIO

Despite the two bullets barely missing my lung, I felt fine. The doctor disagreed, and he had me on bed rest for the past weeks.

I didn't need to heal. I needed to be out there overseeing the search for who paid Zip to touch Chayanne.

The first thing Nikola taught me when searching for hired hits was following the paper trail. I had the best men in Jamaica and Italy searching high and low, but there wasn't a fucking paper trail. It didn't help that Zip was a fucking pro. He'd been a serial rapist for years. It was a miracle we found him.

A crumble yanked me from my thoughts, and I looked at it. I loosened my grip on the paper. I hadn't skipped any meals since receiving this letter yesterday afternoon. Why wasn't she here yet?

As if she could read my thoughts, the door opened. I gulped hard as Chayanne walked into the room toward me. She ignored my gaze while handing me a pill and a glass of water. I swallowed the pill with a gulp of water, then offered the glass to her. She reached for it and I grabbed her wrist. She glared at me, the bags under her eyes making her look older than she was.

"*Fiore...*" I spoke.

"*Chayanne.*" She pulled at her hand while I tightened my grip.

"Did you get the results?" I asked, and she glared.

"Yu have the heart a ask that after yu mek mi shame when the doctor ask if she need fi collect a sample from another man?" she asked, and I glared.

"I asked you a question."

"Maybe if yu leggo mi hand, mi can get it," she snapped. She didn't show a hint of regret for speaking to me like that, and I exhaled a long breath through my nostrils before releasing her. She stomped out of the room, and I looked at the crumbled note.

> Diana tell mi seh yu naa eat. Personally mi nuh care, but Favio stop the foolishness. You're being childish and mi naa mek yu manipulate me into visiting you.
>
> I'm still very upset, and mi doh care if yu waa drop dung and mek the doctor put yu pon drip. Not needle burn thread, so you must know if yago starve before yu get fi see wa yu leff ina mi crochiz.
>
> (PS: I was going to let Diana text you on my phone again, but she told me you still weren't eating because you knew all along that I wasn't the one texting. I don't know how you figured it out, but like I said, I don't care!!! She said I should try doing something sweet to convince you, so when she gives you this letter, smile, eat all of your food, and maybe I'll let you see me and touch my belly.)
>
> -from the person who's in need of a ~~food~~ foot massage

Chayanne returned and threw an envelope at my face. It fell onto my lap. She crossed her arms atop her belly, tapping her foot against the floor while glaring at me. Clenching my jaw, I set the letter aside and broke the envelope's seal. I pulled strings to get the results within twenty-four hours. I didn't sleep at all last night, not that I'd been sleeping. Unfolding the letter, I stopped breathing.

"Yu feel bad, don't?" she hissed, and I looked at her. Her scorching eyes could disseminate a village. She hissed her teeth while I looked away. "Yu deevn a go ask fi fix things? Nothing?!"

Guilt weighed down my body. "I'm thinking about what to say."

"You can start by saying yu shudn put me through that!" she yelled, and I sighed. Hissing her teeth, she sat on the chair beside the bed and rested the glass on the nightstand.

"Ch—" I paused as she held up a hand.

"No. Mek mi talk. Favio, yu too ignorant and have too much anger ina yu. Suppose yu tek out yu anger pon the bab—"

"I wouldn't," I said quickly, but she was unmoved.

"A nuff time yu threaten me."

"Have I ever done anything to you?"

"Not really..."

"You always press my buttons, Chayanne. Yu know mi head easy fi chip, and sometimes mi cya tek yu fuckry."

"Yu think mi can tek yours? You need to work on yourself if yu waa be a good father, that's all me have fi seh."

"I do..." I said, and she glared.

"E nuh look so! Yaa behave like yu bredda! Mi name Chayanne, not Catherine, and mi nago mek yu batta bruise me nuh day!"

A lump formed in my throat, and I swallowed hard. "I'd never hurt you."

"Yu almost strangle me!" she screamed, and my brows furrowed.

"Nuh you like rough up, Chayanne?" I asked. Chayanne never felt wetter than when we had hot, angry sex.

"Yu have sense. Use it and doh further upset me. If we nuh ina bed, yu know yu nuh supposed to put yu hands pon mi certain way," she said, and I sighed. "All now yu nuh feel like apologize? No sah. Mi nuh know why mi still a try."

"You said I should listen." Unease settled on me as she stared at me for a long moment. I held my breath the entire time, worried Chayanne would somehow find the energy to kill me like she'd been tempted to do for the past weeks.

Finally, she spoke. "You need to change, Favio. From we deh, yu eva a cuss seh mi too childish, stubborn, and one bagga things. Mama seh *the older the moon, the brighter it shine*, and I'm living proof of that.

"While you... Yu change fi the worse, Favio. You're not the man I fell in love with. I understand why you try to have complete control over everything in your life, but I shouldn't be one of those things. I'm an individual; I don't belong to you, and you need to understand that. Mi reach a point weh mi nago put up wid the foolishness anymore ina whatever this—" She used her index to point between us. "—is. I love you, Favio, and mi nago ever stop love yu. But if yu continue like this, me afi go love yu from a distance."

A lump formed in my throat as tears formed in her eyes. She quickly blinked them away. Chayanne was never afraid to make me see her cry, and now she was trying not to let me see her at her weakest.

Swallowing the lump, I got out of the bed and kneeled before her. I took her hand in mine, watching my thumb brush over her knuckles. "Please don't leave," I whispered.

"You're not giving me a reason to stay," she said, and my throat tightened. "Favi?" She slipped her hands out of mine, cupping them at the sides of my face. She made me look at her, and her eyes widened while her lips parted slightly.

Try as I might, I couldn't blink away the tears like her.

"Please don't leave me, Chayanne," I whispered, my voice sounding foreign.

Tears brimmed her eyelids, but she didn't blink them away. Instead, she wrapped her arms around my shoulders, burying her face into the crook of my neck. I wrapped my arms around her waist as a wetness seeped into my skin.

Nikola taught me men never cried.

I'd never been this vulnerable before.

But Chayanne made me feel accepted.

Loved.

"I'm going to change," I promised, and she sighed but didn't pull away.

Silence surrounded us for a long moment until she spoke. "I'll give you time like you gave me, but I don't want flowers or sex anymore."

"Nuh want yu attitude and stubbornness no more either," I said, and she chuckled while pulling away to swat at my chest.

"I've been doing better." She used her thumb to wipe away the tears drying on my face. "Go to therapy, please?" she asked, and I sighed. "No rush." She looked at her belly. "As long as it's before they get here."

I rubbed her bump. "We need to get you a better doctor."

She looked at me, her brows furrowing. "Why?"

"She just found out we're having twins. She's no good," I said, smiling as I remembered yesterday's appointment.

Despite Chayanne placing a partition in the room because she didn't want to see me, our shared joy was undeniable when we discovered we were having twins. It only lasted a few minutes because she dived headfirst back into her anger, but it was the happiest either of us had been in a long while.

"That happens sometimes. We naa fire her because Plum and Peanut—"

Kick.

My eyes widened, darting to hers. "Did...?" I asked, and she nodded, resting a hand on mine.

One of our babies kicked again, and my smile stretched. This was the first time I felt the kick.

Moving my hand after they stopped kicking, I lowered my head. I kissed both sides of her belly, and she smiled at me, lifting a weight off my heart and mind. This was the first smile she gave me in weeks, and I wanted to see it for a lifetime.

"Mr. Favio—"

"Be quiet," I said, and silence engulfed us. I needed time to gather my thoughts.

Travis, Chezandra, and Zaveer went to Slovenia a few days after I got shot. Chayanne begged me to give them the private jet and sort out Zaveer's passport as an apology. I didn't want to do it, but I did because I somewhat understood that I shouldn't have taken out my frustration on Travis.

A few hours ago, Chayanne went to the airport with Josiah. After they picked them up, she went to visit her wicked red friend in Portland.

I had the house to myself until Romeo and Renata arrived with a sealed gift box from Nikola.

Patrizia's head.

Her skin was sickly green, her eyes gorged from her head, and her hair matted. She was unrecognizable. If it wasn't for her missing lips, I wouldn't have figured out who she was.

"Are people born twisted or are they made that way?" I looked from the severed head to the woman sitting on the other side of the office desk.

She was Chayanne's therapist. She'd been on Nikola's payroll since *Mamma* joined *la famiglia*. Unbeknownst to Chayanne, her first therapist got replaced as a safety precaution.

"Pardon?" Gaia asked.

"I don't know what I'm supposed to say to you, but my lady thinks you will fix me and our relationship, so fix it."

"That's not how this works, Mr. Favio," she said, and I raised a brow. "You talk, and I listen."

Mamma tried getting me into therapy after Antaro snuck me to Italy for my initiation like he did Fabiano, but I never spoke to the woman. I didn't see the need to. I was a Welsh; I was born fucked. What sense did it make talking about something embedded in my DNA? Today and tomorrow, I'd still be the fuck up from yesterday. Time proved that to me.

But Chayanne had hope, and I had faith in her.

Releasing my breath, I looked away from Gaia to Patrizia's head.

Chayanne reminded me of Catherine.

She didn't at first, but now she did.

Her birthday. Weh she learn tha fuck deh?

Patrizia. Who accused someone of infidelity if they weren't guilty of their own?

Why did she have condoms? Where did she get so much energy? Why mi spliff drop so much when mi ina Italy?

She thought I was a fool, like Fabiano and Catherine did. Deciding I wouldn't allow it this time, I nodded my head.

Travis yanked the bag off the man's head, then walked to the wall behind us. He leaned against it, watching us.

Breathing ragged, the man adjusted his eyes to the torture chamber's blinding light. It took a few seconds for them to settle on me, widening. "N-nuh you a—"

"Chayanne's man?" I smiled wickedly as I stepped forward, dragging the axe against the floor and making it screech. A dark chuckle riveted my chest as he fought against the chair's restraints. "Wapn, mi g?"

Tapping the axe on the ground, I eyed the panting man. He impressed me. It'd been two hours, and he was still going strong. What more should I do to him?

I waterboarded him. Broke his fingers. Made him blind in the right eye — which, in all honesty, was his fault. She said he wouldn't leave her alone, so he must be hard of hearing. I didn't see the need for him to have either ear, so I was trying to deafen him, but the idiot turned, making gunpowder fall into his eye.

I didn't do him badly. This was light work. He should be grateful.

Resting the blade of the axe into the crook of his elbow, I asked, "Do you like this arm?"

Dayshawn didn't answer, so I pressed down harder. Blood trickled from his arm, dripping onto the floor. He winced while I smiled. I loved the sight of his blood.

"Yu sick ina yu fucking head!" Dayshawn exclaimed, tears pouring from both his good and bad eyes as he looked at where I had the blade. "Man like you d-doh deserve woman!"

Maybe fucking so, Dayshawn. But I'd be damned before I allowed anyone to take Chayanne from me.

Call me crazy.

Call me obsessed.

Call me a man who was simply in love, with no intention of letting go. Dead or alive. In this life or the next. I breathed and lived for Chayanne. She was mine until I said when.

If those paternity results dared to say the baby wasn't ours... Well, I guessed I'd let her go be the whore she wanted to be.

With a reminder, of course.

I took the axe off his arm. He released a long, uneven breath as I walked away. I grabbed the heated branding iron and walked toward him.

His eyes widened. "P-please."

"Soon get wa yu want, mi g," I taunted, and he sobbed, hanging his head low. I scanned his body, trying to remember where hurt the most out of all my tattoos. His sweaty inner biceps caught my attention, and I grinned. "Travis," I said, and he walked toward us to hold Dayshawn steady.

I pressed the iron against Dayshawn's inner biceps, laughing as his screams filled the room. Joy flooded me the more he squirmed and screamed like a pussy. I didn't pull away until I was sure it scarred beyond his flesh.

Travis released him, and Dayshawn slumped into the chair, panting. Dayshawn looked at his arm, choking on sobs as he stared through a blurry vision at the 'W' permanently engraved into his skin. I watched him for a while, already feeling more at ease.

Minutes passed until I decided to leave the broken man behind. Travis was out of the room already, but I loitered because I wanted to bask in Dayshawn's cries a little longer. What did Chayanne see in this wuss?

Shaking my head after I got my fill, I walked toward the door.

"None a dis naa change seh mi did a fuck yu gyal, pussy!" Dayshawn spat, and I froze at the door, slowly turning my head to look at him.

"You were going to let him live?" Gaia asked, and I nodded. "Why didn't you?"

"I made a promise to her."

"Why kill him if you thought he was the father of the babies? You say you love her; shouldn't you want her to be happy?"

"Only with me."

"That's selfish."

"I don't care. I want to be her happiness because she's mine."

"Will you confront Miss Chayanne about this?" Gaia nodded toward the head.

"No. She's trying to say we're even." I smiled at what was left of Patrizia, and Gaia sighed.

"You and Miss Chayanne bring out the worst in each other," she said, and I tensed, glaring at her. "And the best, too," Gaia added quickly, and I relaxed. "But with all that's happened lately, you both are becoming destructive to each other."

Why did I agree with Chayanne's stupid idea of therapy? Gaia talked too much. Maybe if I still smoked, this would be half as bearable.

"Why did you make that man rape Zip?" Gaia asked seconds later.

"Exodus twenty-one verse twenty-three."

She took out her phone. After a few taps, she sighed. "I didn't know you're religious."

"Used to be. That's why I know there isn't any salvation for me. But Chayanne thinks I can change, and I want to change for her and our children."

Gaia smiled. "You have a long road ahead of you. I can see you want to let go of the baggage *la famiglia* gave you, but you're still holding yourself back. Recovery doesn't happen overnight. Are you ready to work through your struggle with vulnerability and fear of commitment, Mr. Favio?"

Chapter Seventy-Five

CHAYANNE

Yolo visit fi help with house shopping fi Chezzy. Wi just come from Ochi and go pick up Zaveer from Aunty.

"Like how yaa abstain, yago look a man?" Eltham ask from the driver's seat.

Yolo gagged. "Ew, no! And mi stop abstain."

"Jah know," Zaveer seh, and everybody laugh.

"Cya believe Trav a rub off pon yu crotchfruit already." Yolo tek the blue sweetie outta her mouth fi scowl at Zaveer.

Smiling, Chezzy look round pon we. "Gweh nuh! Him just interested ina yu bag cause it have banana print all over it."

"Him cya see ina this ya bag ya." Yolo hold the backpack close to her chest. She a spend few day wid me. All of her other bags ina the trunk while she hang on pon tha one ya.

Chezzy roll her eyes as Eltham park ina the yard. We enter the house, and Chezzy hand Zaveer him educational toys. Voices drift from the kitchen, and mi smile.

"Unu come meet Favi cousin dem! Dem come yesterday." Mi hold my girls' hands, tugging them toward the kitchen. The twins come visit dem Uncle, but dem say dem naa stay in Jamaica fi long. Entering the kitchen, mi smile widen at Favi, who laugh at sum Romeo say. "Evening," mi seh, and dem stop laugh as dem gaze settle pon me. "Romeo and Renata, these are my friends, Chezandra and Yolanda." Mi point pon the two a dem, pausing at Yolo, who wide-eyed while staring at Ren.

Not in a regular way.

Her face brightened. Her eyes dilated. Her mouth gaped, causing the sweetie to fall out of her mouth.

A tiny smirk crawl pon Ren face. "Nice to meet you," she say ina her thick accent, and Yolo gulp.

"Look how yaa nasty up mi floor!" Mi bend fi take up the sweetie while Chezzy greet dem.

Smaddy approach mi from behind. Mi know a Favi before mi see him.

Favi lay a hand pon mi lower back, stopping me. Him lead me to a chair. "Sit and stop stressing yourself," he ordered, and mi nod as him walk weh fi pick up the sweetie, then throw it away.

Since yesterday, him a act a way. Mi know him get mi likkle gift. Mi did a expect him fi nyam off mi head, but him nuh angry. Him deevn seh nun to me about it, and it a worry mi. If mi neva pregnant, mi crochiz wuda tear out by now.

"Chichi, Mommy seh yu leff yu phone a her yard," Chezzy seh, and mi hear a loud exhale.

"Sorry..." Mi avoid Favi's gaze cause mi nuh waa see if him angry.

"No worries. Me and Yolanda will go fi it." Chezzy pulled Yolo's hand.

Yolo yanked her hand free, adjusting the bag over her shoulder. "You gwan. Me we stay with the baby because I *love* them—"

Chezzy kiss her teeth, grabbing Yolo and pulling her outta the kitchen. Romeo whistle before him seh sum to Ren ina Sicilian. Ren chuckled, glancing toward the kitchen's exit.

Favi walk toward mi, sitting on the chair beside me. Him kiss mi forehead and belly. "*Stai bene?*"

"Yes," mi seh.

"I'm going to Kingston with the twins," him seh, and mi nod.

"Yu alright?" mi ask, and him nod while smiling. "Alright..." Mi a go ask Salvatore fi keep a closer eye pon mi. Mi feel like Favi a plan fi kill mi.

"*Bella*, when we come back from Uncle, where will you bring us?" Romeo ask ina Italian.

"A river," mi blurt, glancing pon Favi.

"Good. Favio seems too busy for us," Romeo seh, and Favi kiss him teeth before pulling out him phone. "I'm so excited to be here! It's my second time visiting Jamaica, and the locals are so nice. Especially the ones at the airport."

Mi raise a brow. "Nice how?"

"A woman said I'm a baddy boi," Romeo seh, and mi gasp while Favi snicker.

"Why did she call you that?"

"She thinks I'm handsome! And my new cologne is a real panty-dropper." He grinned. "But she probably thought I had a girlfriend because I held Ren's handbag when she ran back to the baggage claim. Maybe that's why the woman walked away when I asked for her number."

Mi glare pon Favi while him buss out a laugh, making Romeo's brows furrow. Looking at Romeo, mi smile. "I'll teach you some Patois while you're here," mi seh, and him nod.

We spend the next couple of minutes a mek plans, and Favi caress mi belly the wul time. The baby dem eva active once him close by. When him learn seh it nuh hurt me when dem move, him nuh stop feel me up. Mi nuh see Favi this excited in a long while. Matter a fact, mi neva see him dis excited bout anything before.

Mi naa complain, though. Mi happy him stop treat mi bad. If mi nehna breed and waa him round mi every second, mi wuda keep up the pettiness so him can feel how him did mek mi feel.

Trav kiss him teeth, and mi lean offa Favi shoulder fi look pon him. "Chez, yafi tell Mrs. Simone yaa yu own big woman now... Ah." Him end the call.

"A wa?" mi ask as Trav sidung ina the chair across from me and Favi.

"Mi come here cause she seh shi deh yaso. Now she seh her mother a go somewhere and need her fi watch her brother dem," Trav seh.

"Oh, that's why dem tek so long fi come back. Mi think a did yu friend yu come look fa," mi seh, and Trav and Favi scoff, making me chuckle. Dem have a strange friendship, but mi love it.

Few hours later, night fell. Everybody ina dem room, and Trav and Chezzy leff a few minutes ago. Trav get called to the studio, but him a go drop Chezzy home first. She nuh want Zaveer at the studio round the drinking and smoking, even though him a sleep.

"I'll be here when you wake up," Favi seh as mi lay in bed.

"I know, but why unu a go so late? A eleven and unu naa leave until two. Everything good?" mi ask, and him nod as him phone ring.

"I have to take this."

Mi sigh as him go pon the balcony, closing the door behind him. Him naa come back fi now, so mi a go downstairs fi a snack. These babies mek mi belly nav no bottom. Mi neva use to eat this much before.

Taking time to get out of bed, mi exit the room and walk toward the stairs. Seeing Yolo sneak into Ren room with her bag pon her back, mi chuckle. Shi nuh see me, so mi continue downstairs.

Today was New Year's Eve, and mi a spend it with mi family.

Mi father come offa him undercover case, so mi did have breakfast with him. Wi cudn go wi usual dinners cause mi already mek plans with the twins. Earlier this afternoon, mi carry dem go waa river ina St. Mary. At one point, Ren did afi go to the car fi sum. She carry Yolo with her. When dem come back, Yolo red like tomato juice and have waa scarf round ar neck, even ina the water. Even now, as we deh dinner, she still red.

"Aww." Mi smile at Yolo, who a sit across the table, struggling fi look pon Ren.

"Wicked red gyal," Favio mutter from beside mi, and mi roll mi eyes. Him sigh. "Yu still vex?"

"Yes." Mi cross mi arms atop mi belly.

Him move mi arms. "Stop putting pressure on their heads."

Mi kiss mi teeth, cupping below mi belly as mi look at Romeo. Fi a Christian, Romeo likkle and love sex. Ina the short time him deh ya, him carry five girl come Favio yaad. Based pon how him a eye the server, sum a go give tonight.

"*Ti amo*." Favio lean over fi kiss mi cheek, and mi shrug him off.

"But you wouldn't love me if I were a cow," mi seh, and him sigh before saying him a go the restroom. Mi cya stand him and him big foot! Imagine, afta mi ask if him would love me even if me a waa cow, him seh 'No.'

Tears come to mi eyes, and mi exhale a breath as mi wipe dem away, looking at Trav and Chezzy. Dem a smile and laugh with each other. Dem compliment each other well, and mi cya wait fi see wa the future hold fi dem! "Unu nafi live ina each other skin," I teased, hoping Chezzy memba shi a follow me to the boudoir photoshoot tomorrow.

Chezzy glared playfully. "Mek mi get a deserving love too, nuh."

"Know how long she a wait fi this?" Trav ask, making Chezzy blush.

"Jah know," Zaveer seh, and Trav snicker.

"I'll be back." Ren ran a finger through her hair before standing. She looked at her phone while walking away.

Mi assume Ren a check social media fi the latest pon her friend. Patrizia's publicist reported her missing a few days ago. Apparently, she went to a silent mediation retreat and didn't show up for her return flight.

Yolo sat on Favi's chair. "Me sick?" She grabbed my hand, making me feel her forehead and neck.

"No. Awa?" Mi pull mi hand away, resting it atop my belly.

"Renata obea me! A must waa fake river we go!" Yolo shrieked.

"Yu like her, and that normal—"

"No. This nuh normal! Remember this morning when yu find me a hide ina yu closet and a read the Bible? A cause last night she grip me ina me neck, then seh me fi stop play wid her," Yolo whispered loudly.

"Being controlling deh ina the Welsh dem DNA. A did wa yu do?"

"Block her cause a time fi me explore new pussy."

"Meet yu match." Mi laugh, and Yolo sigh.

"Me can tell yu sum else?" she ask, and mi nod. "Remember the strap me show yu? She use it pon me. Me traumatize bad, me naa lie— Sas Crise! Nuh she dat a come? Me gone back ova deso."

Mi furrow my brows. "Weh yaa run fa?"

"She has me wearing a vibrator," Yolo whisper, and mi eyes widen.

"*Fiore*," Favio seh from behind me, and mi look pon him. Him hold him hand out, and mi roll mi eyes as him help mi stand.

"The firework show is about to start?" mi ask as him lead we outta the restaurant.

"*Sì*," him seh, walking past the people gathered on the beach, while waiting for the fifteen-minute countdown. Him lead we to a quieter part of the beach while the waves crashed on the sand, filling the air with a salty aroma.

Mi smile at the twinkling stars. "The sky's so pretty tonight."

"It is," him seh, and mi chuckle.

"Of course, you wuda say that. A yu favorite thing fi look pon."

"Second favorite," he said, and mi brows furrow as mi look pon him.

"What's your favorite?"

"I'm looking at her," he said, and mi blush, giddy-headed while laying mi head pon him arm.

Ahead, lights flickered in the sand. My eyes narrowed, trying to see better. Realizing what it was, I gasped, my hand slipping out of his to cup my mouth.

'Will you marry me?' was spelled into the sand with tens of white paper lanterns.

"Fa—" Mi look beside me, and mi brows raise.

Favio's down on one knee, staring at me through bright eyes. He gulped hard while holding a closed, black velvet box in his hand. "Chayanne—" He paused, shaking his head. "*Cazzo*, I forgot what I wanted to say."

I laughed, wiping tears from my eyes. My heart raced. Was this real?!

Favio took a sheet of paper out of his pocket, then decided against unfolding it. He slipped it into his pocket, looking at me while he cleared his throat and smiled. "Months ago, I wrote the perfect words to say to you, but I don't want to say those now. I want to go with the flow, so let me do the talking this time," he said, and I glared playfully.

"Chayanne, sometimes I wonder if yu head screw on properly fi deal with a man like me. Whatever it is, I'm happy you put up with me. Happy me have the strength fi put up wid yu on a daily too, cause yu miserableness wuda mad off anybody else long time," he said, and mi chuckle.

He continued speaking. "*Fiore*, I love you more than words can explain, and I love you more than I thought I could be capable of. I love your face and soul. I love how you love me, even when I don't deserve it.

"You make me a better person, and I want to do the same for you and our kids. I'm doing that therapy thing you told me about, and it's... *going*. Dem send yu fi mad mi, but mi nuh want it no other way. I want us to rough out this life together." He opened the box, revealing a gold rose-shaped ring. It glistened beneath the moonlight.

"Can see how yaa swell with unsaid words. Wait nuh," he joked, and I bit into my cheeks, bouncing on my feet. "*Fiore mio*, will you marry me?"

The answer was on the tip of my tongue, but I said something else instead. "Would you still love me if I were a cow?"

Favio heaved a loud breath. "*Sì*, Chayanne. I'd love you if you were a cow. I'd buy you an island so you have grass to eat for the rest of your life."

"Yes!" I answered, holding my hand out.

He chuckled as he took my hand in his, sliding the ring on. It fitted perfectly. *Every ho have him stick a bush.*

He stood, pulling me into a kiss that took my breath away, then breathed life into me. Fireworks erupted in the distance, and we smiled into the kiss.

"Thank you," Favi murmured against my lips, and I pulled away, cupping his face in my hands.

"Favi, don't thank me. You deserve love, and you have all of mine."

Chapter Seventy-Six

FAVIO

"*If she complain to mi bout yu, mi a lock yu up and keep yu far from them,*" *Elder warned, and I scoffed. He'd been fuming since I told him Chayanne was pregnant, but I didn't care.*

Glancing at the men carrying new torture devices into the building, I smirked. The Italians and Blood Paw were on their way with Zip, so I'd have my fun soon. I took the last drag from my spliff, tossing the tail into the nearby bush. I'd have to quit again. "I'm doing my part. Make sure you do yours."

"I'll handle it," Elder promised, and I nodded, foolish to believe him.

Months later, I got a call from him, proving to me why people were incompetent.

"Wa the fuck yu just seh, Elder?" I hissed into the line, and the fucking Pig cleared his throat.

"Fisha is out of prison," he repeated, and I closed my eyes, inhaling a deep breath.

Uno.

Due.

Tre.

Exhaling, I opened my eyes and hung up. It made no sense to stay on the call. He'd piss me off more. I knew this fucking day would come, but I made a promise to Elder. He assured me Fisha would remain imprisoned, so why did Fisha's lawyer get the sentencing overturned because of a biased jury?

Tapping my finger against the wooden table, I looked at the ring around my finger. It'd been three weeks since our engagement, and Chayanne got me this ring. I wasn't one for material things; I was used to it all. A ring couldn't amount to all the love I had for her, but I wore it with pride because it made her happy.

I loved keeping Chayanne happy, but I couldn't keep her happy with this storm brewing.

"*Figlio*," Antaro said, and I looked at him.

We were in his office, waiting for a call from Nikola, Luca, and Alessio. Romeo sat beside me, and Fabiano stood behind Antaro's chair.

I was clueless as to why he wouldn't sit. He wasn't making my life miserable, so I had no desire to kill him. I never kept track of him, but *Mamma* always told me about him when I visited her. Catherine knew there was no way out of *la famiglia* except death, so she gave their relationship another shot. They had a house close to mine, but I didn't care. Wherever Chayanne and our kids were, that would be my home.

"That girl is making you sloppy," Antaro hissed in Italian.

"That *woman* is my fiancée and mother of your grandkids," I said in Italian, and Fabiano's eyes widened.

"Congratulations," Fabiano said, grinning after I nodded.

"Okay, let me rephrase. She's making you soft. If you'd killed Fisha when you had the chance, we wouldn't be waiting for retaliation," Antaro said, and I slid down the chair, looking at the ceiling.

Damned if I did.

Damned if I didn't.

What more did life want from me?

"I don't get why we're worrying about Fisha. He can't go against us and our allies—" Fabiano started, but Romeo interrupted.

"Fisha has an old friend in the Mexican cartel, and they have almost as much power and allies as we do. We're not worried about killing Fisha, we're worried about him sending for protection *before* we get to kill him. Nikola is trying to avoid a war," Romeo said, and I rubbed my temple.

Why the fuck did I agree with Elder's idea? He didn't even get the fucking promotion.

"Rush, too," Antaro added, his gaze snapping to the ringing phone.

Fucking finally.

I walked toward the living room, pausing when I saw Chayanne. Her feet were stretched on the sofa while she ate from the plate resting on her belly. *Mamma* was watching the television on another sofa. Renata lay on the floor, smiling at her phone. I didn't have to guess if she was talking to that wicked red gyal. Nav a clue why the red demon a gwan like she nice.

I sat beside Chayanne, resting her legs across my lap before taking the plate off her belly. I tried taking a bite-sized pizza roll, and she gasped. Yanking the plate from me, she rested it on her other side, out of my reach.

My brow raised. "Yago mek yu man starve?"

She nodded. "Yes."

"Food is in the kitchen, Favio. Help yourself," *Mamma* chimed in.

"You're going to make your son starve?" I asked, massaging Chayanne's swollen feet.

"I have to side with my daughter-in-law. She's eating for three. The only thing you're feeding is your ego," *Mamma* said, and Chayanne nodded while putting three pizza rolls into her mouth.

Glaring at my lady, I considered telling her that a long time she craven. Deciding against it, I looked at *Mamma*. I loved that she and Chayanne were getting along better since I got shot, but I hated that they always teamed up against me. "I'm your washbelly, Diana."

"*Diana?*" Scowling, *Mamma* grabbed at her feet, then she hissed her teeth. "Yu lucky mi nav mi slippers."

"See mi sneakers ya, *Mamma*," Fabiano said from the threshold. He rested a hand on Romeo's shoulder, reaching for his shoe.

Waving a hand, *Mamma* pinched her nose with the other. "Nuh tek off yu shoes and cheesy up the house," *Mamma* said, and I chuckled.

"Nuh you want sum fi slap him?" Fabiano asked, glancing at Antaro, who entered the living room with Catherine by his side.

"Go suck yu madda if yu waa sum fi do. Nuh know weh unu get dem big foot deh from," *Mamma* said, and Chayanne burst out laughing.

"I don't know where we got them, but I know why we have them," Antaro said, making the women — except Renata — blush.

"Stop it, *amore mio*," *Mamma* said, and Antaro chuckled as he sat beside her, kissing her cheek.

"Disgusting," Fabiano muttered in Italian as he and Catherine sat on another sofa.

Rajay returned from the bathroom a few minutes later, sitting between his parents. *La famiglia* chatted and laughed for the next few hours. Most of my focus was on Chayanne. I liked that she was laughing now. She wouldn't be laughing in the next few hours.

Anxiety gnawed at me until we were in bed that night.

Chayanne had her head on my chest, and my arm was around her shoulder. She flicked my nipple, and I slapped her hand away.

"*Chayanne,*" I hissed.

She giggled. "Why yu nuh like when mi feel yu up?"

"Yaa battyman?" I asked, and she huffed, making me smirk. The smirk faded seconds later, and I sighed. "I have something to tell you."

She leaned off me, her brows furrowing. "Why that sound so?" she asked, and I explained everything. Tears sprang to her eyes, and she moved to sit at the side of the bed.

Sighing, I moved to kneel before her. I wiped away her tears, but more replaced them. My shoulders sagged as I took her hand in mine, laying it on the curve of her belly. Our babies had already gone through so much. But Chayanne was strong, so they were still healthy.

"You have to be strong for them, *fiore*..." I murmured.

"How yu expect mi fi stay strong, Favio?! Yu sound like yaa plan fi dead!" she sobbed.

It was hard to remain strong as her words ripped through my defense, obliterating it into shreds and leaving me with an untreatable open wound. One that hurt more than hers did. "I don't plan on dying. How mi fi dead when mi nuh give yu the wedding yu start plan?" I asked, and she chuckled sadly.

"Stop mek mi laugh."

"I want to see you smiling," I said, and she dried her tears to look at me. "If everything goes well, it'll just be for a few days."

"See how far yu gone already? Yu carry wi come a Kingston so it easier fi the guards protect *la famiglia*, when mi think wi did come look fi yu parents. Now yaa tell mi seh unu a go pon a manhunt tonight, and if yu nuh come back by twelve, me afi go Italy."

"Do you trust—" I smirked as she nodded. "Yu love yu man ino."

"I don't love you right now. Mi hate you and yu big foot." She moved out of my hold and lay on the bed, facing away from me. "And yu nuh waa mi tell Chezzy seh me a leave. Mi nuh like this."

Sighing, I settled myself behind her and threw my arm over her waist below the bump. A baby kicked, and I grazed them with my thumb.

She laid her hand atop mine, stilling my actions. "I don't like this, Favio."

I didn't either, but I had to do this.

My brother, father, and I came together for the first time in years. We were cunning in our ways; I believed we could get the job done. Nikola had contacts in Mexico, who were ready to intercept Fisha's message. Travis and Josiah were with the Italians and Rush at the Brown's Town bunker, digitally searching high and low while others scoured the streets.

Jamaica would burn before Fisha lived long enough to tell the tale.

I kissed Chayanne's shoulder. "*Fiore*, you have to be strong for the babies, okay?" I asked, and she nodded slowly.

She turned to face me, taking my face into her hands, and kissing me with trembling lips.

I didn't mind the saltiness of the kiss.

Or how she fucked me back when I moved between her legs.

Tonight might be our last night.

Yet only two words were on the tip of my tongue while I made love to her body like it was the first time: "I'm sorry."

Chapter Seventy-Seven

CHAYANNE

The clock hit twelve.

"We have to leave now," Salvatore stated.

Ignoring him, mi remain frozen ina the same spot mi ina fi the past hours. Mi a wait fi Favi burst through the doors and engulf me in a hug. Him sex mi so good, and we move to the bathtub fi do it again. We talk and play like children, and him mek mi laugh until mi pee miself.

Then he had to leave.

Renata try distract me by making me knit clothes for the babies like I'd been doing since me get back pon good terms with Aunty, but it nehna work. I begged her to leave me alone and go talk to Yolanda, and she did.

I was thankful for the space.

As much space as mi cuda get with Salvatore a breathe dung mi neck. Swallowing a lump, mi look pon Salvatore. His face was a blank slate, like it always was.

"We can wait five more minutes?" mi beg.

Salvatore shook his head, offering a hand to me. "I was given orders."

You have to be strong for them, fiore.

Ignoring Salvatore's hand, mi lay mi hand pon the table beside the sofa, pushing myself to stand. Mi exhale a big breath as mi straighten miself. Mi grab

Marshmallow, who was sleeping on the sofa. Holding her close to mi chest, mi exit the house with Salvatore trailing behind me. Mi enter the armored vehicle, keeping my gaze straight as we drive outta Cherry Gardens.

I barely registered when we arrived at the airport.

Boarded the plane.

Took off.

My heart ached with every mile placed between me and Favi.

Kitania stood beside my seat. "Mrs. Welsh, Mr. Welsh said to give this to you if he never made it—"

"I don't want it," I said.

"I'll keep it for her," Salvatore said.

Favi was fine. He would join me in Italy soon. He promised.

The first thing me wuda do a cuss him fi scare me like that. Then, mi wuda cry. Why Favi love gwan invincible?

Hours later, we landed. Salvatore drove me to Favi's house, and mi mek miself comfortable ina the bed.

Favi would be here soon.

Any minute now...

Any minute turned into one day.

Two.

Three.

A week.

I stopped counting.

I wasn't sure how much time passed, but I kept the faith every day. Favi told me to stay strong, and I'd do that for them and him.

A loud screech jarred me from my thoughts, and I looked in that direction. "What's happening?" I asked Salvatore, my voice raspy.

Staring at the wall before him, he replied, "Patrizia Moretti's presumed dead. They found a suicide letter in her belongings."

"Oh..." I said, and Salvatore glanced at me before looking ahead.

I needed to go to the funeral to support Renata.

My tears would be believable.

"The doctor said your pressure is too high. Please take it easy," Ren begged, and I shrugged her hand off my shoulder.

I couldn't take it easy.

Tomorrow was Favi's birthday.

He'd be here soon, and I wanted him to have a special day for once.

Ren sighed. "Please drink some water, *bella*..."

Looking away from the laptop mi buy last week, mi glance at Ren. "Do you think I should get this watch or the other one? I like the gold one, but I'm leaning toward—"

Ren sighed, reaching over to close the laptop's screen. "Water. Please."

Mi take the bottle from her. Mi drink a few sips and forced a smile. "Happy?"

"Somewhat. Take a break." She rested a sealed envelope atop the laptop. "I hate seeing you like this every day. I know he's not able to talk to you right now, so please read this."

Looking at the envelope, mi heart skip a beat. The handwriting on it was neat, and it said 'FIORE'. Mi always envy him penmanship. Why him write so nice when mine look like chicken scratch? Sighing, I gave in. "Okay."

Ren smiled, hopping off the stool. She squeeze mi shoulder, walking away while pulling out her phone.

I looked at Salvatore, who stood close by. "Can I get some space?"

He nodded, exiting the room. I knew he was standing on the other side of the wall, but I didn't let it bother me. He was used to my constant breakdowns.

Looking at the envelope made unease fill my being. Reading it felt final, and Favi nuh dead. If he was, they would've told me, right?

My throat tightened as I used my shaking fingers to break the envelope's seal and unfold the letter.

Fiore mio,

Before you close the letter without reading the rest, consider the possibility I won't make it back to you. Anything can happen. And if it does, know I tried my hardest to return to you, Plum, and Peanut.

I don't want this to be one of those sappy letters I've written to you before. This one is for the future. I know we agreed to be surprised, but I'd been thinking of names because I feel we'll have a daughter and a son.

For our daughter — Mikeila. She'll be a fighter like your mother was. And no fucking boyfriends until she's 26, Chayanne, I swear. I don't care if you have to lock her in the house until she gets house color. Mi seh wa mi seh and done talk.

For our son — Malakei. Or whatever you want to name him. Except Favio. I won't stand for my son being a junior.

And for you, my beautiful wife, who I had for a moment. I don't want you to grieve me forever. You have to pick yourself up and move on with your life.

Mi naa seh yufi go look next man, but if a so, a so. Ano like mi can fuck him up this time. Still, if you ever find love after me, the bwoy a pussy and I will try to kill him from hell.

Scratch dat, cause mi neevn waa nuh next man round wi youth dem, Chayanne. So might as well yu use one a the hundred toy dem yu wicked red friend gi yu. No other man can fuck and love you like me.

I wish I could've told you one last time, but I can't, so this letter has to suffice. I love you forever, Mrs. Welsh. You're the best thing to happen to me, and I hope I was the same to you.

Before I end this awfully long letter, it's funny, isn't it? I probably couldn't say all of this to you in person.

But what can I say? I'm a Welsh. Nothing but a natural fuck-up. I tried working on it for you, though.

Yours forever,
Favi.

By the end of the letter, the paper damp with tears and mi a smile like crazy.

"Mi cya stand yu, Favi," mi whisper to the quiet room. Holding the paper to my chest, mi smile widen. "I know you're coming back. Thanks, I needed this."

With newfound energy, mi return to mi room. Mi place the letter on my nightstand beside a rose bouquet. Since I came to Italy, mi get rose deliveries every day. The notes nuh personal or handwritten, dem randomly chosen by the florist.

Mi caress mi belly as a baby kicked. "Daddy will be home soon, then you can start kicking him for real." Exiting the room, mi ignore Salvatore, who posted by the door. Mi get used to him, sometimes it feel like him deevn deh here. Mi find Marshy, put her pon her leash, then go outside.

The air was crisp, reminding me of home. The sun was bright, and I basked in it. There were no birds in the sky, but I could hear the tiny critters in the flower bushes. While I yearned for the lively chaos of domino games and the menacing growls of mongrels, this tranquil environment was solace from the anguish I'd been in.

Sitting at the gazebo, I took Marshy off the leash. I looked at Salvatore while she ran away. "Do you have a girlfriend?"

"No. I protect you," he stated, glancing around the garden in Favi's backyard. Ludovica tended to it whenever Favi was in Jamaica. If Aunty Simone see this garden, she'd never leave.

"I'm sorry..."

"I'm doing my job."

Nodding, I looked at Marshy, who was rolling in the dirt. Cho, blousecup! Look how she dirty up! Is a good thing Favi nuh deh here cause him wuda cuss seh him nuh want nuh dutty dog ina him house. Him nav no behavior, and mi never disrespect him snake dem before.

"Salvatore, remind me to fire the caretaker I hired for Favi's snakes. I want to take care of them until he's back," I said, and he nodded. Mi change the topic, telling him seh mago try focus back pon school cause Aunty wuda mad out if she know mi put man over mi book.

Salvatore answered vaguely, but it did nice having a long conversation again.

Hours later, mi ina mi bed, thinking of what else mi can do fi Favi birthday.

Mago mek wi visit a lock bridge; the locks would be symbolic of our relationship and that mi got him forever. Mi cya wait until him come home! If mi neva heavily pregnant, mi wuda practice a new position fi buss pon him. To how long mi nuh sex, mi goodly come when him a remove mi panties.

Mi phone ring, and mi grab it. "Hi, Chezzy!" mi seh with a big smile even though she cya see mi. A long time mi nuh talk to her cause mi did too depressed.

"Chichi!" she cry, and mi stop hug mi pregnancy pillow, sitting up with a huff.

"Wa happen?" mi ask, prepared to put a hit on big head Lamar if a him a mek her cry.

"D-did a go fi mi bredda dem, a-and—" She choked on a loud sob, making my heart thrum wildly.

"Chezzy, talk straight, please," I begged.

"T-them seh pon the n-news that the owner of Welsh's d-dead."

I stopped breathing.

My phone fell from my hand.

The hair rose on my skin and tears blurred my vision.

Dead? Wa Chezzy mean by dead?

I grabbed my sleep shirt, tugging it away from my chest.

It was hard to breathe.

Feel.

See.

I didn't feel alive.

Yet I could still hear Chezzy's distant voice.

"Bus park... Town... To you," she said.

Salvatore must have heard my labored breathing because he rushed into the room. He sat on the edge of the bed, moving a bottle of water to my mouth, but I forced it away while hyperventilating.

"Fav... Favi," I forced out, and Salvatore stared blankly. How could he be so emotionless at a time like this?! I grabbed my phone and tossed it into the wall, shattering it and ending Chezzy's inaudible rant. "Get out!" I screamed, and Salvatore nodded, then left.

Dead?

Dead?!

Dead...

I collapsed onto the bed, clutching at my belly while sobbing loudly. "You said you'd come back to us," I cried into the sheets.

I stayed there for hours, bawling my eyes out. No one checked on me, not that I expected them to. They were used to my crying and knew I'd need time. I bit into my lips, snapping my swollen eyes shut.

I shouldn't have.

Gut-wrenching images flashed in my mind, filled with all the horrible ways Favi could've died.

Alone.

While I was miles away and unable to help him.

Did he die in pain like Asia? Or did he die peacefully like Mommy?

"Why does everyone around me die?" I cried, drifting into a slumber I didn't want to wake from.

A knock on the door snapped me out of it. My eyes were puffy, my throat aching and raw. I didn't have the strength to tell anyone to go away.

The bed dipped, and I tensed as hands pulled me against a hard chest, rubbing my arms and trailing kisses along the skin. I shivered beneath the touch, hair rising as a signature cologne filled my senses.

I was a pathetic mess.

One glance at the clock hanging on the wall made me know it'd barely been an hour since the news, yet I was already hallucinating my deceased fiancé. I sighed, making myself smaller in his hold. Even if I was becoming delusional, it was serene being in his arms again.

The figment of my imagination held me closer, and I smiled as he brushed my hair back. He kissed my temple before his voice came into my ear. "*Fiore.*"

Chapter Seventy-Eight

CHAYANNE

I screamed, tightening my grip on his hand.

"Relax," Favi said comfortingly, and mi nails dig further into his palm.

"Doh tell mi fi relax! Ano your vagina a tear out!" mi scream, and the nurse give him an apologetic smile. Groaning, mi toss mi head onto the pillow. We were in the makeshift hospital room Ren made, per Favi's request. "Get them out!"

"We need you to be more dilated," said the doctor Favi had on standby since I came to Italy.

Groaning, mi look at Favi. Apparently, mi mishear wa Chezzy seh...

Antaro a the one weh get shot days ago, but him neva dead. *La famiglia* made it seem worse than it was cause dem cya find Fisha. Fisha resourceful, so him hold him own without Mexico's help.

Favi was determined to be here for the baby's arrival next week, so him tell *la famiglia* fi pull back. Fisha a go get comfortable, then dem a go find him and kill him. Favi neva tell mi the full plan cause him neva waa get mi hopes up. Ren neva tell mi Favi on him way since yesterday cause she did waa surprise mi.

Goal accomplished. Mi send miself ina labor.

Another contraction hit me, and mi squeeze Favi hand tighter. "You're not getting another one," I said, and him chuckle, staring at me in adoration. "Talk to me, please." Mi wince as another pain shoot through me. Mi a start fi regret not getting the epidural. Why mi so nuff bout mi waa do this naturally? Mi a go stop mek Mama boost mi up!

Rat ketch ina trap, him part wid him tail.

"I can't wait to marry you," he said, and mi smile through the pain, about fi ansa when the doctor stand from the chair at the end of the bed.

"They're coming now! You need to push! Breathe with me, okay?" she said in her thick accent, and I nodded.

Breathing with the doctor, I pushed. The pain was immense, but Favi being here made it somewhat manageable. Still holding my hand, Favi move closer to where my feet were propped up. Him look between mi legs as a head press against mi opening, and him eyes widen.

"Give me a big one this time," instructed the doctor, and I followed suit, exhaling a long breath as the baby's upper body popped out.

"Mi bl—" Favi's grip on my hand loosened and he fell to the floor, bringing down the surgical tray with him.

Mi gasp and stop push fi look pon Favi as the instruments clatter around and on his body, weh sprawl out pon the floor. Him eyes shut, yet him still looked traumatized. A nurse kneeled beside Favi, tending to him. The other nurses hurried to sterilize new instruments in case the doctor needed them.

"Miss Bailey," the doctor said, and mi look away from Favi.

Ren, who was recording from the corner of the room, gave the camera to a nurse. She stood beside the bed, offering me her hand. I smiled, laying my hand in hers and squeezing tightly. She winced, but she withstood the pain as I brought two sweet joys into the world minutes after the other.

"Favi," I croaked, and him look from the small bundles resting on either arm to smile at me.

"Be careful," him seh as mi sit up and press mi back against the headboad. Him stand from the chair and walk toward me. Carefully, him transfer a baby into my arm, then sit beside me.

Tears fill mi eyes as mi smile at the sleeping face. Favi sat beside me, and my smile widened when I looked at the other sleeping bundle. A tear rolled down my cheek, falling on our baby's forehead. I wiped it away gently.

"How are you feeling?" Favi asked, and mi drag mi eyes from the baby I held to look at him.

"Can you kiss me?" I asked, and him chuckle before leaning in fi kiss mi lips, nose, and forehead. Mi beam at him as him pull away. "This doesn't feel real."

"What part?" he asked, looking at the baby in my arm, who yawned.

"All of it. You got your daughters, but who's who?"

"I was waiting for you to name them," he whispered, and my brows furrowed. "You passed out after you breastfed them."

"At least mi neva faint when them a born," mi whisper, and him look away, making me chuckle. "I think we should name Plum, Mikeila. She's the bigger one, right?" mi ask, looking at the baby I held.

"*Sì*. She's the oldest, too," he said, looking at the one in his arm while telling me to name her.

"Mikayla."

He smiled. "They're perfect."

"Like you." I scooted closer, laying my head on his shoulder.

"I'm not perfect, Chayanne. Mi life feel like an action-packed movie more while. Nothing I do is good enough, no matter how hard I try," he confessed, breaking my heart.

I leaned off him, placing a gentle kiss on his cheek. "You're trying your best, and that's good enough for me and them. You've become a better man, but your imperfections make you. I love you for you. Flaws, big foot, and all."

"You got a One in English?" Favi joked.

"Yes. Gweh." Chuckling, I laid my head on his shoulder. The clock on the wall catch mi attention, and mi eyes widen. Mi almost jump up, then mi memba the babies, so mi relax miself. "Happy birthday, Favi!" I whispered as loudly as I could, and he chuckled.

"*Grazie.*"

"Mi deevn get fi give yu nun a yu gifts!" mi complain, pouting.

He stared at our daughters, a smile gracing his handsome face. His cheek had a faint red mark from where a speculum hit him. "No gift is better than our kids."

It was six thirty p.m., and I was anxious. I was getting married! We would've gotten married sooner, but I wanted to lose the baby weight first. It took seven months to go away, but we were finally here.

"Sas Crise," mi curse, fanning mi face.

The door knock, and mi almost jump outta mi skin.

"*Fiore?*" came the voice from the other side of the door, and mi groan.

"Favi! Mama seh it's bad luck for us to see each other before the wedding!" mi hiss, and him kiss him teeth.

"I'm not letting a myth stop me from seeing my wife."

"Fine! Close yu eyes and come in backward."

I closed my eyes as the door opened. I walked in a straight line until I bumped into him, turning and pressing my back against his before opening my eyes. Our hands found each other, our fingers intertwining.

Favi chuckled. "You're sweating, *fiore.*"

"Really?" I fought the urge to release his hand and wipe it against my dress.

"*Sì.* How are you?" he asked in Italian.

"*Sto bene, e tu?*"

"Happy. I get to marry you," he said in English, and I smiled.

"I'm happy I get to marry you, too," I said, and he squeezed my hands. "Have you checked on the girls?"

"Ludovica and Renata are taking good care of them. The red one didn't want to help," he said, and tension left my shoulders.

Fi the next few minutes, we talk and laugh with each other, washing away all

500

the nerves.

Until Chezzy show up.

"Unu stubborn alike!" Chezzy curse, and mi chuckle. She sound like she a go burst a blood vessel. "Favio, leave. Yu crownie dem a look fi yu." Chezzy pry Favi's hand from mine, shoving him outta the room. She closed the door, and I turned to see her big smile while she walked toward me. "You look beautiful, Chichi."

My smile widened as she laced our hands. "Thank you, Chezzy," mi seh, and she smile.

"Al will be here for you soon. I'll meet you at the end of the aisle."

"Sounds like you plan to marry me."

"I married you first, remember?" she asked, and I laughed at the almost-forgotten memory.

When we were seven, Chezzy tied a long grass strand into a circle and slipped it on my finger. She said we were married and mi afi love her forever even when she get pon mi nerves.

A knock came on the door, and Chezzy tell them fi come in. Al entered while Chezzy excused herself.

"*Wow*," Al said in awe, and I blushed. "Do a spin mek mi see yu."

I spun in my lacy, white two-piece wedding dress, getting tangled in the train. Al chuckled while untangling me. "I wish Mikeila was here to see you."

I smiled sadly. "Me, too."

He eased my anxiety with casual conversation and at seven p.m., he led me to the aisle. I smiled at the arrangements Diana helped me to make. Along the stretch of the Sicilian beach, the decor beautifully adhered to the white and gold theme.

"Ready, Pretty Girl?" He smiled after I nodded. "I will shoot him if he makes you unhappy."

"You won't," I teased, bumping his shoulder and making him chuckle.

He and my husband grew close in their pursuit to kill Fisha. When they found him, Favi took a trip to Jamaica so they could torture the man together. Al was now a big fan of Favi's work: his torture methods, his wine company, and the happiness he gave me — which was the most important thing.

Inhaling a big breath, I turned the corner with Al. Through my veil, I saw guests sitting on parallel white chairs. Preserved rose petals covered the silk cloth running down the aisle. They were from the roses Favi gave me when he sent me to Italy, plus the months leading to this moment. An arch of white roses with gold specks was at the end of the aisle. Best man Jelani and bridesmaid Chezzy stood on the opposite ends of it. Beneath it was my groom.

A breath passed my lips as I adored him from head to toe. He was in a white tuxedo paired with gold loafers. Favi was more handsome than I imagined.

Al started leading me down the aisle as Trav cued the music track. The intro to 'One Man' by Gaza Slim featuring Vybz Kartel played, and I froze mid-step.

"I'm going to kill him," I whispered.

"You've done enough," Al muttered, making me remember when Favi begged Al to lecture me about why it was wrong for me to kill people.

I might have gotten Amber slowly poisoned...

She shudn lie seh Favi rape her. If *la famiglia* wasn't rich, that wuda stain him name forever. Mi nuh regret it, and mi wuda do it again. Ten times worse, too. Nikola love how mi bloodthirsty, but Favi seh him a go leff mi if mi keep up the bad behavior. Mi nuh believe him, but mi a relax miself while focusing on launching my crochet company.

"Sorry!" Trav exclaimed.

"Jah know!" Zaveer yelled from beside him, and the crowd chuckled as Trav switched to the traditional song.

Relaxing, I resumed walking. With each step, my heart raced, and I clutched the bouquet tighter. Al transferred me to Favi when we reached the end, and my nerves went haywire. Being this close made his intoxicating cologne flood my senses while I peered at his handsome face.

Favi unveiled me, and my breath hitched as tears brimmed his eyelids. Bowing and holding my stare, he placed a chaste kiss on the back of my hand. He smiled at me while he straightened himself. *"Sei bellissima."*

"Thank you," I whispered, trying my best not to cry. The makeup artist charged an arm and a leg to transform my face into a work of art, but it was hard not to let the tears flow freely. I'd been through so much with this man, and now I was marrying him. I deserved this.

We deserved this.

My lips trembled as the first tear fell, rolling down my cheeks that ached from smiling too hard.

The ceremony flew over my head. I couldn't look away from my husband-to-be, and he couldn't look away from me. He was bursting with love and pride to marry me, and I was the same for him. I couldn't ask for a better life partner.

The officiant told Favi to put the ring on my finger. I smiled while watching him.

My ring had an engraving of our wedding date and initials. Favi didn't have a ring. I joked I wasn't giving him a ring because I wanted him to tattoo my name. I got the idea when he tattooed the girls' names on his abdomen.

Favi took it seriously. He tattooed my name on his ring finger and said he'd get a touch-up whenever it started fading.

Still wanting him to have something physical to symbolize our marriage, I got him a custom-made watch from his favorite brand. It had the same details as my ring.

Cause me nuff, mi tattoo his name on my ring finger, too. It made me cry so hard, only stopping when Favi said, 'You gave birth to two kids at one time. Nuh mek mi see yaa bawl ova dem likkle pain ya like yu nuh militant.'

The officiant smiled after I put the watch around Favi's wrist. "You may now k—"

Favi cupped my face, pressing his lips against mine. I smiled, crying into the kiss as the audience erupted into a chorus of cheers.

I laughed when he broke away. "Couldn't wait?" I teased.

He grinned. "Waited long enough."

We shared another kiss before facing the audience. They mirrored our happiness. I glanced at Favi, who had an unfaltering smile. I'd never seen him smile this much before. It made my heart swell because genuine happiness radiated off him in constant waves.

After the ceremony, we received more congratulations from our guests and family at the reception. All the kids were in a private section, being entertained with cartoons and toys so they didn't have to witness what was happening...

Favi removing my garter. Painfully slow. His fingers trailed up my thighs, stopping at the lace of my panties. He kissed my pussy, and I stiffened.

"Behave," I hissed through a smile.

His chuckle fanned my pussy before he grabbed the garter with his teeth. He moved his head from beneath my dress, then threw it toward the crowd. Jelani caught it.

"Man deh a go be gelding fi life. Nuh know wa kinda foolishness dis," Fabiano said, and the guests laughed.

Afterward, I threw my bouquet. Chezzy caught it.

"Right deso, big batty!" Yolo screamed.

Trav took a big chug from his flute of champagne while pulling at his collar, making me chuckle. Resting the flute atop the table, Trav switched the music to slow, raunchy dancehall.

Yolo danced her way toward me. "Watch wife! What a good thing yu neva listen when me seh fi bun him. Look how me wuda miss out pon nice wedding! No sah, big up we man!"

Mi laugh and hug her.

Favi snuck behind me, wrapping his arms around my waist. Yolo danced away while Favi whispered in my ear. "Give me one of those dances you did in Tavern."

My eyes widened as I looked over my shoulder at him. "H-here? Now?"

He smirked. "Our wedding. Our rules."

I looked around us. Everyone was caught up in conversations or dancing, not giving us any attention.

"Okay," I said, and he pulled away to grab a chair, resting it before me.

He slipped off his jacket and laid it on the back of the chair. He sat down, licking his bottom lip and patting his lap. My heart skipped a beat as I kicked off the heels, modeling toward him. My skin and insides were aflame because of how he looked at me like I was the sexiest, most beautiful woman in the entire world.

Stopping before him, I turned around and parted my feet. I trailed a hand up my leg. The dress lifted, revealing my thighs inch by inch. Favi sucked in a breath, and I smirked as I bent over, showing him my ass. He reached out, rubbing on me.

I swatted his hand away before facing him. "I'm in charge right now."

Eyes darkening, he smirked. "*Dispiace*, Mrs. Welsh."

Throwing a leg over his thigh, I straddled him. I wrapped an arm around his shoulder, grazing his head with the nails of my other hand. Seductively rolling my hips against him, I leaned in to pull his lobe with my teeth.

"Careful..." Favi warned.

Giggling, I pulled away to look at him. "Why?"

"You're making me horny."

"You know how to fix that." I released his hair, moving my hand between us to rub on his hardening dick.

He raised a brow, chuckling. "*You* want me to fuck you here?"

"Our wedding. Our rules." Smirking, I leaned in and placed my lips on his.

Favi kissed me with fervor, and I moaned into the kiss. He pressed his hand on the small of my back, pulling me closer and making my breasts press against his chest. The background chatter faded, shifting my focus to the music and Favi's hands all over my skin. I reached for his belt, and he helped me to undo it.

His hand crept between my thigh, and he broke the kiss to smirk. "Wet already."

"Always wet for you, Favi."

He licked his bottom lip, biting it as he took out his dick. Favi guided me onto it while my eyes fluttered close. His dick pressed against my opening, and we moaned as our bodies became one.

"Still so tight," he said, his voice raspy. His fingers sank into my ass as he directed me up and down his length.

"Ah," I moaned lowly, my fingers sinking into his shoulder as I matched his pace.

"Louder," Favi ordered, and I shook my head.

"The guests," I moaned. I didn't care about them, but if I opened my eyes, all my bravado would fade.

"They're gone."

My eyes snapped open, and I gasped at the empty room. "When—"

"Doesn't matter," he said while standing, making me shriek as he hit my cervix.

"Aye, big hood bwoy! Mind yu mash mi up," I cursed, and he scoffed.

"If two youth neva mash yu up, my dick won't either," him seh, and mi laugh cause mi cya stand how him unfiltered!

My legs wrapped tighter around his body, and he captured my mouth as I held him close. Our tongues tangled in a heated mess. My pussy clamped around his dick as he walked toward a table while guiding me up and down his dick. Favi scraped everything off the table, sending plates and cutlery flying before he lay me on it. I broke the kiss, panting at the ceiling as he ripped my top and exposed my breasts.

"Fucking beautiful," he said, his eyes drinking me in before he leaned down and took my right nipple into his mouth.

I was still breastfeeding, so he swirled his tongue around the sensitive skin instead of sucking on it.

"Oh!" I screamed to the ceiling, loving how he kneaded my other breast and made me desperate for more.

One of his hands moved between us, rubbing at my clit and making my first orgasm come quickly.

But he didn't stop his sweet torture.

He pulled out and flipped me over. Pinning me down by my wrists, he senselessly pounded into me. Our heavy breathing and slapping skin drowned out the music in the background.

"How yu pussy so good, wife?" he asked, his voice deep and sending a jolt between my thighs. My walls clenched around him tighter, and he hissed. "*Fuck*. Yu waa mi come quick?"

I muttered gibberish, and he chuckled as he freed my hands to hold my waist. He pulled me onto him while thrusting, making me grab fistfuls of the decorative cloth atop the table. My face and breasts rubbed against the tabletop. Tears rolled down my cheeks from the overstimulation, but this pain was too good for me to want it to stop.

A drunk guest stumbled in on us, but we ignored them, and they hurried out of the room.

We went round after round, making use of the time we didn't have at home anymore.

On the wall...

The chair...

Until I was kneeling on the floor, my hands resting atop my thighs and my head tilted upward.

Favi stroked his dick above me. His clean-shaven chest peeked out from beneath his shirt. The buttons popped off during our lovemaking, but he didn't bother taking it off. His sex appeal was off the charts. I moved a hand between my thighs, rubbing my aching clit as I waited for him to come.

"Open," Favi ordered, pumping faster while I opened my mouth and stuck out my tongue. He stilled as lines of cum shot out, landing on my hair and face.

I snapped my eyes shut. I didn't want a repeat of the last time when I couldn't explain to Aunty what made one of my eyes red.

Warmth slid down to my breasts, forcing away the thought.

Tonight was our night. With our rules. We could do what we wanted to.

Favi released a heavy breath, and I opened my eyes while smiling at him. His eyes shone as I licked our kids off my lips. "Demon gyal," he said, and I grinned.

EPILOGUE

CHAYANNE

four years later

"Do you want this, *principessa*?" Favi asked Mikayla in Italian while showing her a doll.

"*Papà*, I'm *principessa*." Mikeila pointed at herself.

Laughing, I looked at her. "You're a princess too, baby," I said, and Keila smiled before running toward Favi. Stirring from below capture mi attention, and mi lift the hood of the stroller. I smiled as Cairo yawned at me. "You're awake, sleepyhead?" I rubbed his belly, and he giggled. Adjusting the bib around his neck, I covered him again. "Favi, he's up."

Favi glance over him shoulder pon mi, nodding.

Looking at my family, mi afi smile at how blessed we be these past years...

Mikeila and Mikayla were turning four-years-old next month. Cairo was four-months-old. Apple was still baking cause Favi breed me as the six weeks up.

We didn't plan to have another baby this soon after Cairo, but I kept forgetting to take my pills, so we're pregnant again. Mi nuh waa have no more after Apple, but Favi insist seh him want six pickney. Him nuh ask mi fi much, so whatever the brown man want, the brown man a go get!

Speaking of the girls turning four next month, Favi been a bit more open to his birthdays since our daughters' birth. Me a plan on gifting him a large plot of land in America, which him a debate buy. Him keep on a put it off cause him hate America and nuh waa do business dih deh, despite knowing the investment crucial to the continued success of Welsh's.

Him been a work pon expanding the company. Him have several branches across Europe, and a few in Asia and Africa. In the Caribbean, only Jamaica have a Welsh's branch, and those wineries become a hot spot fi tourists. Mi sister-in-law oversee the tour aspect of the company.

"Let's go." Favi walked toward me, resting him hand pon mi lower back while leading us toward the cashier. After him pay for the toys, we returned to the penthouse and got dressed. "You good?" Favi asked, entering the bathroom.

Nodding, mi look away from mi reflection and meet his worried eyes ina the mirror. "I'm remembering how it was a rough delivery with Cairo, and I had to beg them not to cut me."

If Favi wasn't there, they would have.

After I gave birth and was about to be stitched up, the doctor pull Favi aside to ask, 'Mr. Welsh, would you like to give her a husband stitch?'

In my exhausted state, I heard Favi angrily ask if I requested it, and the doctor said no. Favi hissed his teeth before saying, 'Then nuh give her nun, dunce fuck.'

"When the time comes, everything will go smoothly with the water birth." Favi wrapped his arms around my waist. Him kiss my cheek, then rest him chin atop mi head. "You're strong, Mrs. Welsh."

Mi bout fi answer when crying drift from the bedroom, making me sigh.

Favi pulled away. "I'll do it."

"Thanks." Mi smile, and him nod before leaving. Mi really nuh know how mi wuda survive without my man.

A moment later, Favi enter the room while mi a step ina mi black formal dress. Him a bounce Cairo ina him arm. "No milk's in the fridge."

"Mi forget fi pump before we leave this morning," mi seh, and him shake him head. Mi take the baby, thanking him as him unzip mi dress while we walk into the bedroom.

Once Cairo know me around, him refuse fi tek the bottle. Mi a have waa oversupply right now, and my tender breasts desperately need a break from his gums. Sighing, mi sit on the bed, pulling down my sleeve and directing my breast to Cairo's mouth. Him latch on, suckling roughly and making me wince.

"Yu nuh tired fi bite me?" me ask, and him close him eyes.

"Why yu so wicked to Mommy? Yu nuh waa leff breast fi mi suck afta yu?" Favi ask, and mi chuckle.

"Suppose the girls hear you?"

"They're in the living room watching cartoons. Dem naa hear nun else right now."

Cairo release mi breast with a long pull between his gums, and mi inhale a sharp breath.

"Ow! This likkle bwoy!" mi exclaim, and Cairo laugh, making me glare. "I knew you weren't hungry. You just like torturing me."

Favi chuckled. "How does that taste?"

"What?" I asked, silencing the alarm that went off on my phone.

"Breastmilk."

"Want to taste it?" Mi chuckle when Favi skin up him face. "It won't kill you."

Favi stare at the drop of milk hanging off my nipple before him wipe it off with his finger. Him stick it ina him mouth and gag. "A this Cairo a gwan so ova?" Favi asked, and mi buss out a market laugh.

Putting away my breast, mi hand Cairo to him. "I'm going to use the bathroom. Your pickney a pressure mi bladder."

"*Our*," he said while I walked away.

I did my business, then flushed the toilet and washed my hands. Grabbing the pack of wipes, I returned to the bedroom while spraying the perfume Salvatore give mi as a parting gift. Favi lay pon the bed, moving Cairo in the air like an airplane.

"Did you burp him?" mi ask cause this man will remember fi do everything except burp the baby.

"*Sì...*" Favi seh, and Cairo stop laugh fi puke pon him.

Mi shake mi head as Favi stand with Cairo and walk toward me. I took out a wipe and cleaned them. "It go ina your mouth again?" Mi smile at Cairo as Favi nod. "Good job."

Favi scoff, walking away as I resumed spraying. "Let's go before she kills us."

Rolling my eyes, mi stop spray. Nuh know why everybody love gwan like me use more perfume than anybody else! Mi look round the room fi ensure mi naa leff nun, then go outside to the car. Favi already have the kids strapped in, but me check dem again.

"*Mamma*, where are we going?" Keila ask as mi check the strap on her car seat.

"My graduation, baby," I said, and her brows furrowed.

"What's that?"

"It's like a party for finishing school." I looked at Kayla. "*Stai bene?*" I asked, and she nodded. Mi smile, then sit beside Favi. "I still think we should bring her to speech therapy," I whispered to him as him drive off.

"She's good, Chayanne," Favi said, and mi purse mi lips.

Mi know him nuh like when mi bring up seh sum might be wrong with Kayla, but mi worried. She nuh respond to English or Patois. She only speak ina Italian, and whenever she did, it was only to her twin. It hard fimi understand wa she need sometimes because mi nuh fluent enough fi understand a toddler's broken speech.

Favi nav no trouble understanding her. Him seh shi will grow it out because he was the same as a kid. Italian was his first language, and he struggled with speaking English. He could read it, though, so Diana made him write English as often as possible.

Sighing, mi glance at the kids ina the rearview mirror. Cairo have him fist ina him mouth, making a mess of himself. Keila deh pon her tablet, playing a counting game. Kayla a suck her finger while staring through the window, watching the city pass by.

Mi look away, doing the same as her. Nerves a get the best of mi. Today, mi a go be a college graduate.

After the birth of the twins, I dedicated myself to school, so I was graduating a semester early. As a marketing major, I got a lot of experience by being the assistant to Sergio, the head of Welsh's marketing department.

Well, I was.

Cause me a breed, Favi turn mi ina housewife. Mi just need fi sneeze and this man mek a deposit to mi personal bank account, carry mi pon vacation, or shower me wid push gifts. The soft life nice bad! Mi might become his housewife fi real.

That nuh ideal for me, though. Me a still the CEO of Saanvi's, and mago put this degree to use.

We arrived at the auditorium, and mi find mi place ina the rows of graduates. Mi nuh have any friends here cause mi do alla mi classes online.

The service went smoothly, and I was all smiles when they called my name. Standing, I walked across the stage to collect my diploma. A baby cried from in the crowd, and my breasts leaked. Thankful for the black gown, mi put pep ina mi step. Stopping before the lady, mi accept mi diploma.

Look, Mommy and Mama! I made it!

Every puss have dem four o'clock.

The ceremony finished soon after. I pushed through the crowd of graduates to find my family waiting close to the parking lot.

Keila ran toward me, beaming while showing me a card. "I drew you, *Mamma!*"

I smiled at the drawing of me accepting my diploma. "Thanks, baby!" I stooped to her height, kissing her cheek.

Kayla joined the hug, giving my neck a tight squeeze that made me smile harder. Favi approached while holding a sleeping Cairo, and I stood.

"Congrats, *fiore.*" Favi kissed my cheek, and I smiled.

"Eww!" Keila covered her mouth, and Favi grinned.

"Know wi raise yu right," he said, and I scoffed.

Taking Keila's hand in mine while Favi took Kayla's, we walked toward the car. Mi smile at Aunty, who stood beside our car. Aunty greet the kids before greeting me and Favi.

"I'm so proud of you, Chichi baby!" Aunty pull me into a hug while mi thank her.

"Where's Azera?" mi ask.

"Tate went to get her something to eat."

"We're going to a restaurant, Mrs. Kenzie," Favi seh.

"Oh, okay. I'll let them know where to meet us." Aunty kissed the girls before leaving.

We load the kids ina the car, then drive to the penthouse. Mi run to the closet, swapping the milk-soiled dress for another black one. Throwing myself a kiss in the mirror, I returned to the car. Minutes later, we were at the restaurant, enjoying our meal.

"Slow down," mi seh to Kayla in Italian, wiping her mouth with a napkin before accepting Chezzy's video call.

"Congratulations, best bitch!" Chezzy exclaim, and mi eyes widen.

"Bitch," Kayla tested the word, then laughed.

Mi gasp at Kayla. Mi deevn angry she curse, mi just happy she finally seh sum ina English.

"I'm sorry," Chezzy rushed out, covering her mouth while me lower the phone's volume.

"*Papà*, what's bitch?" Keila asked Favi while chewing on a fry.

"Ask Mommy." Favi smirk at me before returning to his conversation with Aunty and Tate.

"*Mamma*—" Keila look pon mi, and mi tell her fi continue eat. She nod, scooting closer to Kayla. She ask Kayla ina Italian if she waa watch a cartoon pon the tablet, and Kayla nodded.

Trav face filled the screen, smiling. "Watch mi bright sister! Done know wi nuh believe ina dunce!"

Mi laugh. "Nuh swell up mi head," mi seh, laughing.

"Watch ya. Yu better big up yuself! Nuh you seh humble calf suck hood?" Trav ask, and mi facepalm while Chezzy tell him fi leave wid him slackness.

"How are you?" mi ask Chezzy.

Chezzy frown. "Sad. I wish I could've made it. I was watching the livestream, though. When you were walking across the stage, Mommy mek up pay noise with the pot cover."

"Unu a sample." I laughed, happy Chezzy and Aunty back pon good terms.

"And how's our baby?"

"Okay." She smile while rubbing her bump. She seven months along in her high-risk pregnancy, so her husband neva waa put her pon a flight.

Yes, husband! Trav popped the question last year, and their ceremony was beautiful and one to remember. As payback, mi ask the DJ fi play the first few seconds of 'Hold Me' by Vybz Kartel when Trav did a wait fi Chezzy walk down the aisle.

Eltham was the best man. Despite being the bridesmaid, I cried the entire time. Me so happy the two a dem find dem forever person, especially Chezzy! Her seventeen-year-old self would be happy she free from the shackles of big head Lamar, who nuh mine Zaveer since him run off.

I paused at the entrance of the pink-painted tailor room of my Saanvi's boutique in Ocho Rios. "If me neva know betta, wuda swear unu a chat me," I joked with the two women.

"Nun like that, Mrs. Welsh," the designer answered.

Rubbing my bump, I glanced between the cousins and the pink crochet swimsuit. "Sum wrong with it?" I asked Jade Stewart. She was the designer I bought a design from for more practice, and I'd been working on it for her cousin, June Michaels, who was a nail technician.

"No. It's beautiful," Jade answered, staring at it in awe.

"Then?"

Jade exchanged a glance with her cousin, and June rolled her eyes, looking toward the closed door. "She's having *problems* with a guy she likes."

"Man problems." Mi shake mi head, taking a seat. "Me used to have mi fair share of those. Talk to me."

As they spoke, June intrigued me. She reminded me of myself when I was younger — secretive and believed it was my way or no way.

The door open, and Favi enter. Mi smile at him, and him smile back, warming my heart. Mi cya tired of him smile! What a man nice!

"Evening," he greeted my clients, walking toward me. Him kiss mi forehead.

"Evening," June said, standing and offering Favi a hand.

Favi shook it. "How are you?"

"I'm well. Yourself?"

"Same, thanks." He retracted his hand to shake Jade's.

I chimed in. "I'm so sorry, but I have to go. One of my employees will be happy to assist you."

"No. Jade seh yu good, so I only trust you," June said, and I dismissed the flattery.

"Thank you so much for your patience. I'll be sure to visit you before I leave." I accepted June's business card before walking outside. From the time mi buss the style pon Favi, him seh mi only allowed fi get glow in the dark nails. Arriving outside, my brows furrowed at his newest coupe. "Where are the kids?"

"*Mamma,*" Favi said.

"Diana soon thief dem."

"Tell her to keep them tonight so I can make love to you. Mi tired fi thief fuck."

"Mi a mek sure mi carry dem ina the bed tonight," I said, and Favi groaned as if the twins nuh find demself ina wi bed some nights. "Oh, can we stop at a haberdashery? I need to buy a gift bag for Chezzy."

She changed her mind about wanting to be surprised about her baby's gender, so today's the gender reveal party. Trav put together a cool idea, and mi excited fi see how it turn out.

"Where the bag weh yu buy in America?" he asked, and mi nuh ansa. "Soon leff yu fucking self."

"Shut up, big foot."

We stop at a haberdashery, and mi run inside fi buy the gift bag. After mi find one mi like, smaddy tap mi shoulder.

"Miss Bailey?" said an old man, and mi brows furrow. "It's Mr. Black."

"Mr. Black!" mi exclaim, accepting the quick hug from him. "It's so nice to see you, and it's Mrs. Welsh now."

Mr. Black smiled while pulling away. "Congratulations."

"Thank you. How have you been?"

"I've been okay. Yourself?"

"Same." Him ask mi about life after high school, and mi tell him about my business endeavors and seh mi graduate college earlier this week. "I am so proud of you, Mrs. Welsh. Now you see why I was always hard on you about striving for that extra percent? I knew you were capable of great things," Mr. Black said, and tears brimmed in my eyes.

"Thank you, Mr. Black." Mi slip some money ina him hand through a handshake before returning to the car.

We drive to Steer Town and make a detour to the cemetery. Favi follow me to the family plot to replace the withered flowers with fresh ones. Mi sigh while looking at the headstones.

Ishaan Sharma.

Mikeila Sharma.

Saanvi Sharma.

Alphonso Bailey.

My breath hitched upon seeing my father's grave beside Mommy's. After Al died in combat, the police force gave him the highest honor for his contributions to making Jamaica a better society.

Mi shame fi admit it, but mi neva go him funeral. I was in school and pregnant with Cairo, mi cudn bring miself fi do it. Favi handled the funeral for me, and accompanied me to the grave when I got the courage last month.

"Look ya, Elder." Favi pull mi closer by my waist, kissing my lips. Him quickly tear himself away, looking at his feet. "Sum touch mi foot!"

"Al nuh want yu deh ya."

"Well, I'm here. He better stop it before I piss on his grave."

Laughing, mi drag him away from the graves. We went in the car, then drove to Drax Hall. We passed by our house to get to the Bartleys, who live pon the opposite side of the scheme. Trav leff the house a Godsto to Lyrica. Chezzy sell ar house, despite Trav paying off her mortgage.

We hop outta the car and mek way through the mingling crowd. Mi spot

Chezzy, walking with a hand on her back while Trav trail behind her.

"Go get yu friend," mi seh to Favi, and him scoff before taking Trav into the house.

"I'm never getting pregnant again," Chezzy complain as mi help her fi sit.

"So yu seh last time," mi seh, and she chuckle.

"I had to give my husband a baby."

"Hear Mrs. Bartley," mi tease, and she wiggle her ring finger. The sun reflected off the large almond-cut diamond, momentarily blinding me.

"I know that's right!" she brag, and mi smile as we talk fi the next few minutes.

"Where's Yolo?" Mi look around at the festivities. Mi spot Chezzy's friends, and Eltham with some of Trav's other friends.

"Yu yard with Ken face ina her crochiz," Chezzy seh, and mi laugh while standing.

"Mi soon come back. A almost three, so mago change mi clothes."

"Tell my husband I need him."

Entering the house, mi gasp at the kids. The girls were on the sofa, eating chips. Cairo's body was swaddled inside Favi's shirt, his head peeking out of the neck while he struggled to keep his eyes open. Favi and Trav a watch a football match pon the TV.

Chuckling, mi walk toward dem. "He's milk drunk?" mi ask, and Favi nod as mi take Cairo. "Trav, yu wife need yu," mi seh, and Trav sigh as him stand up.

"Jah knows. Wa mi do now?" Trav ask.

"Mi nuh know. Go to her," mi seh, and him dap up Favi before leaving. Me and my crew went upstairs. Dem stay ina the bedroom while me ina the bathroom a put on mi swimsuit. Spotting the minimalistic tattoo on the right side of my waistline, I trailed a finger over each letter of my husband's nickname for me. I got it shortly after Cairo's birth before I knew I was pregnant again. Looking away from it, I yelled, "Where's Diana?"

"Sleeping somewhere. She has a headache," Favi said.

"So weh Rajay and Luna?" mi ask cause Diana have alla her grandbaby dem since morning.

"It look like mi keep track a mi bredda pickney dem?" him ask, and mi kiss mi teeth, making him laugh. "Maybe Catherine came for them. She said they're going to Italy tonight."

Humming, mi look pon Keila, who come ina the bathroom.

She handed a perfume bottle to me. "*Mamma, you forgot this,*" she seh, and mi chuckle.

"Thank you, baby." Mi tek the bottle from her, resting it aside. "Go let Daddy put on your swimsuit."

She nod, leaving the bathroom. Mi use the time fi comb mi hair ina waa nice updo. After me done, mi enter the bedroom. Kayla motion to Favi seh she waa sleep, and mi tell him mi will stay with her. While him carry the other kids outta the room, me and Kayla cuddle ina the bed.

"Take out your finger," mi seh in Italian to her, and she ignore me, making me sigh. Mi a go rub fowl doodoo pon her thumb when Favi naa look.

She like look pon pictures fi fall asleep, so mi open the album Favi and I shared pictures of the kids.

The first picture was when the girls were nine-months-old. Mi miss them being this size. Dem grow up too quickly.

Mi scroll to the next, and mi eyes widen. This one was a somewhat inappropriate picture taken on our wedding anniversary last year. Deevn know how that picture reach ina the kids album, so mi scroll to the next.

"Marshy," Kayla said, pointing at the phone and making me smile. A few minutes later, she exhaled a big puff through her nose, signaling she was asleep.

Carefully, mi lift her, then bring her to the room Diana was in. After mi lay her down, mi go outside.

"Aunty Chi!" Zaveer yell, and mi look round fi see him running toward me.

"Yu cya walk?" mi ask, and him shake him head before dipping his fingers into the bag of banana chips he held. "Excited to be a big brother?" mi ask while we walk toward the backyard.

"Yes!" Zaveer said, unknowingly making me sad.

If only him wuklis Pupa wuda be a part of him life, him wuda know seh him a already waa big brother. The other day, Chezzy hear seh Lamar married and get pickney. It never bother her cause she happily married and Zaveer doh remember him.

"Daddy, Mommy a look fi yu," Zaveer seh.

Trav sigh. "Yu mother a stress ino."

Zaveer nodded. "Jah know."

Trav chuckled. "Go tell her it's time," he said, and Zaveer ran away.

Mi wipe weh fake tears. "Can't believe you a really waa father now."

"Been a father."

"Yu know wa mi mean! As mi deh yaso a look pon yu, maa remember how yu did still mawga nuh matter how much mi feed yu."

"Cause yu cya cook."

"Gweh nuh, Mawga Bwoy! Yu nuh see seh a marriage life yu did need? Mi cya see yu ribs like one time."

Trav roared a laugh, flipping me off. "Fuck off before mi drown yu."

"Yu cya do dat. Yu know you a the godfather," mi seh, and him smile.

"Apple already spoil and she deevn reach yet."

I nodded, thinking of the support system that was my family — both legally and illegally.

My eyes drifted toward Eltham, who was preparing to remove the cover from the pool. Over the years, him nuh pursue any interests besides badness, nuh matter how Trav urge him. Blood Paw and Shottaz were no more — thanks to Trav and Favi — so Eltham joined waa gang ina Ochi.

I heard Favi's voice and looked behind me. Him and Chezzy laughed while walking toward us. Back wheel deh a front fi years now! Favi stop beside me, throwing an arm over my shoulder. Trav and Chezzy walk toward the pool.

"On the count of three," Eltham announced.

The crowd counted down. After a dramatic pause, the cover was removed.

Blue!

We erupted into cheer, congratulating Trav and Chezzy. Afterward, people start mingle and eat. Me grab a nonalcoholic drink, then sit at the poolside, swaying my feet in the cool water.

"Another boy, huh?" mi seh to Chezzy, who a sit beside me.

"Trav wanted a girl, so yu know how that go," Chezzy seh.

"Mi deevn a go pay yu nuh mind cause *cockroach nuh belong ina fowl fight*." Mi glance at Trav while he walked toward us.

"Come here, Fatty." Trav help Chezzy outta the pool, leading her away.

Resting mi drink aside, mi swim toward Yolo, who was at the other end of the pool. "How mi nuh see yu since the party start?"

"Me did a try put pink coloring ina the water, but dem ketch me, so me dee go hide," Yolo seh, making Ren laugh.

"Ren, I might have to steal your girlfriend if you continue keeping her away from me," I warned Ren, and she smirked.

"You can have her for now." Ren kissed Yolo, then swam away, probably in search of her brother. Pity she nuh know Romeo abandon me and Favi ina Ochi cause him see waa girl him like.

"She makes me so happy," Yolo said while smiling.

I grinned. "A long time smaddy fi put yu under manners! Weh unu a go after this?"

"Portland. Mago introduce her to Mommy." She reddened as I smirked. "Don't call me a yamhead, Number One!"

"How Ren a get fi see the big house pon the hill before me? Yu fake," mi seh, and she chuckle.

"I invited you, but yu always busy wid the little walking creampies."

"Mago visit before mi go back to Italy. I promise," I said, and she nodded.

"Girl, me naa tell no lie, me love tha tie dung ya. Me stop go river cause me nuh want it wash off."

"Yaa sample," I laughed, teasing her for the next few minutes until Ren tek her from mi. Mi neva bored and nav nobody fi talk to fi too long cause Favi call mi.

Sitting at the edge of the pool, he placed his feet in the water while I swam toward him. Mi stop between him thighs, and him wrap him arms round mi waist. Mi lay mi head on his chest while him release my hair from the updo. My hair flowed down my back, falling into the water.

"Yu cya leave mi hair alone?" mi ask.

"Should I also leave your hair alone when you need your pussy shaved before you give birth?" he asked.

Pulling away, I glared at him. "Yu know seh yu nav no behavior?"

"I never said I did." He grinned while I rolled my eyes. "Hungry?" him ask, and mi shake mi head. "That's a first."

"The good vibes full mi belly."

"And mi cocky a full yu belly later. *Mamma* is keeping the kids." He slapped my ass, then rubbed away the sting.

"Yu waa live ina mi skin?" I teased as I turned around, resting my arms on his thighs.

He moved his hand to my belly. "And your tight hole."

Watching his hand caress the small bump, I remembered a conversation we had when the girls were born. "Favi?"

"*Sì?*"

"When the girls were born, you said you feel like yu best nuh good enough sometimes. Do you still think so?"

"No. Things worked out well in the end."

"So, yu life nuh feel like a movie anymore?"

"I have a good life with my wife and kids. Of course, it still does," he bragged, and mi roll mi eyes while smiling.

"Your ego, Mr. Welsh. What do you think it'd be called?"

"Your bagga questions, Mrs. Welsh," he said, and I laughed.

"Answer the question, before mi pull yu ina the pool by yu big foot."

Favi stared into nothingness. Seconds passed before he looked at me with a smile. "If it's based on how I met you, it'd be called *The Crossfire*."

GLOSSARY

Amore/fiore mio | My love/flower

Brava ragazza | Good girl

Bugiardo | Liar

Buonanima | God rest his soul

Cazzo | Fuck

Che cosa | What

Come posso dire | How do I say

Figlio/fratello | Son/brother

Grazie mille | Thank you very much

La famiglia | The family

Mi dispiace | I'm sorry

Parli l'italiano | Do you speak Italian

Perché sei qui | Why are you here

Scusati con tuo fratello | Apologize to your brother

Sei bellissima | You're very beautiful

Soldati | Soldiers

Solo Dio può guidicarmi | Only God can judge me

Stai bene | Are you okay

Sto bene e tu | I'm good and you

Stronzo | Asshole

Tanto di cappello | Hats off

Que sera, sera | What will be, will be

ACKNOWLEDGEMENTS

The Crossfire came to me during a time when there was a surge of violence against Jamaican women. I was hesitant about writing it at first because I thought, "Who would want to read a story romanticizing the thing that's killing our women?" I tried to refrain, but Chayanne and Favio refused to leave my mind. Being isolated in my dorm room during the COVID-19 pandemic made me finally bring them to life.

This book wasn't planned to be a happy-ending romance, but I'm thankful I listened to the readers I had on Wattpad who urged me to continue telling this story. Many have supported me since I posted the first chapter, and they witnessed it become a hard copy. I wish I knew your real names so I could say them, but I don't and that doesn't diminish how special you all are to me.

I want to highlight Chenel and Sue because this wouldn't be possible if not for their motivational messages every time I almost gave up. Amelia, my first vote. Christoy, Denay, Dijonae, Jada, Kam, Nia, Paris, Rickayla, Rudesha, Samantha, Samoya, Xeniva, Zodi-Ann, and Zoey, my first set of avid readers. And my parents, who instilled in me the discipline to pursue my passions.

Made in the USA
Columbia, SC
08 September 2024

42006563R00289